I

“The thriller writer ... lon

“A major talent.” —*The Denver Post*

24 Hours

“Iles’s latest brilliantly plotted tale walks the razor’s edge between cinematic excess and bone-chilling suspense. The well-rounded characters are trademark Iles; the plot runs speed-skating smooth. . . . Nasty surprises and perfectly timed terror.” —*Publishers Weekly* (starred review)

“Chilling. . . . The seemingly perfect American family is targeted by a madman who has refined the art of kidnap, and roars into their lives like an avenging angel . . . a memorable trip down paranoia lane.”—*Ottawa Citizen*

“A taut tale, terrifying in its intensity, compelling in its pace. . . . The finale is an amazing scenario with the cinematic flavor of a Bruce Willis caper . . . a good old-fashioned thriller, the likes of which are rare . . . a winner.” —*The Chattanooga Times*

“An enigmatic crime figure, as brilliant as Hannibal Lecter and as seemingly haphazard as Charles Manson. . . . Iles provides enough twists and turns to keep his hair-raising ending unpredictable and the plot surefire grist for a movie.” —*The Memphis Commercial Appeal*

continued . . .

"Greg Iles displays all the well-honed chops that have made him a bestselling author. . . . He achieves a near-perfect balance of high-tech inventiveness and characterization as the plot rushes to its grand—and violent—finale . . . inventive and fast-paced."

—*The New Orleans Times-Picayune*

The Quiet Game

"Suspenseful." —*Kirkus Reviews*

"Grabs you fast and keeps you glued."

—*Entertainment Weekly*

"The climactic unveiling . . . will spellbind readers."

—*Boston Herald*

"Incredibly engrossing." —*The Denver Post*

"A deliciously complicated plot." —*Booklist*

"Fast-paced action, surprise tactics, and down-and-dirty legal maneuvering played out below the surface calm of the deep South will transfix the reader to the very last page." —*Library Journal*

"This ably crafted, richly atmospheric legal thriller is engrossing." —*Publishers Weekly*

"Thriller-meister Greg Iles . . . conveys the darker undercurrents of small-town life, and he doesn't flinch in handling the racial themes." —*Chicago Sun-Times*

"The pace is frenetic, the fear and paranoia palpable, and the characters heartbreakingly honest."

—*The Cleveland Plain Dealer*

Mortal Fear

"An ingenious suspense thriller . . . fascinating."
—*The New York Times Book Review*

"A chilling roller-coaster ride." —*Library Journal*

"Greg Iles mixes action and suspense like a master!"
—Stephen Coonts

"Stay-up-all-night suspense . . . a relentlessly readable thriller." —*Kirkus Reviews*

"Iles displays a flair by pushing topical hot buttons."
—*Booklist*

"Jackhammer pacing . . . addictive. . . . You know you're in Iles country." —*The Clarion-Ledger* (Jackson, MS)

Black Cross

"On fire with suspense." —Stephen King

"A thriller of such accomplishment that it vaporizes every cliché . . . good enough to read twice."
—*Kirkus Reviews*

"A truly fine novel . . . totally absorbing and ingenious."
—Nelson DeMille

"A stunning, horrifying, mesmerizing novel that will keep readers transfixed from beginning to end."
—*Booklist*

continued . . .

"The finest thriller since *Eye of the Needle* . . . vital, compelling, magnificent." —*Romantic Times*

"Henceforth, any recommended reading list of thrillers will have to include this." —*Publishers Weekly*

Spandau Phoenix

"Masterful action and suspense . . . a sizzling-hot read."
—Stephen Coonts

"A terrific thriller in the great tradition of Jack Higgins . . . a remarkable, impressive novel." —Nelson DeMille

"An incredible web of intrigue and suspense, an avalanche of action from first page to last."
—Clive Cussler

"An irresistible plot . . . a scorching read."
—John Grisham

"Amazing . . . a masterwork. A thriller whose depth and scope are sweeping." —*The Tampa Tribune*

GREG ILES

24 HOURS

SIGNET
Published by New American Library, a division of
Penguin Group (USA), 375 Hudson Street,
New York, New York 10014, U.S.A.
Penguin Group (Canada), 90 Eglinton Avenue East, Suite 700, Toronto, Ontario M4P 2Y3, Canada (a division of Pearson Penguin Canada Inc.)
Penguin Books Ltd., 80 Strand, London WC2R 0RL, England
Penguin Ireland, 25 St. Stephen's Green, Dublin 2,
Ireland (a division of Penguin Books Ltd.)
Penguin Group (Australia), 250 Camberwell Road, Camberwell, Victoria 3124, Australia (a division of Pearson Australia Group Pty. Ltd.)
Penguin Books India Pvt. Ltd., 11 Community Centre, Panchsheel Park, New Delhi - 110 017, India
Penguin Group (NZ), 67 Apollo Drive, Rosedale, North Shore 0632
New Zealand (a division of Pearson New Zealand Ltd.)
Penguin Books (South Africa) (Pty.) Ltd., 24 Sturdee Avenue, Rosebank, Johannesburg 2196, South Africa

Penguin Books Ltd, Registered Offices:
80 Strand, London WC2R 0RL, England

Published by Signet, an imprint of New American Library, a division of Penguin Group (USA) Inc. Previously published in a G.P. Putnam's Sons edition.

First Signet Printing, July 2001
20 19 18 17 16 15 14 13 12

Printed in the United States of America

PUBLISHER'S NOTE
This is a work of fiction. Names, characters, places, and incidents either are the product of the author's imagination or are used fictitiously, and any resemblance to actual persons, living or dead, events, business establishments, events or locales is entirely coincidental.

The publisher does not have any control over and does not assume any responsibility for author or third-party Web sites or their content.

ACKNOWLEDGMENTS

Aaron Priest, the Man.

Phyllis Grann, for paving the way.

David Highfill, for bearing with the writer's obsessiveness.

Louise Burke, for her hard work and support.

MEDICAL ADVICE: Jerry Iles, M.D., William Daggett, M.D., Noah Archer, M.D., and Michael Bourland, M.D.

AVIATION: Mike Thompson, Justin Cardneaux, and Stephen Guido.

MISCELLANEOUS: Lisa Erbach-Vance, Glen Ballard, Jon Wood at Hodder, Michael MacInnis, Rush and Leslie Mosby, Ken and Beth Perry, Susan Chambliss, Simmons Iles, Robert Royal, Brent Bourland, Caroline Trefler, Carrie, Madeline, and Mark.

READERS: Ed Stackler, Betty Iles, Michael Henry, and Courtney Aldridge.

To those I have omitted through oversight, my sincere apologies. As always, all mistakes are mine.

For Geoff Iles,
who's been there for me
from the beginning (almost)

He that hath a wife and children
Hath given hostages to fortune.

—FRANCIS BACON

ONE

"The kid always makes it. I told you that."

Margaret McDill had not seen the man in her life until yesterday, but he had dominated every second of her existence since their meeting. He had told her to call him Joe, and he claimed it was his real name, but she assumed it was an alias. He was a dark-haired, pale-skinned man of about fifty, with deep-set eyes and a coarse five-o'clock shadow. Margaret could not look into his eyes for long. They were dark, furious pools that sucked the life out of her, drained her will. And now they carried knowledge about her that she could not bear.

"I don't believe you," she said quietly.

Something rippled deep in the dark eyes, like the flick of a fish tail. "Have I lied to you about anything else?"

"No. But you . . . you let me see your face all night. You won't let me go after that."

"I told you, the kid always makes it."

"You're going to kill me and let my son go."

"You think I'm going to shoot you in broad daylight in front of a freakin' McDonald's?"

"You have a knife in your pocket."

He looked at her with scorn. "Jesus Christ."

Margaret looked down at her hands. She didn't want to look at Joe, and she didn't want to chance seeing herself in one of the mirrors. The one at home had been bad enough. She looked like someone who had just come out of surgery, still groggy with anesthesia. An unhealthy glaze filmed her eyes, and even heavy makeup had failed to hide the bruise along her jaw. Four of her painstakingly maintained nails had broken during the night, and there was a long scratch on her inner forearm from the initial scuffle. She tried to remember exactly when that had happened but couldn't. Her sense of time had abandoned her. She was having trouble keeping her thoughts in order. Even the simplest ones seemed to fall out of sequence by themselves.

She tried to regain control by focusing on her immediate environment. They were sitting in her BMW, in the parking lot of a strip mall, about fifty yards from a McDonald's restaurant. She had often shopped at the mall, at the Barnes & Noble superstore, and also at the pet store for rare tropical fish. Her husband had recently bought a big-screen television at Circuit City, for patient education at his clinic. He was a cardiovascular surgeon. But all that seemed part of someone else's life now. As remote as the bright side of the moon to someone marooned on the dark half. And her son, Peter . . . God alone knew where he was. God and the man beside her.

"I don't care what you do with me," she said with

conviction. "Just let Peter live. Kill me if you have to, just let my son go. He's only ten years old."

"If you don't shut up, I might take you up on that," Joe said wearily.

He started the BMW's engine and switched the air conditioner to high, then lit a Camel cigarette. The cold air blasted smoke all over the interior of the car. Margaret's eyes stung from hours of crying. She turned her head to avoid the smoke, but it was useless.

"Where's Peter now?" she asked, her voice barely a whisper.

Joe took a drag off the Camel and said nothing.

"I said—"

"Didn't I tell you to stop talking?"

Margaret glanced at the pistol lying on the console between the seats. It belonged to her husband. Joe had taken it from her yesterday, but not before she had learned how useless a gun was to her. At least while they had Peter. Some primitive part of her brain still urged her to grab it, but she doubted she could reach the pistol before he did. He was probably waiting for her to try just that. Joe was thin but amazingly strong, another thing she'd learned last night. And his hard-lined face held no mercy.

"He's dead, isn't he?" Margaret heard herself say. "You're just playing games with me. He's dead and you're going to kill me, too—"

"Jesus *Christ*," Joe said through clenched teeth. He turned over his forearm and glanced at his watch. He wore it on the inside of his wrist so that Margaret couldn't see the time.

"I think I'm going to be sick," she said.

"Again?" He punched a number into the BMW's cell phone. As he waited for an answer, he muttered, "I do believe this has been the worst twenty-four hours of my life to date. And that includes our little party."

She flinched.

"Hey," he said into the phone. "You in your spot? . . . Okay. Wait about a minute, then do it."

Margaret jerked erect, her eyes wide, searching the nearby cars. "Oh my God. Peter! *Peter!*"

Joe picked up the gun and jammed the barrel into her neck. "You've come this far, Maggie. Don't blow it now. You remember what we talked about?"

She closed her eyes and nodded.

"I didn't hear you."

Tears rolled down her cheeks. "I remember."

A hundred yards from Margaret McDill's BMW, Peter McDill sat in an old green pickup truck, his eyes shut tight. The truck smelled funny. Good and bad at the same time, like just-cut grass and old motor oil, and really old fast food.

"You can open your eyes now."

Peter opened his eyes.

The first thing he saw was a McDonald's restaurant. It reassured him after his night of isolation. The McDonald's stood in the middle of a suburban strip mall parking lot. As Peter panned his eyes around the mall, he recognized the stores: Office Depot, Barnes & Noble, the Gateway 2000 store. He'd spent hours in that store. It was only a few miles from his house. He looked down at his wrists, which were bound with duct tape.

"Can you take this off now?"

He asked without looking up. The man behind the wheel of the truck was hard for him to look at. Peter had never seen or heard of Huey before yesterday, but for the last twenty-four hours, he had seen no one else. Huey was six inches taller than his father, and weighed at least three hundred pounds. He wore dirty mechanic's coveralls and heavy plastic glasses of a type Peter had seen in old movies, with thick lenses that distorted his eyes. He reminded Peter of a character in a movie he'd seen on the satellite one night, when he sneaked into the home theater room. A movie his parents wouldn't let him watch. The character's name was Carl, and the boy who was Carl's friend in the movie said he sounded like a motorboat. Carl was nice, but he killed people, too. Peter thought Huey was probably like that.

"When I was a little boy," Huey said, peering thoughtfully through the windshield of the pickup, "those golden arches went all the way over the top of the restaurant. The whole place looked like a spaceship." He looked back at Peter, his too-big eyes apologetic behind the thick glasses. "I'm sorry I had to tape you up. But you shouldn't've run. I told you not to run."

Peter's eyes welled with tears. "Where's my mom? You said she was going to be here."

"She's gonna be here. She's probably here already."

Through the heat shimmering off the asphalt, Peter scanned the sea of parked cars, his eyes darting everywhere, searching for his mother's BMW. "I don't see her car."

Huey dug down into his front coverall pocket.

Peter instinctively slid against the door of the pickup truck.

"Look, boy," Huey said in his deep but childlike voice. "I made you something."

The giant hand emerged from the pocket and opened to reveal a carved locomotive. Peter had watched Huey whittling for much of the previous afternoon, but he hadn't been able to tell what Huey was working on. The little train in the massive palm looked like a toy from an expensive store. Huey put the carving into Peter's bound hands.

"I finished it while you was sleeping," he said. "I like trains. I rode one once. When I was little. From St. Louis, after Mamaw died. Joey rode up by hisself on the train and got me. We rode back together. I got to sit in front with the rich people. We wasn't supposed to, but Joey figured a way. Joey's smart. He said it was only fair. He says I'm good as anybody. Ain't nobody no better than nobody else. That's a good thing to remember."

Peter stared at the little locomotive. There was even a tiny engineer inside.

"Whittlin's a good thing, too," Huey went on. "Keeps me from being nervous."

Peter closed his eyes. "Where's my mom?"

"I liked talking to you. Before you ran, anyway. I thought you was my friend."

Peter covered his face with his hands, but he kept an eye on Huey through a crack between his left cheek and palm. Now that he knew where he was, he thought about jumping out. But Huey was faster than he looked.

Huey dug into his coveralls again and brought out his

pocketknife. When he opened the big blade, Peter pressed himself into the passenger door.

"What are you doing?"

Huey grabbed Peter's bound wrists and jerked them away from his body. With a quick jab he thrust the knife between Peter's forearms and sawed through the duct tape. Then he reached over and unlocked the passenger door of the truck.

"Your mama's waiting for you. In the playground. At the McDonald's."

Peter looked up at the giant's face, afraid to believe.

"Go see her, boy."

Peter pushed open the truck's door, jumped to the pavement, and started running toward the McDonald's.

Joe reached across Margaret McDill's lap and opened the passenger door of the BMW. His smoky black hair brushed against her neck as he did, and she shuddered. She had seen his gray roots during the night.

"Your kid's waiting in the McDonald's Playland," he said.

Margaret's heart lurched. She looked at the open door, then back at Joe, who was caressing the BMW's leather-covered steering wheel.

"Sure wish I could keep this ride," he said with genuine regret. "Got used to this. Yes, sir."

"Take it."

"That's not part of the plan. And I always stick to the plan. That's why I'm still around."

As she stared, he opened the driver's door, got out, dropped the keys on the seat, and started walking away.

Margaret sat for a moment without breathing, mistrustful as an injured animal being released into the wild. Then she bolted from the car. With a spastic gait born from panic and exhaustion, she ran toward the McDonald's, gasping a desperate mantra: *"The Lord is my shepherd, I shall not want . . . The Lord is my shepherd, I shall not want . . . The Lord is my shepherd . . ."*

Huey stopped his green pickup beside his cousin Joe with a screech of eroded brake pads. Two men standing under the roofed entrance of the Barnes & Noble looked over at the sound. They looked like bums hoping to pass themselves off as customers and spend the morning reading the papers on the sofas inside the bookstore. Joe Hickey silently wished them good luck. He'd been that far down before.

When he climbed into the cab, Huey looked at him with the relief of a two-year-old at its returning mother.

"Hey, Joey," Huey said, his head bobbing with relief and excitement.

"Twenty-three hours, ten minutes," Hickey said, tapping his watch. "Cheryl's got the money, nobody got hurt, and no FBI in sight. I'm a goddamn genius, son. Master of the universe."

"I'm just glad it's over," said Huey. "I was scared this time."

Hickey laughed and tousled the hair on Huey's great unkempt head. "Home free for another year, Buckethead."

A smile slowly appeared on the giant's rubbery face.

"Yeah." He put the truck into gear, eased forward, and joined the flow of traffic leaving the mall.

Peter McDill stood in the McDonald's Playland like a statue in a hurricane. Toddlers and teenagers tore around him with abandon, leaping on and off the foam-padded playground equipment in their sock feet. The screeches and laughter were deafening. Peter searched among them for his mother, his eyes wet. In his right hand he clutched the carved locomotive Huey had given him, utterly unaware that he was holding it.

The glass door of the restaurant opened, and a woman with frosted hair and wild eyes appeared in it. She looked like his mother, but not exactly. This woman was different somehow. She looked too old, and her clothes were torn. She pushed two children out of the doorway, which his mother would never do, and began looking frantically around the playground. Her gaze jumped from child to child, lighted on Peter, swept on, then returned.

"Mom?" he said uncertainly.

The woman's face seemed to collapse inward upon itself. She rushed to Peter and crushed him against her, then lifted him into her arms. His mother hadn't done that in a long, long time. A terrible wail burst from her throat, freezing the storm of children into a still life.

"Oh, dear Jesus," Margaret keened. "My baby, my baby, my sweet baby . . ."

Peter felt hot tears rolling down his cheeks. As his mother squeezed him, the little wooden train dropped from his hand onto the pebbled concrete. A toddler wandered over, picked it up, smiled, and walked away with it.

TWO

ONE YEAR LATER

Will Jennings swung his Ford Expedition around a dawdling tanker truck and swerved back into the right lane of the airport road. The field was less than a mile away, and he couldn't keep from watching the planes lifting over the trees as they took off. It had been nearly a month since he'd been up, and he was anxious to fly.

"Keep your eyes on the road," said his wife from the seat beside him.

Karen Jennings was thirty-nine, a year younger than her husband, but much older in some ways.

"Daddy's watching the airplanes!" Abby chimed from her safety seat in the back. Though only five and a half years old, their daughter never hesitated to interject her comments into any conversation. Will looked at his rearview mirror and smiled at Abby. Facially, she was a miniature version of Karen, with strawberry-blond curls, piercing green eyes, and a light dusting of freckles across her nose. As he watched, she pointed at the back of her mother's head.

Will laid his right hand on Karen's knee. "I sure wish my girls would come along with old Dad." With Abby present, he often referred to himself as "Dad" and Karen as "Mom," the way his father had done. "Just jump in the plane and forget about everything for three days."

"Can we, Mom?" cried Abby. "Can we?"

"And what do we wear for clothes?" Karen asked in a taut voice.

"I'll buy you both new wardrobes on the coast."

"Yaaayy!" Abby cheered. "Look, there's the airport!"

The white control tower of the terminal had come into sight.

"We don't have any insulin," Karen pointed out.

"Daddy can write me a subscription!"

"*Pre*scription, honey," Will corrected.

"She knows the right word."

"I want to go to the beach!"

"I can't believe you started this again," Karen said under her breath. "Daddy won't be spending any time at the beach, honey. He'll be nervous as a cat until he gives his lecture to all those other doctors. Then they'll spend hours talking about their days in medical school. And then he'll tear up his joints trying to play golf for three days straight."

"If you come," Will said, "we can beat the bushes

around Ocean Springs for some undiscovered Walter Anderson stuff."

"Noooo," Abby said in a plaintive voice. She hated their art-buying explorations, which usually entailed hours of searching small-town backstreets, and sometimes waiting in the car. "*You* won't be playing golf, Mom. You can take me to the beach."

"Yeah, Mom," Will echoed.

Karen cut her eyes at him. Full of repressed anger, they flashed like green warning beacons. "I agreed to chair this flower show two *years* ago. It's the sixtieth anniversary of the Junior League, and I don't know whose brilliant idea it was to have a flower show, but it's officially *my* problem. I've put off everything until the last minute, and there are over four hundred exhibitors."

"You got everything nailed down day before yesterday," Will told her. There wasn't much use in pressing the issue, but he felt he should try. Things had been tense for the past six months, and this would be the first trip he had made without Karen in a long time. It seemed symbolic, somehow. "You're just going to agonize until the whole circus starts on Monday. Four nights of hell. Why not blow it off until then?"

"I can't do it," she said with a note of finality. "Drop it."

Will sighed and watched a 727 lift over the tree line to his left.

Karen leaned forward and switched on the CD player, which began to thump out the teen dance groove of Britney Spears. Abby immediately began to sing along. *"Hit me baby one more time . . ."*

"Now, if you want to take Abby by yourself," Karen said, "you can certainly do that."

"What did you say, Mom?"

"You know I can't," Will said with exasperation.

"You mean you can't do that *and* play golf with your med school buddies. Right?"

Will felt the old weight tighten across his chest. "This is once a year, Karen. I'm giving the keynote speech, and the whole thing is very political. You know that. With the new drug venture, I'll have to spend hours with the Klein-Adams people—"

"You don't have to explain," she said with satisfaction. "Just don't try to make me blow off my obligations when you won't do the same."

Will swung the Expedition into the general aviation area. Lines of single- and twin-engine planes waited on the concrete apron, tethered to rings set in the cement, their wheels chocked against the wind. Just seeing them lightened his heart.

"You're the one who encouraged me to be more social," Karen said in the strained voice she'd used earlier.

"I'm not joining the Junior League when I grow up," Abby said from the backseat. "I'm going to be a pilot."

"I thought you were going to be a doctor," said Will.

"A flying doctor, silly!"

"Flying doctor sure beats housewife," Karen said *sotto voce.*

Will took his wife's hand as he braked beside his Beechcraft Baron 58. "She's only five, babe. One day she'll understand what you sacrificed."

"She's almost six. And sometimes I don't understand it myself."

He squeezed Karen's hand and gave her an understanding look. Then he got out, unstrapped Abby from her child seat, and set her on the apron.

The Baron was ten years old, but she was as fine a piece of machinery as you could ask for, and Will owned her outright. From the twin Continental engines to the state-of-the-art avionics package, he had spared neither time nor expense to make her as safe and airworthy as any billionaire's Gulfstream IV. She was white with blue stripes, and her tail read N-2WJ. The "WJ" was a touch of vanity, but Abby loved hearing the controllers call out *November-Two-Whiskey-Juliet* over the radio. When they were flying together, she sometimes made him call her *Alpha Juliet.*

As Abby ran toward the Baron, Will took a suit bag and a large leather sample case from the back of the Expedition and set them on the concrete. He had driven out during his lunch hour and checked the plane from nose to tail, and also loaded his golf clubs. When he reached back into the SUV for his laptop computer case, Karen picked up the sample case and suit bag and carried them to the plane. The Baron seated four passengers aft of the cockpit, so there was plenty of room. As they loaded the luggage, Karen said:

"You're having pain today, aren't you?"

"No," he lied, closing the cabin door as though the fire in his hands did not exist. Under normal circumstances he would have canceled his flight and taken a car, but it was far too late now to reach the Gulf Coast except by air.

Karen looked into his eyes, started to say something, then decided against it. She walked the length of the wing and helped Abby untether it while Will did his preflight walkaround. As he checked the aircraft, he glanced over and watched Abby work. She was her mother's daughter from the neck up, but she had Will's lean musculature and length of bone. She loved helping with the plane, being part of things.

"What's the flight time to the coast?" Karen asked, joining him behind the wing. "Fifty minutes?"

"Thirty-five minutes to the airport, if I push it." Will was due to give his lecture at the Beau Rivage Casino Hotel in Biloxi at seven p.m., which would open the annual meeting of the Mississippi Medical Association. "I'm cutting it a little close," he conceded. "That aneurysm ran way over. I'll call you after my presentation." He pointed to the beeper on his belt. "If you want me during the flight, use the SkyTel. It's new. Digital. Hardly any dead spots."

"Mr. High-Tech," Karen said, making clear that she wasn't impressed with what she considered boy toys. "I just type in the message at home and send it like e-mail?"

"Right. There's a special Web page for it. But if you don't want to fool with that, just call the answering service. They'll get the message to me."

Abby tugged at his hand. "Will you wiggle the wings after you take off?"

"You mean *waggle* the wings. Sure I will. Just for you. Now . . . who gets the first kiss?"

"Me! Me!" Abby cried.

As Will bent down, she turned aside his kiss and whispered in his ear. He nodded, rose, and walked to Karen. "She said Mommy needs the first kiss today."

"I wish Daddy were as perceptive."

He gently took her by the waist. "Thanks for giving me time last night to finish up the video segment. I'd have been laughed out of the conference."

"You've never been laughed at in your life." Her face softened. "How are your hands? I mean it, Will."

"Stiff," he admitted. "But not too bad."

"You taking anything?"

"Just the methotrexate." Methotrexate was a chemotherapeutic agent developed for use against cancer, but, in much smaller doses, was used against Will's form of arthritis. Even small doses could damage the liver.

"Come on," she pressed.

"Okay, four Advil. But that's it. I'm fine. Good to go." He slipped an arm around Karen's shoulder. "Don't forget to turn on the alarm system when you get home."

She shook her head in a way that conveyed several emotions at once: concern, irritation, and somewhere in there, love. "I never forget. Say good-bye, Abby. Daddy's late."

Abby hugged his waist until at last he bent and picked her up. His sacroiliac joints protested, but he forced a smile.

"I'll be back Sunday night," he said, and kissed her on the forehead. "You take care of Mom. And don't give her any trouble about your shots."

"But it doesn't hurt as much when you do it."

"That's a fib. Mom's given a lot more shots than I have."

He set her down with a muffled groan and gently pushed her toward her mother. Abby walked backward, her eyes locked on Will until Karen scooped her up.

"Oh!" Karen said. "I forgot to tell you. Microsoft is going to split again. It was up twelve points when I left the house."

He smiled. "Forget Microsoft. Tonight starts the ball rolling on Restorase." Restorase was the trade name of a new drug Will had helped develop, and the subject of his presentation tonight. "In thirty days, Abby will be set for Harvard, and you can start wearing haute couture."

"I'm thinking Brown," Karen said with a grudging laugh.

It was an old joke between them, started in the days when they had so little money that a trip to Wendy's Hamburgers was a treat. Now they could actually afford those schools, but the joke took them back to what in some ways had been a happier time.

"I'll see you both Sunday," Will said. He climbed into the Baron, started the twin engines, and checked the wind conditions with ATIS on the radio. After contacting ground control, he waved through the Plexiglas, and began his taxi toward the runway.

Outside, Karen backed toward the Expedition with Abby in her arms. "Come on, honey. It's hot. We can watch him take off from inside the truck."

"But I want him to see me!"

Karen sighed. "All right."

Inside the Baron, Will acknowledged final clearance from the tower, then released his brakes and roared up the sunny runway. The Baron lifted into the sky like a tethered hawk granted freedom. Instead of simply banking to his left to head south, he executed a teardrop turn, which brought him right over the black Expedition on the ground. He could see Karen and Abby standing beside it. As he passed over at six hundred feet, he waggled his wings like a fighter pilot signaling to friendly ground troops.

On the concrete below, Abby whooped with glee. "He did it, Mom! He did it!"

"I'm sorry we couldn't go this time, honey," Karen said, squeezing her shoulders.

"That's okay." Abby reached up and took her mother's hands. "You know what?"

"What?"

"I like arranging flowers, too."

Karen smiled and lifted Abby into her seat, then hugged her neck. "I think we can win the three-color ribbon if we give it half a try."

"I know we can!" Abby agreed.

Karen climbed into the driver's seat, started the Expedition, and drove along the line of airplanes toward the gate.

Fifteen miles north of the airport, a battered green pickup truck with a lawn tractor and two Weed Eaters in back rattled along a curving lane known for over a hundred years as Crooked Mile Road. The truck slowed, then stopped beside a wrought-iron mailbox at the foot of a high wooded hill. An ornamental World War I biplane perched atop the mailbox, and below the biplane, gold letters read: JENNINGS, #100. The pickup turned left and chugged slowly up the steep driveway.

At the top, set far back on the hill, stood a breathtaking Victorian house. Wedgwood blue with white gingerbread trim and stained-glass windows on the second floor, it seemed to watch over the expansive lawns around it with proprietary interest.

When the pickup truck reached the crest of the drive, it did not stop, but continued fifty yards across the St. Augustine grass until it reached an ornate playhouse. An exact replica of the main house, the playhouse stood in the shadow of the pine and oak trees that bordered the lawn. The pickup stopped beside it. When the engine died, there was silence but for birdcalls and the ticking of the motor.

The driver's door banged open, and Huey Cotton climbed out. Clad in his customary brown coveralls and heavy black eyeglasses, he stared at the playhouse with wonder in his eyes. Its roof peaked just above the crown of his head.

"See anybody?" called a voice from the passenger window of the truck.

Huey didn't take his eyes from the enchanting playhouse. "It's like Disneyland, Joey."

"Christ, look at the real house, would you?"

Huey walked around the playhouse and looked across a glittering blue swimming pool to the rear elevation of the main house. Peeking from two of the four garage bays were a silver Toyota Avalon and the white nose of a powerboat.

"There's a pretty boat in the garage," he said distractedly. He turned back to the playhouse, bent, and examined it more closely. "I wonder if there's a boat in this garage?"

As Huey studied the little house, Joe Hickey climbed out of the truck. He wore a new Ralph Lauren polo shirt and Tommy Hilfiger khakis, but he didn't look natural or even comfortable in the costume. The lower half of a crude eagle tattoo showed on his biceps below the band of the polo's left sleeve.

"Look at the real house, Buckethead. See the third downstairs window from the end? That's it."

Huey straightened and glanced over at the main house. "I see it." He laid one of his huge hands on the playhouse's porch roof. "I sure wish I could fit in *this* house. I bet the whole world looks different from in there."

"You'll never know how different." Hickey reached into the truck bed and took out a rusted toolbox. "Let's take care of the alarm system."

He led Huey toward the open garage.

Twenty minutes later they emerged from the back door of the house and stood on the fieldstone patio.

"Put the toolbox back in the truck," Hickey said. "Then wait behind the playhouse. As soon as they go inside, you run up to the window. Got it?"

"Just like last time."

"There wasn't any freakin' Disneyland playhouse last time. And that was a year ago. I don't want you fooling around back there. The second you hear the garage door close, get your big ass up to that window. If some nosy neighbor drives up in the meantime and asks you a question, you're with the lawn service. Act like a retard. It shouldn't be much of a stretch for you."

Huey stiffened. "Don't say that, Joey."

"If you're waiting at the window when you're supposed to be, I'll apologize."

Huey smiled crookedly, exposing yellowed teeth. "I hope this one's nice. I hope she don't get scared easy. That makes me nervous."

"You're a regular John Dillinger, aren't you? Christ. Get behind the playhouse."

Huey shrugged and shambled across the patio toward the tree line. When he reached the playhouse, he looked around blankly at Hickey, then folded his giant frame into a squat.

Hickey shook his head, turned, and walked into the house through the back door.

Karen and Abby sang at the top of their voices as they rolled north on Interstate 55, the tune one from *The Sound of Music*, Abby's favorite musical. The Jenningses lived just west of Annandale in Madison County, Mississippi. Annandale was the state's premier golf course, but it wasn't golf that had drawn them to the area. Fear of crime and the race problems of the capital city had driven many young professionals to the gated enclaves of Madison County, but Karen and Will had moved for a different reason. If you wanted land, you had to move north. The Jennings house sat on twenty acres of pine and hardwood, twelve miles north of Jackson proper, and in evening traffic it took twenty-five minutes to get there.

"That will bring us back to doe, oh, oh, oh. . . ."

Abby clapped her hands and burst into laughter. Breathing hard from the singing, Karen reached down and punched a number into her cell phone. She felt guilty about the way she'd spoken to Will at the airport.

"Anesthesiology Associates," said a woman, her voice tinny in the cell phone speaker.

"Is this the answering service?" asked Karen.

"Yes ma'am. A-1 Answer-all. The clinic's closed."

"I'd like to leave a message for Dr. Jennings. This is his wife."

"Go ahead."

"We already miss you. Break a leg tonight. Love, Karen and Abby."

"With sugar and kisses on top!" Abby shouted from the backseat.

"Did you get that last part?" asked Karen.

"With sugar and kisses on top," repeated the bored voice.

"Thank you."

Karen hit END and looked at her rearview mirror, which was adjusted so that she could see Abby's face.

"Daddy loves getting messages from us," Abby said, smiling.

"He sure does, honey."

Fifty miles south of Jackson, Will settled the Baron in at eight thousand feet. Below him lay a puffy white carpet of cumulus clouds, before him a sky as blue as an Arctic lake. Visibility was unlimited. As he bent his wrist to check his primary GPS unit, a burning current of pain shot up the radial nerve in his right arm. It was worse than he'd admitted to Karen, and she'd known it. She didn't miss anything. The truth was, she didn't want him flying anymore. A month ago, she'd threatened to tell the FAA that he was "cheating" to pass his flight physicals. He didn't think she would, but he couldn't be sure. If she thought Will's arthritis put him—and thus the family—at risk while flying, she wouldn't hesitate to do whatever she had to do to stop him.

If she did, Will wasn't sure he could handle it. Even the thought of being grounded put him in a black mood. Flying was more than recreation for him. It was a physical expression of how far he had come in life, a symbol of all he had attained, and of the lifestyle he had created for his family. His father could never have dreamed of owning a three-hundred-thousand-dollar airplane. Tom Jennings had never even *ridden* in an airplane. His son had paid cash for one.

But for Will the money was not the important thing. It was what the money could buy. Security. He had learned that lesson a thousand times growing up: money was an insulator, like armor. It protected people who had it from the everyday problems that besieged and even destroyed others. And yet, it did not make you invulnerable. His arthritis had taught him that. Other lessons followed.

In 1986, he graduated from LSU medical school and began an obstetrics residency at the University of Mississippi Medical Center in Jackson. It was there that he met a surgical nurse with stunning green eyes, strawberry-blond hair, and a reputation for refusing dates with physicians or medical students. After three months of patience and charm, Will persuaded Karen to meet him for lunch, far from the hospital. There he discovered that the cause of her dating policy was simple: she'd seen too many nurses put medical students through school only to be cast aside later, and others caught in messy triangles with married doctors and their wives. In spite of her policy, she dated Will for the next two years—first secretly, then openly—and after a yearlong engagement, they married. Will entered private practice with a Jackson OB/GYN group the day after his honeymoon, and their adult life together began like a storybook.

But during the second year of his practice, he began experiencing pain in his hands, feet, and lower back. He tried to ignore it, but soon the pain was interfering with his work, and he went to see a friend in the rheumatology department. A week later he was diagnosed with psoriatic arthritis, a severe, often crippling disease. Continuing as an obstetrician was impossible, so he began to investigate less physically rigorous fields like dermatology and radiology. His old college roommate suggested anesthesiology—his own specialty—a three-year program if the university would credit Will's OB experience and let him skip the internship year. It did, and in 1993, he began his anesthesiology residency at UMC in Jackson.

The same month, Karen quit her nursing job and enrolled at nearby Millsaps College for twenty-two hours of basic sciences in the premed program. Karen had always felt she aimed too low with nursing—and Will agreed—but her decision stunned him. It meant they would have to put off having children for several more years, and it would also force them to take on more debt than Will felt comfortable with. But he wanted Karen to be happy. While he trained for his new speciality and learned to deal with the pain of his disease, she racked up four semesters of perfect grades and scored in the ninety-sixth percentile on the Medical College Admissions Test. Will was as proud as he was surprised, and Karen was luminous with happiness. It almost seemed as though Will's disease had been a gift.

Then, during Karen's freshman year of medical school—the third year of Will's residency—she got pregnant. She had never been able to take the pill, and the less certain methods of birth control had finally failed. Will was surprised but happy; Karen was devastated. She believed that keeping the baby would mean the death of her dream of being a doctor. Will was forced to concede that she was probably right. For three agonizing weeks, she considered an abortion. The fact that she was thirty-three finally convinced her to keep the baby. She managed to complete her freshman year of med school, but after Abby was born, there was no question of continuing. She withdrew from the university the day Will completed his residency, and while Will joined the private anesthesiology group led by his old roommate, Karen went home to prepare for motherhood.

They made a commitment to go forward without regrets, but it didn't work out that way. Will was phenomenally successful in his work, and Abby brightened their lives in ways he could never have imagined. But Karen's premature exit from medical school haunted her. Over the next couple of years, her resentment began to permeate their marriage, from their dinner conversations to their sex life. Or more accurately, their lack of one. Will tried to discuss it with her, but his attempts only seemed to aggravate the situation. He responded by focusing on his work and on Abby, and whatever energy he had left he used to fight his slowly progressing arthritis.

He treated himself, which conventional wisdom declared folly, but he had studied his condition until he knew more about it than most rheumatologists. He had done the same with Abby's juvenile diabetes. Being his own doctor allowed him to do things he otherwise might not have been allowed to, like flying. On good days the pain didn't interfere with his control of the aircraft, and Will only flew on good days. Using this rationale, he had medicated himself to get through the flight physical, and the limited documentary records of his disease made it unlikely that his deception would ever be discovered. He only wished the problems in his marriage were as easy to solve.

A high-pitched beeping suddenly filled the Baron's cockpit. Will cursed himself for letting his attention wander. Scanning the instrument panel for the source of the alarm, he felt a hot tingle of anxiety along his arms. He saw nothing out of order, which made him twice as anxious, certain that he was missing something right in front of his eyes. Then relief washed through him. He reached down to his waist, pulled the new SkyTel off his belt, and hit the RETRIEVE button. The alphanumeric pager displayed a message in green backlit letters:

WE ALREADY MISS YOU. BREAK A LEG TONIGHT. LOVE, KAREN AND ABBY. WITH SUGAR AND KISSES ON TOP.

Will smiled and waggled the Baron's wings against the cerulean sky.

Karen stopped the Expedition beside her mailbox and shook her head at the bronze biplane mounted atop it. She had always thought the decoration juvenile. Reaching into the box, she withdrew a thick handful of envelopes and magazines and skimmed through them. There were brokerage statements, party invitations, copies of *Architectural Digest*, *Mississippi Magazine*, and *The New England Journal of Medicine*.

"Did I get any letters?" Abby asked from the backseat.

"You sure did." Karen passed a powder blue envelope over the front seat. "I think that's for Seth's birthday party."

Abby opened the invitation as Karen climbed the long incline of the drive. "How long till *my* birthday?"

"Three more months. Sorry, Charlie."

"I don't like being five and a half. I want to be six."

"Don't be in too much of a hurry. You'll be thirty-six before you know it."

When the house came into sight, Karen felt the ambivalence that always suffused her at the sight of it. Her first emotion was pride. She and Will had designed the house, and she had handled all the contracting work herself. Despite the dire warnings of friends, she had enjoyed this, but when the family finally moved in, she had felt more anticlimax than accomplishment. She could not escape the feeling that she'd constructed her own prison, a gilded cage like all the others on Crooked Mile Road, each inhabited by its own Mississippi version of Martha Stewart, the new millennium's Stepford wives.

Karen pulled into the garage bay nearest the laundry room entrance. Abby unhooked her own safety straps but waited for her mother to open her door.

"Let's get some iced tea," Karen said, setting Abby on the concrete. "How do you feel?"

"Good."

"Did you tee-tee a lot this afternoon?"

"No. I need to go now, though."

"All right. We'll check your sugar after. Then we'll get the tea. We're going to have some fun today, kid. Just us girls."

Abby grinned, her green eyes sparkling. "Just us girls!"

Karen opened the door that led from the laundry room to the walk-through pantry and kitchen. Abby squeezed around her and went inside. Karen followed but stopped at the digital alarm panel on the laundry room wall and punched in the security code.

"All set," she called, walking through the pantry to the sparkling white kitchen. "You want crackers with your tea?"

"I want Oreos!"

Karen squeezed Abby's shoulder. "You know better than that."

"It's only a little while till my shot, Mom. Or you could give me that new kind of shot right now. Couldn't you?"

Abby was too smart for her own good. Conventional forms of insulin had to be injected thirty minutes to an hour before meals, which made controlling juvenile diabetes difficult. If a child lost her appetite after the shot and refused to eat, as children often did, blood sugar could plummet to a dangerous level. To solve this problem, a new form of insulin called Humalog had been developed, which was absorbed by human cells almost instantly. It could be injected right before a meal, during the meal, or even just after. Physicians like Will were some of the first to get access to the drug, and its convenience had revolutionized the daily lives of families with diabetic children. However, Humalog also tempted children to break their dietary rules, since they knew that an "antidote" was near to hand.

"No Oreos, kiddo," Karen said firmly.

"O*kay*," Abby griped. "Iced tea with a lemon. I'm going to tee-tee."

"I'll have it waiting when you get back."

Abby paused at the hall door. "Will you come with me?"

"You're a big girl now. You know where the light is. I'm going to fix the tea while you're gone."

"O*kay*."

As Abby trudged up the hallway, Karen looked down at *The New England Journal of Medicine* and felt the twinge of anger and regret she always did when confronted by tangible symbols of the profession she'd been forced to abandon. She was secretly glad that the flower show had given her an excuse to miss the medical convention, where she would be relegated to "wife" status by men who couldn't have stayed within fifteen points of her in a chemistry class. Next month, Will's drug research would be published in this very magazine, while she would be entangled in the next Junior League service project. She shoved the magazine across the counter with the rest of the mail and opened the stainless-steel refrigerator.

Every appliance in the kitchen was a Viking. The upscale appliances were built in Greenwood, Mississippi, and since Will had done the epidurals on two pregnant wives from the "corporate family," the Jennings house boasted a kitchen that could have been featured in the *AD* that had come in today's mail—at a discounted price, of course. Karen had grown up with a noisy old Coldspot from Sears, and a clothesline to dry the wash. She could appreciate luxury, but she knew there was more to life than a showpiece home and flower shows. She took the tea pitcher from the Viking, set it on the counter, and began slicing a lemon.

Abby slowed her pace as she moved up the dark hallway. Passing her bedroom, she glanced through the half-open door. Her dolls were arranged against the headboard of her tester bed, just as she'd left them in the morning, Barbies, Beatrix Potter bunnies, and Beanie Babies, all mixed together like a big family. The way she liked them.

Five more steps carried her to the hall bathroom, where she stretched on tiptoe to reach the light switch. She pulled up her jumper and used the commode, glad that she didn't tee-tee very much. That meant her sugar was okay. After fixing her clothes, she climbed up on a stool before the basin and carefully washed and dried her hands. Then she started for the kitchen, leaving the bathroom light on in case she needed to come back.

As she passed her bedroom, she noticed a funny smell. Her dolls all looked happy, but something didn't seem right. She started to walk in and check, but her mother's voice echoed up the hall, saying the tea was ready.

When Abby turned away from the bedroom, something gray fluttered in front of her eyes. She instinctively swatted the air, as she would at a spiderweb, but her hand hit something solid behind the gray. The gray thing was a towel, and there was a hand inside it. The hand clamped the towel over her nose, mouth, and one eye, and the strange smell she'd noticed earlier swept into her lungs with each gasp.

Terror closed her throat too tightly to scream. She tried to fight, but another arm went around her stomach and lifted her into the air, so that her kicking legs flailed uselessly between the wide-spaced walls of the hallway. The towel was cold against her face. For an instant Abby wondered if her daddy had come home early to play a joke on her. But he couldn't have. He was in his plane. And he would never scare her on purpose. Not *really*. And she was scared. As scared as the time she'd gone into ketoacidosis, her thoughts flying out of her ears as soon as she could think them, her voice speaking words no one had ever heard before. She tried to fight the monster holding her, but the harder she fought, the weaker she became. Suddenly everything began to go dark, even the eye that was uncovered. She concentrated as hard as she could on saying one word, the only word that could help her now. With a great feeling of triumph, she said, "Mama," but the word died instantly in the wet towel.

Huey Cotton stood outside the Jennings house, nervously rubbing his palms against the legs of his coveralls and peering through Abby's bedroom window. *Abby.* Unlike most names, he could remember that one without trouble. His mother had once read letters to a woman named Abby out loud to him. *Dear Abby,* she would drawl in her cigarette-parched voice, sitting at the kitchen table in her hair-rollers and housecoat. The people who wrote to that Abby never signed their real names. They were embarrassed, his mother said. They signed big words instead of names, and sometimes they signed places, too, like *Bewildered in Omaha.* He always remembered that one.

Huey heard the scuff of a heel on wood. He looked up to see his cousin walking through the pink bedroom with the little Abby in his arms. She was fighting, kicking her skinny legs to beat the band. Joey held her at the center of the room so that her feet wouldn't hit the furniture or the tall bedposts. The kicks got weaker and weaker until finally they were just little jerks, like a hound's legs when it dreamed of hunting.

The little girl looked like another of the hundred or so dolls that lay around the room like the sleeping occupants of some fairyland, only bigger. Joey walked to the open window and passed her through it. Huey accepted

Abby as gingerly as he would a wounded bird, his mouth open in wonder.

"You're a genius," Joey said, a crooked grin on his face. "I apologize, okay? She'll be out for two to four hours. Plenty of time."

"You're going to call me, right?" Huey asked.

"Every thirty minutes. Don't say anything but 'hello,' unless I ask you a question. And shut off the cell phone when you get there. Just cut it on for the check-in calls. And remember the backup plan, right?"

"I remember."

"Good. Now, get going."

Huey turned away and started to walk, then stopped and turned back.

"What's wrong now?" Joey asked.

"Can she have one of her dolls?"

Joey leaned back inside the window, snatched up a gowned Barbie off the bed, and handed it out. Huey took it between Abby's hip and his little finger.

"Don't crank the truck till you hit the road," Joey said.

"I know."

Carrying Abby with maternal care, Huey turned and lumbered toward the playhouse and his concealed pickup truck, the gold lamé gown of the Barbie fluttering behind him like a tiny flag.

Karen stood at the kitchen counter, thumbing through the *NEJM* in spite of her resentment. Two sweating glasses of iced tea stood on the counter beside her, bright yellow lemon rinds hooked over the rims. Beside the glasses lay a plastic device for pricking Abby's finger; it looked like a ballpoint pen. Without taking her eyes from the magazine, Karen called: "Abby? You okay, sweetie?"

There was no answer.

She took a sip of tea and kept reading, thankful for a few moments of silence before the maddening last-minute details of the flower show would have to be dealt with.

Beneath the tall, sweet-scented pines behind the playhouse, Huey opened the driver's door of his pickup and slid Abby's unconscious body across the bench seat to the passenger side. She lay still as a sleeping angel. Huey watched her for a while. He liked standing on pine needles. They were cushy, like deep carpet. He wished he was barefoot.

Suddenly, an image of his cousin filled his mind. Joey would be really mad if he messed up. He reached into the truck, shifted it into neutral, and pushed it backward around the playhouse like a normal-sized man pushing a motorcycle. After the truck cleared the playhouse, he stopped, shifted his weight forward, and began pushing again, steering the pickup across the yard toward the steep driveway. The yard had a pitch to it, for drainage, and gravity soon began to help him.

When the wheels hit concrete the truck gathered momentum, and Huey tried clumsily to climb inside. He got one foot up on the step, but as he tried to pull himself through the open door, his boot slipped. He stumbled forward, trying to keep his feet under him as the old

Chevy raced down the hill. Only the strength in his huge hands kept him and the truck joined as it careened down toward Crooked Mile Road.

Three quarters of the way to the bottom, Huey flexed his wrists with enough power to snap the tendons of a normal man and dragged himself into the cab by main strength. He hit the brakes just before the truck shot into the road, and the vehicle shuddered to a stop. Abby was thrown forward against the dash, but she did not wake up. Huey pulled her back across the bench seat, her head pillowed on his thigh, then put his hand to her mouth to make sure she was breathing.

After his nerves settled a little, he pulled his door shut, cranked the engine, and turned onto Crooked Mile Road, which led to Highway 463, and from there to Interstate 55. He had a long night ahead.

Karen's ears pricked up at the rumble of a starting engine. It seemed out of place at this time of day. Her neighbors' houses were too far away for her to hear that sort of thing. She glanced through the kitchen window but saw nothing, as she'd expected. Only one curve of Crooked Mile Road was visible from the house, and the height of their hill hid the intersection of the road and the driveway. Maybe it was a UPS truck running late, making a turn in the drive.

She looked back at the hall door and called, "Abby? Do you need help, honey?"

Still no answer.

A worm of fear turned in Karen's stomach. She was compulsive about controlling Abby's diabetes, and though she hated to admit it, panic was always just one layer beneath the surface. She put down the magazine and started toward the hall. Relief surged through her as she heard footsteps on the hardwood. She was laughing at herself when a dark-haired man of about fifty walked through the hall door and held up both hands.

Her right hand flew to her heart, and in some sickening subdivision of a second, her mouth went dry, her throat closed, and sweat broke out from the crown of her head to her toes. Almost as quickly, a desperate hope bloomed in her brain. Hope that the stranger's presence was merely a mistake, some crazy mixup, that he was a workman to whom Will had given a key.

But he wasn't. She knew it the way you know about the lump in your breast, an alien thing that shouldn't be there and isn't going anywhere soon except by very unpleasant means. Karen had lost a sister that way. And her father—a Korean War veteran—had taught her very young that this was the way fate came at you: out of the blue, without warning, the worst thing in the world appearing with a leer and a ticking clock.

"Stay calm, Mrs. Jennings," the man said in a reassuring voice. "Abby's fine. I want you to listen to me. Everything is *o-kay.*"

At the word "Abby," tears filled Karen's eyes. The panic that lived beneath her skin burned through to the surface, paralyzing her where she stood. Her chin began to quiver. She tried to scream, but no sound came from her throat.

THREE

As Karen stood gaping, the stranger said, "My name's Joe, Mrs. Jennings. Joe Hickey. I'm going to help you through this thing. And the first thing to remember is that Abby is *absolutely fine*."

The temporary paralysis caused by seeing a strange man where she had expected Abby finally broke, and Karen jerked as though she had taken a physical blow.

"Abby!" she screamed. "Come to Mama!"

"Calm down," the stranger said softly. "Look at me, not the door. I'm Joe Hickey, okay? I'm telling you my real name because I'm not worried that it's going to matter later. You're never going to report this, because Abby's going to be fine. Everybody's going to be fine. Abby, you, me, everybody. The kid always makes it through. That's my rule."

Absurdly, Karen flashed onto the movie *The Jungle Book*, which she had watched at least fifty times with Abby. Listening to this man was like listening to Kaa the cobra, who hypnotized you with his voice while he waited for the perfect moment to strike. She shook her head and fixed her mind on Abby's face, and her fear dissolved in a violent rush, replaced by a fury beyond any she had known. The man before her stood between her and her child. If he wanted to keep them apart, he would have to kill her.

Hickey seemed to sense this. "Abby's not here, Mrs. Jennings. She's—"

Karen charged, batting him aside like an old man as she raced into the hallway. She yanked open the bathroom door and, though she found it empty, cried, "Abby! Abby? Where are you?"

She stood blinking for a moment; then she tore through the ground floor, checking every room and closet. With each empty space that greeted her, dread settled deeper into her bones. She raced up the back stairs and began searching the second floor. Every room was empty. She ran into the main upstairs guest room, picked up the nearest phone, and dialed 911. Instead of a dispatcher's voice, she heard a man speaking in a deep piney woods drawl: "*. . . Preacher Bob's Fount of Life Church is a Full Gospel church, with no wishy-washy bending of the Word, no newfangled editions of the King James—*"

She clicked the DISCONNECT button, but the voice droned on. Hickey must have dialed the prayer line from the kitchen phone and left it off the hook. She slammed down the phone, ran around the bed and picked up the private line. This time a female voice that sounded like an android was speaking.

". . . the satellite farm forecast is made possible by a grant from the ChemStar corporation, maker of postemergent broad-spectrum herbicides—"

Karen dropped the phone and stood staring at herself in the bureau mirror. Her eyes were frantic, blanked out like those you saw in the ERs after motor vehicle accidents. Relatives. Victims. Walking wounded. She needed to calm down, to try to think rationally, but she couldn't. As she struggled to gain control, an image came into her mind with the power of a talisman.

She ran to the back stairs again, but this time she crept down the carpeted steps. When she reached the first floor, she swept up the hallway on tiptoe and darted into the master bedroom, locking the door behind her.

Her heart thumped as though to make up for the beats it had skipped when the stranger first appeared. She put her hands on her cheeks, which felt deathly cold, and took three deep breaths. Then she walked into the closet and stood on the inverted wooden box that gave her access to the top shelf.

Her hand barely reached over the edge, but she felt what she wanted: Will's .38 revolver. She had pleaded with him a hundred times not to keep the pistol in the house with Abby. Now she thanked God he hadn't listened. She pulled down the gun and opened the cylinder, as her father had taught her long ago. *A gun is just a tool, hon, like an ax or a drill. . . .* The .38's hammer rested on an empty chamber, but five rounds filled the others.

Karen snapped the cylinder home and walked to the bedroom door, steeling herself with each step, clenching the pistol's checked grip like a lifeline. She was about to face the man who had taken Abby, and she would do whatever was necessary to make him give her back. There was no room for hesitation. Or for mercy.

She quietly opened the door, then edged along the hallway toward the rectangle of light that was the kitchen door. Her breath coming in little pants, she stopped just outside the door and peered into the kitchen.

Joe Hickey was sitting calmly at the kitchen table, drinking from one of the glasses of tea. The realization that she had made that tea for Abby brought a lump to Karen's throat. She stepped into the kitchen, raised the gun, and aimed it at his face.

"Where's my daughter?"

Hickey swallowed some tea and slowly set down the glass. "You don't want to shoot me, Karen. Can I call you Karen?"

She shook the .38 at him. "Where's my little girl!"

"Abby is perfectly safe. However, if you shoot me, she'll be stone-dead within thirty minutes. And there won't be a thing I can do about it."

"Tell me what's happening!"

"Listen carefully, Karen. This is a kidnapping-for-ransom. Okay? It's about money. M-O-N-E-Y. That's all. So, the last thing I want is for anything to happen to your precious little girl."

"Where is Abby *right now*?"

"With my cousin. His name's Huey. Right after you got here, I passed her outside and Huey drove her off in his pickup truck. He's got a cell phone with him. . . ."

Hickey kept talking, but Karen couldn't make sense of

the words. She couldn't get past the image he'd just described. Abby alone with a stranger. She'd be whimpering in terror, crying for her mother. Karen felt as though she had been pushed from a great height, her stomach rolling over and over as she went into free fall.

"Are you listening, Karen? I said, if I don't call Huey every thirty minutes, he'll kill her. He won't want to, but he will. That's rule number two. So don't get any crazy ideas about calling the police. It would take them an hour just to get me fingerprinted and into lockup, and by the time I saw a pay phone, Abby would be lying dead beside the highway."

Karen snapped out of her trance.

"But that's not going to happen," Hickey said, smiling. "You're a smart girl. And Huey's a good boy. Loves kids. He's practically a kid himself. But he's a little slow. Since I'm the only person who was ever nice to him, he always does exactly what I tell him. So you want to be real careful with that gun."

Karen looked at the weapon in her hand. Suddenly it seemed more of a threat to Abby than to the man in front of her.

"You pick things up real quick, I can tell," Hickey said. "So keep paying attention. This is a kidnapping-for-ransom, like I said. But it's not like you've seen on TV or in the movies. This isn't the Lindbergh baby. It's not some Exxon executive buried-alive bullshit. This is a work of art. A perfect crime. I know, because I've done it five times before and I haven't been caught yet. Not even a whiff of Johnny Law."

Karen pointed to Hickey's left arm, where the poorly

inked needlework showed below the band of his sleeve. An eagle holding an iron cross in its talons. "Isn't that a prison tattoo?"

Hickey's face tightened, then relaxed. "They busted me for something else. How'd you know that was done in the joint?"

"I don't know." Karen had seen several tattoos like it on surgical patients in the OR. "I just know."

"You're smarter than the average June Cleaver, aren't you? Well, it won't help you any. I own you, lady. And your little girl. You need to remember that."

Karen forced back fresh tears, unwilling to give Hickey the satisfaction of seeing them. The gun wavered in her hand. She steadied it.

"I know what you're thinking," he said. "What happened to the kids those other five times, right?"

She nodded slowly.

"Right this second, every one of them is living a carefree life, watching *Barney* or *Rugrats* or swimming in their private freakin' swimming pool. You know why? Because their mamas didn't shoot me and their daddies were calm and methodical after the first few minutes. Just like you're going to be." He took another slow sip of tea. "Needs sugar. I can tell you weren't raised in the country."

Karen had been raised on rural army bases, but she saw no reason to correct Hickey's impression.

"If that gun happens to go off by accident," he said, "Abby will be just as dead as if you shot her. The bullet in that chamber will kill two people, Karen. Something to think about."

She didn't want to put down the gun, but she saw no choice. She tossed it onto the table beside Hickey, cracking one of the white tiles of its surface.

"Good girl," he said, leaving the .38 where it had fallen. "Yes, ma'am, that's exactly what a good mother does in a situation like this. I hope your husband's as smart as you are."

New fear gripped Karen. "Where's Will? What have you done with him?"

Hickey made an elaborate show of looking at his watch, which he wore on the inside of his wrist, like certain military officers, as though time were his province alone, and not to be shared with anyone else. "Right about now, hubby's winged most of his way to Biloxi's *beautiful* Beau Rivage Casino Resort."

Hickey said this with the exaggerated enthusiasm of a game show huckster, but it was the level of his knowledge that crystallized the fear in Karen. He knew their lives, their plans, their exact schedules—

"After hubby gets checked in, we're going to let him shower up and give his little speech. Then he's going to get a visit from a partner of mine, and he'll find out where things stand. The way you just did. Then we're all going to wait out the night together."

Terror ballooned in Karen's chest. "Wait out the night? What are you talking about?"

"This operation takes exactly twenty-four hours. I'm talking from the time Huey and me cranked up this morning. A day's work for a year's pay." Hickey chuckled. "We've got about twenty hours left to go."

"But why do we have to wait?" The old panic had

come back with a vengeance. "If you want money, I'll get it for you. All you want. Just bring my baby back!"

Hickey shook his had. "I know you would, Karen. But that's not the way this operation works. Everything's set up according to a timetable. That way there's no surprises."

"But we *can't* wait twenty hours!"

"You'd be surprised what you can do for your kid. This is a nice place. We'll get to know each other a little, have supper, pretend everything's fine. Abby can watch Huey whittle. Before you know it, I'll have my money and you'll have Abby back."

"Listen to me, you stupid son of a bitch!"

Hickey paled. "You want to watch what you're saying there, Mom. It's not smart under the circumstances."

Karen tried to keep her voice under control. "Sir—Mr. Hickey—if we wait until tomorrow, Abby is going to die."

His dark eyes narrowed. "What are you talking about?"

"Abby's a diabetic. A juvenile diabetic. She'll die without her insulin."

"Bullshit."

"My God . . . didn't you *know* that?"

"Talk's cheap. Let's see some proof."

Karen went to a kitchen drawer and pulled out a plastic bag full of orange-capped syringes with 25-gauge needles. She threw the bag onto the table, then opened the refrigerator, where a dozen glass vials waited in compulsively organized rows. She took out a vial of long-acting insulin and tossed it at Hickey.

He caught it and stared at the label. It read: *Humulin N.* PATIENT: Abigail Jennings. PRESCRIBING PHYSICIAN: Will Jennings, M.D.

"Damn," Hickey said under his breath. "I don't believe this."

"Please," Karen said in the most submissive voice she could muster. "We *must* get this medicine to my daughter. She—My God, I didn't check her sugar when we got home." Karen felt herself falling again, as though the floor beneath her feet had vanished. "Abby's due for her shot in an hour. We've *got* to get this to her. How far away is she?"

"We can't go," Hickey said in a flat voice.

Karen grabbed the .38 off the table and pointed it at his chest. "Oh, yes, we can. We're going right now."

"I told you about that gun."

She cocked the revolver. "If Abby doesn't get her insulin, she's going to die. Now you *do what I say!*"

Something flickered in Hickey's eyes. Amusement. Perhaps surprise. He held up his hands, palms toward Karen. "Take it easy, June. I meant we can't go *yet.* Abby's being transported to a safe place. Maybe we can go later. Tell me about her condition. How critical is it?"

"How critical? She could *die.*"

"How long before she's in trouble?"

Karen did the math in her head. If Abby ate only normal food before falling asleep—if she could sleep at all—she could make it through the night. But Karen had no intention of taking that risk. What if Hickey's cousin fed her candy bars?

"Juvenile diabetics are very unstable," she said. "If

Abby eats too much sugar, she could get in trouble very quickly. She'll get dehydrated. Then comes abdominal pain and vomiting. Then she'll go into a coma and die. It can happen *very* fast."

Hickey pursed his lips, obviously doing some mental math of his own. Then he reached over the little built-in desk where Karen paid the household bills, hung up the cordless phone, and punched in a new number.

Karen stepped up to the desk and hit the SPEAKER button on the phone. Hickey looked down, trying to figure out how to switch it off, but before he could, a deep male voice said: "Joey? Has it been thirty minutes?"

"No. What happened to 'hello'?"

"Oh, yeah. I'm sorry." The man's voice had an incongruous sound, like the voice of a fifty-year-old child. *He's practically a kid himself,* Hickey had said.

"How does the kid look?"

"Okay. She's still sleeping."

Karen's heart thudded. She jerked the gun. "Let me talk to her."

Hickey warned her back with a flip of his hand.

"Who was that, Joey?"

"Betty Crocker."

"Give me the phone!" Karen demanded.

"Abby can't talk right now. She's sedated."

Sedated? "You son of a bitch! You—"

Hickey half rose and slugged Karen in the stomach. The breath left her in an explosive rush, and she dropped to the kitchen floor, the gun clattering uselessly in front of her.

"Touch the kid's chest, Huey. She breathing okay?"

"Kinda shallow. Like a puppy."

"Okay, that's fine. Look, don't give her any candy bars or anything like that. Okay? Maybe some saltines or something."

"She needs fluids," Karen gasped from the floor. "Plenty of water!"

"Give her some water. Plenty of water."

"Saltines and water," Huey echoed.

"I may be coming out to see you tonight."

Karen felt a surge of hope.

"That'd be good," Huey said. "I wouldn't be so nervous."

"Yeah. Drive slow, okay?"

"Fifty-five," Huey said dutifully.

"Good boy."

Hickey hung up and squatted before Karen. "Here's the deal. Before we do anything, we have to let my partner make contact with your husband. We've got to make sure old Will's on the same page with us before we move. Because those first few minutes are the shocker. Nobody knows that better than you, right? And with this diabetic thing, he might just flip out. I hope not, because if he does, all the insulin in the world won't save Abby." Hickey stood. "We'll take care of your little girl. It's just going to take a couple of hours. Now, get up off that floor."

He offered his hand, but Karen ignored it. She got her knees beneath her and used the edge of the table to pull herself to her feet. The gun remained on the floor.

He walked past her to the opposite wall of the kitchen, where a four-foot-wide framed silk screen hung. It was a semiabstract rendering of an alligator, brightly colored like a child's painting, but with the unmistakable strength of genius in it.

"You've got paintings by this guy all over your house," he said. "Right?"

"Yes," Karen replied, her thoughts on Abby. "Walter Anderson. He's dead."

"Worth a lot of money?"

"That silk screen isn't. I colored it myself. But the watercolors are valuable. Do you want them?"

Hickey laughed. "Want them? I don't give a shit about 'em. And by morning, you're going to hate every one. You're never going to want see another one again."

He turned from the painting and smiled.

Forty miles south of Jackson, a small, tin-roofed cabin stood in a thick forest of second-growth pine and hardwoods. An old white AMC Rambler rested on cinder blocks in the small clearing, blotched with primer and overgrown by weeds. A few feet away from the Rambler stood a rusting propane tank with a black hose curled over the valve mechanism. Birdcalls echoed through the small clearing, punctuated by the rapid-fire *pock-pock-pock* of a woodpecker, and gray squirrels chased each other through the upper branches of the oaks.

The animals fell silent. A new sound had entered the woods. A motor. An old one, its valves tapping from unleaded gasoline. The noise grew steadily until the green hood of a pickup truck broke from beneath the trees into dappled sunlight. The truck trundled down the rutted lane and stopped before the cabin porch.

Huey Cotton got out and walked quickly around the hood, the Barbie still sticking out of his pocket. He opened the passenger door and lifted Abby's limp body off the seat. Cradling her like an infant in his massive arms, he closed the truck's door with his hip and walked carefully up the porch steps.

The old planks groaned beneath his weight. He paused before the screen door, then bent at the waist, hooked his sausagelike pinkie in the door handle, and shuffled backward until the screen opened enough for him to thrust his bulk between it and the main door. The main door yielded to one shove of his size-16 Redwing boot. He carried Abby through it, and the screen door slapped shut behind him with a bang.

Will landed the Baron behind a vintage DC-3 he would have loved to get a look at, but today he didn't have the time. He taxied to the general aviation area and pulled into the empty spot indicated to him by a ground crewman. The Gulfport-Biloxi airport housed units of the Army and Air National Guard. There were fighter jets and helicopters stationed around the field, and the resulting high security always gave Will a little shock.

He had radioed ahead and arranged to have his rental car waiting at U.S. Aviation Corp., which handled the needs of private pilots. As soon as the props stopped turning, he climbed out and unloaded his luggage from the cabin. Hanging bag, suitcase, sample case, notebook computer case, golf clubs. Schlepping it all to the blue Ford Tempo made his inflamed sacroiliac joints scream, even through the deadening layer of ibuprofen.

A security guard told him that Interstate 10 East had been closed due to a jackknifed semitruck, so he would have to take the beachfront highway to Biloxi. Will hoped the traffic was not too bad between the airport and the casino. He had less than an hour to reach the meeting room, and he needed to shower and shave before he took the podium before five hundred physicians and their wives.

It took him five minutes to reach U.S. 90, the highway that ran along the Gulf of Mexico from Bay Saint Louis to the Alabama border and Mobile Bay. The sun was just starting to fall toward New Orleans, sixty miles to the west. It would still be light when he began his lecture. Bathing-suited families walked and flew kites along the beach, but Will saw no one in the water. There were no waves to speak of, and the "surf" here had always been brown and tepid. The gulf didn't turn its trademark emerald green until you hit Destin, Florida, two hours to the east.

Will didn't particularly like the Mississippi Gulf Coast. He never had. The place had a seedy, transient air. A peeling, tired-out atmosphere that drifted over the trucked-in sand and brown water like a haze of corruption. In 1969, Hurricane Camille had torn through the beachfront communities at two hundred miles per hour, and after that things were the same, only worse. There was a pervasive sense that the best times had come and gone, never to return.

But two decades after Camille's fearsome passage, casino gambling changed everything. Glittering palaces rose off the beach like surrealistic sand castles, employing thousands of people and pollinating all sorts of service industries, particularly pawn shops and "Cash

Quick" establishments where you could cash your social security check or hock your car title for money to blow at the craps table. But at night you didn't see all that. You only saw the line of sparkling towers, their Vegas-style signs blazing over the night waters of the gulf as thousands of cars crawled up the coast highway, filled with the desperate and the gullible.

Will felt strange being by himself, away from home. Having the simple freedom to stop anywhere he chose, to take an unplanned turn without having to explain or to answer to anyone. Of course, that freedom was illusory. There were people waiting for him, and he was late already. He pressed down the accelerator, figuring it was worth the risk of a ticket.

As he neared the casino, traffic slowed to a crawl, but he was already in sight of the words BEAU RIVAGE glittering high in the fading sunlight. He turned off the highway and pulled up into the tasteful entrance of the casino resort, thankful for the bellboys who stood waiting to take his bags. Keeping the computer and sample cases for himself, he gave his keys to a valet and walked through the massive doors.

The interior of the Beau Rivage was built on the colossal scale of post-mafia Las Vegas casinos. A fantasy re-creation of the antebellum South, with full-size magnolia trees growing throughout its lobby, the casino hotel struck Will as a cross between Trump Tower and Walt Disney World. He picked his way through the gamblers in the lobby and walked over to the long check-in desk. When he gave his name, the hotel manager came out of an office to the left and shook his hand. He was tall and too thin, and his name tag read GEAUTREAU.

"Your colleagues have been getting a little nervous, Dr. Jennings," he said with a cool smile.

"I had a long surgery this afternoon." Will tapped his computer case. "But I've got my program ready to go. Just get me to a shower."

Geautreau handed over an envelope containing a credit card key. "You've got a suite on twenty-eight, Doctor. A Cypress suite. A thousand square feet. Dr. Stein instructed me to give you the red-carpet treatment." Saul Stein was the outgoing president of the Mississippi Medical Association. "Are you sure I can't have a bellman take those cases up for you?"

Will strained to maintain his smile as he realized that his privacy had been violated. He could hear Dr. Stein telling the hotel manager about his arthritis, warning Geautreau not to let Will carry a single bag upstairs. All with the best of intentions, of course.

"No, thanks," he said, tapping his case again. "Sensitive cargo here."

"Our audio-video consultant is waiting for you in the Magnolia Ballroom. You'll find the VIP elevators past the jewelry store and to the right. Don't hesitate to call for anything, Doctor. Ask for me by name."

"I will."

As Will crossed the lobby, making for the elevators, a heavyset man in his forties shouted from an open-air bar to his left. It was Jackson Everett, an old medical school buddy. Everett was wearing a Hawaiian shirt and held an umbrella drink in his hand.

"Will Jennings!" he boomed. "It's about damned time!" Everett shouldered his way across the lobby and slapped Will on the back, sending a sword of pain down his spine. "I haven't seen you since the scramble at Annandale, boy. How's it hanging? Where's Karen?"

"She didn't make it this trip, Jack. Some Junior League thing. You just get here?"

Everett laughed. "Are you kidding? I flew in two days ago for some early golf. You're giving the speech tonight, I hear."

Will nodded.

"Hey, without Karen, you'll have to hit the casino with me. High rollers, stud!"

"I'd better pass. I had a long surgery, and then the flight. I'm whipped."

"Pussy-whipped, more like," Everett complained. "You gotta live a little, son."

Will gave an obliging laugh. "Let's get a beer tomorrow and catch up."

"How are your hands? Are you up for eighteen holes?"

"I brought my clubs. We'll just have to see."

"Well, I hope you can. Hey, don't put us to sleep tonight, okay?"

"But that's my specialty, Jack."

Everett groaned and walked off gulping his drink.

As Will waited for an elevator, he saw a few more faces he recognized across the lobby, but he didn't make an effort to speak. He had twenty-five minutes to get dressed and down to the meeting room, where he would still have to set up the notebook computer for his video presentation.

On the twenty-eighth floor, he opened the door to his suite and found his bags and golf clubs waiting for him. The manager had not exaggerated. The suite was large enough for permanent residence. He set his cases on the sitting room sofa, then walked into the marble-floored bathroom and turned on the hot water. As the bathroom filled with steam, he unzipped his suit bag, hung a blue pinstripe Lands' End suit in the closet, and unpacked a laundry-boxed shirt, which he laid out on the coffee table. Then he stripped to his shorts and lifted his sample case onto the bureau beside the television. From it he removed a bound folder and laid it on the desk. The title on the cover read: "The Safe Use of Depolarizing Paralyzing Relaxants in the Violent Patient." The paper summarized three years of work in the laboratory and in clinical trials, as well as in the conference rooms of pharmaceutical companies. The culmination of that work—a drug that would trade under the name *Restorase*—represented potential profits on a vast scale, enough to make Will a truly wealthy man.

Nervous compulsion made him check the other contents of the sample case: a video-adapter unit, which would allow his computer to interface with the hotel convention room's projection TV, several drug vials, some of which contained prototype Restorase; and some high-tech syringes. Will counted the vials, then closed the case and hurried into the steamy bathroom, pulling off his underwear as he went.

Hickey and Karen sat facing each other across the kitchen table. A few moments before, Karen had picked up the .38, and he had made no move to stop her. She pointed it at his chest as they talked.

"That gun makes you feel better?" Hickey said.

"If you tell me we're not taking the insulin to Abby, it's going to make me feel a lot better. And you a lot worse."

He smiled. "The Junior League princess has guts, huh?"

"If you hurt my baby, you'll see some guts. Yours."

Hickey laughed outright.

"I don't understand why we have to wait until tomorrow," she said. "Why don't you just let me empty our accounts and give you the money?"

"For one thing, the banks have closed. You can't come close to the ransom with automated withdrawals. Even if the banks were open, just pulling out the money would cause a lot of suspicion."

"What will be different tomorrow morning? How do you plan to get the ransom money?"

"Your husband is going to call his financial advisor here—Gray Davidson—and tell him a great little story. He's just discovered the missing centerpiece of Walter Anderson's largest sculpture. It's a male figure with antlers called 'Father Mississippi.' Only one photograph of it exists, and many people believe it was stolen from Anderson's house. The value is—"

"Higher than any painting he ever did," Karen finished. "Because he didn't do much sculpture."

Hickey grinned. "Pretty good, huh? I do my homework. These goddamn doctors, I tell you. Every one of 'em collects something. Cars, boats, books, whatever.

Look at this kitchen. Every gadget known to man. I bet you got eighty pairs of shoes upstairs, like that Filipino hog, Imelda Marcos. You can't believe the money these guys piss away. I mean, how many freakin' gallbladders can you take out in a month?"

"Will's not like that."

"Oh, no, he doesn't spend more money on paintings every year than he pays all his employees put together. These guys . . . a slip of the knife, somebody dies, and it's 'Gee, sorry. Couldn't be helped. Wish I could stick around, but I've got a two o'clock tee time.' "

Karen started to argue, but she sensed that it wouldn't help her situation. Hickey knew a lot about their lives, yet there were huge gaps. Abby's diabetes. Will's work. Will didn't even use a scalpel. He was an anesthesiologist. He used gases and needles. She watched Hickey closely, trying to get a handle on the man beneath the bluster. One thing she knew already: he carried a chip on his shoulder the size of the Rock of Gibraltar.

"Anyway," Hickey said, "tomorrow morning, Will's gonna call Davidson and tell him he needs two hundred grand wired to him in Biloxi. He's got a one-time opportunity to buy this statue, and the owner wants cash. And just in case Mr. Tight-Ass Gray Davidson is suspicious, Will's lovely wife, Karen, is coming down to the office to authorize the wire. It isn't strictly required, but it's a nice touch. Then you and I are going to drive down to Davidson's office. I'll wait outside while you go in and bitch a little. 'That Will, he goes absolutely off his head when he makes a discovery, but what can you do? Boys will be boys.' Then you sign off on the money, and the two hundred grand is off to Biloxi at the speed of light. My partner drives Will to the bank in Biloxi, Will goes in, comes out with the cash, and hands it to my partner. And that's all she wrote."

"You're doing all this for two hundred thousand dollars?"

Hickey laughed and shook his head. "See? That's what I'm talking about. To you, two hundred grand is nothing. A down payment on a house. You won't even *feel* two hundred. And that's the point. The money's liquid. You can get it easy, and you don't feel any pain when it's gone. You're happy, I'm happy, and your kid's back safe at home. What more could you ask for?"

"Abby here now! Why can't she stay with us? Or us with her? That won't hurt your plan a bit."

Hickey's smile vanished. "This whole little machine runs on fear, Karen. Your fear for Abby. Will's fear for you, and for Abby. Fear is the only thing keeping you from pulling that trigger right now. Right?"

She didn't answer.

"Most kidnappers are brain-dead," he said. "They get busted the minute they go for the ransom. Or right after. They try all kinds of complicated shit, but the truth is, no ransom pickup method is safe from the FBI. Not even wiring the money to Brazil. The technology's just too good now. You should see the statistics. Damn near *zero* kidnappings-for-ransom succeed in this country. Why? The drop. Picking up the ransom. But I'm not picking up any ransom. Your husband's doing it for me. You're sending it, he's picking it up. I'm not even *involved.* Is that beautiful or what?"

Karen said nothing, but she saw the merit in his plan. Like all great ideas, it had the virtue of simplicity.

"I'm a goddamn genius," Hickey went on. "You think your old man could've dreamed this up? Fucking gas-passer's all he is. Pass the gas, pick up the check. And a fine wife like you waiting at home. What a waste."

She forced herself not to look away as Hickey appraised her body. She would not let him believe she was intimidated by anything but his control of Abby.

"The other way people screw up," he said, "is taking the kid off with them and sending a ransom note. That leaves the parents at home, alone and scared shitless. Then they get a note or a call—both traceable—asking for more ransom money than they could raise in a week. What else are they going to do but call the FBI? My way, nobody calls anybody but me and my partners, every half hour like clockwork. And as long as we do that, nobody gets hurt. Nobody goes to prison. Nobody dies."

"You like listening to yourself talk, don't you."

He shrugged. "I like doing things right. This plan is as clean as they come. It's run perfectly five times in a row. Am I proud of that? Yeah. And who else can I talk about it to but someone like you?"

Hickey was talking about kidnapping the way Will's partners bragged about inside stock trades. "Don't you have any feelings for the children involved?" she asked. "How terrified they must be?"

"A kid can stand anything for twenty-four hours," Hickey said softly. "I stood a lot worse for *years.*"

"But sooner or later you'll make a mistake. You're bound to."

"The parents might. Not me. The guy I got keeping these kids? He loves 'em. Weighs about three hundred fifty pounds. Looks like goddamn Frankenstein, but he's a giant teddy bear."

Karen shut her eyes against the image of Abby being held prisoner by a monster. The image did not vanish but instead became clearer.

"Don't worry," Hickey said. "Huey's not a child abuser or anything. He's too slow. Only . . ."

Her eyes flew open. "What?"

"He doesn't like kids running away from him. When he was little, kids at the regular school treated him pretty bad. When he got bigger, they just yelled things and ran. Then his mama put him in a retard school. Kids are pretty damn cruel. When Huey sees kids run, it still makes him lose his head."

Hot blood rushed to her face. "But don't you think it's natural for a child being held prisoner by a stranger to try to run?"

"Your kid the panicky type?"

"Not usually, but . . . God, can't we please spend the night wherever they are?"

"I'm getting hungry," Hickey said. "Why don't you see about fixing some supper? I'll bet you were a natural with an Easy-Bake oven."

Karen looked at the gun in her hand. A less useful thing she could not imagine. "When can we take Abby the insulin?"

"Food," Hickey said, rubbing his flat belly. "F-O-O-D."

FOUR

Will ate a bite of redfish and looked out over an audience of close to a thousand people eating the same dish. To his right, at the podium, Dr. Saul Stein was giving a rather digressive introductory speech. At last, like a man making a sudden left turn, he veered back onto the point.

"Ladies and gentlemen, we are very lucky to have with us tonight a physician of the first caliber. A man whose pioneering work on the clinical frontiers of anesthesiology will be published in next month's *New England Journal of Medicine*."

A burst of applause stopped Stein for several moments, and he smiled.

"Tonight, we will be treated to a précis of that article, which describes fundamental work carried out at our own University of Mississippi Medical Center. What's amazing to me is that our speaker—a native Mississippian—entered his field as a second specialty, out of unfortunate necessity. We are very lucky that he did, because—"

A high-pitched beep stopped Stein in midsentence. Five hundred doctors simultaneously reached for their belts, Will included. General laughter rolled through the huge room as most of the physicians remembered that they were on vacation, their pagers back in their hometowns. Will was wearing his, but it had not produced the offending beep. Still, he moved the switch on the SkyTel from BEEP to VIBRATE.

"Who the hell's on call down here?" Stein barked from the podium. "There's no getting away from those damn things." As the laughter died away, he said, "I could easily talk about our speaker for another hour, but I won't. Dessert is coming, and I want to let Will get started. Ladies and gentlemen, Dr. Will Jennings."

Applause filled the darkened ballroom. Will rose, speech in hand, and walked to the podium, where his notebook computer glowed softly. He sensed the expectation in the crowd.

"They tell me you should begin a speech with a joke," he said. "My wife tells me I'm not much of a comedian, so I shouldn't risk it. But flying down here today, I was reminded of a story an old paramedic told me about Hurricane Camille."

Everybody thought about Camille when they came to the coast. You could still see trees that had been twisted into eerie contortions by the mother of all hurricanes.

"This guy was driving an ambulance down here in sixty-nine, and he was one of the first to go out on call after the storm surge receded. There were dead animals everywhere, and it was still raining like hell. On his second call, he and his partner saw a young woman lying beside the road in a formal dress. They thought she might be one of those fools who tried to ride out the hurricane by throwing a party. Anyway, he figures the girl is dead, but he doesn't want to let her go without a fight, so he starts CPR, mouth-to-mouth, the whole bit. Nothing works, and he finally gives up. The next day, they're hearing who died in the hurricane, because relatives of the missing are coming back to view the bodies in the morgue. The EMT asks about the girl he tried to save, but nobody's come forward to identify her. A week goes by, and he still can't forget her. Then the word comes down from the morgue. The girl's mother finally ID'd her. She'd been dead for two years. The hurricane had washed her up from the cemetery."

Squeals of revulsion were drowned by a wave of male laughter. No one appreciated morbid humor more than a bunch of docs with a couple of drinks under their belts.

"My presentation will be brief and to the point. The emergency physicians and anesthesiologists should find it provocative, and I hope the rest of you find it interesting. I'm going to try something new tonight, a bit of high-tech wizardry I've been toying with." Will had videotaped his past year's clinical work on a Canon XL-1, a broadcast-quality digital video camera that Karen had tried to talk him out of buying. He'd worked dozens of hours on his computer, editing it all down to the program that would accompany tonight's talk. The finished product was seamless. But any time you worked with hard drives and video, glitches lurked in the wings. "If it doesn't work," he added, "at least nobody dies."

More laughter, wry this time.

"Lights, please."

The lights dimmed. With a last flutter of nerves, Will clicked a file icon with his trackball, and the 61-inch Hitachi television behind him flashed up a high-resolution image of an operating room. A patient lay unconscious on the table as the OR team prepared for surgery. Wonder lit the faces in the crowd, most of them doctors with minimal computer knowledge. Their ages varied widely, with couples in their sixties seated beside others in their thirties. Some of the younger wives looked a lot like Karen.

Will glanced at his large-font script and said, "This patient looks thoroughly prepped for surgery, doesn't he? Twenty minutes before this picture was taken, he assaulted a doctor and two nurses with a broken coffee carafe, causing serious injuries."

The image on the Hitachi smash-cut to a jiggling, handheld shot that looked like something out of a Quentin Tarantino film. A wild-eyed man was jabbing a broken coffee carafe at whoever was behind the camera and screaming at the top of his lungs. *"Satan's hiding inside you, motherfucker!"*

The audience gasped.

The man in the video swung the jagged carafe in a roundhouse arc, and the camera jerked wildly toward the ceiling as its operator leaped back to avoid being slashed. Only Will knew that the cameraman had been himself.

"It's the end times!" the man shrieked. *"Jesus is coming!"* In the background, a nurse cried, "Where the hell is security?" The man with the carafe charged her and began weeping and howling at once. *"Where's my Rhelda Jean? Somebody call Rhelda, goddamn it!"*

Suddenly the video cut back to the man lying prostrate and prepped in the OR.

"If I were to tell you that this man was subdued in the ER not by police, but by me—using a drug—you might guess this was accomplished with a benzodiazepene, a barbiturate, or a narcotic. You would be wrong. No doctor can hit the vein, or even the muscle, of a PCP-crazed man who is trying to kill him with a coffee carafe, not without grave risk to himself and other staff. The ER docs among you might make a more experienced guess and assume that it was done with a paralyzing relaxant like pancuronium bromide, curate, or succinylcholine. And you'd be right. Nowadays, emergency physicians routinely resort to the use of these drugs, because they sometimes offer the only means of compelling violent patients to accept lifesaving treatment. And though they don't talk about it much, they sometimes use paralyzing relaxants without first administering sedatives, as a sort of punishment to 'repeat offenders'—violent addicts and gangbangers who show up in the ER again and again, causing chaos and injury to staff.

"All of you know how dangerous the paralyzing relaxants are, both medically and legally, because they leave patients unable to move or even breathe until they're intubated and bagged, and their breathing done for them."

The Hitachi showed a nurse standing over the patient in the ER, working a breathing bag. Will glanced into the crowd. At the first table, a stunning young woman was staring at him with laserlike concentration. She was twenty years younger than most of the women in the audience, except the trophy wives escorted by those doctors who had ditched the loyal ladies who put them through medical school, in favor of newer models. This woman wore a tight black dress accented by a diamond drop necklace, and she seemed to be alone. Older couples sat on either side of her, framing her like bookends. Since she was sitting in front of the first table, Will had an unobstructed view, from her tapered legs and well-turned ankles to her impressive décolletage. The dress was shockingly short for a medical meeting, but it produced the desired effect. She was distracting enough that he had to remind himself to start talking again.

"Tonight," he said, "I'm going to tell you about a revolutionary new class of drug developed by myself and the Klein-Adams pharmaceutical company, and tested in my own clinical trials at University Hospital in Jackson. This drug, the chemical name of which I must keep under wraps for one more month, can completely counteract the effects of succinylcholine, restoring full nerve conductivity in less than thirty seconds."

Will heard murmurs of disbelief.

"Beyond this, we have developed special new compressed-gas syringes that allow the safe injection of a therapeutic dose of Anectine—that's a popular trade name for succinylcholine—into the external jugular vein, with one half second of skin contact."

The Hitachi showed the screaming man with the broken carafe again. This time, as he charged a female nurse, a tall man in a white coat stepped up behind him with something that looked like a small white pistol in his hand. The white-coated doctor was Will. As the patient jabbed the glittering shard at the brave nurse who had agreed to distract him, Will moved in and touched the side of neck with the white pistol, which was in fact a compressed-gas syringe. There was an audible hiss, and the man's free hand flew up to his neck. The dramatic fluttering of his eyelids and facial muscles was hard to see in the handheld camera shot, but when he threw up both arms and crossed them over his chest, the audience gasped. As he collapsed, Will caught him and dragged him toward a treatment table, and two nurses hurried over to help.

The ballroom was silent as a cave.

On screen, two nurses restrained the patient with straps. Then Will stepped up and injected him in the antecubital vein with a conventional syringe.

"I am now injecting the patient with Restorase, the first of these new drugs to be approved by the FDA. Now, if you'll look at your watches, please."

The camera operator moved up to the treatment table and focused on the patient's face. His eyes were half closed. Every doctor in the audience knew that the man's diaphragm was paralyzed. He could not move or breathe, yet he was fully conscious of what was going on around him.

Will heard shuffles and whispers as the seconds ticked past. At twenty-five seconds, the patient's eyes blinked, then opened. He tried to raise his hand, but the arm moved with a floppy motion. He gasped twice, then began to breathe.

"What's your name, sir?" Will asked.

"Tommy Joe Smith," he said, his eyes wide.

"Do you know what just happened to you, Mr Smith?"

"Jesus Lord . . . don't do that again."

"Are you going to try to stab anyone else, Mr. Smith?"

He shook his head violently.

The image cut to a shot of drug vials—Anectine and Restorase—sitting beside a compressed gas syringe on a soapstone surface.

"I know how shocking that footage can be," Will said. "But remember the scene that preceded it."

On the Hitachi, Tommy Joe Smith charged the nurse again with the shard of glass.

"The potential applications are limited, thank God, but their necessity cannot be argued. In emergency rooms, psychiatric wards, and prison infirmaries, health-care workers are suffering grave injury at the hands of violent patients. Now their safety can be insured without resorting to greater violence to restrain the out-of-control patient. Very soon, physicians will be able to use depolarizing relaxants without fear of fatal outcomes or costly lawsuits."

A collective murmur of approval swept through the darkened room, followed by a wave of applause. Will had known the video would disturb them—as it should have—but he also knew they would recognize the enormous potential of the drug. He glanced to his left and saw Saul Stein grinning like a proud parent.

"As you know," he said, checking to be sure that the Hitachi showed an anatomical diagram of a hand, "the relaxants work primarily at the myoneural junction, interrupting the normal flow of impulses from the brain to the skeletal muscles. . . ."

He continued almost without thought, thanks to the rehearsals he had done with Karen and Abby. The woman in black was still staring from the front table. She wasn't smiling exactly, but there was a suggestive curve to her lips that signaled interest in more than drug therapy. He tried to make eye contact with several other audience members, but every few seconds his gaze returned to the young woman. And why not? It was natural for a lecturer to pick out an individual and speak directly to him—or her. It eased the nerves and gave the voice an undertone of intimacy. Tonight he would speak to the woman in black.

Whenever he turned back from pointing out something on the Hitachi, she was watching him. She had large eyes that never seemed to blink, and a mane of blond hair that fell to her shoulders in the style of Lauren Bacall in *To Have and Have Not.* Blondes had never done much for Will, but this one was different. What struck him—even in the dim spill of light from the big Hitachi—was her remarkable symmetry. His eyes followed the curve of her long legs as they rose to feminine hips, the hips curving into an hourglass waist. Her breasts were not too large, but almost too perfect. The strapless black dress revealed fine collarbones and strong shoulders. Her neck was long and graceful, her jaw defined, her lips full. But what held him was her eyes. They never left his face, even as he studied her from head to toe.

He turned to the Hitachi to check the video feed, and when he turned back, she shifted in her seat, uncrossed her legs, then recrossed them with the languid grace of a lioness stretching her flanks. The shortness of the cocktail dress gave him a brief but direct sight line between her legs, even from the podium. He felt blood rush to his face. It wasn't quite Sharon Stone in *Basic Instinct*—this woman was wearing panties—but she had made sure he could see everything but the brand name on the silk. Those dark panties were a far cry from the white cotton "granny" panties Karen had taken to wearing the past couple of years. As Will dropped his gaze to look at his speech, he realized that he had fallen behind the video. He looked back up and skipped ahead to the proper cue line.

The ghost of a smile touched the woman's lips.

Huey Cotton stood on the cabin porch, looking into darkening trees as the sun sank behind them. Tiny flashes of greenish yellow light floated beneath the branches like phosphorescent sparks from an unseen fire.

"Lightnin' bugs," he said, his voice filled with pleasure. "I wonder if there's a mason jar in the kitchen."

As he watched the little flares winking in the shadows, a soft groan came from inside the cabin. Huey's smile vanished, replaced by something like fear. He took a deep breath, then turned slowly and looked at the door with trepidation.

"I wish you was here, Mamaw," he said softly.

The groan came again.

He reached out and opened the screen door, then pushed open the main door and walked inside.

* * *

Hickey sat at Karen's kitchen table, eating a huge muffaletta sandwich and drinking iced tea.

"Damn, that's good," he said, wiping his mouth. "You got the dressing just right. Reminds me of New Orleans. That grocery store down in the Quarter."

"Are you from New Orleans?" Karen asked. She was standing at the island, opposite the refrigerator, packing syringes and insulin into a small Igloo ice chest.

"You hear a New Orleans accent?"

"Not really." She couldn't classify Hickey's speech. There was some Mississippi in it, but other inflections, too. He had to have spent some time outside the South. In the service, maybe.

"We'll just skip over my biography for now," he said, chewing another bite of the big sandwich. "Maybe we'll get into it later."

Karen was closing the ice chest when the garage doorbell rang.

Hickey was instantly on his feet, Will's gun in his hand. "Who's that?" he asked, his eyes flicking around the room as though a SWAT team might burst in. "You expecting somebody?"

Karen shook her head. She had no idea who it could be.

"Don't answer it. We'll just let them go on their merry way." He took a step toward the pantry. "Which door are they at?"

"The garage," she whispered, shocked by the sense of conspiracy she felt with Hickey. But the last thing she wanted was someone disrupting his carefully organized plan while Abby was under his control.

The bell rang twice more. The urgency of the ringer was like a finger poking Karen in the side.

"How come I didn't hear a car?" Hickey asked.

"Sometimes we don't." As she spoke the words, she realized who the visitor might be. Stephanie Morgan, the cochair of the Junior League flower show. Stephanie drove a Lexus that ran so quietly Karen never heard it pulling up the driveway. And of everyone she knew, Stephanie had the most reason to drop by over the next couple of days.

She and Hickey jumped when the kitchen window rattled. Karen turned and saw Stephanie Morgan's face pressed against the glass. She was shaking a reprimanding finger, and beside her was the little moon face of her eleven-month-old son, Josh.

"Open the door," Hickey said in a flat voice.

"Hide," Karen told him.

"I can't. She's looking at me right now." He slid the gun behind his right leg. "Go open it."

Karen didn't want to invite Stephanie into her nightmare, but if she refused to open the door now, Steph would throw a fit, and Hickey's plan would come apart. She held up her hand and motioned toward the garage. Stephanie nodded and disappeared from the window.

"Let me handle this," Karen told him. "Please."

He looked skeptical. "Let's see if you can."

When Karen opened the door, Stephanie pushed right past her with Josh in her arms, talking as she went. "Karen, you've *got* to come down to the Coliseum in the morning. I mean *first thing*. I've been down there all day, and the place is a wreck. They were supposed to have those livestock people out of there by lunch today, but there are still cows on the floor. *Cows,* Karen."

Stephanie had reached the kitchen. "Hello," she said to Hickey. "Are you Karen's secret lover? I always knew she had one. It's the quiet ones you have to watch out for."

Karen stepped into the kitchen and rubbed Josh's arm. The little guy was obviously exhausted from his day at the flower show venue, and he was resting his head on his mother's shoulder. Or had he sensed something frightening in Joe Hickey?

"Stephanie, this is Joe, my second cousin. He's from Washington State. Joe, Stephanie Morgan, Junior League soccer mom."

"Puh-*lease*," Stephanie said, giving Hickey a little wave and turning back to Karen. She obviously hadn't seen the gun. "I want to know why you didn't answer that doorbell."

Hickey was watching Karen over Stephanie's shoulder. His eyes had gone dead the moment she turned away from him. "I had some Mormons around before," Karen said. "I thought they'd come back for another try."

Stephanie pulled a wry face. With her overdone makeup, it made her look like a circus clown. "Likely story. *I* know what you're doing. Hiding from me. But I've got news for you, honey. You *can't.* You're the queen bee of this show, and I need you. When I saw those cows on that floor, I said, 'There's only one woman in the Junior League for this job, and that's Karen Jennings. She'll have those damn bovines out of here before another cow patty hits the floor.' "

Karen didn't know what to say. The only thing in her

mind was getting Stephanie and Josh out as quickly as possible. She felt a frightening energy radiating from Hickey, a sort of survival desperation. It was in his eyes, in the set of his shoulders and mouth. Something he'd developed in prison, maybe. If he perceived Stephanie as a threat, he would kill her. And eleven-month-old Josh? Karen didn't want to think about that.

Josh began to cry. Stephanie gave his back a perfunctory pat and began rocking on the balls of her feet.

"I'll be down there in the morning," Karen promised. She took Stephanie by the arm and began walking her back toward the pantry. "But Joe's father passed away recently, and he's down here to work out some estate problems with me. We only have tonight and the morning to do it."

"Karen." Stephanie planted her feet at the kitchen door. "You know how important this is. Lucy Childs is just waiting for us to screw this up."

Good God, Karen thought. *Junior League politics. Could anything in the world be less important?* She kept moving Stephanie toward the door. "I'll take care of the cows. You take Josh home and get him some supper. Where's Caroline?"

The second she asked, she wished she hadn't. Because Stephanie would now ask where Abby was.

"With my mother," Stephanie replied. "Which is another reason I'm so stressed. Mom was all set to get her highlights done this afternoon, and then she had to cancel to keep Caroline. Guilt trip from hell, of course. Where's Abby?"

"With Will's mother, in the Delta." They had reached

the laundry room. Karen looked back and saw Hickey silhouetted in the kitchen door. Her eyes searched for the outline of the gun.

"Nice meeting you, Joe!" Stephanie called.

"Yeah," he said.

Karen pushed her into the garage. Sure enough, Stephanie's white Lexus was parked just behind the Expedition.

"Your cousin looks interesting," Stephanie said, her eyes twinkling. "A little rough, maybe, but interesting. You sure I didn't just stumble onto a *tryst*?"

Karen forced a laugh. "Positive. Joe can't stand me. He's just here to settle the estate."

"Well, I hope you get some money out of it." She pointed at the Avalon parked beside the Expedition. "You need to upgrade your transportation, girl."

"I'll see you in the morning, Steph. I may be a little late."

Stephanie had leaned down to strap Josh into his car seat. "Don't you *dare*. I cannot handle cow shit, okay? That is not in my contract."

Karen forced another laugh. Stephanie got into the Lexus, started it, and backed around to go down the hill.

Something brushed Karen's shoulder. Hickey was standing beside her, and she hadn't even realized it. He waved at the Lexus. Stephanie honked her horn in reply, then disappeared over the lip of the drive.

"Not bad, Mom," Hickey said. "That skinny bitch owes you her life, and she doesn't even know it."

Karen realized she was shaking.

Hickey slapped her lightly on the behind, exactly the

way Will would have. "Let's get back inside. My muffaletta's getting cold."

Will's lecture was nearly done. The first susurrant sounds of dresses shifting on seats had reached his ears from the floor of the darkened ballroom. He had timed the program just right. Behind him, the Hitachi showed a maternal-fetal medicine specialist injecting Restorase into a fetus still in the womb. The fetus had been paralyzed before undergoing a blood transfusion to save its life. Restorase would bring it out of paralysis in a tenth of the time it would normally take.

"And while this particular injection required a good deal of comment," Will said, "I think this last shot is pretty self-explanatory."

The pregnant woman's belly was replaced by a wide-screen sequence of Will teeing off at the Annandale golf course, one recognized by most doctors in the audience. With creative editing, he had made his perfect drive appear to conclude with a stunning hole-in-one. When the ball hit the pin and dropped into the cup—to the accompaniment of Tex-Mex music from Kevin Costner's *Tin Cup*—a wild whoop went up from the dark (probably from the throat of Jackson Everett) and enthusiastic applause followed. The lights came up and revealed a laughing, exhilarated audience.

"I'll be at the Klein-Adams booth for two hours tomorrow afternoon," Will said. "I've brought samples of Restorase with me, as well as some of the gas-injection systems I've discussed tonight. I look forward to speaking with all of you."

This time the applause was more sedate, but also more sustained. Saul Stein stood and patted him on the back. Will shook Stein's hand, then began disconnecting his computer while the MMA president waited for the applause to die. Stein gushed over the presentation, then moved on to announcements regarding the next day's seminars. Will zipped up his computer case and stepped down from the podium.

He was immediately swallowed by a congratulatory mob that swept him out of the Magnolia Ballroom and into the atrium area. A visual echo of the woman in black remained in his mind, but he saw no sign of her among the smiling faces. For fifteen minutes he shook hands and accepted compliments, but before the real gabbers could trap him, he made for the escalators.

Like all casino hotels, the Beau Rivage made sure its guests had to pass through a carnival of slot machines and gaming tables on their way to and from the meeting rooms. Will's joints were giving him trouble, but he walked briskly. He wanted to get up to the room and take some more Advil.

He had planned to use the VIP elevators, but as he passed the main elevators, Jackson Everett reached out and pulled him into the waiting area. Everett had another drink in his hand, and the smell of rum came off him like Caribbean perfume. He opened his mouth to say something to Will, but just then an elevator opened and disgorged an elderly woman holding a cigar box full of quarters.

"Take 'em to the cleaners, Grandma!" he yelled. "Break the bank!"

The woman grinned and hurried toward the lobby. Everett pushed Will into the elevator, then followed him. Two more doctors wearing name tags stepped in after them, and the door began to close.

"Hold the door!" cried a female voice.

Will's right arm shot out to stop the sliding door, despite the pain the sudden move caused him. As the door retracted, the blond woman in the black dress stepped into the elevator.

"Thanks," she said. Her cheeks were flushed as though she had been running.

"You're welcome," Will replied.

The woman immediately turned and faced the closing doors, leaving him to study the wave of Lauren Bacall hair. The elevator was lined with mirrors and burled wood. Will looked to his right and studied her reflection in profile. The first thing he noticed was Everett and the other two doctors staring at her behind. She clutched her small handbag and looked at the floor, seemingly oblivious to the men behind her. Everett's gaze was openly lascivious.

"Did you set up that video display, Jennings?" asked one of the docs, whom Will vaguely recognized. "Or did you get some talented secretary to do it?"

"Karen probably did it," interjected Everett.

"No, I did it. It's easier than you think."

"Maybe," said the first man. "But where do you get the *time*?"

"I don't have Jack's bad habits."

"Hah," said Everett. "That from the guy who just developed the ultimate date-rape drug."

The men fell uncomfortably silent, and the elevator

stopped on the eighth floor. The doctors waited, giving the woman time to exit first, but she didn't move. The one who'd spoken to Will excused himself and brushed past her. Everett reached down and made as if to squeeze her exquisitely round derriere, then laughed and followed the other man out. Instead of walking to his room, he turned back to the elevator and pointed at Will.

"Come on to the casino with us! You'll love it. And even if you don't, we're going to take in a little *dancing* later. Know what I mean?"

The woman stiffened.

"I've got to call Karen," Will said, before Everett could get more explicit. "And I'm getting up early for golf. You guys knock the walls out."

"We always do." Everett smirked and flicked his eyebrows up and down like Groucho Marx.

Will leaned forward and hit the CLOSE DOOR button.

"Thanks," the woman said as the doors slid shut.

"He's okay, really. Just a little drunk."

She nodded and gave Will a look that told him she was used to such things. The elevator began to ascend. Between floors, Will caught himself staring at her trim figure again. When he looked up, her reflected face was watching him. He blushed and looked at the floor.

Someone behind Will cleared his throat. He'd forgotten the other doctor was still aboard. The elevator stopped again, this time on the thirteenth floor. The stranger got out, but the woman stayed put.

"What's your floor?" she asked.

"I'm sorry?"

"There's no floor button lit."

"Oh. I forgot to hit it. Still nervous, I guess. Twenty-eight, please."

"You've got a Cypress suite? So do I." She half-turned to him and smiled. "Your program was great, by the way. I can't believe you were nervous."

"Are you a physician?" he asked. He didn't like to think he believed in stereotypes, but he'd never met a woman doctor who looked like this.

"No. I'm with the casino company."

"Oh. I see. Hey, what's your floor? There's no button lit but twenty-eight."

"I'm twenty-eight, too. Most of the Cypress suites are up there."

He nodded and smiled politely, but when the woman turned away he gave her a hard look. *A hooker?* he wondered. The desk manager had told him Saul Stein said to give him the red-carpet treatment. Did that include a beautiful call girl?

The elevator opened on twenty-eight.

"Bye," the woman said. She got off and walked briskly down the hallway to the left. Will got off and watched her seductive motion, then turned left and counted the numbers down to suite 28021. He was inserting his credit card key when a female voice called, "Dr. Jennings?"

He looked up the long corridor. The blonde in the black dress was walking hesitantly toward him, gripping her small handbag in front of her.

"Can I help you?" he asked.

She fidgeted with her bag, then stopped as a door

opened opposite Will. A heavyset man wearing a plaid sport coat came out and hurried toward the elevators.

"My key doesn't work," the woman said, after he'd passed. "Could you try it for me?"

"I doubt I can do any better than you. I'll give it a shot, though."

"No pun intended?"

Will laughed, then put his computer case inside his room and followed her past the heavyset man waiting for the elevators.

The elevator bell dinged as Will inserted her card key and watched for green LED lights. But when he removed the key, only one LED flashed—red—and there was no click of tumblers. He tried again, seating the card squarely and firmly, but no matter what he did, the lock refused to open.

"I think you're out of luck," he told her.

"Looks like it. Would you mind if I used your phone to call the desk?"

He started to say he didn't mind, but something stopped him. A sense of something out of place, not quite logical. "I think there's a house phone by the VIP elevators. I'll be glad to wait with you."

She looked momentarily confused, but after a moment she smiled. "That's right. I appreciate you waiting with me. You never know who's creeping around the casino. My name's Cheryl, by the way."

Will accepted her proffered hand, which was cool, almost to the point of coldness. It felt like the hand of an anxious patient, someone terrified of needles. He dropped her hand and escorted her back toward the elevators, walking a little ahead.

The heavyset man was gone. Will glanced into the waiting area and saw what he was looking for: a cream-colored house telephone.

"Here it is," he said, turning back to her. "They'll have a new key up here in no—"

The words died in his throat. Cheryl was pointing an automatic pistol at his chest. She must have taken it from her handbag. Her eyes were resolute, but there was something else in them. Fear.

"What is this?" he asked. "I've only got a few bucks on me, but you're welcome to it. Credit cards, whatever."

"I don't want your money," she said, looking anxiously at the elevators. "I want you to go in your room."

"What for?"

"You'll find out. Just hurry up."

Something in Will's mind hardened to resistance. He wasn't going to start blindly obeying orders. If you did that, the next thing you knew, you were lying facedown on some dirty bathroom floor while they shot you in the back of the head.

"I'm not going anywhere. Not until you tell me what's going on. In fact"—he stepped toward the phone—"I'm going to call the front desk and have them call the police."

"Don't touch that."

"You're not going to shoot me, Cheryl." He picked up the telephone.

"If you call the police, Abby is going to die. And there's nothing I can do to stop it."

His arm froze. "What did you say?"

"Your daughter was kidnapped two hours ago, Doctor. If you want her to live, take me into your room right now. If you call the police, she'll die. I'm serious as a heart attack."

A paralyzing numbness was spreading from deep within Will's chest. It was disbelief, or perhaps the brain's attempt at disbelief in the face of knowledge too terrible to accept.

"What are you talking about?"

Cheryl glanced at the elevator again. He sensed the fear inside her metamorphosing into panic.

"Doctor, if somebody gets out of that elevator and sees me with this gun, the whole thing's going to come apart. Abby's going to die, okay? And I don't want that to happen. I'll tell you everything you want to know, but you'd better get me into your goddamn room right now."

Will heard a squawk and realized the phone was still in his right hand. He brought it slowly to his mouth.

"Talk, and you put a bullet in Abby's brain."

He hung up.

"Hurry," she said. "If I don't make a phone call soon, she's going to die anyway."

He stared at her for another few seconds, looking for options. He had none. He walked down to his door, unlocked it, and held it open for her.

Cheryl walked past him, holding the gun close against her, as though she expected Will to try to take it. Once inside, she walked all the way across the sitting room and into the bedroom. He closed the door and followed her.

Cheryl put the bed between herself and Will. She was

still pointing the gun at him, but he walked to the edge of the bed anyway. His fear for Abby was burgeoning into an anger that would brook no delay.

"Get back!" she cried. "Stay back until I explain!"

"Tell me about my little girl!"

"This is a kidnapping-for-ransom," she said, like a grammar-school girl reciting from memory. "Right now my partner is with your wife, at your house in Madison County. Someone else is holding Abby at a third location. This is what's going to happen from this point on. . . ."

Will listened like a man being given a clinical description of a disease that would shortly kill him. His disbelief quickly gave way to horror at the way his family's lives had been studied and deconstructed, all in preparation for a plan designed to separate him from two hundred thousand dollars.

"Listen to me," he interrupted. "We don't have to wait twenty-four hours. I'll get you the money right now—"

"The banks are closed."

"I'll find a way." He tried to keep panic out of his voice. "I can make it happen. The casino has money. I'll call down—"

"No. It doesn't work that way. It has to be tomorrow. Now, let me finish."

He shut up and listened, his brain working frantically. Whoever was behind this plan knew his business. He—or she—had turned the normal mechanics of a kidnapping inside out, creating a situation in which any aggressive response was impossible. Cheryl's gun was only there to control Will's initial panic. The real coercion was Abby. He could pick up the telephone and call the police right now. But if they came and arrested Cheryl, and she didn't call her partner on their thirty-minute schedule, Abby would die.

"If I do what you want," he said, "what guarantee do I have that we'll get Abby back?"

"No guarantee. You have to trust us."

"That's not good enough. How are we supposed to get her back? Tell me the details. Don't think! Tell me right this second."

Cheryl nodded. "Abby and your wife will be driven to a public place and set free within sight of each other."

She sounded like she believed it. And she'd told him they'd carried out the same plan five times before. He thought back over the past few years' headlines in Mississippi. He didn't remember hearing about any kidnapped children who were found murdered. Not kidnappings-for-ransom, anyway. And that would definitely have made headlines across the state.

"What's to keep me from going to the police after you let Abby go?" he asked.

"The fact that two hundred thousand dollars is nothing to you. And because if the police start looking for us, we'll know. We'll know, and my partner will come back and kill Abby. In the playhouse in your backyard, at her school, after church . . . anywhere. Believe me, he'll do it. We've done this to five other doctors just like you, and none of them have reported it. Not one. You won't, either."

He turned away from her in frustration. Through the bedroom's picture window, he saw the lights of a freighter out on the darkening gulf, plying its way westward. He had never felt so impotent in his life. One simple dictum had carried him through many life-or-death situations: *There's always a way. Another option. Drastic, maybe, but there.* But this time there didn't seem to be one. The trapped feeling made him crazy with rage. He whirled back to Cheryl.

"I'm supposed to just sit here all night while some stranger holds my little girl prisoner? Scared out of her mind? Lady, I will rip your head off before I let that happen."

She jerked the gun back up. "Stay back!"

"What kind of woman are you? Don't you have any maternal feelings?"

"Don't you say anything about my feelings!" Cheryl's face reddened. "You don't know anything about me!"

"I know you're making a child suffer pure terror."

"That can't be helped."

He was about to respond when a thought burst into his mind like a star shell. "Oh Jesus. What about Abby's insulin?"

Cheryl's face was blank. "What?"

"Abby's a juvenile diabetic. You didn't know that? You didn't *plan* for that?"

"Calm down."

"You've got to call your partner. I've got to talk to him right now. Right now!"

The telephone beside the bed rang loudly.

They stared at it. Then Cheryl walked to the phone and laid her free hand on the receiver.

"You want to talk?" she said. "Here's your chance. But be cool, Doctor. Very cool."

FIVE

Will took the phone from Cheryl and held it to his ear.

"This is Will Jennings."

"*Doctor* Will Jennings?" said a male voice.

"That's right."

"You got some unexpected company down there, Doctor?"

Will looked over at Cheryl, who was watching intently. "Yes."

"She looks hot in that black dress, doesn't she?"

"Listen, I need to explain something to you."

"You don't explain anything, college boy. *I'm* in charge tonight. You got that?"

"I've got it, but—"

"But nothing. I'm going to ask you a question, Doc. Kind of like the *Match Game*. Remember that one? That freakin' Richard Dawson—what a fruitcake."

Will heard eerie laughter.

"Anyway, we're going to see if your answer matches

your wife's. This is really more like the *Newlywed Game*, I guess. *Uhh . . . that would be the butt, Bob.*" The man broke up again.

Will breathed deeply, his entire being concentrated on understanding whom he was dealing with.

"The question is . . . does your child have any serious medical condition?"

A trickle of hope flowed into his veins. "She has juvenile diabetes."

"That's a match! You just won the all-expense paid trip to *beautiful* Puerto Vallarta!"

The man sounded like Wink Martindale on speed. Will shook his head at the surreal horror of the situation. "Abby needs that insulin, sir. Immediately."

"Sir?" The man laughed darkly. "Oh, I like that. This is probably the only time you'd ever call me 'sir.' Unless you had to tell me I was dying or something. *Sir*, I'm afraid you've got terminal pecker cancer. Stand two steps back please."

"I'm an anesthesiologist. I don't handle things like that."

"No? You never told anybody they were dying?"

Will hesitated. "When I was an OB/GYN, I did."

"Ahh. So, no means yes. You ever kill anybody, Doc?"

"Of course not."

"Really? Nobody ever died on the table while you were passing the gas?"

"Well, of course. But not as a result of my actions."

"No? I've got to wonder how honest you're being about that. I really do."

"Would you mind telling me your name?"

"Joe Hickey, Doc. You can call me Joe."

"All right, Joe. Are you a former patient of mine? Or a relative of a patient?"

"Why would you ask that? I mean, you never killed anybody, right?"

"It's just that you seem to have a lot of animosity toward me personally."

"You feel that? Huh. Could be, I guess. Well, let's leave that for now. 'Cause I'm about to show you what a nice guy I am. I'm about to set it up so your little princess gets her insulin."

"Thank God."

"God's got nothing to do with this. Let me talk to my partner."

"Joe, could I speak with my wife for a moment?"

"Put Cheryl on, Doc."

Will held out the phone.

"Get in the bathroom while I'm talking," she said.

"Your partner didn't tell me to go in the bathroom."

She shook the automatic at him. "Get in the goddamn bathroom!"

Will held up his hands and backed into the spacious cubicle of white marble and gold fixtures. He kept the knob turned as he closed the door, and after he heard Cheryl's voice resume, opened it a couple of inches and put his ear to the crack.

"Why didn't we know about this medicine thing?" she asked. "Well, I don't like it. Getting on the road with her is dangerous. What if a cop stops you? . . . Okay. . . . I'm all right, I guess. But this guy isn't like the others, Joey. . . . I don't know how. His eyes are on me every second. He's like a wolf, waiting for his chance. . . . I know. I *know.* Okay. Thirty minutes."

Will put his eye to the crack and saw Cheryl grimace as she hung up.

"All clear?" he asked, pushing open the door.

"Yeah."

"What did he say?"

"He's taking the medicine to your little girl. I mean, he's taking your wife to give her the shot. See? If we didn't care what happened to her, would we take a risk to get her medicine to her?"

"Yes. Because you know if anything happened to Abby during the night, you wouldn't get your money."

"You wouldn't know whether anything had happened to her or not."

"If I don't get confirmation that Abby's gotten her insulin within seven hours, I'll assume she's gone into ketoacidosis. And you'll talk then. You'll talk if I have to break every bone in your body, one at a time."

The threat seemed to have no effect on Cheryl. From her expression, he got the feeling she'd heard such things before. Maybe she thought he wasn't capable of such barbarity. Or maybe she knew he wasn't.

"You think Joey hasn't thought of that?" she asked. "I don't even know where your kid is. But even if I did, and you tortured it out of me, the police couldn't possibly get there in thirty minutes. I know that for sure." With the gun still in her right hand, Cheryl rubbed both arms as if she were cold. "And you don't want to start making threats to Joey, Doctor. He could do a lot of things to your little girl besides kill her, you know? You're not holding any cards here."

Will closed his eyes and fought a nauseating rush of terror. "Who the hell is this Joey?"

Cheryl looked at him like he was an idiot.

"He's my husband."

Abby lay sleeping on an old sofa in the cabin. A crocheted comforter lay over her. Huey sat on the floor beside her, whittling slowly at a piece of cedar. Huey was nervous. He knew the little girl was going to be scared when she woke up, and that scared him. He wished she was a boy instead of a girl. Boys were easier. Three of the five times they had taken boys. Girls made him think too much, and thinking made him sad. He barely remembered his sister now, but he remembered some things. Coughing, mostly. Long, terrible coughs with wheezing whistles between them, whistles with every breath. Thinking of those whistles made him cringe. Huey had slid Jo Ellen's little bed over by the woodstove to keep her warm, but it hadn't done any good. His mother and the first doctor kept saying it was just a bad cold until it was too late. By the time they got her to the city doctor in a neighbor's pickup, she was stone dead. She looked like a little china angel lying across the seat, bluish white, one of God's chosen, just four years old. Diphtheria, they said. Huey hated the word. Someone had said it on TV once, years afterward, and he'd picked up the TV and smashed it to kindling. Joey had never known Jo Ellen. He was living in Mississippi then.

Abby groaned again, louder this time, and Huey

picked up the Barbie doll Joey had passed him through the window.

"Mama?" Abby moaned, her eyes still closed. "Mama?"

"Mama's not here right now, Abby. I'm Huey."

Her eyes popped open, then went wide as she focused on the giant sitting before her. Tears pooled instantly in her eyes, and her lower lip began to quiver.

"Where's my mama?" she asked in a tiny voice.

"She had to go somewhere with your daddy. They asked me to babysit you for a while."

Abby looked around the dilapidated cabin, her cheeks turning bright red. "Where are we? Where is this place?"

"A cabin in the woods. Not very far from your house. Your mama will be back soon."

Her lip quivered harder. "Where *is* she?"

"With your daddy. They're both coming soon."

Abby closed her eyes and whimpered, on the edge of panic now. Huey took the Barbie from behind him and set it gently before her. When her eyes opened again, they locked onto the doll, drawn to the tiny piece of home.

"Your mama left this for you," Huey said.

She snatched up the Barbie and clutched it to her chest. "I'm scared."

He nodded in sympathy. "I'm scared, too."

Abby's mouth opened. "You are?"

He nodded again. His eyes were wet with tears.

Abby swallowed, then reached out and squeezed his little finger as if to reassure him.

* * *

Forty miles northeast of the cabin, still in Jackson, Joe Hickey drove Karen's Expedition southward on Interstate 55. Karen sat beside him, the small Igloo in her lap. Hickey reached into his pocket and pulled out a long silk scarf he'd taken from the Jenningses' laundry room.

"Put this over your eyes."

Karen tied the scarf around her head without argument. "Are we getting close?"

"Less than an hour. Don't ask me anything else. I might change my mind about the insulin."

"I won't talk at all."

"No, talk," he said. "I like your voice. It's got class, you know?"

Though blindfolded, Karen turned to him with amazement.

In the heart of Jackson, in the elite subdivision of Eastover, a white-columned mansion stood gleaming in the beams of spotlights fixed to stately oak trees. On the circular driveway before the house sat a yellow 1932 Duesenberg, the dazzling cornerstone of a vintage car collection of which its owner had spent the better part of the last year divesting himself.

Inside the mansion, Dr. James McDill, owner of both the Duesenberg and the mansion, sat across the dinner table from his wife, Margaret. He felt a deep apprehension when he looked at her. Over the past twelve months, she had lost twenty pounds, and she'd weighed only one hundred twenty-five to start with. McDill wasn't in the best shape himself. But after weeks of personal struggle, he was about to speak his mind on a very sensitive matter. He knew the reaction that would follow, but he had no choice. The closer the convention got, the more convinced he became that he was right. Time and reflection had brought it all back to him, particularly the things they had said in passing.

He put down his fork. "Margaret, I know you don't want me to bring this up again. But I've got to."

His wife's spoon clattered against her bone china plate. "Why?" she asked in a voice that could have shaved glass. "*Why* do you have to?"

McDill sighed. He was a cardiovascular surgeon of wide experience, but he had never approached any surgery with the trepidation with which he now faced his wife. "Maybe because it happened exactly a year ago. Maybe because of the things they told us. I couldn't get it out of my mind in the OR this morning. How this thing has affected our lives. Poisoned them."

"Not mine. Yours! *Your* life."

"For God's sake, Margaret. The convention started tonight on the coast. We're not there, and for one reason. Because what happened last year is still controlling us."

Her mouth opened in shock. "You wish you were there now? My God!"

"No. But we were wrong not to go to the police a year ago. And I have a very bad feeling now. That woman told me they'd done it before, and I believed her. She said they'd done it to other doctors. They took advantage of the convention . . . of our separation. Margaret, what if it's happening again? Right now?"

"Stop it!" she said in a strangled whisper. "*Don't you remember what they said?* They'll kill Peter! You want to go to the police now? A year after the fact? Don't you know what would happen? You're so naive!"

McDill laid both hands on the dinner table. "We've got to face this. We simply cannot let what happened to us happen to another family."

"To *us*? What happened to you, James? You sat in a hotel room with some slut for a night. Don't you ever think for one minute of anyone but yourself? Peter was traumatized!"

"Of course I think about Peter! But I refuse to let another child go through what he did because of our cowardice."

Margaret wrapped her arms tight around herself and began rocking back and forth in the chair, like schizophrenics McDill had seen in medical school. "If only you hadn't left us here alone," she murmured. "All alone . . . Margaret and Peter . . . alone and unprotected."

McDill fought the stab of guilt this produced. "Margaret—"

"Medical convention, my foot," she hissed, her eyes going narrow. "It was that goddamned *car* show."

"Margaret, please—"

He fell silent as their eleven-year-old son appeared in the dining room door. Peter was a pale, thin boy, and his eyes never settled in one place long.

"What's the matter?" he asked timidly. "Why are you guys yelling?"

"Just a misunderstanding, son. I had a tough surgery today, and we were discussing some tax problems. I lost my temper. Nothing for you to worry about. What time are you going over to Jimmy's?"

"His dad is picking me up in a minute."

Margaret took a gulp of wine and said, "Are you sure you want to spend the night over there tonight, darling?"

"Yeah. Unless . . . unless you don't want me to."

"I like having my baby under this roof," Margaret cooed.

"Nonsense," said McDill. "Go have some fun, son. You've been studying too hard this week."

A car horn sounded outside.

Peter looked uncertain. "I guess that's them."

"You'd better run, son. We'll see you in the morning."

Peter crossed the room and kissed his mother. Over his shoulder, Margaret glared at McDill.

"We'll be right here if you need us for anything," she said. "Just call. We'll be right here. *All night.*"

McDill stared dejectedly at his plate. He had lost his appetite.

The Expedition jounced and jumped along rutted ground beneath black trees, Hickey sitting stiff behind the wheel. Karen gripped the handle on the windshield frame, the ice chest cold between her legs. She was terrified that Hickey would wreck the Expedition before they reached Abby. He had let her remove the blindfold after the last turn, but she felt like she was still wearing it. He refused to use the headlights, and with only the running lights on, she was astonished that he could pick his way through the dense trees. Wherever this place was, Hickey must have spent a lot of time here.

"We're going to meet Huey on this road," he said.

"You and I will walk forward with the ice chest. You will not get emotional. You will not freak out. You hear? You can hug your kid long enough to calm her down. Then you take her blood sugar and give her the shot. After that, one last hug, then we go."

"I understand."

"Be sure you do. She's going to go crazy when you start to leave, but you'd better tough it out. Just like the first day of school. Huey's told her he's babysitting her for one night. You reinforce that. Tell her everything's okay, we're all friends, and you're going to pick her up in the morning. If you flip out . . ." Hickey turned to her for an instant, his eyes hard as agates. "If you flip out, I'll have to hurt you right in front of her. She'll have nightmares all night. You don't want that."

A pair of headlights flashed out of the dark and speared Karen's retinas. As she threw up her hand to shield her eyes, Hickey stopped the Expedition and blinked the headlights twice. Then he left them on, creating a long tunnel of halogen light that merged with the dimmer headlights pointing at them.

"Come on," he said, shutting off the engine. "Bring your stuff."

Karen picked up the ice chest and climbed out. When she got to the front of the Expedition, Hickey grabbed her arm and said, "Start walking."

Night mist floated through the headlight beams as they walked along them, and the humidity was heavy on Karen's skin. She was straining for a sight or sound of Abby when a giant form blotted out the other pair of headlights.

The silhouette was about thirty yards away, and it looked like the outline of a grizzly bear. Karen stopped in her tracks, but Hickey pushed her on. Suddenly a squeal cut through the night.

"Mama? *Mama!*"

Karen rushed forward, stumbling in the ruts, picking herself up, going on. She fell to her knees and embraced the tiny shadow that had emerged from behind the massive one.

"I'm here, honey!" she said, squeezing Abby as tight as she dared and choking back a wave of tears. "Mama's here, baby!"

Abby keened and cried and screeched all at once. She wanted to speak, but each time she tried, her little chest heaved and caught, and she kept repeating the same syllable over and over.

"Wh—wh—wha—"

Karen kissed her cheeks and nose and forehead and hair. Abby was almost hyperventilating, mucus and tears running down her face, sheer panic in her eyes.

"It's okay, baby. Take your time. Mama's here. I can hear you, baby."

"Wh-why did you leave me here, Mama? Why?"

Karen forced herself to appear calm. She couldn't let Abby see how terrified she was. "I had to, honey. Daddy and I have an important meeting. One we forgot about. It's only for grown-ups, but it won't last long. It's only for tonight."

"Are you *leaving* again?" The confusion in Abby's eyes was the most wrenching sight Karen had ever seen. Terror of abandonment was something she had known herself, and seeing it in her daughter made her bones ache.

"Not for a while yet," she said. "Not for a while. We need to check your sugar, baby."

"Nooooo," Abby wailed. "I want to go home!"

"Is Mr. Huey being nice to you?" Karen looked fearfully at the huge shadow standing a few yards away.

Abby was too upset to answer.

Karen opened the ice chest and took out the spring-loaded finger-stick device, which she had already loaded with a needle. Abby halfheartedly fought her, but when Karen took firm hold of her hand, she let her middle finger be immobilized. Karen pressed the tip of the pen to the pad of the finger and popped the trigger. Abby yelped, though the pain was negligible, and Karen wiped off the first drop of blood and forced out another. She wiped that against a paper test strip, which she fed into a small machine containing a microchip. After fifteen seconds, the machine beeped.

"Two hundred and forty. You need your shot, sweetie."

Karen drew three units of short-acting insulin from one vial, then, using the same syringe, added five units from the long-acting vial. This was more than usual, but she suspected that Abby would sleep little during the night, and would probably be given food of some kind.

"Has Mr. Huey fed you anything, sweetie?"

"Just some crackers."

"That's all?"

Abby looked at the ground. "And a peppermint."

"Abby!"

"I was hungry."

Karen started to pull up Abby's jumper to inject the insulin into her stomach, but with Huey standing so near, she decided to inject it right through the material. She pinched up a fold of fat and shot the insulin into it. Abby whimpered softly and locked her arms around Karen's neck. Karen threw the used syringe into the woods and lifted Abby into her arms. There, on her knees in the dirt, she rocked her daughter back and forth like an infant, singing softly Abby's favorite childhood rhyme.

The itsy-bitsy spider climbed up the water spout.
Down came the rain and washed the spider out.
Out came the sun and dried up all the rain,
And the eensy-weensy spider climbed up the spout again.

"I love you, punkin," she murmured. "Everything's going to be all right."

She felt Hickey brush past her as he walked forward to speak to Huey.

"Keep singing, Mama," Abby said.

Karen started the song again, but as she sang, she tuned her ears to the male voices drifting back to her on the night air.

"You doing okay?" Hickey asked.

"Uh-huh," said a much deeper voice. Deeper but more tentative. "She's nice."

Hickey took out a cigarette and lit it. The match flared like a bonfire in the blackness.

"I thought you quit, Joey."

"Give me a freakin' break."

The orange eye of the cigarette waxed and waned like a little moon. Karen knew Hickey was watching her, transfixed in the headlight beams with her child, as vulnerable as a deer under the hunter's gun. She put her mouth to Abby's ear.

"Do you remember what I taught you about calling the police? What numbers to call?"

"Nine?" Abby thought aloud. "Nine-nine-one?"

"Nine-*one*-one."

"Oh. I know. When I'm nervous I forget. I know our phone number."

"Good, honey. Don't be nervous, now. Mr. Huey has a cell phone. If he goes to the bathroom, he might forget it. If he does, you use it to call nine-one-one. Run and hide outside with it, tell them you're in trouble, and then hide the phone. Don't hang it up. If you can do all that, people will come and bring you home to Mommy and Daddy early. Do you understand?"

Abby's eyes were wide. "Will the policeman hurt Huey?"

"No, baby. But don't even try it unless you can call without him knowing. Okay? It's like a game."

Tears shone in Abby's eyes. "I'm scared, Mom. I want to go home with you."

"Listen to me, honey. If you have to do number two, you wipe yourself. Don't ask Mr. Huey for help. Even if he's nice. You don't know him well enough."

Hickey dropped his cigarette and stubbed it out with his foot. "Old home week's over," he called. "Let's mount up."

Abby screamed and grabbed Karen's neck.

"Let's go," said Hickey, walking toward her. "Tell princess bye-bye."

"Nooo!" Abby wailed. *"Nooooooo!"*

Karen looked over her shoulder at Hickey, her eyes pleading. "I'm *begging* you. Let me stay here with her until morning. What can it possibly matter?"

"I told you about this crap." He held out his arms. "Hand her over."

Karen backed away, clutching Abby in her arms. She knew it would do no good, but the decision was not hers to make. Two million years of evolution would not let her voluntarily give up her child. Hickey lunged forward and grabbed Abby under the arms, then yanked at her as if pulling on a sack of feed. Abby shrieked like she was being flayed alive.

"Stop!" Karen yelled at Hickey. *"Stop it! You're hurting her!"*

"Then let go, goddamn it!"

With a cry of desolation, Karen let go.

A heart-wrenching scream burst from Abby's lips.

Karen snatched up the ice chest, then ran to Huey and hooked the handle of the Igloo around his huge fingers. There were more syringes inside, and five vials of insulin, including one of Humalog. "Please keep this! If Abby gets sick or passes out, call me and I'll tell you what to do!"

The giant's face was a mask of bewildered fear. "Yes, ma'am. I—"

"Shut up!" Hickey shouted. "Get the kid back inside, retard!"

Karen laid both hands against Huey's chest. "I know you're a good Christian man. Please don't hurt my baby!"

Huey's mouth fell open, exposing his yellow teeth. "Hurt your baby?"

Hickey thrust Abby into Huey's arms, then grabbed Karen by the elbow and dragged her toward the Expedition.

"I'll be back in the morning, Abby!" Karen promised. "I'll be the first thing you see tomorrow!"

Abby continued to shriek with air-raid intensity, so loudly that Karen finally put her hands over her ears to blunt the agony of hearing her child's terror. But even that didn't work. Ten yards from the Expedition, she slammed her right elbow into Hickey's head and charged back toward the other pair of headlights.

She was halfway there when Hickey cracked her on the back of the head with what felt like a hammer, sending her sprawling onto the hard dirt. She heard a door slam, then the squeal of a loose fan belt as Huey's truck backed slowly down the road.

High in the Beau Rivage Hotel in Biloxi, the phone rang in suite 28021. Will grabbed it before Cheryl could.

"Joe?" he said. "Is this Joe?"

"Will?" said an uncertain voice.

"Karen!"

The sound of weeping came down the line, and it nearly unmanned him. It took a lot to make Karen Jennings cry.

"Did you see Abby?" he asked through the lump in his throat. "Did you get her the insulin?"

"Will, she's so scared! I gave her eight units and left some extra vials and syringes. It was awful—"

Karen screamed; then her voice was replaced by Hickey's. "You can calm down now, college boy. Your kid got her medicine. It's sayonara for now."

"Wait!"

Will was shouting at a dead phone. He exhaled slowly, trying to control the wild anger swelling in his chest. It was simply not in his nature to endure anguish and frustration without acting.

"Hey," said Cheryl. "Everything's gonna be okay. It is." She reached out to touch his shoulder.

Will slammed the phone into the side of her head. As she fell across the bed, he tried to wrench the gun from her hand, but she held it tight. They wrestled over the bedspread, clawing and fighting for the weapon. Will's joints shot fire through his limbs and trunk, but they kept functioning. Cheryl was clutching the gun beneath her breasts with both hands. Abandoning caution, he grabbed it blindly with both hands and yanked as hard as he could.

Something ripped, Cheryl screamed, and the gun came away in his hands. He jumped up and pointed it at her. She was cradling her bloody right hand.

"What the hell?"

Cheryl's dress had torn, exposing her from the waist up. She wore a sheer black bra, but Will wasn't looking at her breasts. He was staring at a blue and green montage of bruises that covered her abdomen and ribs like stains, one of which continued up into the bra.

"What happened to you?"

She backed against the ornate headboard, the movement instinctive, animallike. "Nothing."

"That's not nothing. That's a beating."

She picked up a pillow and covered her chest. "It's nothing. And you just screwed up big-time."

After venting his rage in the attack, Will found himself puzzled about what to do next. "I want to ask you something, Cheryl."

"Fuck you."

"Are you committed to this kidnapping?"

She said nothing.

"Because I have a feeling you're not. I have a feeling this kind of thing is what Joe gets off on, but not you. I think you tried to talk him out of it. That's why you got the beating, isn't it?"

Her face was as closed as a tribal mask. "Don't need no reason for a beating," she said, all her earlier elocution gone. "Ain't never no reason."

Will flashed back to his days as a resident, working the Jackson ERs. He'd seen more physical abuse in six months than he'd thought existed in the world at the time. And many of the responses he got from women sounded exactly like Cheryl's. Sullen, angry, resigned. But he couldn't solve her marital problems in one night. He couldn't even solve his own. With that thought, a new idea entered his mind. And with it a new fear.

"Why are you here with me?" he asked.

Cheryl looked blank.

"I mean, why isn't Joe here with me? He obviously resents the hell out of me. If he was here, he could piss on me all night, beat the hell out of me. I'd have no choice but to take it. But he passed up that chance." Will lowered the gun and stepped closer to the bed. "It doesn't make sense, Cheryl. Why not man-man, woman-woman? You know? A man has a lot more chance of controlling an angry father than a woman does. Has Joe done it this way every time? Is he always with the wife?"

She wiped her bloody hand on the pillow. "Putting me with the husband avoids the whole macho thing. A type A jerk like you doesn't feel as threatened by a woman. You're less likely to blow up and do something stupid." She gingerly tested her right wrist. "Only you just did. You hurt me, you bastard."

"What do you expect? You kidnapped my daughter. Don't worry about your hand. I can fix it."

"You stay the hell away from me."

"Whatever you say." He walked over to the window and looked out over the gulf. There were more lights now, ships making steady headway, oblivious to the drama unfolding in the glittering tower on the beach.

"That's Joe talking," he said, thinking aloud. "About who stays with whom, I mean. I've talked to him less than five minutes, but I know one thing about him. He *loves* the macho thing. He'd like nothing better than to be here rubbing my face in it. That's half the point of all this. So, if he's not here . . . he's somehow rubbing my face in it *more* by being there." Will turned back to Cheryl, who jerked up the pillow. "How could he be doing that?"

"You think he's tearing up all your precious paintings or something? That's not Joey."

Will pulled a chair over beside the bed. "I want you to tell me everything you know that *is* Joe, Cheryl. Start talking."

"I'm not telling you shit. You'll find out more than you want to know when he calls back and I tell him what you did."

Another black wave of rage rolled through him. "If you *can* talk."

She laughed outright. "There's nothing you can do to me that hasn't been done before, Doctor. I mean *nothing*." She tossed the pillow aside, exposing her breasts and the relief map of bruises. "Face it. Joey's got you beat, right down the line."

In an upstairs bathroom of the McDill mansion, Margaret McDill sat at a vanity table, taking off her makeup with cold cream. She looked into the mirror at her husband, who hovered in the door behind her like an accusing ghost.

"I refuse to discuss it," she said. "How many times do I have to tell you that?"

Dr. McDill gave a long sigh. "I just want to—"

"What? Drive me back to a bottle a day?" She threw a mascara-stained Kleenex onto the floor. "I can't stand this, James. It's sadistic!"

"Margaret, for God's sake. I'm just trying to understand." He took a deep breath and pushed into forbidden territory yet again. "Is there something more? Something I don't know about?" He'd asked this before and been rebuffed. Tonight he would press it. He had to. "Did this man hurt you?"

"Hurt me?" Her lips tightened to white. "Did he *hurt* me?"

"I'm your husband, Margaret. I only want to help you."

She whirled from the mirror, her eyes wild. "All right! All *right*! You want to know why I won't report it? Because he raped me."

McDill flinched.

"He raped me, James. Do you feel better now? Is that what you wanted to hear? What you want to tell the police? All the gory details?"

McDill stared openmouthed at his wife.

"He told me to take off my clothes and I did. He told me to kiss him and I did. He told me I'd have to do things I'd never done before"—she covered her face with her hands—"and I did. I *did*. And I'd do it again! All I could think of was Peter. *They had my baby!*"

She exploded into unintelligible screams, thrashing her head and arms until McDill rushed forward and, oblivious to the blows he was taking, hugged her so tightly that she couldn't move. He spoke in a reassuring voice as she continued to shriek.

"It's all right, Margaret. . . . It's going to be all right. You didn't do anything wrong. You did nothing wrong." Tears stung his eyes. "God help me, I thought it might be something like this. It's all right. . . ."

As her screams subsided, Margaret descended into a near catatonic state.

"Can you hear me?" asked McDill. "Margaret?"

She nodded like an Alzheimer's patient.

"I'm afraid the same thing is happening again. Do you understand? To another family. Another mother. Another child." He took her firmly by the shoulders and peered into her eyes. "We can't let that happen. It wouldn't be Christian. Would it?"

Margaret slowly shook her head, her eyes glassy.

"I'm going to call the FBI," McDill said. "But we don't have to tell them anything about what happened to you. You understand? It's irrelevant to the situation."

His wife's only response was fresh tears sliding down her cheeks.

"I love you, sweetheart," he assured her. "More than I ever have."

McDill pulled her close. When he squeezed her shuddering body, something inside him came loose. Something came loose and a fearful darkness poured out. James McDill read the Bible every night, no matter how tired. He went to church every week, taught Sunday school to his son's class. He spent every day but Sunday bringing people back from the edge of death with his hard-earned skills. But when he thought of the faceless man who had brutalized the girl he had loved since high school—the mother of his child—something deeper than reason spoke from within him. Something deeper even than God. When he opened his mouth, what emerged was a whispered vow.

"I am going to kill that son of a bitch."

SIX

Being forced to leave Abby behind had shattered Karen. She sat in the Expedition in a sort of detached haze, like a disembodied brain floating in ether. She was wearing the blindfold again, but she sensed that there was little traffic. The whooshes of cars passing were far apart.

"You taken a vow of silence or what?" asked Hickey.

Karen let her mind reach into the starless night beneath the blindfold.

"Hey. I'm talking to you."

The voice was like a face obscured by fog.

"You're upset, I know. But it had to be that way. You'll get over it."

"I'm not sure I will."

"See? You can talk."

She heard him light another cigarette. The smell of burning tobacco filled the air.

"You can take off the blindfold now."

"I prefer it on."

"I prefer it off."

Karen unwrapped the scarf. The dash lights shone like a coastal city viewed from the sea. Glancing up, she saw that the digital compass between the visors read "E" for east. That was information she could use. They were on a two-lane road, and she knew by the speed and sound of the outgoing trip that they had driven on an interstate for at least half an hour after leaving Jackson. That left two options: they were still on I-55, which ran north and south, or they had turned onto I-20, which ran east and west. That meant Abby was being held somewhere south of Jackson and west of I-55, if Hickey had taken that interstate. If he'd taken I-20, it was harder to make assumptions. But if he left the blindfold off, she might soon know for sure. She decided to make an effort to keep him in a good mood.

"Thank you for letting me give Abby the shot."

Hickey rolled down his window a crack and blew cigarette smoke outside. "That's what I like to hear. Gratitude. You don't see much of it these days. It's a forgotten courtesy. But you're an old-fashioned girl. I can tell. You know how to show appreciation for a good deed."

Karen waited a moment, then looked left. Hickey's profile was like a wind-eroded boulder. Heavy brows, the nose a bit flat, the chin like an unspoken challenge. It looked like a face that could take a lot of punishment, and probably had.

"We've got a whole night to kill," he said, glancing away from the road long enough to find her eyes in the dark. "Why make it like breaking rocks, you know? Let's be friends."

Her internal radar went to alert status.

"You're a beautiful woman. You got that red hair, but not the coarse kind, you know? Strawberry blond, I guess they call it. And I'm not a bad-looking guy, am I?"

"Look, I don't know what you've done in the past, but—"

"I want to see that bush, girl." Hickey's eyes glinted in the dash lights. "I *know* you got a good one."

The words shocked and frightened Karen more than she would have believed possible. She didn't want to show fear, but she had already pressed herself against the door.

"You got some good tan lines, too, I bet. With that pool out back."

She stared straight ahead, her cheeks burning.

"I've got something for you, too, Karen. A lot more than you're used to, I bet."

With every remark she left unanswered, she felt Hickey's confidence growing. "I wouldn't count on that," she said. "My husband got lucky with those genes."

Hickey gave a self-assured laugh. "That right? Somehow I don't picture old Will having the goods. Seems like the tennis player type to me. Mr. Average in the showers. See, that's why I never back off. On that elemental level, I got what it takes." He threw his cigarette butt out of the window and pressed the dashboard cigarette lighter. "I heard this story about LBJ once. During the Vietnam thing, McNamara was giving him some shit about how Ho Chi Minh has this, Ho Chi Minh has that. LBJ unzips his fly, whips out his Johnson and says, 'Has old Ho got anything like *this*?' "

He broke up laughing.

"Right there in the freakin' Oval Office. Hey, I wonder if that's why they call it a Johnson?"

"LBJ lost that war, didn't he?"

Hickey stopped laughing. "Get those jeans off. You're gonna be walking bowlegged for a week."

A ball of ice formed in Karen's chest.

"You think I'm kidding? We've done this gig five times, and every time the wives and me had a little party. A little bonus for the executive in the operation, and nobody the wiser."

"No party tonight, Joe."

"No?" He laughed again. "In thirty minutes I'm gonna be banging on your tonsils, lady. Get those jeans off."

"Here?"

"Like you never done it in a car before?"

She sat rigidly in the seat, refusing to acknowledge the remark.

Hickey shook his head and tapped a finger on the cell phone. "Lose the jeans. Or I reach out and touch your precious princess."

Karen held out for another few seconds. Then she unsnapped her jeans, arched in the seat, and pulled them off.

"Happy now?"

"Getting there. Keep going."

A cold trickle of sweat ran down her rib cage. "Not in the car."

He looked down and punched a number into the Expedition's cell phone.

"Don't!"

He cut his eyes at her. "Still dressed?"

She folded her jeans and laid them in her lap, then slid the panties off and put them on top of the jeans.

Hickey laughed and hit END on the phone, then picked up the cotton panties and knocked her jeans to the floor. "Not exactly Victoria's Secret. You trying to discourage interest with these things?"

She felt an irrational prick of guilt. As Hickey laughed, she arranged the tail of her blouse so that it fell into her lap. But no sooner had she done this than he reached up and hit the passenger reading light switch, flooding her side of the interior with yellow light. She felt as she had as a little girl, playing hide-and-seek with her older male cousins. She'd hidden in the basement once, at the house at Fort Leavenworth, and as she heard them approach, she backed deeper and deeper into the dark recesses of the mildewed room. Yet no matter how far she went, the footsteps followed. And in the dark basement, far from the adults, she knew what they would do. Pressure her into "show-me" games, whether she wanted to play or not.

"Nice legs," Hickey said. "Far as they go."

She shivered in the air conditioning. "Why are you doing this?"

He sniffed and reached down for the cigarette lighter, then shook another Camel from the pack in his shirt pocket and ignited the tip. A stream of smoke clouded the windshield like dissipating fog.

"Does there always have to be a why?"

"Yes." She felt his gaze on her lap like the heat from a lamp.

"We've got time for all that. Slide that shirttail over."

She wanted to refuse. But how could she? She breathed slowly and deeply, trying not to let him rattle her. "Are you going to leave the light on all the way back? It seems dangerous."

"I gotta admit, I'm tempted. But it wouldn't be too smart, would it?" He reached out and traced a fingernail along her outer thigh. "Like I said, we've got all night. What the hell."

He flicked off the light, and the protective blanket of night closed around her again. But she was not safe. Nowhere close. Of course, *safe* didn't really matter, not in the usual sense. What mattered was survival. For once in her life, it was that simple. There was only one priority: Abby. Other mothers had walked through fire for their children; she could do the same. She could endure the worst that an animal like Hickey could dish out, and be there to hug Abby when it was over. But that didn't mean she would stop looking for a way to fight back. Because Hickey was arrogant. And arrogant men made mistakes. If he did make one, God and all his angels wouldn't be able to help the son of a bitch who made Abby Jennings suffer pain.

Another hope burned in her heart, small but steady. Wherever Will was, he was thinking. And not the way Karen was. She had outscored her husband by five percentile points on the MCAT test, and she could balance a checkbook twice as fast as he could. But there was another kind of intelligence, and Will had it in spades. It was speed of thought, and not just down one pathway, but several simultaneously. Karen thought logically, examining each option from beginning to end, then accepting or rejecting it before moving on. Will could look at a situation and see the end points of a dozen possible choices in the blink of an eye, then from instinct choose rightly. He wasn't always able to explain his choices, but they were almost inevitably correct. He told her once that they weren't correct in any objective sense. Sometimes, he said, simply *making* a choice—any choice—and following through with absolute commitment *made* it the right choice.

That's the kind of brain I need now, she thought.

At that moment, Will was staring at the telephone in the bedroom of his suite. It had just rung, and though he was holding Cheryl's Walther in his hand, he knew it was useless. If she told Hickey he had assaulted her, anything could happen. Yet if he didn't let her answer, Hickey would assume things were not as they should be, and he might retaliate against Abby.

The phone rang again.

"What are you going to do now, smart-ass?" Cheryl asked. She was leaning against the headboard of the bed, her torn dress around her waist, the road map of bruises on her torso left exposed like a silent "go to hell."

He tossed the gun into her lap.

She laughed and picked it up, then answered the

phone. After listening for a few moments, she said, "It is now. The doc flipped out. . . . He hit me and took my gun. Just like the guy from Tupelo. . . . Okay." She held out the receiver to Will. "He wants to talk to you."

Will took the phone. "Joe?"

"Doc, you screw up again, and the biggest piece you find of your little girl will fit in a thimble."

"I hear you, Joe."

"You hit my old lady?"

"It doesn't look like I was the first."

Silence. Then, "That ain't your business, is it?"

"No."

"You remember what I said about your little girl."

"I understand. I made a mistake. I just want my daughter back."

The phone went dead.

"You're pathetic," Cheryl said. "Like some kid stopped by a highway patrolman. Totally submissive."

"You know all about that, don't you? Submission."

She shrugged. "So he smacks me around sometimes. You never smacked your wife?"

"No."

"Liar."

Will saw no point in arguing. "Those bruises weren't caused by a couple of smacks. I see signs of systematic abuse."

"You don't argue with your wife?"

"We argue. We don't hit each other. What did you and Joe argue about last? Was it about going through with this kidnapping?"

"Hell no. We've done this lots of times."

"Maybe you're tired of it." He let that simmer for a few moments. "I can see how you would be. Realizing how much pain you're putting people through. Especially the kids."

She looked away. "Talk all you want. You know what I was doing before Joe found me?"

"What?"

"I was a bar girl in a truck stop. A full-service bar girl."

"You mean like—"

"Yeah, like that."

"How did you end up there?"

"You sound like some frat-boy john. 'Oh, Cheryl, you're so sweet, how'd ever you end up doing this?' Well, I ain't blaming nobody. My stepfather, maybe, but he's dead now. My mother had it worse than I did."

"Being a whore is a lot more respectable than what you're doing now."

"You ever been a whore?"

"No."

"Then you don't know. Every time I see a hooker in a movie, I want to throw something at the screen. When I saw *Pretty Woman*, I wanted to puke. You know the part in that movie when Richard Gere's friend tries to make Julia Roberts do him? The guy from *Seinfeld*? It's like the only uncomfortable part of that whole movie."

"I remember."

"That's what being in the life is like all the time. Except no movie star busts in to save you from his friend. He probably bought you for his friend." Her eyes burned into Will's with disturbing intensity. "Think about sitting somewhere all day, all night, available to any scummy, shit-breath, disease-ridden son of a bitch who walks in the door with the price of admission. That's being a hooker."

"You didn't have any choice about clients?"

"Clients?" She barked a little laugh. "I wasn't a lawyer, okay? It's *johns.* And, no, I didn't have any choice. 'Cause if I said no, I didn't get the good thing."

"The good thing. Cocaine?"

"My pimp used to say we were just trading crack for crack."

"Joe got you out of that life?"

"That's right. He got me clean. It was the hardest thing either of us ever did. So, if you think you're gonna talk me into betraying him, or bribe me into it, think again. If he smacks me around now and then, you think I care?"

"Yes, I do. Because you know that's not love. You don't owe Joe a life of servitude because he got you off crack. You deserve to be as happy as anybody else."

She shook her head like someone listening to a salesman. "My stepfather always said everybody gets what they deserve."

"He sounds like an asshole."

A bitter laugh. "You got that right. You ever go to a hooker?"

"No."

"What guy admits it, right? I believe you, though. You're one of those one-in-a-million guys who were meant to be husbands, aren't you?"

"And fathers."

She winced.

"You never had a child of your own?" Will asked.

"I'm not talking about that."

"Why not?"

"Let's just say I've been pregnant enough times that I can't have kids."

What did that mean? Multiple abortions? One bad one? "Are you sure? I was an obstetrician before I was an anesthesiologist. There are lots of new therapies for—"

"Don't ask me any more about it," Cheryl said in a desolate voice.

"All right."

He turned and walked over to the picture window. There wasn't much moon over the gulf. It was hard to see where the dark water ended and the sky began. Far below him, the lighted blue swimming pool undulated at the center of the plaza, with the paler Jacuzzi beside it. To his right lay the marina, with its stylized lighthouse and million-dollar cabin cruisers. A few bright stars shone high in the sky, but the glare from the casino sign drowned the rest. Changing focus, he saw Cheryl reflected in the glass, sitting on the bed with the gun in her lap, looking as lost as anyone he'd ever seen. He spoke without turning.

"I don't want to beat a dead horse here. And I don't want to pry. But I would really like to know how you ended up in prostitution. I mean, you just don't look like one. You look too fresh. You're beautiful, for God's sake. How old are you?"

"Twenty-six."

"How old is Joe?"

"Fifty."

Twenty-four years' difference. "Where are you from?"

Cheryl sighed. "Do we have to play *Twenty Questions?*"

"What else is there to do?"

"I could use a drink."

Will walked over to the phone.

"What are you doing?" she asked, laying a hand on the gun.

"Ordering you a drink. What do you like?"

She looked suspicious. "I guess it won't hurt anything. I like rum and Coke."

He called room service and ordered a bottle of Bacardi, a two-liter bottle of Coca-Cola, and a pot of tea for himself.

"You English or something?" asked Cheryl.

"I just like tea." What he wanted was caffeine, enough to get him through whatever was going to be required of him in the next twelve hours. He needed a pain pill, too, for his joints, but he wasn't going to take anything that might dull his mind. He needed his edge tonight.

"So, where are you from?" he asked again.

"Nowhere. Everywhere."

"What does that mean?"

"My dad was in the army. We moved a lot when I was a little girl."

"My wife grew up the same way. Moving from base to base."

She gave him a skeptical look. "I doubt much was the same about it. She was probably the colonel's daughter or something."

"No. Her father was a master sergeant."

"Yeah? My father was a captain. Or so I'm told. He screwed up some way, so they never let him go to Vietnam. He took it out on my mom for one too many years, and she finally left him. We went back to her hometown, little nothing of a place in Marion County. Then she hooked up with my stepfather." Cheryl's eyes glazed. "That was a whole new thing. I was about ten, I guess. After he got tired of Mom in the sack, he turned to me. She was so scared he'd leave us, she wouldn't listen to anything I said. When I turned sixteen, I got the hell out of there."

"Where'd you go?"

"I had a girlfriend who'd gone to Hinds Junior College. She had an apartment in Jackson with two other girls. I crashed with her for a couple of weeks, got a job waiting tables. I was barely making enough to help with the rent, and her roomies got mad. One of them was dancing at this club in Jackson. She was making three hundred bucks a night. Straight, you know? Just lap dances and stuff, no tricks out back. A couple of nights, just for kicks, a bunch of us went in there and watched her dance. It wasn't at all what I thought. I mean, some of the men were pathetic and all that, but it wasn't humiliating. The girls were in control. For the most part, anyway. Or that's what it looked like."

"You started stripping?"

"Not right away. But my girlfriend got pregnant, and her boyfriend ran offshore. She went back home to Mayberry RFD, and suddenly my share of the rent went up. So I gave it a try. And it worked. I was a natural, they said. Plenty of nights I made six hundred bucks. Of course, I had to kick half of that back to the club."

"That sounds like enough money to eventually move up to a different kind of job."

"That's not how it works. See, stripping is like any night job. Musician, whatever. You've got these long shifts. You sleep all day, so you don't really meet normal people. You get tired as hell. I mean, have you ever danced for eight hours straight? Drinking beer and mixed drinks? Plus, you find out it's not exactly what you thought. You've got your lap dances, which are fine. But then you've got sofa dances. A sofa dance is a little more involved. The guys want to make it, you know? It's hand jobs on the outside of the pants, or dry humping till they get off. What you try to do is get them almost there just as the song ends. Then they'll come across with another thirty bucks to get off at the start of the next song. You do that for eight hours, you start needing something to keep you going. To keep you from sinking too far down, you know?"

"Cocaine."

A hint of a smile animated her lips, like a ghost smiling from within her. "The sweet thing."

"And once you got on coke, they had you."

"Yep. Pretty soon you're only breaking even on the dancing, just to keep up your habit. Then you're into *them* for money. Dancing eight hours a day, just to pay the vig on what you owe. And that's when they hit you. There's ways to pay off the principal."

"Turning tricks."

"Blow jobs in the bathroom. Half-and-half in the cars

out back. Around the world in the motel up the street, after your shift."

"Jesus."

Her eyes looked ancient in her young face. "Girls don't last long doing that, Doc. These are people, you know? Single mothers trying to raise kids. Girls working through junior college."

"And Joe got you out?"

A cynical smile. "Sir Galahad to the rescue. That's Joe. One night he paid for a trick at the motel, packed me into his car, and hauled me all the way down to New Orleans. He had a house in Gentilly. He put mattresses on the walls, boarded up the windows, and locked me in." She shuddered at the memory. "Cold turkey. He cleaned up the vomit and brought me soup. Talk about a nightmare."

Will tried to imagine how Joe saw this drama in his mind. He probably did see himself as some sort of knight, rescuing the fair damsel from the dark castle. And Cheryl was fair, all right. It was difficult to believe that she had endured the ravages of the life she described. Working the ERs as a resident, Will had seen twenty-six-year-old whores who looked fifty. Cheryl looked like a sorority girl from Ole Miss, poised in that bloom of youth between college and marriage. Maybe a little hard around the jaw and eyes, but otherwise unmarred.

"How the hell did you wind up kidnapping kids? Is that what Sir Galahad rescued you for?"

"It wasn't like that. Not at first. But we needed money. Joe tried some straight things, but they never seemed to work out. And I knew how to strip. He put me in a club in Metairie, just outside New Orleans. Nice club. He stayed every night watching over me. No drugs, no drinking. I was making so much money, we couldn't believe it. Everybody said I was better than the featured dancers who came through, you know, Penthouse pets, girls like that. So I got into that for a while." Cheryl's eyes suddenly lit up, the way Abby's did when she was telling someone about her doll collection. "I had a dozen different outfits, props, the whole works. I had a Jeep Grand Cherokee, and we'd drive around the country, following my club tour. Texas, Colorado, Montana . . . Man, it was something."

"But?"

She looked down at the gun in her lap. "Joe got jealous. I was good enough that people started talking to me about other things. Movie people. Not like Sandra Bullock, you know, but still Hollywood. Soft porn stuff, like you see on Cinemax. And Joe got nervous about that. He didn't . . . He—"

"He didn't want you out from under," Will said. "He wanted you all to himself, all the time."

She nodded sadly. "Yeah."

"You couldn't break loose?"

"I owed him, okay? I owed him in a way only me and him understood."

"For getting you off crack?"

"Not just that, okay?"

"What do you mean?"

"Where's my damn drink?"

As though in answer to her question, a knock sounded

at the door. Will walked through the sitting room of the suite and accepted the tray from a young Mexican girl. He tipped her liberally, then hung out the DO NOT DISTURB sign and carried the tray in to Cheryl.

"How did you owe Joe?" he asked, pouring Bacardi and Coke over the small hotel ice cubes.

She took the glass and drank a long sip of the sweet mixture. Then another. She clearly meant to finish the drink before continuing. Will poured himself a steaming cup of tea, added sugar and lemon. The scent of Earl Grey wafted through the bedroom.

Cheryl finished her rum and Coke and held out the glass for a refill. Will mixed another—stronger this time—then took a sip of tea and sat on the edge of the bed.

"How did you owe him, Cheryl?"

"You don't just walk away from the kind of work I was doing at the club in Jackson," she said quietly. "I owed them money, and they wanted me working it off. When I started dancing in Metairie, they heard about it. They sent a couple of guys down to get me. Joe offered to pay my debts, but they wouldn't go for it. They wanted me back at the club. The guy who owned the place . . . he had a thing for me."

"So what happened?"

A little laugh rippled the bruised flesh of her abdomen. "Joe convinced these guys to change their minds."

"How did he do that?"

"Convincingly."

"And they left you alone?"

"Those guys did."

"And?"

"The owner sent another guy for me. To bring me back. A really bad guy."

"And what happened?"

Another swallow. "Joe punched his ticket."

"You mean he killed him?"

Cheryl looked Will right in the eye. "That's what I mean. Messy, too. So that anybody else they sent would know what he was getting into. You know? And it worked. Nobody else came. I was free."

"You weren't exactly free. You'd just traded one master for another."

"Hey, I ain't nobody's slave."

"Who are you trying to convince?"

"Shut up."

"You carry a lot of pain around, don't you?"

"Don't we all?"

"Yes. But I don't think Joe understands that. He thinks he's got a monopoly on suffering. That everything's stacked against him from the start."

"How do you know it wasn't? You sit up there in your perfect little house, with your money and your kid and your paintings and your swimming pool and your cars. Everything laid out just right since the day you were born. Well, some people don't have it that way."

"Is that what you think? You think I started rich? My father worked in a mill for eighteen years, Cheryl. No college degree. Then the mill shut down. He put his life savings into his dream, a music store. Every dollar he had went into Wurlitzer organs, Baldwin pianos, and brass band instruments. Five months after he opened it, the store burned to the ground. His insurance had lapsed two days before." Will reached out and took a shot from the Bacardi bottle. "He drove off a bridge a week later. I was eleven years old."

Cheryl shook her head. "You must have inherited something. You're silver spoon all the way."

Will laughed bitterly. "My wife's mother was a waitress. Karen was the first woman in her family to go to college. Then nursing school. Then medical school, but she had to drop out because she got pregnant. And her father died before he could see how well she did. She fought for everything she has. So did I."

"The American dream," Cheryl mumbled. "Get out the violins."

"I'm just pointing out that Joe seems to have a personal problem with me. Some kind of class thing. And he's way off base."

She looked up, her eyes alert. "How much money do you make a year?"

"About four hundred thousand dollars."

"He's not that far off."

Will had understated his income, and he doubted Cheryl had any concept of the kind of royalties he would earn from Restorase. "I can give you a lot more money than that, Cheryl. If you'll help me save Abby, I mean. Enough to get you away clean. Really free. Forever."

A faint flicker of hope lighted her eyes, then died. "You're lying, sweetie. You'd rat me out the first chance you got."

"Why would I? I'd have nothing to gain."

"Because it's the nature of things. I'd do the same. If you had my kid, I'd be over there right now giving you the sofa dance of your life. I'd take you to bed and give you around-the-world like you never imagined it before." A note of professional pride entered her voice. "I can do things for you that your wife never even heard of. That your wildest old girlfriend never heard of. When was the last time you got off four times in one night?"

Will treated this as a rhetorical question.

"I thought so. But you could. I could make you. And if you had my kid, I would. Gladly. But as soon as I had my kid back, I'd rat you out."

He started to argue, but there was no point. She would not be persuaded.

Cheryl held up her drink in a mock toast. "Don't feel bad, Doc. Like I said, it's just the nature of things."

Will had stopped listening. He was thinking about what Cheryl had said she would do to save her child, if she had one. And about why Hickey had chosen to spend the night with Karen rather than with him. And what Karen would or would not do to save Abby.

SEVEN

Hickey pulled the Expedition into the garage and shut off the engine. In the ticking silence, with the leather seat clammy against her backside, Karen felt dread settle in her limbs like cement.

"Party time, *cher,*" Hickey said. He opened his door and climbed out, then waited in the glow of the dome light. "You're not doing anybody any good sitting there. You or me."

She folded her panties into her jeans and got out. As she walked to the laundry room door, she could feel the tail of her blouse covering her behind, and she was thankful for that. At the door she stopped and waited for Hickey to open it, but he walked up and handed her the key ring.

"You do it," he said. "Your house."

She tucked her jeans under her arm, then bent and took hold of the doorknob with her left hand. When her palm touched the brass, a mild shock went through her. Before this house existed, she had drawn it on a piece of paper. Every room. Every window. She had chosen the knob in her hand. Worked with the architect on the blueprints. Badgered the subcontractors. Mortared the patio bricks. Painted the interiors. If any place on earth belonged to her, personified her, this house did. And now it was about to be violated. In point of fact, it already had been when Abby was taken. But the violation to come would be more profound. She could read the thoughts in Hickey's mind as though no border of flesh and bone concealed them. He wanted her body, yes. But his intent was more complex than that. He wanted more to desecrate her marriage.

"Come on," he said. "Meter's running."

A desperate thought flashed through her mind. She could shove open the door just far enough to slip inside, then lock it behind her. Lock it and call the police. But what would that accomplish? Nothing but pain or death for Abby. Hickey had his pocket cell phone, and he could be talking to his giant of a cousin in seconds. No. There was no choice but to obey.

She turned the key and walked inside, right through the laundry room and pantry to the kitchen. Every instinct told her to pull her jeans back on, but that might prompt Hickey to retaliate. She simply stood there, on the oven side of the island, waiting for a command.

He walked up slowly and smiled. "Up the hall. To your bedroom."

She turned and walked up the hallway, heavy-footed as a zombie. She was walking in Abby's tracks, in the last footsteps her child had taken in this house. That knowledge infused her with guilt, but also hardened her will to resist. The scent of Abby's room was strong here, even with her door closed. The comforting smell of toy animal fur and little girls' makeup kits.

"Stop," Hickey said.

Karen stopped. He reached around her left side and opened Abby's door. Faint moonlight shone through the window, falling upon the countless inhabitants of the room.

"Take a good look, Mom. This is why we're not going to have any trouble being friends tonight."

Karen looked. Here was the justification for whatever she would have to do to get through the night. To bring Abby back to this sanctuary.

Hickey's cupped hand flashed up under her shirttail and slapped her flank, hard. He laughed when she jumped, then poked her between the shoulder blades, pushing her until she reached the master bedroom.

Not wanting to enter it in the dark, she reached out and rotated the dimmer switch on the wall. The sight of the bedroom startled her. Everything was in its proper place, yet nothing seemed familiar. Not the antique sleigh bed. Not the overstuffed chair and ottoman. Not the matched Henredon dressers or the cherrywood cabinet that held the television. Not even the Walter Anderson watercolors on the walls. All struck her as furnishings in some nameless hotel, not objects she had chosen with the greatest care.

"The lap of luxury," Hickey said. "Looks like a nice place to pass an evening."

He walked past her, fell back into the oversized chair, and kicked his feet up on the ottoman. His Top-Siders were so new that there were no marks on the soles. Only dirt from the trip to the cabin.

"I could use a drink," he said. "Bourbon. Kentucky bourbon, if you got it."

The bourbon was kept on a sideboard in Will's study. Karen laid her jeans on the foot of the bed and went back up the hall, thankful for a chance to postpone what seemed inevitable. Had five other mothers submitted to this?

In the study, she saw Will's computer glowing softly. For a moment she considered trying to send a message to his pager via the SkyTel, but she had never used it before. And besides, what could she say? I'm about to be raped? If she did, Will would probably do something heroic and stupid, and get Abby killed. As she poured a shot of Wild Turkey, she realized that bourbon might accomplish what defiance could not. If Hickey drank enough whiskey fast enough, he might not be able to perform. It was probably a long shot, though. Karen thought the old saying about alcohol increasing desire but decreasing ability was exaggerated. Some of the best sex she and Will ever had was consummated when they were drunk. Of course, that had been a while back, when Will was in his midthirties. This thought disturbed the deep well of guilt inside her, but mixed with it was enough resentment to force the guilt down.

She picked up the Wild Turkey bottle and walked back toward her bedroom. Unexpected images flashed in her mind, scenes from a film she had seen long ago and forgotten until now. It starred Nicole Kidman. She couldn't remember its name, but Nicole and her husband had been blue-water sailing and had rescued a man in a life raft. The man turned out to be psychotic, and sailed off from Nicole's husband with her aboard. To go back and save her husband, Nicole had to get control of the boat again. But the psychopath had the gun. Before long, he decided to rape her, and what Karen remembered about the film—what had stayed with her long after—was that Nicole had let it happen. She had known it was the wrong moment to resist, and she had endured the rape in the hope of surviving until the right moment came. And it had arrived, finally, proving her sacrifice worthwhile.

As Karen neared the bedroom, words from her dead mother rose in her mind. A genteel woman speaking of rape in the language of older generations of southern women. The "fate worse than death," they called it. But they were wrong. Pride had bred a lot of wrong notions, and that was one. Karen had lived long enough to know that. Rape could scar forever, but it was not death. *Where there's life, there's hope,* her father had always said. And whatever it cost, she and Abby were going to live through this night.

Hickey was smiling when she stepped through the door. "Wild Turkey!" he cried. "I'll be damned. Bring that here!"

She crossed the room and gave him the bottle, then took three steps back.

"Scared I'll bite?" He unscrewed the cap and drank liberally from the wide glass mouth, then set the bottle between his legs. "I'll tell you a little secret. I *do*."

She looked away.

"Put your pants back on," he said.

What should have been a welcome command only

made her more anxious. She went to the bed and slipped her panties on, then slid her jeans up and snapped them.

"Look at me," Hickey said.

She looked.

His black eyes seethed. "You know what a lap dance is?"

Lurid images from HBO movies went through her mind. Scantily clad women hunching over bar patrons in chairs, wiggling their silicone-enhanced breasts in the faces of bachelor party boys and rheumy-eyed older men.

"No," she replied.

"You're lying. You know what one is. What you don't know is, my wife had to do them for a living for a while. That bugged me, Karen. That she had to do that."

So why didn't you get a decent job? she thought. But what she said was, "I'm sorry she had to do that."

His face went sullen. "All those bastards feeling her up, slobbering all over her. Your husband was probably one of them. She danced right here in Jackson."

"Will doesn't go to those places."

Hickey's eyes glinted. "Who you think you're kidding? You think hubby never had a lap dance?"

"No. At least I don't think so."

"You're living in a dream world. Ten to one, he'd have gotten one tonight on the coast, if this thing hadn't come up. Hell, a weekend away from the old lady? Even one who looks like you do . . . a man needs a little variety."

"That's your wife with Will right now?"

"That's right."

Every time Hickey confided another detail, Karen became more convinced that he didn't intend to let her live through this ordeal.

"What's going on in that little head of yours?" he asked. "Trying to think your way out of the box?"

"Your wife doesn't see anything wrong with kidnapping?"

"She doesn't see anything wrong with anything I do. And if she does, she keeps quiet about it. Get the picture?"

"I think so."

He took another slug of Wild Turkey. "We need some music. You got a stereo in that TV cabinet?"

Karen walked over and switched on the CD player. "What do you want to hear?"

"Something with a steady beat. You need a good beat for a lap dance. Not too fast, but not too slow either."

With a growing sense of unreality, she scanned the CD rack. Will collected everything from classic rock to country and New Age. There was music here that made her feel sexy, but she didn't want to taint it by being raped to its accompaniment. At a loss, she finally chose a *Best of the 80s* compilation. The first song was "Every Breath You Take" by the Police. The bass and drums began to pulse sinuously from speakers Will had mounted in the ceiling. When she turned, Hickey was nodding to the beat.

"That's it," he said. "Yeah. Come over here."

She took a step closer to the ottoman.

"Dance."

She would have laughed, were the situation not so desperate. It was like the old Westerns her father had loved so much, where the black-hatted gunfighter said the same line to the frightened homesteader.

"I said *dance*," Hickey repeated.

Karen began to sway to the music, but she felt awkward.

She had never been a good dancer. Will claimed she was, but she knew she lacked the effortless grace of some girls she had known growing up. Long-limbed creatures who, through some physical alchemy, absorbed sound waves and transformed that energy into purely sensual motion.

"Closer," Hickey said.

Karen danced nearer the chair, but jerked back as Hickey's hand reached toward her.

"It's just money," he said.

He was telling the truth. In his hand was a folded one-dollar bill.

"Come over here."

She danced closer, and he stuffed the bill into the front pocket of her jeans.

"That means you gotta take something off," he said, as though explaining the rules of a game.

She hesitated, then slowly unbuttoned her blouse until it hung from her shoulders.

"Shake it off."

She did. Goose bumps raced across her back and shoulders.

"Those aren't half bad," Hickey said, staring at her bra.

Karen focused on the wall and kept swaying to the music, but her mind was spinning. How fast could the Wild Turkey dull his senses? How long could she distract him from what he really wanted?

"Lean over," he ordered.

She bent slightly at the waist, and he rose up and stuffed a dollar bill into her bra.

"You know what that means, babe."

She unsnapped her jeans, but Hickey shook his head. "The bra. The bra next."

She almost stopped dancing. Part of her—the part that took no nonsense from anyone, man or woman—wanted to scream, *If you're going to rape me, just get it over with!* But a wiser part of her knew that would be a mistake. Anything could happen between now and the moment he actually forced himself on her. Miracles could happen. Her bra hooked in front. Dancing a little more enthusiastically, she reached up and undid the catch, then threaded her fingers under the shoulder straps and slid off the cups with exaggerated sensuality.

"That's better," Hickey intoned. "Jesus, you look good. For a mother, I mean. You ought to get some implants, though."

I don't want any damn implants! she screamed silently. But she let the music penetrate further into her, and gave more of herself to it.

"Yeah," he encouraged, holding up another bill. A five this time. She danced closer, close enough for him to slide the five into her pocket, but he shook his head.

"Lean over. And don't use your hands."

It took her a moment to figure out what he wanted, but it was simple enough. She bent over and used her upper arms to bring her breasts together, creating a soft niche for Hickey to stuff his five-dollar bill into. He immediately made use of it.

"Now the jeans."

She unzipped the jeans but left them on. As she spun slowly, he took another slug of Wild Turkey and stared mesmerized at her chest. The effect was almost comical, one that Karen had never really understood. Men stared at naked breasts the way LSD trippers stared at the sun, as though mammary glands held the secret of the universe. As Hickey stared, she saw that his dazed fascination gave her a certain amount of control. Instead of removing her jeans, she licked her forefinger and brought it down to her right nipple, then traced a small circle around it. When it responded, Hickey's nostrils flared and his eyes widened. He took another long pull from the bottle.

She raised both arms and began swaying to "Hold Me Now" by the Thompson Twins. She thought she must look like a go-go girl in one of those hanging cages from the sixties. Hickey was nodding in time to the beat, gripping the bottle by its neck and drinking from it every few seconds. His eyes looked darker than before, if that was possible. No longer bottomless pools, but flat disks of slate. Shark's eyes. No knowledge in them, only hunger. A vast, insatiable appetite.

"Come on," he rasped. "Let's see the goods."

She didn't want to take off her jeans. The vulnerability she had felt without them was dehumanizing. But she couldn't afford to make him truly angry. Then she would lose any semblance of control. She had to keep him drinking, convince him that she was going along. She let the jeans ride down her hips, then lifted her knees one at a time and kicked her feet out of them. That she managed this without falling on her butt was a miracle in itself—she hoped not the only one of the night.

That thought evaporated as Hickey slid down in the chair so that his legs were fully extended, his hips and thighs stretched like a bridge between the chair and ottoman. "Stand over me," he said. "Then you sit down and dance. That's called a sofa dance."

Sofa dance?

"Hurry," he said insistently. "Right here."

He meant his lap. Karen was nearing the limit of her tolerance. She stepped over his outstretched legs but did not sit down. She could no longer dance in any real sense, only sway from the waist up. But Hickey seemed content for the moment.

"Turn around," he said.

She thought she detected a slur in his pronunciation. She stepped over his legs, then back over them so that she was facing his feet. She had never been more thankful for underwear. She focused on the "L" of light that was her almost-closed bathroom door.

"Damn," Hickey said softly. "That's a work of art. Bend over. Slow."

Karen shut her eyes and bent toward his feet, knowing she was fully exposed now, terrified that he would touch her.

He did. But with paper, not his hand. Another bill. This one slid between her panties and her skin. She shuddered with disgust, thinking of where that money might have been, who might have touched it. Then she realized that her disgust was not even a fraction of what she would feel when he violated her.

"Turn around again."

She obeyed. To her horror, Hickey had laid a hand in his lap and begun rubbing himself. Her stomach turned a somersault. She was thankful she hadn't eaten in a while. Or perhaps it would be better if she had. She'd heard that vomiting was a good defense against rape, but she'd never understood how you could do it at the right time. If Hickey touched her now, though, she just might manage it.

"That was a twenty," he said. "Twenty for the panties."

She couldn't do it. She could not remove the last barrier between herself and total nakedness. "We've got all night," she said. "Don't rush it."

"Sit!" Hickey commanded, as he would a dog.

Karen tried to steel herself to obey, but it was no use.

He took hold of her hips with powerful hands and yanked her down against him. In the first instant of contact, a torrent of emotions raced through her. Terror first, because now it was real. Whiskey wasn't going to keep this man from performing. Nothing was, except death, and if she somehow managed to kill him, Abby would die, too. With the terror came dazed disbelief. She had not felt any other man but Will in that place for fifteen years, and only two before him. To be touched there by someone she had not chosen was an affront to her most secret self. But most deeply she felt guilt, for allowing it to go this far. Even though logic told her she had no alternative, her insecurity said there had to be one. One that a braver or more moral woman would have seen without thought. But the only alternative she could see was death for Abby.

As Hickey groaned in rapture, a cold certainty crystallized in Karen's brain. No matter what Nicole Kidman had done in the movies, she could not endure being raped by this man. By any man. For any reason. Her answer to the eternal female question—would I fight or submit?—was an unequivocal *fight.*

Hickey groaned again, and this time the sound pierced her to the marrow. Will sometimes made exactly the same sound during sex. The thought that there was any connection between her marital lovemaking and what was happening now nauseated her. But of course there was. Will was as human as any man, and he wanted sex all the time. Much more often than she did, anyway. And not just lovemaking. He wanted physical sex, an outlet for his drives and frustrations, and she resented that. There had been a time, just before and after their marriage, when she had felt a powerful urge to make love. But that had slowly faded with time. Not that she loved him less. But after she was forced to give up medical school, her desire flatlined. She couldn't voice the reason to Will, but the fact was that submitting to his sexual desires seemed the ultimate expression of the terrible sacrifice she had made. Because it was sex, at bottom, that had made that sacrifice necessary. And just because Will got an erection every morning and night was no reason she had to wait at his beck and call like some nineteenth-century *hausfrau*—

"Get up!" Hickey ordered. "That's enough foreplay."

She practically leaped off him and retreated toward the TV cabinet.

He thrust himself to his feet and carried the bottle of Wild Turkey to the bedside table. Then he walked back toward her, pulling off his polo shirt as he came, revealing a pale, wiry torso. Only his neck was tanned, and his arms from the elbows down. A farmer's tan, her father had called it. When he reached for his belt, Karen looked at the carpet.

"Watch," he said, his voice full of pride.

She took a deep breath and looked up as Hickey's khakis hit the floor. A tingling numbness began to creep outward from some place deep within her. The act would be bad, she knew, but the anticipation was worse. The knowing—while you were still intact—that absolute suffering was inevitable. That the place you had protected all your life was about to be violated. That no help would come. There was only Hickey. And Abby. Abby hanging over her head like a sword, enforcing every command he gave.

The numbness continued to spread through her, and the temptation was to let it come, like a freezing person giving in to the cold. *Let it penetrate into my bones,* she thought. *Into my heart and soul, so that whatever happens will be unfelt, a crime committed upon another person, an insensate body. A cadaver.* And yet, if she let the numbness that far in, could she ever get it all out again?

As Hickey stared at her with his stupid schoolboy grin, something stirred deep within her. Not quite a thought, but the seed of one. A tiny spark of awareness, smoldering and darkly feminine. A ruthless, chthonic knowledge of male vulnerability.

Her moment would come.

EIGHT

Huey sat across from Abby on the linoleum floor of the cabin, whittling slowly. He had dragged an old saddle blanket in from the bedroom and set her on it, so she wouldn't have to sit on the bare floor. She clutched the Barbie in her little hands like a talisman.

"Do you feel better now?" asked Huey.

Abby nodded. "A little bit."

"Are you hungry? I'm hungry."

"Kind of. My tummy hurts."

A knot of worry formed in Huey's stomach. "What do you like? I got baloney. You like Captain Crunch? I love Captain Crunch."

"I have to eat Raisin Bran."

"You can't eat Captain Crunch?"

"No."

"How come?"

Her lips puckered and moved to one side as she thought about it. "Well, when you eat, the food puts sugar in your blood. And you've got stuff in your body to make the sugar go away. But I don't have any. So, the sugar gets more and more until it makes me sick. And if I get too sick, I'll go to sleep. Sleep and maybe never wake up."

Fear passed into Huey's face like a shadow falling over a rock. He rubbed his hands anxiously across his putty-like cheeks. "That happened to my sister. Jo Ellen. I wish I could give you some of my blood to make your sugar go away."

"That's what's in my shots. Stuff to make the sugar go away. I don't like needles, but I don't like being sick, either. It hurts."

"I hate needles," Huey said forcefully. "Hate, hate, hate."

"Me, too."

"*Hate* needles," Huey reasserted.

"There are big ones and little ones, though," Abby said. "My shots have the littlest kind. Some shots have really big ones. Like when they take your blood. And sometimes my dad has to stick people in the back. In the spine cord. Or in the nerves sometimes. That hurts the worst. But he does it to make a bigger hurt go away."

"How do you know so much?"

Abby shrugged. "I don't know. My mom and dad are always telling me stuff. People at school say I talk grown-up all the time."

"Are you going to be a doctor when you get big?"

"Uh-huh. A flying doctor."

Huey's eyes got bigger. "You can't fly, can you?"

"In an airplane, silly."

"Oh."

"My tummy still hurts."

Huey's mouth fell open. "You just play here with your doll. I'm gonna make you the biggest bowl of Captain Crunch you ever saw!"

Before Abby could remind him that she couldn't eat Cap'n Crunch, the giant got to his feet and walked toward the kitchen. After three steps, he stopped and put his hand to his head as though he had forgotten something.

"Dumb, dumb, dumb," he said.

He came back to Abby, bent down, and picked up the Nokia cell phone he'd left beside her. "Joey said, take this with me everywhere. Don't leave it anywhere. He gave me a extra battery, too."

Abby looked forlornly at the phone. She was thinking about what her mother had said about calling the police.

"I'll be right back," Huey promised. "You just wait."

He walked into the kitchen, leaving Abby alone in the front room with his whittling knife and his shapeless chunk of wood. She could see his back as he opened a cabinet. Then he moved out of the doorway, and she couldn't see him anymore. She heard a sucking sound. A refrigerator door.

She turned to the cabin window. It was pitch-black outside. She hated the dark, but her mother's voice was playing in her head. *Take the phone and hide. . . .* She wouldn't have said that if she wanted Abby to stay with Huey. But if she went outside, what could she do? She didn't know the way home, or even how far away home was. And without the phone, she couldn't call anybody.

She heard a clink, then Huey humming something.

She liked Huey. But he was a stranger, and her daddy had told her over and over how strangers could be bad, even when they seemed nice. She felt sorry for him, but whenever she looked up and saw him watching her, she felt something funny in her stomach. Like a big bubble pressing up against her heart. In a moment he would walk through the door with a bowl of cereal that could kill her. Abby closed her eyes and pictured her mother's face. *What would she say if she could talk to me now?*

Run.

Abby stood up with her Barbie and took a tentative step toward the door. Looking back toward the kitchen, she saw Huey's shadow moving on the floor. She walked very fast to the front door, picked up the small ice chest her mother had left, and slipped outside without a sound.

Joe Hickey took two steps toward Karen, a lopsided grin on his face. She kept her eyes on his and tried to keep the fear out of her voice as she spoke.

"Will you please wear a condom?"

"Sorry, babe. Not tonight."

A shudder of revulsion ran through her. God only knew what diseases Hickey carried. He had been in prison, and the HIV infection rate behind bars was astronomical.

"Please," she implored. "I don't want to—"

"I ain't worn a rubber since junior high, and I ain't starting now."

She fought down a wave of nausea. "I need to use the bathroom."

"I'll go with you."

"For God's sake. Give me that much privacy."

"What's in the bathroom? Another gun?"

"My diaphragm, okay? I don't want to get pregnant."

Hickey's grin returned. "Well, now, I don't know. You look like you got good genes. Maybe you and me should *pro*-create. Do the global gene pool a favor."

She closed her eyes, praying he wasn't serious. "May I please use the diaphragm?"

"What the hell." He waved his hand. "Hey, maybe I should put it in for you."

She struggled to keep her face impassive.

"Fine. Go do whatever. But when you come out of there, I don't want to see those panties. It's Lady Godiva time."

As she walked toward the bathroom, he picked up the Wild Turkey bottle and stretched out on the sleigh bed, his face glowing with anticipation.

Huey came out of the kitchen carrying a bowl of Cap'n Crunch as big as a colander in his left hand and his cell phone in his right. He looked down at the saddle blanket Abby had been sitting on and blinked in confusion. Then he peered around the room. After several seconds, a grin lighted his face.

"Are you playing hide-and-go-seek? Is that what you're doing?"

He carried the cereal and the phone into the bathroom. Finding it empty, he checked the bedroom. He had to set the bowl on the mattress and lie prone to look under the old iron frame bed, groaning as he squeezed his oversized body between the side rail and the wall.

There was nothing under the bed but what his mother used to call "slut wool."

He got to his feet again, picked up the cereal bowl, went to the bedroom door, and stared at the empty saddle blanket again. Then he cocked his head and listened hard.

"Abby?"

His voice sounded lonelier than it had when she was in the room. The silence just swallowed it up.

"Abby?"

The screen door banged softly in the wind.

Huey looked to his right and saw the door hanging open. His face went slack. After a long sequence of thought, doubt, and realization, he dropped the bowl and the cell phone and charged onto the porch.

The second Karen closed the bathroom door, her survival instinct kicked into overdrive. She turned on the sink taps, then opened the cabinet behind the mirror, revealing bottles of vitamins, drugs, facial cleansers, gauze bandages, and all the other sundries of a doctor's home medicine cabinet. On the bottom shelf was a stack of Lo-Ovral birth control pills. She grabbed them and threw them into the cabinet under the lavatory so Hickey wouldn't see them if he came in.

She scanned the drugs in the cabinet. Zithromax, an antibiotic. Naproxen for Will's arthritis. Methotrexate. Stuck behind the gauze bandage pack was a small brown prescription bottle. Her heart quickened as she picked it up and read the label: *Mepergan Fortis.* Demerol. But when she opened it, she saw only two red pills in its bottom. Not enough to put Hickey out quickly, even if she found a way to slip them into the Wild Turkey bottle. Raking frantically through the cabinet, she saw nothing that could help her. As she closed the door, she caught her reflection in its mirrored surface. She looked like a ghost of herself.

Splashing water on her face, she reached down for a hand towel and froze. Standing in a ceramic cup by the sink were three toothbrushes. But beside their blue and orange handles, a different sort of handle stuck up. A thinner one. She reached down and lifted it out of the glass. It was a disposable scalpel, its thin blade shielded by a plastic sheath. As she studied it, an arc of instinct closed, completing the circuit begun when Hickey dropped his pants.

"Christ, how long can it take?" he complained.

Hickey sounded like he was right outside the door. Dropping a washrag over the scalpel, Karen yanked off her panties, sat on the commode, and watched the doorknob.

It didn't move.

She got up and took the scalpel from beneath the rag, then removed the clear protective sheath from the blade. Its edge was twice as bright as its side, honed to a sharpness that could lay open the human dermis like the skin of a peach. She straightened before the mirror and looked at herself. Was the scalpel concealable? After a moment's thought, she raised it point-first toward her forehead and slid it neatly into her hair.

It vanished.

She turned her head right and then left, to see whether the scalpel was visible. It wasn't. She felt her hair to see how obvious it was. Too obvious. If Hickey held her head for any reason, he would instantly discover the blade.

She pulled the scalpel from her hair and looked at it again. Six inches of plastic and surgical steel, flatter than a key and lighter than a pencil. The Papillon solution was not an option. She turned away from the mirror and looked back over her shoulder. She could see down to the upper cleft of her buttocks. For the first time in her life, she was glad to be carrying a few extra pounds. Using the mirror as a guide, she slid the scalpel, handle first, down between her cheeks. It felt cold and alien, but only the silver tip of the blade was visible at the base of her spine.

It would have to do.

All she could hope for now was to stack the odds a little in her favor. She opened the dirty clothes cabinet and stood on tiptoe. In the top section were two shelves she used to store clothes she rarely wore. She reached up and dug through them with feverish intensity.

There.

She wriggled into the claret-colored teddy Will had bought at the mall last year, a garment she'd never even tried on. The top half must have been designed by Wonderbra, because it lifted and pressed her modest breasts together until the cleavage reminded her of the beach bunnies on *Baywatch.* The bottom half was ridiculously tight, with a sheer lace triangle over the crotch, leaving her fully exposed.

She looked like a French whore.

Perfect.

* * *

Crouching in a lightless thicket, Abby watched Huey lumber past her in the moonlight.

"Abby?" he called. "Why did you run away? You're scaring me."

She looked down at her doll, which she had laid across the ice chest to keep it out of the briars. She was trying hard not to make a sound, but her shins had already been scratched bloody, and they stung like a thousand paper cuts. She hadn't wanted to go far from the lights, but she knew Huey would find her if she didn't get into the dark.

He paused twenty feet to her left, looking into the wall of trees. "Abby? Where are you?"

She wondered how long she could wait here. The woods didn't scare her. Not usually, anyway. Their house was in the middle of the woods. But she'd never spent the night in them, at least not alone. Only with her dad, at the Indian Princess campout. Already she'd heard sounds that made her shiver. Scuttling in the undergrowth, like armadillos, or maybe possums. There was a possum that kept eating the cat's food at Kate Mosby's house up the road. Abby had seen the cat fight it once, and the long, needlelike teeth of the possum as it hissed at the cat. If a possum came close now, she wouldn't be able to sit still.

The other thing was her sugar. She felt like it was okay, but her mother wasn't there to measure it, and if she started to "go south," as her daddy put it, she would need a shot. She had never given herself a shot before.

"Come out!" Huey yelled, sounding really mad now.

Abby watched him pick up a big stick and poke some

bushes with it. Then he moved off farther to her left, going along the line of trees.

She looked at the cabin, the lovely yellow light streaming from the windows. She wished she could wait inside, where there were no animals or bugs. Huey's voice floated back to her on the wind.

"There's bad things in the woods at night! Wolves and bears and things! You need Huey to look out for you!"

She hugged herself and tried not to listen. There might be bears in these woods, but she didn't think so. And certainly not wolves. There weren't any more wolves.

"There's snakes, too," Huey called. "Creepy crawly snakes looking for warm bodies in the dark."

A chill shot up Abby's spine. There were snakes in Mississippi, all right. Bad ones. She'd learned about them at Indian Princesses. Copperheads and cottonmouths and ground rattlers and coral snakes. They'd seen a coral snake on one campout, sunning itself on a rock by the creek. The fathers didn't even try to get close enough to kill it. They said if it bit you, you could die before you got to the hospital. Her dad had taught the Princesses a rhyme to help them tell the difference between a coral snake and a scarlet king snake, which looked almost exactly like it: *If red touches yellow, it can kill a fellow.*

"If the snakes get you, it won't be my fault!" Huey yelled, beating the bushes off to her left.

Abby shut her eyes and tried not to cry.

When Karen emerged from the bathroom wearing the teddy, she saw Hickey lying under the covers in the middle of the bed. The only light came from the lamp on the end table. He gave a long, low wolf whistle.

"Man *alive*. That's better than naked. Talk about getting with the program."

As Karen moved toward the bed, she saw Will's .38 lying on the floor by the dust ruffle. That was how confident Hickey was in the diabolical cage of circumstance he had constructed.

He patted the side of the bed.

As she moved toward him, she slid the gun under the bed with her foot, then turned her back to him and slipped under the covers, being careful to keep her legs together as she moved. She tried not to stiffen as her hip and shoulder touched Hickey's side, but she knew that her tension would be transmitted to him in a thousand subtle ways.

"Damn, you're cold," he complained.

"Sorry." He smelled like a stale ashtray. She stared up at the ceiling as though she had nothing in her mind but enduring what was to come with stoicism. "What do you want me to do?"

"You're not gonna whine about it?"

"Not if it keeps you from hurting Abby."

"Thank God for small favors." He turned sideways and propped himself on an elbow, and she felt him press against her hip. A deep shudder rippled through her.

"Are you ready down there?" he asked.

Unbelievable. How could he possibly think that an impending rape could arouse a woman? She had to distract him from his immediate goal. "Is that what you want first? Straight to business? I thought you'd want something else."

"Like what?" He reached up and cupped her left breast with a sweaty hand.

Every fiber of instinct told her to jerk away from the offending touch, but she forced herself to lie still and turn her face toward his. "Something you fantasize about when you see women like me in the grocery store."

He squeezed the breast. "Like what?"

"Lie back and relax. You'll see."

A slow smile spread his lips. "Oh, man . . ."

She rolled onto her stomach, pulled the covers over her shoulders, and slid down toward Hickey's midsection. She hoped he would leave the comforter where it was, but he lifted it so that he could watch what he believed was to come. She was foolish to have expected anything else.

"I'm cold," she said, looking up.

"You'll warm up." His black eyes were bright. "And don't think you're going to get out of anything by doing this."

She swallowed her revulsion, then straddled his legs and took hold of him with her left hand.

"Mmm," he moaned.

She had to get him to look away. Closing her eyes, she worked her left hand a little, the way Will liked it. Hickey groaned but did not look away. He wouldn't, she realized, until she progressed much further. This was what he got off on: watching a "society" woman pleasure him.

"Good," he murmured. "Good girl."

She slid her right hand down beneath her stomach.

"Yeah," he said. "I want to see you do that."

"After you finish," she said, feeling sweat break out on her face. It was hot in the bedroom, but it was fear, not the temperature that had brought moisture to her skin.

He groped for the back of her head.

Panic shot through her. "I know what to do. Lie back and relax. You don't want it to be over too fast."

"Yeah." After a moment, his head lolled back, and his eyes rolled up toward the ceiling.

She quickly slid her right hand up around her hip. Her forefinger touched the scalpel blade. Very carefully, she felt her way down the plastic handle, which was slick with perspiration. Closing her first and second fingers around the handle, she drew the scalpel from its place of concealment and set it firmly in her fist, the flat of the blade wedged between the pad of her thumb and her forefinger.

"Come *on*," Hickey urged, his voice brimming with impatience.

She brought the blade smoothly along her right side and underneath her right breast. When it was beneath her chin, she slid her knees up under her chest, as though to position herself for oral sex.

"Finally," he grunted.

She had to get between his legs. Straddling him this way, he could easily buck her off in the initial moment of panic. Without breaking her rhythm, she lifted one knee and wedged it between his thighs, then followed with the other.

"Go for it," he said.

Karen gripped him as hard as she could with her left hand and pressed the blade against his urethra with her right, anchoring the point in a few millimeters of skin. It would take several seconds for him to register the pain of the puncture.

"Look down, Joe," she said in a cold voice. "And don't make any sudden moves."

"What?"

"If you move, you're going to lose this organ you're so proud of."

She felt his abdomen tighten as he raised his head to look. "What? Hey, whatever you're doing, it hurts."

"I'm holding a scalpel against your penis, Joe." She prepared herself for a reflex jerk of panic. "You *really* don't want to move, okay?"

His eyes went from blank confusion to shock in less than a second. At last he had seen and understood the scalpel. His whole body went rigid, but his pelvis didn't move an inch.

"What the—" he blurted in a stage whisper.

He raised his hand to strike her, but didn't have the courage to do it. Karen looked straight into his eyes. Fear crackled there like electricity. The power was intoxicating. She had gone from helpless supplicant to total dominance in seconds. If she had held the gun to Hickey's head, he would have laughed in her face. But the threat to his manhood paralyzed him. She could almost feel his heart squirming in his chest.

"This is a Bard-Parker Number Ten scalpel," she said. "We keep them around to take out splinters, stuff like that. But it'll take off your equipment just as easily. I bet you'd hardly even feel it. Just a quick sting."

"I'm gonna kill you," he said in a matter-of-fact voice. "You and your kid."

She pushed the scalpel point deeper, drawing blood.

"Stop!" he shouted, his face contorted in terror. His skin had gone as white as that of a man on his deathbed.

"You're bleeding, Joe. So listen very closely. You're going to pick up that telephone, call your cousin, and tell him to bring my daughter back here."

Hickey's eyes flicked from the blade to her face. "You won't do it. If you do, your kid dies."

"Oh, I'll do it." Karen's heart felt like it was beating at random, firing off drumrolls between dangerous silences. She had to hold her nerve. "I'll do it, and if you live through it, you'll be peeing through an indwelling catheter for the rest of your life. No more making women walk bowlegged for a week. No more banging tonsils."

She thought she saw a flicker of fear, but Hickey covered it quickly.

"Your hand's shaking," he said. "Feel it?"

"Pick up the phone!"

"Goddamn women. You ain't got the guts."

Something in his voice ignited an anger so deep that Karen had never even attempted to express it. She squeezed him with all the power in her left arm, and his skin went purple.

"I was a surgical nurse for six years, Joe. I'll castrate you with no more regret than slicing a chicken neck. And it won't be like that Bobbitt guy. No sewing it back on. Because while you're spurting blood all over my percale sheets, I'll throw it in the garbage disposal and flip the switch. Now *pick up that fucking phone!*"

"Take it easy!" Hickey grabbed the phone off the

bedside table. "I'm dialing!" He punched wildly at the keypad. "What do you want me to say?"

Karen struggled to rein in her anger. The fierce pleasure she felt at seeing him broken had her muscles twitching like they did after four sets of tennis. Some primal part of her *wanted* to cut him.

"Tell him you already have the ransom money. Tell him to put Abby in the truck and drive her back here."

"He won't do it. We've never done it that way. He'll know something's wrong."

"You told me he always does everything you say!"

Puzzlement came into Hickey's face. "He's not answering."

"You didn't dial it right!"

"I swear to God I did!"

"Then why hasn't he answered?"

"How do I know?"

"Dial it again!" She pressed the blade deeper. There was a steady stream of blood now.

"Shit! Wait!" He hung up and redialed the number, then waited for an answer.

Karen's nerves were fraying fast. Despite her immediate control over Hickey, she had put herself in an untenable position if Huey didn't answer the phone.

"He's not picking up," Hickey said, looking worried enough for it to distract him from his immediate peril. "What the hell?"

"He hasn't missed a call yet! Why this one?"

Hickey shrugged. "How do I know? He's a damn retard. Now get that knife away from me, will you? We've got to figure out what's happening up there."

"Shut up," Karen snapped. "Let me think."

"What are you going to do? You can't sit like that all night."

"I said, 'Shut up'!"

"Okay. But why don't you go ahead and give me that blow job while you're deciding?"

Karen blinked in amazement, and Hickey slammed the telephone into the side of her head.

Huey had circled back around the cabin, poking at bushes and trying to scare Abby, but now his voice had faded to almost nothing as he worked his way along the dirt road leading away from the cabin.

She crouched in the dark, her head filled with images of snakes curling and uncurling like whips in the weeds around her. During the last few minutes, beetles had crawled over her feet, and fat mosquitoes had feasted on her exposed arms and face. She was afraid to swat them, because Huey might hear the sound and come running back. Part of her wanted to find a tree and climb it, but that would surely make too much noise. Besides, snakes could climb. She didn't think they *slept* in the trees, though.

As she squashed a mosquito bloody against her forearm, a faint ringing sounded in her ears. She tried to focus on it, but it disappeared. Then it came again—louder, she thought—or maybe it just seemed louder because she was listening for it. Her heart thumped.

It was a telephone.

The ringing was coming from the cabin. Huey must have left his phone inside when he went looking for her!

She got up to run to the cabin, then stopped. What if he had gone back to the cabin without her seeing him? What if he was inside now? No. The phone was still ringing, and if Huey was inside, he would have answered it. She grabbed her doll and the ice chest and raced out of the trees toward the glowing windows.

White light exploded in Karen's brain. As her thoughts scattered into meaningless electrochemicals, her cerebellum executed the impulse her cerebral cortex had been holding in check for the past minute. Like a frog's leg touched by an electrode, the hand holding the scalpel jerked back toward her stomach.

Hickey shrieked like a hog having its throat cut.

The white light shattered into stars, then faded to an unstable image of a screaming man. Karen looked down.

All she saw was blood.

Abby couldn't find the phone. It wasn't on the table or the broken old couch. But it was still ringing.

She looked at the floor. There was a big puddle of spilled milk and Cap'n Crunch by the bedroom door. The phone was lying half under the upside-down salad bowl Huey had put the cereal into. Abby darted to the puddle and reached for the wet cell phone, but even as she did, she knew something wasn't right. The phone's numbers and window were dark. She pressed SEND and put the phone to her ear.

She heard only silence. *"No,"* she keened, terrified that her mother had hung up.

The phone rang again.

"Hello? Hello! Mama?"

The ringing bell sounded again. It wasn't coming from the cell phone. It was coming from the bedroom. She ran in and looked around. An old-timey black phone sat on the floor on the far side of the bed. It rang again.

She grabbed the receiver. "Hello? . . . Hello!"

She heard a dial tone.

"Hello?"

The phone did not ring again. She stared at it in disbelief. How could her mother stop ringing, just when she was about to pick up? Shaking with fear, she stared at the rotary dial and spoke softly as she tried to remember. "Nine-nine-one? Nine . . . nine-*one*-one. Nine-one—"

"Abby?" Huey's voice floated into the bedroom. "Don't run away from Huey! You're going to get me in trouble. Big trouble."

She froze.

The voice sounded close, but she didn't hear footsteps. She was too afraid to peek outside the bedroom door. She grabbed the Barbie and the cell phone off the bed and ran flat-out for the back door.

Outside, she ran past a small shed and crouched beside a tree. There was just enough moonlight to see the POWER button. "Nine-one-one," she said with certainty. She switched on the phone, carefully punched in 911, pressed SEND, and put the phone to her ear.

"Welcome to CellStar," said a computer voice. "You are currently in a nonemergency-service zone. Please—"

"Is this the police?" Abby cried. "I need a policeman!"

Tears formed in her eyes as the voice refused to

acknowledge her. She hit END and began to dial the only number she could think of: home.

"Six-oh-one," she whispered. "Eight-five-six-four-seven-one-two."

She hit SEND again.

A man's voice answered this time, but it was a computer, too. "We're sorry," it said. "You must first press a one or zero before making this call. Thank you."

"Press one first?" Abby echoed, feeling panic in her chest. "Press one first. Press one first. . . ."

Karen and Hickey knelt three feet apart on the bed. Karen was holding the scalpel up defensively; Hickey clutched a pillow to his groin. His face was a mask of rage and agony.

"You've got to get to a hospital!" she told him. "You could bleed to death."

He lifted the pillow away from his skin and looked down, then laughed maniacally. "You missed! You *missed*. Look at that!"

He lifted the pillow higher, and his smile vanished. His right thigh had been laid open from groin to knee. Blood was pulsing out at an alarming rate.

"Oh God," he whispered. "Oh God."

"You did it!" Karen told him. "You hit me with the phone!"

"Your kid is dead, bitch. *Dead!*"

Her heart turned to stone. She had gambled and failed. As Hickey tried to stanch the flow of blood with the pillow, she jumped off the bed and scrabbled under it for the gun. She had to keep him from bleeding to death, but she didn't want to be at his mercy while he was in a fit of rage.

"Go in the bathroom!" she said, getting to her feet with the pistol. "Tie a towel just above the laceration. You've got to slow the arterial flow."

"Look what you did!" he screamed, his eyes wide with shock.

She was going to have to tend to the wound, but she didn't think she could bring herself to touch him yet. She didn't even want to get close to him.

"Get a towel!" she yelled. "Hurry! Make a tourniquet!"

Hickey hobbled into the bathroom with the pillow pressed to his thigh, groaning and whining and cursing at once. Karen grabbed the bedsheet and wiped his blood off her thighs, then pulled her discarded blouse over the teddy, went to the bathroom door, and held the gun on Hickey while he tied a towel around his thigh. He was doing a fair job, good enough to slow the bleeding anyway.

"Why didn't Huey answer?" she asked. "Why aren't they at the cabin? Has he taken Abby somewhere?"

Hickey looked up, his face red with strain. "You don't need to worry about that. No point at all. You just bought yourself a world of pain, lady. A *world* of pain."

"What do you expect? You steal my child and try to rape me, and I'm supposed to lie down and take it?"

He shook a bloody washrag at her. "Look at this goddamn leg! I'm bleeding to death here!"

"You need a hospital."

"Bullshit, I need a hospital. I need some stitches is all. You were a nurse, you said. You do it."

"It would take fifty stitches to close that." She was exaggerating. A butcher could bring the edges of the wound together with ten.

"So get the stuff! Your husband's got a black bag or something, right? To take care of the neighborhood brats?"

Will did keep a bag at home for Abby's soccer games, but Karen didn't want to get it. She didn't want to hold the gun or look at Hickey's nakedness or anything else anymore. She just wanted Abby locked tight in her nurturing arms.

"Why are you doing this?" she screamed. *"Why my little girl? It's not fair! It's not right—"*

Hickey slapped her. Then, his jaw set tight against the pain, he said through clenched teeth: "Lady, if you don't get your shit together and sew me up, Huey will snap your little girl's spine like a twig. One phone call will do it. One fucking call."

"You can't even get him on the phone!"

"I'll get him."

Karen stood shaking in the aftermath of her fit. Blood was soaking through her blouse from the teddy beneath, and Will's gun quivered in her hand. She had to keep herself together. Or Abby wouldn't make it.

"Move your ass!" Hickey yelled. "Get the bag!"

She nodded and hurried out of the bathroom.

Abby thought she'd heard Huey outside again, so she crept into the little shed behind the cabin. There was a tractor in it, like the one her daddy used to cut the grass at home, only bigger. She climbed up onto its seat and started pressing numbers on the cell phone's lighted keypad. She began with "1," then moved on to the area code of Mississippi. "Six-oh-one," she said as she dialed. Then she pressed the other seven numbers, hit SEND, and prayed that the answering service wouldn't answer.

The phone began to ring.

Karen was rummaging through Will's medical bag when the phone rang on Will's side of the bed. Hickey was still in the bathroom, loosening the towel tourniquet as she had advised. Though the caller was almost surely Hickey's wife, Karen answered, hoping against hope that her desperate act had somehow paid off.

"Hello?"

"Tell her to give me a minute," Hickey called from behind the half-closed bathroom door.

"Mama?"

Karen's hands began to shake as if with palsy. "Abby?"

"Mama!"

Karen had to swallow before she could continue. "Honey, are you all right? Where are you?"

Abby's voice disintegrated into sobs before she could answer. Karen heard her hiccupping and swallowing, trying to control herself enough to speak.

"Take your time, baby. Tell me where you are."

"I don't *know*! I'm in the woods. Mama, come get me! I'm *scared*."

Karen glanced at the bathroom door. "I'm going to come, honey, but—" She paused, unsure what to say. How much reality could a five-year-old absorb and still function? "Baby, Mama doesn't know how to get to where you are. Are you still at the place where I gave you the shot?"

"Uh-huh. I ran outside the cabin. I was hiding in the woods and Mr. Huey yelled that there's snakes and bears. Then I heard the phone inside."

"Listen, honey. Do you remember how to call nine-one-one? If you do that, the police can come get—"

"I already *did* that. The lady wouldn't listen! Mama, help me."

"What the hell are you doing? Give me that goddamn phone!" Hickey was coming through the bathroom door, trying to move quickly but not wanting to put too much weight on his injured leg.

"Mama?" cried Abby.

"Give me the phone!" Hickey roared.

Karen grabbed the .38 off the bed, pointed it at him, and fired.

Hickey hit the floor like a soldier under incoming artillery and covered his head with both hands.

"TELL ME WHERE MY BABY IS, YOU SON OF A BITCH!"

"Mama? Mama!"

Hickey didn't speak or move. Karen fired into the floor, missing him by inches. "ANSWER ME, GODDAMN IT!"

"Stop shooting!" he screamed. "If you kill me, your kid is dead!"

"RIGHT ALONG WITH YOU! GET IT?" Karen tried to speak calmly into the receiver. "Stay on the phone, baby. Mama's fine, but she's busy. Are you in the cabin now?"

"I'm in a little shed outside. I'm on a tractor."

Abby's captor was certain to focus on any structures as

he hunted for her, no matter how simpleminded he was. It was like looking for your car keys under the streetlight.

"I want you to go back outside, Abby, into the woods. Make sure Mr. Huey isn't around, then sneak out of the shed, get down in some bushes, and stay down."

"But it's nighttime."

"I know, but tonight the dark is your friend. Remember Pajama Sam? No need to hide when it's dark outside?"

"That's on the computer. That's not real."

"I know, baby, but the woods are the safe place for you now. Do you understand?"

"I guess so."

"Do you think your sugar's okay?"

"I guess."

"Don't you worry, sweetie. Mama's going to come get you."

"You promise?"

"I promise. Now, I want you to look outside, and then run into the woods. Take the phone with you, and stay on the line. Don't hang up, okay? *Don't hang up.*"

"Okay."

Karen covered the phone with her hand and pointed the gun at Hickey's head. "Get up, you bastard."

He looked up, his eyes bright with anger. Maybe with surprise, too, she thought.

"I SAID, 'GET UP'!"

Hickey flattened his hands on the floor and raised himself slowly, then leaned against the frame of the bathroom door for support.

"What the hell do you think you're doing?" he asked.

She gave him a cold smile. "I'm changing the plan."

NINE

Dr. James McDill and his wife sat across from Special Agent Bill Chalmers, a bland-faced, sandy-haired man in his early forties. Agent Chalmers's tie was still neatly tied despite the fact that it was 11:30 P.M. McDill had called the Jackson Field Office of the FBI a few minutes after Margaret's mini-breakdown, and that call had resulted in this meeting.

He had planned to come to the Federal Building alone, but Margaret had insisted on accompanying him. Chalmers met them in the empty lobby, escorted them through the unmanned security post and up to the FBI floor. They arrived to find most of the office complex empty and dark: a government-issue cube farm lit by glowing computer screens. Chalmers led them back to the office of the SAC, or Special Agent-in-Charge. A nameplate on the desk read FRANK ZWICK.

The Jackson FBI office had a distinguished or notorious history, depending on what part of the country you were from. It had been established by J. Edgar Hoover himself during the terrible civil rights summer of 1967.

"I'm not quite clear about some of the things you said on the phone," Chalmers said from behind his boss's desk. "Do you mind if I ask some questions?"

"Fire away," said McDill.

"We're talking about a kidnapping-for-ransom, correct? And wire fraud, it sounds like."

"Yes, to the first question. To the second, I imagine so."

"And this happened one year ago today?"

"Give or take a few days. It happened during the same annual medical convention that's going on right now in Biloxi."

Chalmers pursed his lips and gazed through the window, toward the old Standard Life Building, illuminated now by cold fluorescent light. After a few moments' thought, he looked the heart surgeon directly in the eye.

"I've got to ask this, Doctor. Why did you folks wait a whole year to report this kidnapping?"

McDill had rehearsed his answer during the drive over. "They threatened to come back and kill our son. We'd paid the ransom. It was a hundred and seventy-five thousand dollars, which, frankly, isn't much money to me. Especially weighed against the life of my son."

"But didn't you tell me the kidnappers told you they'd done the same thing before?"

"Yes."

"So you must have feared from the first that they would do it again, to another child. Another family."

McDill looked at the floor. "That's true. The hard

truth is, I'm more selfish than I'd like to think. If I had it to do again—"

"I was raped," Margaret said quietly.

McDill froze with his mouth open, but Agent Chalmers settled back into his boss's chair, as though the situation was at last becoming clear.

"I see," he said. "Could you tell me a little more about that?"

McDill laid a hand on his wife's forearm. "Margaret, you don't have to do this."

She waved off his hand, then gripped the arms of the chair. It was clear that she meant to tell the truth, no matter what it cost her. As she spoke, she did not quite look at Chalmers, but into some indeterminate space beyond him.

"I wouldn't let James report what happened. I was alone with the man who was running the kidnapping, and my son was being held at another location. Peter was at the mercy of these people. My husband was also. The man with me . . . he was in telephone contact with his partners. He could have told them to hurt or kill either Peter or James. He made very sure that I understood that, that I believed he was capable of it. Then he used that fact to extort sex from me."

McDill tried to comfort her, but she shrunk away and kept talking. "Very painful, dirty sex," she said. "I was terrified that would be made public. I know now that I was wrong to keep it quiet, but—" She wiped one eye but kept going, like a marathon runner forcing herself to reach the finish line. "Combined with the threat to come back and kill Peter, I simply couldn't deal with the idea.

I couldn't take that risk. But I couldn't stop thinking about it, either. I haven't thought about anything else since it happened. I can't even make love with my husband. I—I'm going to pieces, I think."

McDill took her hand and squeezed it hard. This time she didn't pull away.

Agent Chalmers picked up his pen and tapped it on the table. He suddenly seemed much more convinced by their story.

"The truth is," said McDill, "it was just easier for us to try to forget it. To pretend it never happened. But it did."

"And now you think it's happening again."

"Yes."

"Tell me why."

McDill took a deep breath and marshaled his thoughts. "I have no objective evidence. I admit that right up front. But the woman holding me at the hotel said they'd done the same thing before, more than once. I believed her. She also said no one had ever reported them. And knowing what I know now about the leader's tactics, I believe that, too. I mean, *we* didn't report it. The man who conceived of this damned scheme—Joe, or whatever his real name is—is clearly a psychopath. He kidnaps children to get money, and to commit rape as some sort of bonus. And so far he's gotten way with it. I guess what I'm saying is, what reason does he have to stop?"

Chalmers put down his pen and laid his hands flat on the desk. McDill had the sense that the agent was deciding whether to engage the full resources of the FBI in the middle of the night, or to take a more conservative approach.

"Mrs. McDill, you were with this man for a considerable period of time. Did you have a feeling about whether the name he used was his real name?"

Margaret had begun weeping softly. McDill and Chalmers waited.

"I think Joe was his real name," she said. "I think it was some perverse point of pride with him. Like he could do all this to us without any fear that we would report him. The fact that he used his real name demonstrated his superiority. That's what I think, anyway."

"Did he say anything about where he was from? What state, for example?"

"No."

"Did he say the other kidnappings had taken place in Mississippi?"

"No. But I assumed they had."

"Did you have any feeling about what part of the country he might be from?"

"The South," Margaret said. "Definitely the South. I won't say Mississippi for sure, because the accent was . . . too hard. Like he was from the South but had been away for a long time. Or maybe the reverse. A man who was from someplace else but had spent a lot of time in the South. Does that make any sense?"

"Yes," Chalmers replied. "What about you, Doctor? Did the woman you were with say where she was from? Something about family, anything like that?"

"Nothing useful. She seemed frightened by the whole experience. But she was obviously committed enough to go through with it. I had the feeling she was dominated by this Joe character. I also thought—a couple of times, anyway—that the two of them might be married. She never said it in so many words, but the way she spoke about him gave me that impression."

"How old was she?"

"Early to midtwenties."

"Really?"

"She was quite attractive, to be honest." McDill gave his wife an uncomfortable look. "I mean, you wouldn't have expected someone who looked like her to be involved in something like that. She looked like a Junior League wife, or even a model. Swimsuit model, anyway."

Agent Chalmers turned to Mrs. McDill. "What about Joe? The leader. How old was he?"

"Fifty. Somewhere around there."

"Could you give a good description of him?"

"Yes."

"Recognize him from a photo?"

"Yes."

"Any distinguishing marks?"

Margaret covered her face. "He had a tattoo on his arm. An eagle. Very crudely done."

"Do you remember which arm?"

"Left. Yes, the left."

"And the girl?" Chalmers asked McDill.

"I'd know her anywhere. If you want to put me on a plane and fly me down to the coast, I'll go through that whole hotel looking for her."

"I'm not sure that's the most efficient way to go about it. If she is in the hotel, she's probably in a room by now.

We can't go through every room in the place looking for someone we don't even know is there."

"Not even for a kidnapping?"

"The Beau Rivage has eighteen hundred rooms. No judge would give us a warrant for that. Not without more evidence."

"What about a bomb threat?" McDill asked.

"What do you mean?"

"You're the FBI. You could say you had a bomb threat on the casino. They'd have to evacuate the hotel. I could stand outside, watching as you bring the people through the front door. You could videotape them."

Chalmers looked at McDill with a combination of surprise and respect. "You're talking about a felony, Doctor. And violating people's civil rights."

McDill shrugged. "Desperate times, desperate measures."

"I wish it worked that way sometimes. We'll start by going through the Jackson police department mug books. And the NCIC computer." He ran his tongue over his lips and glanced away from the McDills. Somehow this action telegraphed his next question.

"No," the surgeon said.

"No, what?"

"No, we're not going to involve our son at this point. The third member of this group was a semiretarded giant who claimed to be the leader's cousin. He called himself Huey. He kept Peter in a cabin in the woods, somewhere within two hours of Jackson. He called the leader Joey. That makes me think Joe was the leader's real name. From what my son described, the retarded man might have had trouble remembering an alias. He spent all night whittling. But that's all Peter could tell you. We don't want him involved."

"Not even to look at mug books?"

"Not at this point."

"But, Doctor—"

"If you try to involve our son, I'm going to call my attorney and break off contact with you. I've already spoken to him tonight, and he urged me not to speak to you without him present. I disregarded that advice. However, if you try to involve Peter, I will call him. He's awake at home, waiting for just such a call."

Chalmers started to respond, then apparently decided that McDill was not the sort to be intimidated by threats.

"Well, then. The next step is to go over to the JPD and go through some of their mug books. There'll be a homicide shift working, and I know some of the guys over there. I can access NCIC from there, as well. Are you two ready to look at a hell of a stack of pictures?"

"We're prepared to do anything you require, short of involving Peter. The sooner the better. I really think there are people in danger as we speak."

Chalmers nodded. "From all you've told me, I'd say we have a few hours before they try to wire and collect the ransom. I'm going to wake up my boss and outline the situation. We can alert the coastal banks to flag all wire transfers of any size coming in tomorrow morning. We can have agents from the New Orleans office ready to respond the moment a suspicious wire comes in. We can also have a tactical squad here in Jackson, ready to hit whatever bank is the source of the wire, and arrest the leader while the wife is inside trying to send it. There are lots of ways to come at this thing—"

"Just a minute," McDill interrupted. "You're forgetting something."

"What? The hostage?"

"Yes. If you arrest any of these people, the schedule of thirty-minute telephone calls they keep will be broken, and the man in the woods will kill the child."

"Doctor, a minute ago you were talking about calling in a bomb threat to ID the woman involved."

"Yes, but only to confirm that it's really happening again. And they use cell phones, so that wouldn't break their schedule."

"What exactly do you expect us to do with the information you've given me? Nothing?"

"I'm not sure. But you can't just ride into the middle of this thing like the Seventh Cavalry. You'll get people killed."

"That's not how we operate, Doctor. We might follow them from the ransom pickup at the bank, using a helicopter. We could put a GPS tracking device on the doctor's car while it's parked at the bank. The leader and the woman are eventually going to meet somewhere with the money. Maybe even at the same McDonald's restaurant where your wife got your son back."

A disturbing current of anxiety was flowing through McDill. "Agent Chalmers, my child lived through his kidnapping precisely because I did not attempt to involve the police. I've come forward now to try to prevent another family from going through the same experience we did. But the fact is, they're probably going through it already. And if your people attempt to intervene, you could cause the death of a child who otherwise would probably live. And please don't start talking to me about 'acceptable risk.' Because I'm old enough to remember Vietnam."

Chalmers blew air from his cheeks in frustration. "You're saying we should let these kidnappers get away in order to be absolutely sure the hostage makes it. But if they get away with it again, they'll simply keep doing it. If you're right about any of this, I mean. And sooner or later, they'll make a mistake. Or some parent will crack under the pressure, and their child will be murdered. It's got to stop here, Doctor."

McDill wrung his hands, a gesture he despised but at this moment was powerless to stop. "I understand that. It's just . . . I know the potential for human error. If you involve a large number of people in any process, you exponentially increase the risk of mistakes. The kind of surveillance you're talking about, planting bugs, following cars with helicopters—"

"We're the FBI, Doctor," Chalmers said. "We're professionals."

McDill sighed heavily. "No offense, but that doesn't exactly fill me with confidence."

TEN

"Go to the other side of the bed," Karen ordered. "Move."

Still rattled by the gunshots, Hickey edged around the foot of the bed, leaving her between the bathroom and Will's side of the bed.

"Pick up that phone," she said, pointing at the cordless beside Hickey. "That's the private line."

"Who am I calling?"

"Pick it up!"

Hickey obeyed, but his eyes had a manic gleam that kept Karen's finger on the trigger.

"Call my husband's hotel room."

"You're making a mistake, Karen."

She raised the gun until it was pointed at his face, then spoke into the phone in her left hand. "Abby, are you outside yet?"

"Yes."

"Good. Get down out of sight." She shifted the phone

into the crook between her right shoulder and cheek. Now she could keep the pistol in her right hand while taking the private line from Hickey with her left. The phone on which Abby waited—Will's phone—handled both lines, but she didn't want to put Abby on hold unless she absolutely had to. "Are you down in some bushes?"

"Uh-huh. They're itchy."

"You sit tight right there. I'm calling Daddy, and we're going to straighten this out and come get you. Don't hang up, remember?"

"I'm not."

"Have you got Will yet?" she asked Hickey.

He raised his hands as though to negotiate. "I'm bleeding to death here. Can't you stitch up my leg first?"

"The sooner you get Will on the phone, the sooner you stop bleeding."

Hickey dialed a number and asked for suite 28021.

"Throw the receiver onto the bed."

He did. She picked it up with her left hand and heard the phone ringing. Then a female voice said, "Hey."

"Put Dr. Jennings on the phone."

"Who is this?"

"This is Mrs. Jennings. And if you don't put him on the phone, I'm going to shoot your husband in the head."

There was a stunned silence. Then the woman said, "You can't do that. We've got your little girl."

"Your husband's bleeding pretty badly right now, missy. You'd better get a move on."

She heard a fumbling with the phone. Then Will said, "Karen?"

"Will, thank God."

"What's going on? Is Abby all right?"

"She's free. I mean—"

"Free?"

"She got away from the man guarding her. She's hiding in the woods with a cell phone. I'm talking to her right now."

"My God! Where's the man now?"

"Hunting for her. But she's hunkered down in some bushes."

"Where's Joe?"

"I'm holding a gun on him. And I'm very tempted to blow his goddamn head off."

"Don't do that, Karen."

"I know. But what can we do? If we call the police, can they trace the cell phone Abby's using? Can they find her?"

"I think they can triangulate cell phones pretty well. But if she's out in the country somewhere . . . I don't know. I don't know if they use towers or trucks or what. How far away from Jackson do you think she is?"

"An hour. Maybe more, maybe less."

"It won't work," said Hickey.

"Sixty miles," Will mused.

"It won't work," Hickey said again. "What you're thinking won't work."

"Shut up!" Karen snapped.

"What's the matter?" asked Will.

"Hickey says tracing the phone won't work."

"To hell with him. Look, I know the guy who runs CellStar. I did a gallbladder on his wife, and I played in a golf tournament with him."

"Call him! He'll know what the police can do."

"We need to know what cellular company Hickey's people are using. CellStar is the biggest, and he might have picked it for anonymity. Tell him to give you his cell phone."

Karen gestured at Hickey's pocket with the pistol. "Give me your cell phone."

"What for?"

"To keep me from shooting you! I'm losing my patience here."

Hickey took a small Nokia from his pocket and tossed it across the bed.

"I've got it," she told Will.

"Turn it on and dial— Wait. Is it already on?"

Karen used the barrel of the .38 to flip the phone over. The lights of the LED display were dead. "No, it's off."

"Damn. Okay. Dial star-eight-one-one and see who answers."

"I'm doing it right now."

"Mama?" Abby said in her other ear.

"Hang on, baby, I'm talking to Daddy."

Karen used her trigger finger to switch on the phone and punch the keys. Hickey watched her with a puzzled look in his eyes.

"Welcome to the CellStar customer service line," said a computerized voice.

Karen hit END. "It's CellStar."

"Yes!" Will exulted. "We finally caught a break. Stay on the line. I'll use Cheryl's cell phone to call my guy."

"Don't worry. I'm too scared to hang up."

She heard Will tell Hickey's wife to call directory assistance for the home number of a Harley Ferris in

Ridgeland, Mississippi. Then he said, "Karen, ask Hickey why he thinks we can't trace the phone."

"Why can't we trace Huey's phone?" she repeated.

Hickey's eyes glowed with a strange sort of amusement. "You're about to kill your kid," he said, "and you don't even know it. You'd better let me talk some sense into that husband of yours."

"He wants to talk to you," she told Will.

"Fine. Just be careful passing the phone."

Karen tossed the phone onto the bed. Hickey picked it up.

"Doc? You there?"

Karen said to Abby: "I'm going to put you on hold for a few seconds, honey. I'm not hanging up, I'm just going to listen to Daddy for a minute. Okay?"

Abby's voice rose to a frantic whisper. "Don't hang up, Mama!"

"I'll be right back." She hit the button that switched that phone to the private line.

"You're screwing up, Doc," Hickey said to Will. "All you had to do was follow the rules, and you'd have got your kid back in the morning. But now you're trying to pull a fucking John Wayne. And your old lady thinks she's Wonder Woman."

"Sometimes I think she is, too. The simple truth is that I don't trust you to keep your word."

"Let me explain something to you, Doc. In some ways tracing a cellular call is easy. 'Cause a cell phone ain't nothing but a radio. Right?"

"Right."

"And you can triangulate a radio just like in the old

World War Two spy movies. That's what you're thinking. You look at the relative signal strengths between towers and figure a location down to yards. The problem, Doc—for you, I mean—is that not many towers are equipped to measure that stuff yet. All this is under legislation right now. People *want* cell companies to be able to do that kind of tracing, so people making nine-one-one calls can be found before they bleed to death. Great idea, right? The problem is the equipment. And Mississippi's five years behind the rest of the country. As usual, right? That's why I feel okay using cell phones in this operation. So, if you think the cops are gonna find your kid before Huey does, you're out of your mind. And if you're wondering why I'm telling you this, it's simple. I still want this thing to work. I still want my money. But if you bring in the cops or the FBI, you're taking control out of my hands. It's like bringing divorce lawyers into a marriage. It's the irrevocable step. There won't be anything I can do. I've got to cut my losses and run. That means when Huey finds the kid, he kills her."

"But we know who you are," Will pointed out. "If you kill Abby, you're opening yourself to murder charges."

"You're not thinking, Doc. Kidnapping alone is a death penalty offense. So I've got nothing to lose by killing her. And by killing her, I kill any chance that she can identify Huey."

"My wife saw him, too."

"Did she? Gee, I don't recall that." Hickey smiled at Karen. "You starting to get the picture?"

There was a hissing silence as Will considered his

options. Karen was about to switch back to Abby when he said, "Screw you, Joe. Put my wife back on."

"I'm here," said Karen. "Abby's on hold. Let me get her back." She switched her phone back to the main line. "I'm back, baby. Are you okay?"

"No! I was scared. Don't get off anymore."

"I won't." She motioned for Hickey to toss his phone back to her. When it landed beside her, it was smeared with dark blood. She wiped it on the comforter, then held it to her mouth. "Go ahead, Will."

"I already called my guy on the hotel phone. I'm getting an answering machine."

"No. Oh God."

"It is after midnight. And they may not have a phone in their bedroom. I'll keep calling back till they wake up." He fell silent for a moment. "Look, you saw the guy who was holding Abby, right?"

"Yes."

"Do you think he would kill her if Joe told him to?"

Images of a giant standing in the dark flashed through Karen's mind. The startled eyes as she shoved the ice chest into his hands and begged him not to hurt her baby. *Hurt your baby?* Huey had echoed, as though the idea had never entered his head. But what had he really meant? Had the idea of hurting Abby been so alien that he'd been shocked by the suggestion? Or was Huey just too simpleminded to do anything but repeat what was said to him?

Karen covered the mouthpiece of the phone that connected her to Abby. "I can't answer that. He's huge, and he's simpleminded. Hickey says he gets angry when children run from him, something about the way he was treated growing up. And Abby just ran from him."

"Jesus. Do you think Abby could hide from him until dawn? Or maybe walk to a road?"

"It's the middle of nowhere, Will."

"But you left some insulin with her, right?"

"Yes. Hang on." She uncovered the mouthpiece of the other phone. "Abby? Do you have your ice chest with you? The one I left with Mr. Huey?"

"No. I picked it up when I first ran. But when I went back inside for the phone, I forgot it."

"That's all right. You're doing great. I'm talking to Daddy."

"Are y'all coming to get me?"

"Yes. We're figuring it out right now. Where's Mr. Huey?"

"I'm still getting the answering machine," Will said.

"I don't know," said Abby. "He stopped yelling."

A shiver ran through Karen. "Don't make a sound, baby." She covered the phone again. "She doesn't have the insulin. She doesn't know how to inject herself even if she had it."

"I think she could do it if she had to. I just don't know if she'd know she was in trouble in time."

"She's only five years old, Will. Do we have any alternatives?"

"Abby gives herself up and we trust Joe to give her back after he gets the money."

Karen looked across the bed at Hickey's glittering eyes, his prison tattoo, the bleeding leg. "No. We've got to try to save her now."

"Let me talk to him again," Hickey said.

Karen threw the phone across the bed.

"Doc? Let me tell you a quick story. Me and Huey are cousins. We grew up in different states, but our mamas were sisters. They both married sons of bitches, only Huey's daddy was the leaving kind of son of a bitch, and mine was the ass-whipping kind. After Huey's little sister died, he had to move down to Mississippi with us. He'd got in some trouble up there trying to talk to little girls after that. Hurt some of their parents. Anyhow, my old man could be okay when he wasn't drunk—which wasn't often. He was nice to Huey, but when he was loaded he'd lay into him over being useless. Then he'd whale on me, just for kicks."

Karen wanted to hear Will's responses, but she knew Abby might break down if she was put on hold again. She hoped Will was still ringing the president of CellStar.

"So, Pop takes us deer hunting one day," Hickey said. "We didn't let Huey carry a gun, of course, but we always took him. You couldn't beat him for hauling dead deer out of the woods. Anyhow, I was climbing through this bobwire fence, and my gun went off. Pop was drunk, and he started yelling how he'd felt the bullet pass his cheek. He threw down his rifle and started whalin' on me right there in the woods. I was about thirteen. Huey was twelve. He was a big boy, though. So, Pop whales on me till he runs out of wind, then he stops to rest. I try to go for my rifle on the ground, but soon as I do, he gets between me and it. Then he takes a sip from his flask and starts whalin' on me again. Huey has this funny look on his face. Then, real slow like, he walks up behind Pop and grabs him around the arms, like he's hugging a tree. And he just holds him there. Pop goes crazy. He's kicking and screaming how he's gonna kill us both when he gets loose. I pick up my rifle and point it at him. I know when he gets loose he's gonna tear me to pieces. But I can't shoot him too easy with Huey holding him, except point-blank in the head, which wouldn't look right."

Karen made sure her palm was sealing the phone Abby waited on.

"So Huey gets this scared look on his face and says, 'I just wanted him to stop hitting you, Joey. I don't want to hurt him none.' I say, 'He ain't ever gonna stop. Not till he's dead. You kill him, Buckethead, and we'll be done with it. We're blood brothers, boy, you gotta listen when I tell you something.' So Huey thinks for a minute. Then he picks Pop up where his legs won't touch the ground and carries him over to this big rock and lays him down and smashes his head against it till he stops wiggling. He carries the body the top of a ridge, just like I tell him to, and drops him down onto the creek rocks. Like he fell there."

Karen closed her eyes, praying for Abby with all her being.

"Now, Huey didn't *want* do that, Doc. But he did it. He won't want to hurt your little girl, either. But if I tell him to, he will. 'Cause he can't envision a world without cousin Joey in it. And if he thinks your little girl living means me going to Parchman, she'll die sure as old Pop did." Hickey winked at Karen as he spoke into the phone. "He could break Abby's neck without even meaning to. Like dropping a china vase."

Hickey listened to whatever Will said, then laid the phone near the middle of the bed, a confident smile on his face. Karen picked it up.

"What are we going to do?" she asked.

"While Hickey was telling his story, I called CellStar and tried to find out if Ferris is even in town. I told them it was a medical emergency. Their security department said he should be at home."

"But you're still getting the machine?"

"Yes, but I'm going to keep ringing it. Somebody's bound to wake up eventually. I want to talk to Abby right now. I need to hear her voice. Can you hold the phones together?"

Karen raised the gun to Hickey's face. "Sit on the floor by the wall."

"Why?"

"Sit!"

He backed to the wall and slid down it, keeping both hands pressed to his lacerated thigh. Karen laid the .38 on the comforter, then inverted one of the phones and held them together.

"Punkin?" Will said, sounding like a transistor radio. "This is Daddy. Are you all right?"

Karen heard Abby sobbing. It made her want to pick up the gun and blow a hole in Hickey's heart.

"I'm coming to get you, baby," Will said, his voice cracking with emotion. "But what I need now is for you to stay hidden. It's just like the Indian Princess campout. Just another game. It may take a little while, but Daddy's going to be there. Do you hear me?"

"Yes." The voice sounded tiny and alone.

"I want to ask you a question. Has there ever been a time when you really needed me and I didn't come?"

"No."

"That's right. And there never will be. I swear that on the Bible."

"You're not supposed to swear on the Bible."

"If it's real important, you can. I'm coming to get you, baby. If you get scared, you just remember that. Daddy's coming."

"Okay."

"I need to talk to Mom again. I love you, baby."

"Please hurry, Daddy."

Karen separated the phones. "Will?"

"It would be good if we could get Abby to shut off that phone for a while," he said, "to conserve the batteries. But I don't think she could handle it. Just keep her calm and quiet. I'm doing everything I can."

"Hurry, Will."

Huey Cotton paused in the rutted road leading to the cabin and looked up at the sky. His heart was full of sadness, and his eyes felt fuzzy from staring into the dark trees. Huey experienced much of the world as colors. A doctor had questioned him about it once. Like the woods. The woods had a green smell. Even at night, when you couldn't see the green, you could smell and taste it. The clean green of the oak leaves overhead. The thick jungly green of the vines tugging at his pant legs.

Joey was two colors. Sometimes he was white like an angel, a guardian who floated at Huey's shoulder or walked in his shadow, ready to reveal himself when needed. But there was red in Joey, too, a hard little seed filled with dark ink, and sometimes it burst and bled out into the white, covering it completely. When Joey turned red, bad things happened, or had already happened, or were coming down the road. When Joey turned red, Huey had to do things he didn't like to do. But by doing them, he helped the red fade away, like blood on a shirt in a wash bucket.

Sometimes he couldn't see color at all. There was a shade between brown and black ("no-color," he called it) that hovered at the edges of everything, like a fog waiting to blot out the world. He saw it when he stood in line to order a hamburger and heard people whispering behind him because he couldn't make up his mind about what he wanted. The order-taker seemed to float in a tiny, faraway circle at the center of his vision, and all he could keep in his head was what the people behind him were saying, not whether he wanted pickles or onions. He knew they said mean things because they couldn't see inside him, past how big he was, but whenever he tried to explain that, he scared people. And the more afraid they got, the more the no-color seeped in from the edges.

School was the worst. He had tried with all his might to forget the things children had said to him at the school in Missouri. But he couldn't. They lived inside his head, like termites in the support beams of a house. Even when he got so big that teenage boys wouldn't stand toe-to-toe with him, they teased him. Teased him and ran before he could make them pay for it. Girls teased him, too. *Retard, retard, retard.* In his dreams they still ran from him, and he never caught them. In real life, though, he caught one once. A teenage boy. That was one reason he'd had to come to Mississippi to live. His mother never told his aunt about it. She was afraid her sister wouldn't take him. But Huey had told Joey. And Joey had understood.

Huey lowered his head and breathed deep. He could smell people sometimes, the way he smelled animals. Some smelled bad, others nothing special. Abby smelled like a towel fresh out of the clothes dryer. Cleaner than anything he'd ever smelled. And she sparkled. He didn't understand why he couldn't find her in the dark, because she was silver and gold, and should be reflecting the moonlight.

Maybe the no-color was hiding her. It had been seeping into his eyes since the moment he realized she'd run away. He had tried hard not to be scary, but he'd seen the fear in her eyes. Maybe she couldn't help it. She was so tiny. Joey said she was six years old, but her head was smaller than Huey's hand.

"Abby?" he called halfheartedly.

Nothing.

He walked back toward the cabin, sniffing and listening, but nothing registered. Cutting around the cabin, he looked into the tractor shed. The clean towel smell hovered around the tractor. He leaned down and sniffed the seat.

Abby had sat there.

He crept out of the shed and looked into the dark mosaic of foliage, straining his eyes. Some greens looked gray at night. The tree trunks looked silver-black. Moonlight dripped down the black leaves and hanging branches. He relaxed his eyes, which was a trick he had learned while hunting with Joey. Sometimes, if you let your eyes relax, they picked up things they never would if you were *trying* to see. As he looked into the shadows, something yellowy and far dimmer than a lightning bug winked in the darkness.

His heartbeat quickened. He focused on the spot, but the yellowy light was gone. He relaxed his eyes again.

The light winked and disappeared.

He was close. The light was important, but something else had stirred the blood in his slow veins. The green smell had changed.

Twenty yards from the tractor shed, Abby crouched in the sweltering darkness, clenching the cell phone as hard as she could. The thick branches of the oak above blocked the moonlight. She couldn't see anything beyond the bushes that shielded her. She wished she was still up on the tractor seat. It was dry and safe there, not itchy like the briars clawing at her now. She had no idea where Mr. Huey was. There were too many noises around her to tell anything. Only the reassuring glow of the phone's readout panel kept her from bolting toward the lights of the cabin. It was like looking at the kitchen window of her house when she was playing outside after supper.

A soft squawk from the phone startled her, and she put it to her ear.

"Abby?" said her mother.

"What?" she whispered back.

"Are you okay?"

"I guess so."

"Where's Mr. Huey?"

"I don't know."

"You haven't heard him?"

"He stopped yelling a while ago. Maybe he's gone."

"Maybe. But we don't know that for sure. You have to stay down."

"I'm sitting on my knees."

"That's good. Daddy's calling a man right now who's going to help us find you. Do you know how he's going to do that?"

"No."

"The phone in your hand is like a radio. As long as it stays on, the police can find you. It's the same as if you were standing there yelling, 'Mama, Mama.' "

"Do you want me to stand up and yell? I can yell loud."

"No! No, honey. The phone is yelling for you, okay? People can't hear it, but computers can."

"Like a dog hearing a whistle?"

"Exactly like that. Now— Hang on, Daddy's talking to me."

"Okay."

Abby held the phone against her ear so hard it hurt. She wanted to hear her father's voice again.

Hickey was still sitting against the bedroom wall. Despite his wounded leg, he watched Karen like a hyena waiting for its chance to strike.

"You going to sew me up or what?" he asked, holding up his bloody palms.

"I haven't decided."

"I'm getting exactly nowhere," Will said in her ear, his voice tight with frustration. "Goddamn answering machine. I can't believe the president of a cellular phone company doesn't have a service."

"Maybe we should call the police. Or the FBI."

"I don't think we can risk that. If Huey—"

"Mama?" Abby said in her other ear.

"What is it, baby?"

"I think I heard something."

Karen's heart fluttered. "Whisper, honey. What did you hear?"

"I don't know." Abby's voice was a thin filament stretched over a vast chasm of fear. "How long till you get here?"

"Not long. Has the noise stopped?"

"I don't hear it right now. I'm scared it's a possum."

Karen felt a hysterical relief. "It's okay if it's a possum. They won't hurt you."

"They won't bite me?"

"No. They're more scared of you than you are of them."

"One bit Kate's cat last week."

"That's different."

"What if it's a snake?"

"It's not a snake," Karen assured her, even as she panicked at the thought. "Snakes are sleeping right now."

"Uh-uh. Snakes hunt at night. I saw it on Animal Planet."

Jesus. "That's just in other countries, like India. And Sri Lanka. Cobras and things. We don't have cobras here."

"Oh."

"Our snakes sleep at night."

"Mom, I heard it again." Her whisper was barely audible now. "Like somebody sneaking up."

Karen fought a surge of panic. "You have to be *quiet.* I want you to stop talking."

"I feel better when we talk."

"I know, sweetie, but—"

"Mama—"

In two nearly silent syllables, utter terror traveled from child to mother. Karen squeezed the phone tight enough to bruise her hand. "Abby? Say something!"

There was only silence. Then she heard breathing, and she understood what was happening. Abby was sitting motionless in the dark, scared out of her mind. Huey was close. Praying that Abby still had the phone to her ear, Karen whispered, "I'm with you, honey. I'm here. Sit very still. You're going to be fine. Remember what Daddy said."

She listened with every fiber of her nervous system.

Out of the breathing, she heard a whimper, so soft that Abby had to be fighting a heroic battle to suppress it. Karen was about to reassure her again when a crash like breaking branches came down the line and Abby screamed.

"I found you, didn't I?" Huey said loudly.

Karen's heart turned to ice. *"Abby?"*

"I saw the light," Huey said, his voice exultant. "Why did you run, Abby?"

"ABBY!"

"What is it?" Will shouted in her ear.

"Joey?" said Huey.

"Put Abby back on!" Karen demanded. "Please!"

"Where's Joey?"

"Well, well," said Hickey. He pressed his bloody palms against the carpet and stood. "The worm has turned."

Karen grabbed the .38 and pointed it at his chest. "MAKE HIM PUT ABBY BACK ON!"

Hickey walked fearlessly around the bed. "If you shoot me now, she's as dead as a hammer. Give me the phone."

"Get back!"

He brushed the gun aside and slapped her face, then stripped the phone from her hand.

"Huey? This is Joey. If you hear a shot, strangle that brat. Don't even wait to ask me a question, because I'll be dead. This bitch already stabbed me. She tried to kill me."

Hickey's face hardened as he listened to his cousin's reply. "You goddamn retard. I give the orders and you follow them. Period." He grabbed Karen's wrist and squeezed until her hand opened of its own accord and she dropped the .38. He bent and picked it up. "Tie the kid and gag her, Huey. I'll call you back."

Without warning, Karen snapped. She flew at Hickey's face, meaning to claw out his eyes, but before she reached them, he slammed his fist into her sternum. The blow drove the wind from her lungs and dropped her to the floor. As she lay there gasping, he picked up the phone that had connected her to Will and spoke in a savage voice.

"Huey just found your kid, Doc. I hope you haven't talked to anybody yet, because if you have, Abby won't ever see second grade. . . . Calm down. I don't want you to stroke out on me. I just hope this wildcat you're married to has learned her lesson."

"Please," Karen pleaded, struggling to her knees. "Don't let him tie her. Don't let him hurt her. She—"

"Shut your mouth." Hickey hung up. "And stitch up this goddamn leg already."

She stared up at him, panting like a winded runner. Tiny points of light danced at the centers of his eyes.

"I own you," he said in a quiet voice. "You know that now, don't you?"

"I just want my little girl safe. Whatever that takes."

"That's a good answer. But first things first." He pointed at his lacerated leg. "Get to work."

Karen tried to put Abby out of her mind. If she didn't, she wouldn't be able to function. Bracing her hand on the bed, she got to her feet, then picked up the forceps she'd dropped earlier and opened Will's black bag.

"No needles," Hickey said, as she removed a vial of lidocaine and a syringe. "I don't trust you far as I can throw you."

"Fine with me. Forty stitches without anesthetic will burn like the hinges of hell."

Hickey laughed. "You should enjoy it, then. But don't worry, babe. I'm gonna pay you back for every stitch."

ELEVEN

Huey stumbled through the dark with Abby in his arms and fear bubbling from his heart. The no-color was all around, flooding in from the edges of his sight, leaving only the glowing cabin windows swirling in the dark. Abby shrieked endlessly, so long and so loudly that he didn't know how she was breathing. He wished to God he could put his hands over his ears, but he needed them to carry her.

Her screams were like water he had to run through. And the fear in them was the same fear he had known as a little boy. It set something vibrating in his chest, like a bell struck with a hammer. Joey had said to tie her up, but Huey didn't want to tie her up. Joey said to strangle her if he heard a shot, and Huey thanked Jesus he hadn't heard one. The only way he could hurt Abby was if he saw another face on top of her face, some other girl's face. An older girl had once taken him into the woods and showed him things, then asked him to pull down his pants. After he did, she yelled to a dozen boys who came running out of the trees, laughing and jeering at him. He wanted to twist that girl's head around and around until it came right off, like a chicken's.

Huey had never felt so twisted up inside, but he knew one thing. He couldn't live without Joey. Life before Joey was a fearful blur, and the idea of life without him would not even fit into Huey's head. Creatures like Abby were like lanterns in the dark, but he could never keep them. In the end, Joey was all he had.

Midnight had passed, and the Jenningses' Victorian house stood dark and silent on its hill. Crickets cheeped in the pine trees; a truck droned out on the interstate; but the house itself was silent.

A scream pierced the night.

Inside the master bedroom, Karen crouched over Hickey's wounded thigh on the sleigh bed. Naked but for a towel she had laid across his midsection, Hickey held the bottle of Wild Turkey in his left hand and a halogen lamp from Will's study in his right. He aimed the light wherever she told him to, keeping silent during most of the work, but occasionally yelling when the needle pierced his unanesthetized flesh.

Karen worked the U-shaped suture needle with almost careless speed, mating the edges of the wound, tying knots, moving on. It was amazing how much damage one slash with a good scalpel could do. Hickey hadn't lost enough blood to threaten his life, but he'd bled enough to scare the hell out of someone unused to trauma. Karen was grateful to see that she had in fact nicked the base of his penis with her panicked stroke (a wound that required two stitches) and hoped this would discourage him from trying to force her to finish what she'd begun earlier.

"How many to go?" he asked in a taut voice.

"We're only half done. You should have taken that lidocaine."

He gulped another slug of Wild Turkey as she jabbed the needle through his skin. "This is all the shot I need. Just hurry it up."

She sewed five more stitches, then paused to stretch her wrists. As she did, something that had been bothering her from the beginning slipped out. "Why us?" she said softly.

"What?"

"I said, 'Why us?' "

Hickey reached out with the bottle and forced her chin up, so that she was looking at his face. "Are you that dumb? Are you that fucking dumb?"

"What do you mean?"

"Why *not* you? Huh? You think because you live out here in this suburban palace, you're immune to pain? My mother had throat cancer. That's the worst, man. *'Why me?'* she'd rasp all the time. *'Dear Jesus, why me?'* I'd ask the same thing. Why my mother? Why not my shit-for-brains old man? I'd look at the ceiling like God was up there listening and ask why. Then I finally figured it out. The joke was on me." Hickey shook his bottle, spilling amber fluid on Karen's knee. "The joke's on you, too, June Cleaver."

"Why?"

"You're a human being, that's why. So why not you, okay? Why *not* you?"

Karen bit her lip and gazed intently at Hickey. Bitterness was etched in every line of his face, and his eyes were like black wells with a film of oil floating on them. "It must be awful to be you," she said.

"Sometimes," he conceded. "But tonight it's worse to be you."

Will stood at the picture window of the bedroom, staring out over the Gulf of Mexico. The Cypress suite, despite its luxurious appointments, had begun to close around him like a prison cell, and the knowledge that the dark gulf stretched south to the Yucatan somehow calmed him.

The first seconds after he realized that Huey had recaptured Abby had been hellish. Even armed with a pistol, Cheryl had felt compelled to lock herself in one of the marble bathroms for protection, so terrible had been his rage. He could have killed Hickey at that moment, if the man had appeared before him. But of course he hadn't. Hickey had designed his Chinese box precisely so that this scenario would never occur.

Even as Will's rage dissipated, his frustration grew. There was so much he didn't know. How had Karen gotten the drop on Hickey? Probably by sneaking the .38 from the top of their closet. But even so, why would Hickey respond to her threat? He had control over Abby, and so long as he did, a gun would do Karen no good. But apparently it had. Or *something* had. Before Hickey hung up the telephone, Will had heard him yell something about being stabbed. Had Karen stabbed him? Had she snapped under the stress and tried to kill him? No. Karen never lost control. That was axiomatic. Her father, the master sergeant, had drilled into his daughter a self-discipline that was unnerving. Whatever had happened, Will had no way to discover it. He would just have to wait.

The only lights on the gulf now belonged to a lone freighter sailing west, probably to off-load coffee or bananas or God-knew-what-else in New Orleans. There were men sleeping on that ship, a full crew less than three miles away, men who knew nothing of his problem and could do nothing to help him if they did. There were several hundred doctors in this very hotel, many of whom Will knew personally—yet none could help him. He was trapped in an unbreakable cage constructed by a madman named Joe Hickey.

No, he thought. *"Madman" is probably inaccurate.* True madness was rare, if you barred disorders caused by organic disease. During his psychiatry rotation in medical school, Will had treated patients at the state mental hospital at Whitfield, several of them classified as criminally insane. After a while, he had come to the conclusion that some of the men were quite sane. They had pursued their goals and desires with the single-minded drive of men who succeeded in business or the arts or politics. It was simply that society found itself unable to admit that their chosen goals could be the goals of sane men. But Will knew different. All men had atavistic desires, sometimes savage ones. Some were merely better at suppressing them than others. And Hickey did not belong in the first category. He acted on his impulses, regardless of law or danger. His overt motive was simple enough: money. But it seemed to Will that if a man was willing to flout the law, there were easier and less risky ways to steal large amounts of money. Hickey's plan was constructed to satisfy deeper urges than money. And Will needed to figure out what those were. Very soon.

He was having trouble keeping his mind on track. He remembered the ride to the airport that morning, when he'd asked Karen to bring Abby to the convention at the last minute. He'd had a bad feeling about her refusal. A premonition. Nothing melodramatic, just a feeling that if Karen wasn't with him on this trip, their lives might skew farther apart than they already had. In his wildest flights of paranoia, he could not have imagined something like this. But he *had* imagined that without Karen at his side this weekend, he might find himself in one of those situations he'd experienced many times before. Situations in which he had always chosen to spend the night alone rather than accept an offer of female company. But during the ride to the airport, something had been whispering below the level of consciousness, a voice born during long months of miscommunication and silent rejections, whispering that a channel for release was presenting itself. And a part of him had heeded that voice. That knowledge now ate like acid at his heart.

It was a cliché of a cliché. You never knew what you had until it was gone. The idea that Abby could be murdered was so paralyzing that Will did not allow himself to consider it a real possibility. He would get her back, no matter what it cost him. Money. Blood. His life. But even with the best possible outcome, something irrevocable had already occurred. He had left his wife and child alone. Exposed. It was nothing that millions of fathers didn't do every week, but in this case, some part of him had *wanted* to be alone on this trip. He could have pushed Karen harder—and earlier—really convinced her that he wanted her with him on this weekend. But he hadn't. It wasn't solely his fault. Organizing the Junior League's sixtieth anniversary flower show was comparable to planning double-blind trials for a new drug, and missing the event itself would be Junior League suicide for the chairperson. But deep down, Will suspected, Karen *wanted* to commit Junior League suicide. And he had not done enough to help her.

"What are you thinking about over there?" asked Cheryl.

She came out of the bathroom and climbed back into the bed, using the oversized pillows to prop herself against the headboard. The torn cocktail dress was tied around her waist. She wore the black bra as though it were a Madonna-style bustier. Will supposed that to a girl who had turned tricks in cars behind a strip club, wearing only a bra in front of a stranger was no big deal.

"Not speaking to me?" she asked.

Cheryl was the kind of person who couldn't tolerate silence. Will shrugged and turned back to the lights of the freighter.

"Look, you're going to get your daughter back," she said. "It's just a waiting game. You pay some money—which you don't give a shit about compared to your little girl—and you get her back in the morning. You ought to try to sleep. I've got to take the calls from Joey, so I have to stay awake. But you should crash. I'll wake you up when it's time."

"You think I can sleep with this going on?"

"You need to. You're going to be a basket case in the morning if you don't."

"I can't."

"Yes, you can."

"Leave me alone, okay?"

"Look, you're just standing there blaming yourself and trying to figure out a way to rescue your little girl. That's what they all do. But you can't. You're not Mel Gibson, for Christ's sake. Mel Gibson isn't even Mel Gibson, you know? You save your little girl by paying Joey the money. It's that simple."

"I should trust Joe?"

"Joey's got a motto on this deal, Doc. You know what it is?"

"What?"

"The kid always makes it."

Will turned from the window.

"I'm serious," she said. "He's said it a hundred times. That's how we've managed to keep on doing this. That's how we made all our money."

"And every child you've done this to has lived? Been returned to its parents?"

"Good as new. I'm telling you, you've got to chill." She barked a laugh that gave the lie to the classic beauty of her face. "You gotta *chill*, Will!" she sang out, delighted by the rhyme. "You're going to give yourself a stroke."

He turned back to the window. Cheryl's reassurances didn't mesh with the voice on the other end of the phone. There was hatred in Hickey's voice, a resentment so deep that Will could not see it stopping short of the maximum pain it could inflict. Yet in the other cases, it had. If Cheryl and Hickey could be believed.

"You want me to help you calm down?" Cheryl asked.

He looked at her reflection in the window. She had taken a brush from her purse and was pulling it through her blond hair. "How?" he asked. "Drugs?"

"I told you, I'm clean now. But I can chill you out. Whatever, you know. Back rub?"

"No, thanks."

"Front rub?"

He turned to her, unsure he had heard correctly. She stopped brushing her hair.

"It's no big deal," she said. "You'll sleep like a baby. All guys do."

"Are you kidding?"

She smiled knowingly. "Don't worry. Wifey won't ever know about it."

"I said no, okay? Jesus."

"I was just trying to help you relax. I know you're upset."

"What's the deal here, Cheryl? Is sex the only way you know how to relate to men?"

She turned to the television, her lower lip pooched out like an angry child's. "Not quite, Oprah."

"A while ago you gave me your sob story about how terrible it was to be a whore. Now you're acting like one."

"Hey, I was just trying to make this easier on you."

"Do you make the same offer to all your victims?"

The word "victim" didn't sit well with her. "I saw you

looking at me during the speech, and I knew you were interested."

"Bullshit."

She cut her eyes at him, and they held a disturbing knowledge. "My mistake, I guess. What do I know? I'm just a dumb stripper, right?" She picked up the remote and flipped through some channels, finally settling on the Home Shopping Network.

Will turned back to the window. As he searched for the tiny lights of the freighter, he saw movement in the reflection of the room. Focusing on it, he saw Cheryl remove her bra. He didn't turn, but he saw her settle deeper on the pillows and begin slowly stroking her breasts. He tried to watch the freighter, but he couldn't concentrate. It was absurd. This woman had helped kidnap his daughter; now she was coming on to him as if they'd just met in the casino downstairs. Cheryl moaned softly, drawing his eyes to her reflection again. Her movements were impossible to ignore.

"Why are you doing that?"

"To show you you're no different than the rest. And that it's okay."

"Put your bra back on."

She didn't stop moving her hands. "You're saying that, but you'd rather I left it off."

"Put it back on, Cheryl."

"They look good, don't they?"

He turned toward the bed at last. "If you like implants."

She laughed. "Sure they're implants. But they're good. Not like the local junk you see around here. Joey flew me out to L.A. to have it done, when I was a featured dancer.

I got the same doctor that did Demi. He said mine looked just as good." She cupped them in her palms. "*Just* as good."

They did look like perfect male fantasies, but they did not look natural. As a doctor, Will had seen more breasts than he cared to think about, and Cheryl's *Penthouse*-style showpieces had almost nothing in common with the female form in its natural state.

"Cover yourself," he said.

"Are you sure?"

"I don't care what you do." He turned back to the window.

"Why don't you at least face the truth about something, Will?"

It wasn't the first time she had used his Christian name, but he still didn't like it. "What?"

"When you were first giving your speech, and you saw me down there watching you, you were fantasizing about me."

"You're wrong."

"You can't lie about that. You checked me out from head to toe. Then you stared at my panties when I uncrossed my legs."

"You made them too obvious to ignore."

"But you were interested. A lot more interested than you were in your speech. And if it wasn't for the reason we're in this room together now, we might be here for another reason."

"You're wrong," he said again, annoyed by the accuracy of her instincts.

"Am I?"

"Yes."

"What I saw in your face tonight I've seen in lots of guys' faces. Decent guys, I mean. I know you. For a few years now, you've been wishing you had someone like me to sleep with. You love your wife, you wouldn't trade her for anything, but she just doesn't do it for you. She doesn't understand what you need. How you need it, and how often. Nothing, really. She's making a nest, adding twigs, thinking about the little chickadees. You're helping with the nest, but you miss hunting."

"Where'd you get that? *Cosmo?*"

"I don't remember. But it's on the money, isn't it?"

He turned back to the bed, where Cheryl was enacting a fifteen-year-old boy's dream of paradise. "This isn't going to happen. You don't want sex. And you don't want to 'relax' me. What you really want is to somehow make me culpable in what you're doing."

"What's culpable?" She looked genuinely confused.

"You want to make me part of this. To involve me, to pull me down to your level, so that what you're doing doesn't seem so horrible. But it *is* horrible. And you know it."

Cheryl jerked the bra up over her breasts and stared at the television.

He turned and laid his palms flat on the windowpane. The thick glass was cool from the air conditioner, but he knew there was a warm wind blowing outside. Cool compared to the stagnant air hanging over the scrub and stunted pines growing inland from the beach, but warm compared to the frigid air in the casino suite.

"We never finished our conversation from before," Cheryl said.

"What are you talking about?"

"When you asked how I wound up doing this. Kidnapping kids."

"You told me your story."

"I left out a few things." She looked the way Abby did when she was trying to conceal some surprise. "After Joey made me stop being a featured dancer, he put me back into Jackson. New Orleans and Jackson. Sometimes the club down in Hattiesburg, but that was down-market. Mostly college kids, lining up to get off in their pants."

"You should go on Howard Stern."

"Maybe I should. But you should listen to me, Doc. There's a lesson here for you."

"I'm on pins and needles."

"Joey put me back in the clubs, but not really to dance. He started coming in every night I was on, but not to watch me. He came to talk to the people. The owners, the bouncers, the customers. He bought rounds for everybody. Bought them sofa dances. Pretty soon he got a handle on who was coming in there. And it would blow your mind, Doc. Lawyers, doctors, stockbrokers, aldermen. *Ministers,* for Christ's sake. Ministers sneaking in there to get a sofa dance. What a crazy kick. Anyway, Joey got a handle on all these guys. And then we started up a little business on the side."

"What business was that?"

"Blackmail. These guys got addicted to me, see? I mean, I may not like doing it, but I can *give* a sofa dance. I took those guys places they'd never even dreamed about. They're dropping fifty bucks a pop for three minutes, and happy as pigs in slop. Pretty soon they're offering lots more and asking if I do any after-hours dancing." She wrinkled her nose. "Dancing, right? So, to the right ones—the rich, married ones—I said, Sure, honey. And I let them take me to a motel after work. A motel run by a guy who was tight with Joey, who had special cameras set up in a certain room. Once we got inside that room, I got those guys to do things they would die before they let their wives or bosses see. They left there with their minds blown and their lives in Joey's pocket. And you know something? I never felt sorry for them. Not once. Every one of those bastards left his wife and kids at home to come into that club. They took me back to that room to screw me senseless, not giving a damn if I lived or died after. Every one of them begged me to do it without a condom, and most of them wanted . . . God, I don't even want to think about it. And these were pillars of the community, you know? So, when you stand there acting like you're above it, I know it's bullshit, okay? You play your little game, but I *know*."

"I'm not above it," Will said. "No man is. Or woman, for that matter. It's called human frailty. It's pathetic, but it's the story of life. You don't have any special knowledge. I think my wife knows everything you just told me, even without experiencing it. She just chooses not to let it touch her."

"So, she's above it, huh? Maybe that's why she isn't doing it for you in the bedroom."

"You still haven't told me how or why you switched from blackmail to kidnapping."

Cheryl drank off what was left of her rum and Coke. "Blackmail gets messy. You can't predict what guys will do when you hit them with the pictures. The reality of it. The end of life as they know it. Most of them can't wait to pay, of course. But you never know. One guy wanted copies to give to his wife and everybody at his office." She smiled at the memory. "But some of them freak. They run home and confess to their wives, or try to kill Joey, or . . ."

She trailed off, and in the moments of silence that followed, Will knew what she had not said. "Some of them kill themselves," he finished. "Right?"

She squinted at the television. "One guy did. It was bad. He left his copy of the tape playing on the VCR when he shot himself. His wife found him. Can you imagine?" She poured more rum into her glass, straight this time. "The cops nearly got us for that one. After that, Joey decided we were going about it the wrong way. The thing to do, he figured, was a small number of jobs, but get the maximum bang for the risk."

"Kidnapping?"

She nodded. "When he was working the blackmail gigs, he saw that what these guys were most scared of—way more than hurting their wives—was their kids. They couldn't take the idea that their kids would lose all respect for them. Their kids were what they lived for. So, the way to get the most money was to make the guys pay for their kids."

"That's a hell of a lot riskier than blackmail."

"It is if you do it the way everybody else does it. That's like asking the FBI to stomp on you with a SWAT team. Joey's smarter than that. But I don't have to tell you, do I?"

Will stepped to his left and collapsed into the chair by the window. After all that had happened, it was Cheryl's last story that brought the full weight of reality crashing down upon him. He wasn't special. He was merely the latest in a long line of fools victimized by a man who specialized in exploiting human weakness. Hickey had made a profession of it, an art, and Will couldn't see any way to extricate himself or his family from the man's web.

"Tell me one thing."

"What?"

"Did any of the other fathers take you up on your offer?"

Cheryl intertwined her fingers and put her hands behind her head, which showed her implants to best advantage. A strange smile touched her lips. "Two out of five. The others tortured themselves all night. Those two slept like babies."

Despite his speech about human frailty, Will couldn't believe that fathers whose children were in mortal danger would have sex with one of their kidnappers. It seemed incomprehensible. And yet, he knew it was possible. "You're lying," he said, trying to reassure himself.

"Whatever you say. But I know what I know."

Special Agent Bill Chalmers thanked a black homicide detective named Washington and closed the door of the police interrogation room. Dr. McDill and his wife had followed the FBI agent's car the few blocks from the Federal Building to police headquarters, and what they had come for now lay on the metal table in front of them. A stack of mug books two and a half feet high.

"I know it's not great," Chalmers said. "But it's more private than the squad room."

"There must be thousands of photos here," McDill said.

"Easily. I'll be outside, accessing the National Crime Information Center computer. I'll check all past records of kidnappings-for-ransom in the Southeast, then hit the names 'Joe,' 'Cheryl,' and 'Huey' for criminal records under actual names and aliases. 'Joe' is common as dirt, but the others might ring a bell. Also, I talked to my boss by cell phone on the way over. We may see him down here before long. Right now he's waking up some bank officers to set up flags on large wire transfers going to the Gulf Coast tomorrow morning." Chalmers looked at his watch. "I guess I mean this morning."

McDill sighed. "Could we have some coffee or something?"

"You bet. How do you take it?"

"Black for me. Margaret?"

"Is it possible they might have tea?" she asked in a soft voice.

Chalmers gave her a smile. "You never know. I'll check."

After he went out, Margaret sat down at the table and opened one of the mug books. The faces staring up from the page belonged to people the McDills used all their money and privilege to avoid. The faces shared many features. Flash-blinded, dope-fried eyes. Hollow cheeks. Bad teeth. Nose rings. Tattoos. And stamped into every one, as though dyed into the skin, a bitter hopelessness that never looked further than the next twenty-four hours.

"Are we doing the right thing?" Margaret asked, looking up at her husband.

McDill gently squeezed her shoulder. "Yes."

"How do you know?"

"The right thing is always the hardest thing."

Abby sat scrunched in the corner of the ratty sofa, crying inconsolably, her Barbie held tight against her. Huey sat on the floor six feet away, looking stricken.

"I didn't mean to scare you," he said. "I just did what Joey told me to. I have to do what Joey says."

"He stole me from my mom and dad!" Abby wailed. "You did, too!"

"I didn't want to! I wish your mama was here right now." Huey squeezed his hands into fists. "I wish *my* mama was here."

"Where is she?" Abby asked, pausing in midwail.

"Heaven." Huey said it as though he didn't quite believe it. "How come you ran away? It's because I'm ugly, isn't it?"

Abby resumed crying, but she shook her head.

"You don't have to say it. I know. The kids in my school ran too. Nobody liked me. But I thought we was friends. All I wanted to do was be nice. But you ran. How come?"

"I *told* you. You stole me away from my mom."

"That's not it. You don't like me because I look like a monster."

Abby fixed her swollen eyes on him. "What you *look* like doesn't matter. Don't you know that?"

Huey blinked. "What?"

"Belle taught me that."

"Who?"

Abby rubbed her eyes and held out her gold-lamé-gowned Barbie. "This is Belle. *Beauty and the Beast* Belle. She's my favorite Disney princess because she reads books. She wants to be something someday. Belle says it doesn't matter what you look like. It only matters what you feel inside. In your heart. And what you do."

Huey's mouth hung slack, as though he were staring at a magical fairy risen from the grass.

"You never saw *Beauty and the Beast*?" Abby said incredulously.

He shook his head.

"Let's pretend I'm Belle, and you're Beast."

"Beast?" He looked suddenly upset. "I'm a beast?"

"*Good* Beast." Abby wiped her runny nose. "Beast after he turns nice. Not mean like at first."

She slid off the couch and held Belle out to him. "Say something Beast says in the movie. Oh, I forgot. You missed it. Just say something nice. And call me 'Belle,' remember?"

Huey was at a loss. Tentatively, he said, "I'm not going to let anything happen to you, Belle. I'm going to keep you safe till morning comes, and your mama comes to get you."

Abby smiled. "Thank you, Beast. And if the villagers come and try to kill you, me and Mrs. Potts and Chip will make them go away. They won't get you!"

Huey swallowed, his eyes bright.

"Now you say, 'Thank you, Belle.' "

"Thank you, Belle."

Abby petted the doll's hair. "Do you want to brush her hair? Just pretendlike."

Huey reached out shyly and petted Belle's hair with his enormous hand.

"Good, Beast," Abby murmured. "Good Beast."

TWELVE

Karen watched the digital clock beside her bed flash over to one a.m. She was sitting in the overstuffed chair in the corner, hugging her knees; Hickey lay on the bed, his injured leg propped high on some pillows. The Wild Turkey bottle sat beside him, along with Will's .38. His eyes were glued to the television, which was showing the opening credits of *The Desperate Hours* with Humphrey Bogart and Fredric March. She was glad he hadn't yet realized there was a satellite dish connected to the bedroom television; she didn't want him flipping through to Cinemax and getting more ideas from the T&A movies they seemed to run all night.

"Bogey's good," Hickey drawled, sounding more than half drunk. "But Mitchum was the greatest. No acting at all, you know? The real deal."

Karen said nothing. She had never known time to pass so slowly. Not even when she was in labor, screaming for Abby to be born. It was as though the earth itself had slowed on its axis, its sole purpose to torment her family. She had entered that realm of timelessness that exists in certain places, a few of which she had visited herself. Prisons were like that. And monasteries. But the ones she knew most intimately were the waiting rooms of hospitals: bubbles in time where entire families entered a state of temporal suspension, waiting to learn whether the heart of the patriarch would restart after the triple bypass, whether a child would be saved or killed by a well-intentioned gift of marrow. Her bedroom had now become such a bubble. Only her child was not in the hands of a doctor.

"You alive over there?" Hickey asked.

"Barely," she whispered, her eyes on Fredric March. March reminded her of her father; he was a model of male restraint and dignity, yet he would do whatever was required when the going got tough. She still cried when she saw *The Best Years of Our Lives*, with March and that poor boy who'd lost both hands in the war trying to learn to play the piano—

"I said, are you alive over there?"

"Yes," she replied.

"Then you ought to feel lucky."

She sensed that Hickey was looking for a fight. She didn't intend to give him one.

" 'Cause a lot of people who ought to be alive aren't," he said. "You know?"

She looked over at him, wondering who he was thinking of. "I know."

"Bullshit you know."

"I told you, I was a nurse."

He glanced at her. "You proud of it? People in agony

waiting for pain medicine while nurses sit there painting their fucking fingernails, watching the clock, waiting for their shift to end."

She could not let that pass. "I am proud I was a nurse. I know that happens. But nurses are stuck with doctors' orders. If they break them, they get fired."

Hickey scowled and drank from the Wild Turkey bottle. "Don't get me started on doctors."

Karen thought she remembered him saying that all the previous kidnappings had involved children of doctors. He'd said something about doctors collecting expensive toys. But that couldn't be the only reason he targeted them. Lots of people collected expensive things. Somehow, doctors were part of a vein of suffering that ran deep in Hickey's soul.

"When did your mother pass away?" she asked.

He turned his head far enough to glare at her in the chair. "What the fuck do you care?"

"I am a human being, as you so eloquently pointed out before. And I'm trying to understand what makes you so angry. Angry enough to do this to total strangers."

He wagged a finger at her. "You're not trying to understand anything. You're trying to make me think you actually give a shit, so I might feel enough for you that I won't hurt your kid."

"That's not true."

"The hell it's not." He drank again, then let his eyes burn into her. "I'll let you in on a little secret, Sunshine. You ain't strangers."

"What?"

He smiled, and a wicked pleasure came into his face. "The light dawning up there?"

A shadow seemed to pass behind Karen's eyes, a flickering foreknowledge that made her shudder in the chair. "What do you mean?"

"Your husband works at University Hospital, right?"

"He works at several hospitals." This was true, but University provided the facilities for Will's drug research. He also held a faculty position, and did quite a bit of anesthesiology there.

Hickey waved his hand. "He works at University, right?"

"That's right. That's where we met."

"How romantic. But I have a little different feeling about the place. My mother died there."

The transient fear that made her shudder before now took up residence in her heart.

"She was in for her throat cancer," he said, almost to himself. "They'd cut on her a bunch of times before. It was no big deal. But they were supposed to put some kind of special panty-hose things on her during the operation. STDs or something."

"SCDs," Karen corrected him. "Sequential compression devices. Along with T.E.D. hose, they keep the blood circulating in the legs while the patient is under anesthesia."

"Supposed to, anyway," Hickey said. "But they left them off, and she got some kind of clot. Sounds like Efrem Zimbalist."

"An embolus."

"That's it."

"Will was the anesthesiologist?"

"Fuckin'-A right he was. And my mother died right

there on the table. They told me nothing could be done. But I went back later and talked to the surgeon who'd done the operation. And he finally told me. It's the gas passer's job to make sure those SCD things are on the patient."

"But that's not true!" Karen cried. "The anesthesiologist has nothing to do with that."

"Oh, yeah. What else are you going to say?"

"That's the job of the circulating nurse—*if* the surgeon has written the proper orders. The surgeon himself should check to be sure they're on."

"The cutter told me there's some kind of box under the table, and the gas passer's supposed to check for it."

"He was probably scared to death of you! He was shifting the blame wherever he could."

A dark laugh from Hickey. "He was scared, all right." He leaned up on his elbow. "Don't worry. That asshole paid, too. In full."

"You sued him for malpractice?"

"Sued him?" Hickey laughed. "I said he paid *in full.*"

"What do you mean?"

"What do you think I mean?"

"You killed him?"

Hickey snapped his fingers. "Just like that. No telling how many people I saved by wasting that butcher."

Struggling to keep her anxiety hidden, Karen tried to remember Will mentioning a case like the one Hickey had described. But she couldn't. And it didn't surprise her. Her resentment about leaving med school made her a poor listener when Will wanted to discuss work.

"When exactly did this happen? I mean, when did your mother pass away? Will—"

"She didn't *pass away*, okay?" Hickey sat up in the bed. "She was murdered. By doctors who didn't give a shit. Your old man wasn't even in the room when she started to go. He was there at the start and the end. Some assistant was in there the rest of the time."

Nurse anesthetist, Karen thought, her heart sinking. More and more, nurse anesthetists were handling the bulk of routine operations. It lowered the cost to the patient and freed up time for the doctor to concentrate on difficult cases. But the custom had always worried her. In an empirical sense, there was no such thing as a routine operation.

"Probably talking to his fucking stockbroker through most of it," Hickey said, lying back on the pillows. "Yapping on his cell phone while my mother was croaking. The bottom line is, your husband murdered my mother. And that's why we're here tonight, babe. Instant karma."

Karen tried to think of a way to convince him of Will's innocence, but it was useless. His mind was made up. She shook her head, trying to resist the change that had already taken place within her, the instant reappraisal of Abby's chances. Until now, Abby's kidnapping had seemed a stroke of fate, terrible but random, like being blindsided by a bus. But this was infinitely worse. Because every moment of the crime, from the moment it was born in Hickey's fevered mind to the conclusion waiting out there in the dark, was suffused with malice, driven by hatred, and focused on revenge.

"How long have you been planning this?" she asked

softly. "I mean, you said you've done this to other doctors. Were they all involved in your mother's case?"

"Nah. I picked doctors for the reason I told you. They collect expensive toys, go off to meetings all the time. They're perfect marks. It's strange the way it happened, really. Your husband was already on my short list when he killed my mother. He just went to the top of the list."

Karen hugged her knees tighter. Hickey had already returned his attention to the movie. He seemed enthralled by the paranoia and hatred crackling off of Humphrey Bogart, an inchoate anger that quite by chance had found a target in the family of Fredric March, a man whose loving family Bogie's character had never known and never would. She recalled Hickey's story of the death of his father. Hickey had ordered his cousin to kill the man who brought him into the world, and Huey had obeyed him. Patricide. A man capable of that was capable of anything.

"You just want the money, right?" she said, watching his face in the light of the television.

Hickey glanced away from the screen. "What?"

"I said, you just want the money, right?"

"Sure." He smiled, but his eyes were dead. "What else?"

Karen kept her face motionless, but her soul was falling down a dark shaft. Abby wasn't meant to survive the kidnapping. She would live until Hickey's wife got the ransom money. Then she would wind up a corpse in a ditch somewhere, waiting for the inevitable deer hunter to stumble across her body. Hickey's other victims might have lived, but this time was different. This time it was not about money.

He wants to punish Will, she thought. *That's why he wanted to rape me. And how could he be sure Will would know he'd done it? By killing me. Because when the medical examiner performed the required autopsy, he would find Hickey's semen—*

It was hard to believe that a simple chain of thoughts could incapacitate a person, but Karen felt her mind and body shutting down as surely as if Hickey had cracked her skull with a hammer. She had to keep functioning. She had to shed her fear for herself. Hickey meant to kill Abby: that was the critical fact. That alone had to determine her actions from this moment forward. The first thing to do was to warn Will. He had to know that waiting out the night and paying the ransom wasn't going to bring Abby back to them. She wasn't sure how to warn him yet, but she knew one thing absolutely: if morning dawned without them any closer to saving Abby, she would have to kill Hickey. If he wasn't alive to give the death order, the giant in the forest might just falter at the brutality of his appointed task. But first she had to get out of the bedroom.

Alone.

Will lay on the sofa in the sitting room of the suite, a hot towel over his face. He was tired of looking at Cheryl in her bra. Tired of listening to her street analysis of his marriage and his present situation. He had paced out a couple of miles on the sitting room carpet, circling the furniture groups, trying to burn off the desperate energy produced by his inability to help Abby. That exercise, combined with his earlier wrestling match with Cheryl, had aggravated his joints to the point that he had to take a powerful painkiller that he kept for emergency situations. The drug and the hot towel had tamped down the pain, but his brain was humming like an overloaded circuit. The QVC shopping network babbled incessantly from the bedroom, where Cheryl lay drinking her rum and Cokes.

His mind was working strangely, like the jump cuts he saw whenever he flipped through MTV on the way to VH1 or CNBC. He saw himself walking into the bedroom, jamming Cheryl's gun underneath her jaw, and forcing her to tell him where Abby was, the way Clint Eastwood would do it. But Cheryl had hit the nail on the head before. This was no movie. As long as Abby was under Hickey's control, Will could yank out Cheryl's fingernails with pliers and it would get him nowhere. When the thirty-minute check-in call came, Abby would suffer horribly or die.

For a while, he'd tried to view his situation as an exercise in problem-solving. It was like a chess game, with only six pieces. But the stakes were so high that he couldn't make a move. He couldn't even *see* a move. Cheryl claimed she didn't know where Abby was being held. Will wasn't sure he believed her, but even if she did know—and he somehow forced her to tell him—she claimed it was impossible for police to reach the location within the thirty-minute window. He did believe that. It only made sense—from Hickey's point of view—and it dovetailed with what Karen had said about where Abby was being held. So, in order for Will to save Abby, Cheryl would not only have to know where Abby was—and tell him—she would also have to pretend to Hickey that everything was fine while the state police or the FBI raced to rescue her.

What could convince her to do that? Fear? He doubted it. Any torture he was capable of inflicting would almost certainly fall short of what Cheryl believed Hickey would do if she betrayed him. A bribe? It was an option, but one he'd have to be careful with. The previous fathers had undoubtedly tried it. Yet they had failed. Why? Why should Cheryl remain loyal to Hickey? A man who, by her own admission, still beat her? What would it take to erode that perverse loyalty? A million? Will could get a million dollars cash. It would take a few days, though. Which killed the idea. To be effective, bribe money would have to be in his hands before the ransom pickup tomorrow morning. Or simultaneously. Karen was supposed to wire the ransom to a bank on the coast. There were branches of Magnolia Federal—the main state bank—all over Biloxi and Gulfport, and the odds were that Hickey would pick one of them to handle the receipt of a large wire transfer. Most of Will's money was in the stock market, but he had $150,000 in CDs at Magnolia Fed. But would the promise of $150,000—plus the $200,000 ransom—be enough to turn Cheryl against her husband? Unlikely. The other fathers had probably suffered from the same lack of liquidity.

The towel had gone cold on Will's face. He got up and went to the bathroom, then ran the tap as hot as it would go and held a washrag under it. The reflection that stared back from the mirror was not the one he saw every morning; it was the face of a lab rat trapped in a maze, forced to jump through hoops laid out for it by an unreachable adversary.

He wrung out the washrag, then returned to the sofa and laid the cloth across his eyes. Images of Abby in pain rose in his mind but he forced them down. Why had he and his family been targeted? Had his art collection really been the determining factor? All Hickey's victims had supposedly been doctors who collected things, all of them hit on occasions when they left their families for more than forty-eight hours. Cheryl wouldn't reveal how they knew when these physicians were traveling, but Will assumed Hickey had a mole in one of the hospitals, a nurse or an aide, probably. Someone who heard the chitchat around the ORs and doctors' lounges. Not that it mattered. They were in the eye of the storm now, and everything hung in the balance. Will had seen enough parents lose children to know what it did to families. The death of a child was an emotional Hiroshima, leaving utter devastation in its wake. The world became a shadow of itself. Marriages failed, and suicide began to look like sweet release, a path back to the one who was lost.

As a doctor, Will had often speculated about the worst disease. Was it ALS? A lingering cancer? Soldiers pondered wounds the same way. Was it a Bouncing Betty in the balls? A disfiguring facial wound? But in truth there was no worst wound, or worst disease. The worst wound was the one *you* got. The worst disease was the one that got you.

But among all the evils of the world, there was one worst thing, and he had always known what it was. It grew out of a single image: a child hunched in the dark, alone and in pain, whimpering for help where no help would come. That child had a thousand faces, plastered on bulletin boards in the entrances of Wal-Marts, on milk cartons, on desperate flyers in the mail. *Have you seen this child?* The abandoned. The kidnapped. Runaways. But worse than being that child crying in the dark was being the parent of that child. Pondering forever the moment you let your attention wander in the mall, or that you'd said yes to that out-of-town trip, conjuring scenes of cruelty beyond Goya himself, living and reliving them in the everlasting torment of self-inflicted damnation.

Lying on the couch in his luxury suite, Will knew he was one step away from that eternity of guilt. He could not have known, of course, that someone like Hickey waited in the wings to take away everything he had during a convention weekend. Yet on some level, he had. He had always known. Yeats had said it long ago: *things fall apart.* It was the human version of the entropy that powered the universe as it ticked down toward cold death. Just as some people always built things, organized, nested, and planned, there were those serving the function of chaos: stealing, tearing down, killing. It was a paranoid worldview, but at the deepest level Will had always embraced it. Only recently had he become soft. Complacent. Lulled by material success. He had let down his guard, and now chaos had ripped into his life like a tornado.

He had to respond, and forcefully. He had never believed that by simply letting events take their course, things would work out for the best. That view was held by people who accepted whatever fate handed them and called it "the best" in a pathetic attempt to cope. Will

Jennings *made* things come out for the best. His father's failures had taught him the necessity of that attitide.

He had to detach himself from the situation. Karen always said that his instinct was his most valuable asset. But instinct, he believed, was integrally bound up with emotion. And emotion had no place in solving a problem like this one. What he needed now was logic. Pure reason.

Of course, there *were* situations in which doing nothing was the wisest response. Any doctor could tell you that. But when doctors chose the option of "inaction," they were actually choosing to get out of the way of an immune system perfected over millions of years. For Will, on this night, doing nothing meant relying on a system created by Joe Hickey, a man he did not know or remember, yet who harbored a deep resentment of him and all he stood for. He could not do that. In spite of Cheryl's assurances that waiting out the night was the way to get Abby back, he was certain she was wrong. He would trust his instinct that far.

The washrag on his eyes had gone cold again. The QVC hawker's voice floated in from the bedroom, where Cheryl was watching a presentation on "faux sapphires," whatever they were. He threw the cloth on the floor and sat up on the sofa. He needed more information. Cheryl claimed this kidnapping was exactly like all the others, but it wasn't. What made it different? Was it something Cheryl herself did not know? Or something she did not know she knew? With a groan of pain, Will got up and walked into the bedroom.

In downtown Jackson, Dr. James McDill was working his way through police mug books, sliding his hand down each page to isolate the lines of photos. Tired of the claustrophobic interrogation room, he and Margaret had moved out to the squad room, with the late homicide shift. Agent Chalmers had been working the NCIC computer but hadn't come up with anything yet. The number of "Joes" who had committed crimes in the South was astounding, and most had compound names. Chalmers had shown Margaret photos of Joe-Bobs, Joe-Eds, Joe Dees, Joe Jimmys, Joe Franks, Joe Willies, and even a Joe DiMaggio Smith. But none brought even a flicker of recognition to Margaret's eyes. McDill had asked his wife to lie down on the Naugahyde sofa by the wall, but she refused. She sat at another empty desk, doggedly searching through book after book. Her eyes had a strange glint, and McDill was glad to see it. Perhaps, after the long year in purgatory, that light signaled a return to the world of the living.

He took a sip of cold coffee and looked down at the book before him. Female offenders, harshly lit. The smug grins of check kiters. The gaunt, pocked faces of coke whores. None was nearly as attractive as "Cheryl." In his memory, the woman who had forced him to sit all night in the Beau Rivage looked like a high school prom queen. He knew he must be exaggerating her beauty, yet his mental picture was as clear as the room he was sitting in now. He was sure of one thing. If "Cheryl" was in one of these books, she would stand out like a rose in a field of garbage.

He rubbed his eyes and turned another page. As he scanned the photos, Agent Chalmers's voice intruded into his concentration. The FBI agent was talking to the black JPD detective named Washington about the

McDills' experience. Chalmers had enough tact not to mention the rape with Margaret in the room, but he seemed very impressed by the kidnappers' plan.

"There *is* no ransom drop," he was saying. "Not in the classic sense. See? The ransom is low enough so that it's liquid. The target can get it without any trouble. Two, the husband's out of town when it goes down. The kid vanishes, poof, and the mother finds herself stuck with one of the kidnappers for the night. A female member of the team hits the husband on the coast, while the kid's with a third member at an unknown location. From then on, the thirty-minute check-in calls work like an unbreakable net. It wipes out the classic model. I mean, it *neutralizes* the risk. In the morning, pretty as you please, the wife goes down to her bank and wires the ransom to her own husband. Ba-da-bing, it's over. Jackpot."

Detective Washington nodded thoughtfully. "You're dealing with a smart son of a bitch. What you gonna do if you find out who he is? That thirty-minute thing has you boxed. Anything you do could kill the hostage before you even figure out where he is."

"We have to go high-tech, all the way. If we can confirm that this thing is going down, Frank Zwick is going to get a chopper, GPS homers, the works, everything by dawn."

"Do you think it's going down?" Washington asked.

Chalmers nodded. "I've never known a criminal to stop something that was working for him. They always push it till they get bit. That's their nature."

"You're right about that much."

"We just need to catch a break. If we still don't know

who they are when that ransom wire hits the coast in the morning, we'll be way behind the curve."

McDill closed his eyes and tried to shut out their conversation. In Chalmers's voice, he recognized the sound of a man who believed he could impose his will on the world. McDill knew how illusory that belief was. Every day he cut into the thoracic cavities of human beings, and it was difficult enough to impose his will on simple human tissue. When you brought large numbers of people into a dangerous situation—each acting independently—the best you could hope for was that nobody would die. McDill didn't just remember Vietnam, as he'd said before. He had served there as a medical corpsman. And he had seen more situations go to hell in a handbasket because of the good intentions of men like Agent Chalmers than he cared to recall. Chalmers was the classic second lieutenant, green and hungry for action. His faith in technology also struck a dark resonance with Vietnam. McDill hoped that the Special Agent-in-Charge had been tempered by more experience.

He opened his eyes and looked down at the rows of unfamiliar women, then wearily turned another page. His breath caught in his throat. Staring up from the mug book like a graduation portrait was Cheryl's innocent face.

"Agent Chalmers! This is her!"

The FBI agent stopped in midsentence and looked over. "Are you sure?"

"Positive."

Chalmers walked over and looked down at the photo beneath McDill's index finger.

"Who is she?" McDill asked.

Chalmers took the photo out of its plastic sleeve and read from its back. "Cheryl Lynn Tilly. I'll be damned. She *did* use her real name. Maybe the others did too. I wonder why she didn't pop up on NCIC?"

He walked over to the computer he'd been using and began typing in the information off the photo. The JPD detective stood behind him with his arms folded. After several seconds, data from Washington began flashing up onto the CRT.

"She's got some small-time collars," Chalmers said. "Passing bad checks, forgery. One prostitution arrest. She did thirty days in a county jail. Nothing violent. You're positive it's her?"

"Absolutely."

"I'll make a copy of this photo and fax it down to the Beau Rivage. Maybe someone on staff down there has seen her."

"What will you do if they have?"

Chalmers raised his eyebrows and took a deep breath. "Call in the troops. If she's down there this weekend, we have to assume you're right. There's a kidnapping in progress. And that is a major situation. Right now, we need to see whether known associates can lead us to the man behind all this."

Chalmers turned to Margaret McDill, who was watching them with a look of apprehension. "Are you awake enough to keep helping us, Mrs. McDill?"

"Whatever you need," she said softly.

McDill walked over and put his hands on his wife's shoulders.

Chalmers picked up a telephone, then paused. "These

people have some nerve. To repeat the same crime in exactly the same place, a year after the fact?"

"You didn't talk to them," McDill said. "They think they're invincible."

The FBI agent smiled. "They're not."

Karen rocked slowly but ceaselessly in her chair, her arms around her shins, her chin buried between her knees. Hickey was still lying on the bed, his eyes glued to Bogart and Fredric March as they played out the final minutes of *The Desperate Hours.* Karen sensed that she was close to a breakdown. She had been pulling hairs from her scalp, one at time. Externally, she could maintain calm, but inside she was coming apart. The knowledge that Hickey meant to kill Abby to punish Will was unendurable.

She had to warn him.

Food was her best excuse to get out of the bedroom, but there was no guarantee that Hickey wouldn't follow her into the kitchen. For a while she had entertained the hope that the whiskey might put him to sleep, but he seemed immune to its effects. He'd gone into the bathroom twice during commercials, once to urinate and once to check his stitches, but she hadn't felt confident enough to risk using the phone, much less to try to reach the computer in Will's study.

She stopped rocking. She had the feeling that Hickey had said something to her and that she'd been concentrating so hard that she missed it.

"Did you say something?" she asked.

"I said I'm starving. Go fix something."

She wanted to jump out of the chair, but she forced herself to sound peeved. "What would you like?"

"What you got?"

"A sandwich?"

Gunshots rang from the television. Bogey fell to the ground. "Goddamn it," Hickey said. "I don't know. Something hot."

"There's some crawfish étouffée I could heat up."

"Yeah." He glanced over at her, his eyes bleary. "Can you put it in an omelet?"

"Sure."

"What was I thinking? I got Betty Crocker here. Weaned on an Easy-Bake oven, right?"

Karen tried to laugh, but the sound died in her throat. She got up from the chair and walked toward the door. "Anything else?"

"Just hurry it up."

She nodded and went out.

As soon as she cleared the door, she sped to a silent run. In the kitchen, she slid a skillet onto the Viking's large burner, switched the gas to HIGH, then opened the refrigerator and took out three eggs, a bottle of Squeeze Parkay, and a Tupperware dish half-filled with seasoned crawfish tails in a roux. The eggs went into the pocket of her housecoat, the étouffée into the microwave, and a glob of margarine into the skillet. Then she grabbed the cordless phone off the wall and punched in the number of Will's office.

"Anesthesiology Associates," said the answering service operator.

"This is Karen Jennings. I need to—"

"Could you speak up, please?"

She raised the volume of her whisper. "This is *Karen Jennings*. I need to get a message to my husband on his SkyTel pager."

"Go ahead, ma'am."

"You've got to do something. They're going to . . ."

"Just a second. Is that the message?"

"Yes—no, wait." She should have thought this out more carefully. She couldn't simply state the situation to a stranger. The operator was liable to call the police herself. With shaking hands she broke the three eggs and dropped the yolks into the skillet. "The message is, 'You've got to do something before morning. Abby is going to die no matter what. Karen.' Do you have that?"

"Yes, ma'am. This sounds like a real emergency."

"It is. Wait, I want to add something. Add 'Confirm receipt by e-mail.' "

"I don't take many messages like this, Mrs. Jennings. Shouldn't you maybe call nine-one-one?"

"No! I mean, that's not appropriate in this case. This is a little girl with liver cancer. Will's working with the transplant team, and things are very dicey right now."

"Lord, lord," said the operator. "I know about livers. I got a brother with hepatitis C. I'll get this entered right away."

"It's got to go to his SkyTel. It's a brand-new pager."

"I've got that noted on my screen. Don't you worry. If he's got the pager on, he'll get the message. I think those SkyTels can even access missed messages."

"Thank you." Another thought struck Karen. "If he doesn't call you to confirm that he's received this message, would you call his room at the Beau Rivage in Biloxi and give it to him?"

"Yes, ma'am. The Beau Rivage. Half our doctors are down there right now."

"Thank you. Thank you so much." Karen hung up the phone, her hand shaking. The concern in the operator's voice had been like salve on a burn. She'd wanted to pour out the whole horrible story to her, tell her to call the police and—

"That doesn't smell half bad."

Karen froze.

Hickey was standing in the kitchen door in his bloody towel. He looked into her eyes for a moment, then past her. His eyes went cold. "What are you doing by that phone?"

She felt a fist crushing her heart. To avoid Hickey's gaze, she turned and looked at the phone. Tacked and taped around it were greeting cards, photographs, and Post-it notes. She reached into the midst of them and pulled a small photo off the wall.

"I was looking at Abby's school picture. I still can't believe this is happening."

The microwave beeped loudly. She went to it and took out the étouffée, then spooned it into the rapidly firming omelet. She sensed Hickey moving closer, but she didn't look up. With shaking hands she folded the egg over the crawfish.

His fingers fell on her forearm, sending a shock up her spine. "Look at me," he said in a hard voice.

She did. His eyes were preternaturally alert, the eyes of a predator studying its prey.

"What?" she said.

Hickey just stared, registering each movement of her facial muscles, every pulse beat in her neck.

"It's going to burn," she said, pulling her arm away and reaching for the spatula. As she slid it under the omelet, he slipped his arms around her waist, as though he were a loving husband watching his wife make breakfast. His touch made her light-headed, but she forced herself to continue the motion, lifting the omelet from the pan and turning to drop it onto a plate. Hickey stayed with her as she moved.

After the omelet hit the plate, he said, "You're a little wildcat, aren't you?"

She did not reply.

"I still own you. Don't forget that."

She looked him full in the face at last. "How can I?"

His expression hardened, and she had a sudden premonition that he was going to push her to her knees. She didn't know what she would do if he did.

"Bring the food back to the bed," he said finally. Then he let his hands fall. "And bring a bottle of Tabasco with it."

He turned and limped up the hallway.

She had no idea how long she'd been holding her breath, but it must have been a while, because after she exhaled, she couldn't seem to get enough oxygen. Her legs became water. She gripped the counter to hold herself up, but it wasn't enough. She had to lie across the Corian and grab the top of the splashboard to keep from falling.

THIRTEEN

Will sat in the chair by the bed, facing Cheryl. She was still propped against the headboard—gun beside her, QVC chattering in the background—but she had finally slipped on one of Will's white pinpoint button-downs. For an hour he had probed her about Hickey, but to no avail. She had given him all the biography she felt safe giving, and beyond that she would only discuss her own interests, such as aromatherapy and Reiki.

Cheryl had somehow got it into her head that the jump from sofa dancing and prostitution to the laying on of hands required in Reiki energy therapy was a natural one. Will tried to lull her into carelessness by telling her about the success of certain alternative therapies with his arthritis, but once he got her on that subject, he couldn't turn her back to what mattered.

He changed his tack by asking about Huey instead of Joe, but suddenly something buzzed against his side. He jumped out of the chair, thinking it was a cockroach, but when he looked down he realized it was the new SkyTel. The pager was still set to VIBRATE mode from the keynote dinner.

"What's with you?" Cheryl asked.

"Something crawled over me." He made a big show of looking under the chair cushion. "A damn roach or something."

She laughed. "I wouldn't be surprised. Hey, this brochure over here says they close the swimming pool at eight p.m. That's kind of cheap, isn't it?"

"They don't want you swimming, they want you gambling in the casino downstairs."

"Yeah." Her eyes brightened. "You like gambling?"

Will was dying to check the pager. He wasn't on call, so the message had almost certainly come from Karen. The only other people who would be able to persuade his service to page him at this hour would be his partners, most of whom were at the convention. "Not really," he said, trying to remember the thread of the conversation. "Life's uncertain enough without that."

"Party pooper."

"Do you mind if I use the bathroom?"

Cheryl shrugged and returned her attention to a display of Peterboro baskets on QVC. "Hey, if you got to go . . ."

Will walked into the bathroom with the Jacuzzi and closed the door, then whipped the pager off his belt and punched the RETRIEVE button. The green backlit screen scrolled:

YOU'VE GOT TO DO SOMETHING BEFORE MORNING. ABBY IS GOING TO DIE NO MATTER WHAT. KAREN. CONFIRM BY E-MAIL.

He scrolled the message again, staring in shock at the words as they trailed past. *Abby is going to die no matter what.* What did that mean? Was Abby having some sort of diabetic crisis? Karen had given her eight units of insulin in the early evening, and that should hold her until morning. Had Karen learned something new about Hickey's plan?

You've got to do something before morning. What the hell could he do without risking Abby's life? But the answer to that question was contained within the message. *Abby is going to die no matter what.* Karen *had* learned something. And her meaning was clear: he would have to risk Abby's life to save her life.

He looked around the bathroom as though something in it could help him. The only potential weapon he saw was a steam iron. As he stared at the thing, the phone beside the toilet rang. He looked at his watch. Three a.m. Hickey's regular check-in call. He heard Cheryl's muffled voice through the bathroom door. A few words, then silence again. Or rather the droning chatter of the television. He turned on the hot water tap and waited for steam to rise from the basin.

Wetting another washcloth, he wrung it out and pressed it to his face. As the blood came into his cheeks, something strange and astonishing happened. His mental perspective simultaneously contracted and expanded, piercing the fog that had blinded him for the past hours.

He suddenly saw three separate scenes with absolute clarity: Abby held hostage in the woods, Karen trapped in their house at Annandale, and himself standing in the marble-floored bathroom. He saw these scenes like a man in the first row of a theater, yet at the same time he saw the relationships between them as though from satellite altitude: visible and invisible filaments connecting six people in time and space, a soft machine with six moving parts. And burning at the center of his brain was awareness of a single fact: he had exactly thirty minutes to save Abby. That was all he would ever have. The thirty minutes between check-in calls. Whether it was this half hour or the next, that was the window of opportunity Hickey had left him.

He threw the washrag into the basin. He had to know what Cheryl knew. *Everything* she knew. There was a chance that she'd lied before, that she knew exactly where Abby was being held. But probably she didn't. None of the previous fathers had dragged it out of her, and he was sure some had tried. How would they have tried? The gun was the obvious tool. But Abby gave Cheryl immunity to the gun, and to everything else. Because the effectiveness of any threat—torture with a steam iron, say—lay in the victim's belief that his tormentor would follow through. And while they had the children, no one could.

Even if he somehow broke Cheryl, it wouldn't be enough for her to spill what she knew. She would have to cooperate until Abby was found. Play her role for Hickey during the check-in calls—at least three of them, probably more. What could possibly persuade her to do that? The bruises on her body proved she could take punishment, and God alone knew what horrors Hickey had visited upon her in the past. Yet she stayed with him. She felt a loyalty that Will would never understand. And yet . . .

Her eyes had shone when she told him about the contact she'd had with Hollywood producers, the contact Hickey had acted so decisively to terminate. And she hadn't tried to make it more than it was. She admitted the potential roles were soft-core porn, late-night cable stuff. But that had been fine with her. It was a step up, and Cheryl had known it. It was also a step away from Joe Hickey, and on some level she must have known that, too. Known it, and believed she'd been born for more than prostitution and crime.

But to betray Hickey, she would have to believe she could escape him. And that would take money. Enough to not merely run, but to vanish. To become someone else. She might like that idea. Leaving Cheryl the sofa dancer in the ashes of the past. But by the time Will got his hands on that much money, the final act would be playing itself out, and by Hickey's rules. Earlier, while Cheryl made a trip to the bathroom, he had called downstairs and asked about cashing checks. The casino used TelChek, and that company had a $2,500 limit over ten days. Given his credit rating, he could probably persuade the casino manager to take a promissory note for a larger cash advance, but only if he intended to gamble that money in the casino.

"You okay in there?" Cheryl called.

"Fine." Maybe he could take the $2,500, max out his

credit cards at the ATM, and then parlay that stake into the kind of money he needed—

"Dumb," he muttered at his reflection. The only games he knew how to play were blackjack and five-card-stud, and he hadn't played either since medical school.

His right eye suddenly blurred, and a pain like the sharp end of a poker woke to life behind it. The prodromal phase of a migraine. The euphoric clarity he'd experienced moments ago began to evaporate like drunken insight in the haze of a hangover. His thirty-minute window was ticking away. *Abby's going to die no matter what. . . .*

He had never felt such desperation. A paralyzing mixture of terror and futility that cornered animals must feel. Abby was his flesh, his blood, his spirit. Her survival was his own. Will had never seen Joe Hickey's face, but it floated just beyond his blurred vision, dancing like the hooded head of a cobra. The pain behind his eye ratcheted up a notch. He reached into his dop kit and gobbled four Advils. Then he flushed the toilet and opened the bathroom door.

Cheryl didn't bother to look away from the television.

"Was that Joe?" he asked.

"Yeah. Everything's cool, just like I said it would be."

Will looked at her there, wearing his button-down and the remains of her black cocktail dress. The gun lay beside her.

Sensing his eyes upon her, she glanced over at him. "What are you looking at? You changing your mind about getting calmed down?"

"Maybe."

She gave him a strange look. A hurt look. "Maybe I changed my mind, too. You said some mean things before."

Mean things. This woman had helped kidnap his daughter. Now she was talking about meanness on his part.

Will walked into the bedroom, his eyes on the gun. But as he neared the bed, something made him continue around it. Past the chair, past the window where he watched the gulf, into the spacious sitting room. Here was the sofa, the wet bar, the desk, the dining table. He looked at his notebook computer on the desk. Eight hours ago he had been running video clips from the hard drive on that machine, proud and self-satisfied, dreaming of stock options and the royalties he would realize on the drug he had worked so hard to develop. What a pathetic joke. What would that money be worth if Abby lay in a coffin beneath the ground? How much time had he spent away from home, away from her, working on the trials for Restorase? How many hours wasted thinking up the stupid name? Fighting with the Klein-Adams marketing people over it? *Restorase*, *Neurovert*, *Synapticin*—

His rambling train of thought crashed to a halt like a locomotive hitting a wall. His eyes went from the computer case to his sample case. *Restorase.* He had four vials of the prototype drug inside the case. But more importantly, he had two vials of Anectine. It was all part of the display for the Klein-Adams booth. Doctors would recognize Anectine, which was the trade name for succinylcholine, the depolarizing relaxant Will had developed Restorase to counteract. There was also a package of syringes: two conventional, and two of the special contact syringes the Klein-Adams engineering people had manufactured to Will's specifications. The compressed gas syringes could deliver a therapeutic dose of Anectine in a half second of skin contact.

"Succinylcholine," Will murmured, and a strange chill went through him. With the chill came visions from the clinical trials of the past year, images that would scare the living hell out of a layman.

"What are you doing in there?" Cheryl called from the bedroom.

"Thinking."

"Don't strain your brain."

He opened the sample case and made sure everything that was supposed to be there *was* there. Then he closed his eyes and summoned Abby from memory, bringing her to center stage in his mind. Her smiling face and sturdy little body, her beyond-her-years determination, forged during her constant battle with juvenile diabetes. She lived on the knife edge of disaster, yet considered herself far luckier than most children. Will's pride in her was boundless. Abby was the nourishing flame that burned at the center of his soul. And the woman in the next room had put her life at risk. Dropped her down a black hole of terror. Whatever disadvantages fate had handed Cheryl, she had chosen to help Hickey of her own free will—not once, but six times, by her own admission. Six children put through hell. Twelve parents. Whatever she had to endure now was only what she had asked for.

He walked back into the bedroom as though everything

was fine. But instead of stopping at the chair, he walked to the edge of the bed and looked down at Cheryl, much as he might have at Karen when he wanted to make love with her.

She looked up, her eyes curious. "What?"

"I want to kiss you."

Her cheeks went pink. "You what?"

"I want to kiss you."

"I don't do that," she said in a flustered voice. "That's too personal."

"But I want to."

She bit her lip. "No kiss." But then she undid the top four buttons of the dress shirt and slid down a cup of her bra. "You can kiss here."

He smiled and bent toward her breast.

"What changed your mind?" she asked in a softer voice.

As his cheek brushed her skin, he put his hand across her as though to prop himself on the bed, then closed his hand around the butt of her Walther. When he rose up and pointed the automatic at her face, she blinked with incomprehension.

"What are you doing?"

"Pull up your bra."

She did..

Will took the pager from his belt and handed it to her. "Read the last message."

"What?"

An ex-hooker would know all about pagers. "Hit the RETRIEVE button!"

She fumbled with the device, then found the button.

He could see the words scrolling on the LCD screen, her eyes narrowing as she read them.

"I just got that message from my wife. Do you understand what it means?"

She shook her head.

"Joe is going to kill my little girl. No matter what I do. Whether he gets the ransom or not."

"He is not!"

"If Karen says he is, he is."

"Joey would never let her send this message. This is some kind of mistake."

"No mistake, Cheryl. Karen is smarter than Joe, and she found a way. It's that simple. Now, you're about to tell me where Abby is."

She blinked at him. "I can't. I don't know where she is."

"For your sake, I hope you do."

Confidence suddenly returned to her face. "Are you going to shoot me? Come on, Doc. We've been over this."

"I'm not going to shoot you. Not with a bullet, anyway."

Something in his eyes must have gotten through, because a shadow of fear played over her face. "What do you mean?" she said in a higher voice. "I told you before. Even if I did know, and you made me tell, the cops couldn't get to her in time. Joey's going to call back in twenty-five minutes. If I don't answer, Abby's dead. It's that simple. And if I do, and I say one word, the same thing. And you don't know what that word is. So give me back my gun, and let's forget this happened."

A surreal sense of detachment was settling over Will. "Remember when you said there was nothing I could do to you that hadn't been done before?"

She gave him a blank look. "Yeah?"

"You were wrong about that. Do you remember my presentation last night?"

She bit her lip as she thought back.

"Stand up," he said.

"Screw you."

He transferred the Walther to his left hand and grabbed her arm with his right. He was surprised to feel no pain. His brain had to be pumping out endorphins at five times the normal rate.

"Unhook my belt," he said.

"What?"

"Do it!"

She reached up and unfastened his belt.

"Pull it out."

"What?"

"The belt, damn it. Pull it out of the loops."

She did.

"Bring that chair over here." He pointed not at the French chaise he had been using, but at a straight-backed chair against the wall. "Put it here by the bed and sit down."

"Why?"

He slapped her face.

A bitterness beyond anything he'd ever seen came into her eyes. But with the bitterness came something else. Familiarity. This was a language she understood. She climbed off the bed, picked up the chair, and brought it back.

"Sit in it."

She did.

He put down the gun and wrapped the belt around her torso and the chair back, then buckled it. From the bathroom closet he took a terry-cloth robe belt and used it to tie her lower legs to the legs of the chair.

"I'm going to scream," she said.

"Go ahead. Scream your head off. Then you explain to Joe why he won't be getting his money in the morning."

"You're killing your kid," she said, as though talking to a man who had lost his reason. "Don't you get that?"

Will stood back and considered his handiwork. Screaming could become a problem, even if Cheryl didn't mean for it to. Fear was an unpredictable thing. He went into the other room and brought back a pair of socks with his sample case, then stuffed them into Cheryl's mouth. Her eyes went wide.

He dragged the chair against the bed, then bent and flipped Cheryl and the chair up onto the mattress. From there it was simple to rock the chair legs and move her to the middle of the bed. She lay with her legs molded in the shape of the chair, feet sticking into the air like a woman in stirrups.

"If you listened to my speech," he said, "you know a little about paralyzing muscle relaxants."

Cheryl looked confused. She probably hadn't listened to his program. She had been trying to seduce him with her eyes, all the time thinking about the moment when she'd have to pull the gun upstairs. Unless she could con him into taking her into his room in the hope of sex, which had probably been her original plan.

Will removed a vial of Anectine and a conventional syringe from his sample case. Cheryl's eyes locked onto the syringe as he popped off its cap, poked the needle through the rubber seal of the vial, and drew sixty milligrams of Anectine into the barrel. Many people had an irrational fear of needles. It was something you dealt with all the time in anesthesiology.

"This is succinylcholine," he said in a calm voice. "Shortly after I inject it, your skeletal muscles will cease to function. The skeletal muscles are the ones that move your bones. But your diaphragm is also made of skeletal muscle. So, while you'll be able to see, hear, and think normally, you won't be able to breathe. Or move."

There was more white than color showing in her eyes now.

"You don't have to go through this," he said. "All you have to do is tell me where Abby is, and I'll put this syringe back in the case."

She nodded frantically.

He leaned over and pulled the socks from her mouth. She gasped for air, then said, "I swear to God, I don't know! Please don't stick me with that!"

Will picked up the remote control and raised the volume of the television. The QVC huckster was selling "limited edition" china plates ("only 150 firing days!") bearing likenesses of Ronald and Nancy Reagan. As he shoved the socks back into Cheryl's mouth, she tried to bite his hand. He climbed onto the bed and sat on her rib cage. Her upraised thighs held his back like the back of a chair.

"You can scream," he said. "But the sound won't last five seconds after I stick you. Listen to me, Cheryl. I first saw this drug used as an intern. An ER doctor used it to restrain a crack addict who'd stabbed a cop in the emergency room. It was awful. I've seen murderers turned into whimpering babies by this stuff. They lay there paralyzed, soiling themselves, turning blue. Then you bag them and breathe for them, but the whole time they know that if you stop pumping that bag, their brain is going to shut off like a cheap lightbulb. It must be like being buried alive."

Cheryl fought the restraining belts like a madwoman, rocking Will and the chair in her attempt to get loose. He jabbed the point of the needle into her external jugular vein, and she stopped instantly.

"You have a choice. You can help me save my little girl. Or you can find out what it's like to be dead."

She closed her eyes, then opened them again. Tears ran from their corners down into her ears. *"I nono!"* she choked through the socks. *"I sweahta gaa!"*

"You know something."

She shook her head violently.

Will depressed the plunger of the syringe.

"Helll," Cheryl screamed. *"Someodeee—"*

The scream died in her throat. Her eyelids began to flutter, and her facial muscles twitched far too rapidly to be controlled by conscious thought. Her arms flew up and across her chest; then her body went rigid as the signals reaching its muscle fibers became a garbled storm of misfiring electrochemicals. The smell of human waste reached him, a common side effect of Anectine. It was all familar to Will, though the context was alien. He'd seen this happen to mice, pigs, rhesus monkeys, and homo sapiens, but always in a controlled environment. Cheryl's eyes were frozen open, filled with limitless horror.

He pulled the socks from her mouth, then climbed off her chest and sat beside her. "I know it's bad. Maybe you feel as scared as my little girl feels right now."

Cheryl lay as still as a stone angel on a grave. An angel with screaming eyes.

"We're going to do this over and over until you tell me where Abby is, so you'd do well to tell me everything as soon as you can."

Her face was going gray. He checked her fingernails for cyanosis. Hypoxia was taking its toll, and consciousness would soon wink out. In the time it took him to reach down to the sample case for a vial of Restorase, Cheryl's skin took on a bluish cast. Loading the contact syringes would take more time than he had, so he drew fifty milligrams into a conventional syringe and shot the drug into the antecubital vein at the crook of her elbow. Twenty seconds later, her eyelids fluttered. She blinked, and then her lacrimal glands began draining tears again.

"I didn't like doing that," he said. "But you forced me to. *Joe* forced me to." He patted her upper arm, then used his sleeve to wipe away her tears. "I know you don't want to go through it again. So, talk to me."

"You buh . . . bastard," Cheryl whispered. "You made me mess myself. You're *worse* than Joey. Worse than any of them!"

"Where's Abby, Cheryl?"

"I told you I don't know!"

"You know more than you're telling me. You couldn't have pulled this off five times before without knowing something. Where's the pickup? Where are you going to meet Joe to give him the money?"

"A motel," she said. "Near Brookhaven."

Brookhaven was fifty minutes south of Jackson.

"You see?" he said. "That's something I didn't know before. That's a good start. Keep talking."

"That's all I know."

"You know a lot more than that. What's the name of the motel?"

"The Truckers' Rest." She shook her head. "*Please* don't do it again. I'm begging you."

Will steeled himself against pity. She sounded like a child herself, a little girl begging not to be hurt by a monster. Was he a monster? Abby might be begging the same way right now, pleading not to be hurt. And that was partly the fault of the woman before him. An image came to him from somewhere, a man waiting in an airport for a defendant to be escorted through by deputies. He stood at a pay phone, pretending to talk, then drew a pistol from his coat, a pistol that had lain in a cabinet in his home for twenty years, waiting for the day when it would be used to kill a man who had molested a little boy. Will didn't know if he could commit murder out of revenge. But he could kill to prevent a murder. He could torture to spare his daughter pain.

With the coldness of a Nazi doctor he stuffed the socks back into Cheryl's mouth and injected her with seventy milligrams of Anectine. He looked straight into her eyes as her face began to twitch and her muscles turned to stone. The terror in them predated human consciousness by millions of years. It was like watching someone drown from six inches away. He loaded another dose of Restorase and watched Cheryl's fear race up an unimaginable scale, then slow and fade as her brain cells slowly starved of oxygen. She was blue when he shot the Restorase into her arm, and when she came out of the paralysis, her entire body was shivering.

"Where is Abby?" he asked. "Right this minute?"

Cheryl seemed to be trying to speak. He pulled the socks from her mouth.

"Wuh . . . *water,*" she croaked.

Will went to the sink and moistened a clean washcloth, then came back and squeezed a few drops into her mouth. "Careful."

"More," she begged, coughing violently.

He squeezed a few more drops from the cloth.

Deep sobs racked her chest. Cheryl had seen a glimpse of hell few people ever would, and the experience had shattered her.

"If I tell you anything," she said, "Joey will kill me."

"Joe is two hundred miles away. I'm right here. If you tell me where Abby is, the needle goes back into the case, and you can have all the money you need to start over somewhere else. Anyplace you want."

"You've forgotten something, Doctor. When Joey calls back, I can kill your kid with one word. And I think I'm going to, for what you did."

Will kept his face calm. "You don't want Abby to die.

I sensed that before, when we were talking about kids. About being pregnant."

She looked away.

"And you don't want to die yourself. If you kill Abby, you will. One way or another. It's one thing to talk about death, or to flirt with it when you're depressed. But you've got a taste of it now. And it's bad. Isn't it?"

She closed her eyes.

"You think that because nothing happened to the kids those other times, nothing will happen to Abby. But you're wrong. There's something different about this time. And Karen found out what it is. That's why she sent me that message. What is it, Cheryl? What's different about this time?"

"Nothing."

He reached out and pulled her chin over until she faced him. "Open your eyes and tell me why this time is different. Don't make me inject you again. To be honest, it's getting dangerous."

She opened her eyes. For the first time, he thought about their color. They were grayish blue, not the cornflower you expected to go with her hair. "Tell me," he said.

"You killed Joey's mother."

Will blinked. "What are you talking about?"

"Last year, Joey's mother died during an operation. The doctor who did the surgery told Joey it was your fault. He said you weren't paying attention. You weren't even in the room."

"What?" He thought back over the past year's cases. Some were clear, others a blur. He did about eight

hundred fifty a year, but he almost always remembered the deaths. "Was her name Hickey?"

"No. She'd remarried. Simpkins was her name."

"Simpkins . . . Simpkins?"

"Joey said you wouldn't remember it. That's how little it mattered to you. But it matters to him."

"I do remember! The SCD case."

"The what?"

"SCDs. Sequential compression devices. The surgeon operated without them, and Mrs. Simpkins developed a pulmonary embolus."

"Embolus," Cheryl said. "That's it. A blood clot."

"Viola Simpkins," Will said.

"That's her."

It was all coming back now. The surgeon had been a visiting professor, and the accident had caused a big rift between UMC and his institution. "I had nothing to do with that death. It was a terrible mistake, but it wasn't my responsibility."

"The surgeon told Joey it was."

"Well, I'll tell him it wasn't. I'll make the damn surgeon tell him."

"That might be tough. He's dead. Joey killed him."

Will suddenly felt cold. Hickey had murdered a surgeon because his mother died on an operating table? "Karen must have found this out," he thought aloud. "That's why she sent the message. And that's why Joe is going to kill Abby. To punish me."

"He never told me that," Cheryl insisted.

"Because he knew you might not go along." Will gripped her arms. "Cheryl, you've got to tell me where

Abby is. Joe's going to murder her. She's only five years old!"

She looked him dead in the eye. "I told you. *I—don't—know—where—she—is.*"

Will drew seventy milligrams of Anectine into the syringe and climbed back onto her chest. She began to fight beneath him.

"Please, *please*," she begged. "Don't do it!"

Streaks of blood marked the previous puncture sites on her neck and arm. Will moved the needle toward her neck and pressed it against her flesh.

"She's somewhere west of Hazlehurst!" Cheryl cried. "Do you know where that is?"

He kept the needle against her vein. "Where Highway 28 crosses I-55?"

She nodded violently. "That's it! There's a shack ten or fifteen miles up that road."

"Ten miles? Or fifteen?"

"I don't know! I've never been there. It's not on the main road. You go down two or three logging roads before you get to it."

"That's useless. There are a hundred logging roads through those woods. Hunting camps, everything."

"That's all I know! For Christ's sake, I'm trying to help you!"

"How is Joe calling Huey?"

"What?"

"Is Huey using a landline or a cell phone?"

"Cellular. There's no regular phone out there."

"What else?"

She shook her head. "That's all I know! I swear to God!"

Cheryl was exhausted, that was plain. But there was still a private knowledge in her eyes. Something she was holding back. He considered injecting her again, but he didn't really want to risk it. He had never put a human being through three consecutive cycles, and he needed her alive and cooperative for Hickey's next call. The important thing was to get a cellular trace started around Hazlehurst, if it was possible. He took the torn sheet of hotel stationery from his pocket and dialed Harley Ferris's number yet again.

"Are you going to leave me like this?" Cheryl asked.

"I'll untie you in a second." Ferris's phone rang four times. Then the answering machine began its spiel. Will had expected it, but even so, it was like someone slamming a door in his face at the moment he saw a way out. He hung up and redialed, taking care to enter every number correctly.

"Joey's going to be calling in a couple of minutes," Cheryl said.

Will's watch read three twenty-six a.m. By the time Ferris's phone began ringing, he was practically hyperventilating. Three rings. Four. The answering machine clicked and began speaking. Will's finger was on the DISCONNECT button when he heard a click, then a clatter.

"Hello?" said a male voice. "Hello! I'm here."

"Is this Harley Ferris?"

"Yes. Who's this?"

"Thank God. Mr. Ferris, this is Dr. Will Jennings. This is an emergency. I want you to listen very carefully."

"Oh my God. Oh no. Is it one of my kids?"

"No, sir. It's not your family. It's mine."

"What?"

"Do you remember me, Mr. Ferris? I was the anesthesiologist on your wife's gallbladder surgery. She requested me."

"I know you," Ferris said. "We played in that scramble at Annandale a few months back. But it's three-thirty in the morning, Doctor. What the hell's going on?"

"My daughter's in trouble. Desperate trouble. You can help her. But before I tell you anything, you've got to promise not to call the police."

"The police? I don't understand."

Will decided to go for broke. "Mr. Ferris, my daughter was kidnapped yesterday evening. I can't go to the police because the kidnappers will kill her if I do. Do you understand?"

There was a delay as Ferris processed this information. "I heard you," he said finally. "I'm not sure I understand you."

"I'm in a casino hotel in Biloxi right now. The Beau Rivage. My wife's at home in Annandale. One of the kidnappers is with her. My daughter is being held at a third location. Somewhere in the woods around Hazlehurst, Mississippi. Every thirty minutes, the leader of the kidnappers calls the location where my daughter's being held. I know they're using a CellStar telephone. You're the president of CellStar. Can you trace that call for me?"

"Not without a court order, I can't."

"My daughter will be dead long before anyone gets a court order."

"Jesus. Is this some sort of prank? Is this really Will Jennings?"

"I wish it were a joke. But it's not. On the soul of my daughter, it's not."

"Are both parties using cell phones?"

"The man on the receiving end is using one. There's no landline where he is. He's ten or fifteen miles west of Hazlehurst, down some logging road. That's all I know at this point."

"There's not much activity around there this time of night," Ferris said. "We've only got one tower down that way, an older one. Our coverage is pretty thin around there, to be honest. I'd have to get a vehicle down there to trace it, and I don't know where our vans are right now."

"Where could they be?"

"Anywhere in the state."

"How many do you have?"

"Two."

"Harley, if we don't find that phone, my five-year-old daughter will be dead by morning. Even if I pay the ransom."

"How much are they asking for?"

"Two hundred thousand."

"That doesn't seem like much."

"That's part of their plan. It's not really the money they want. They want to hurt me. Can you help?"

"Doctor, it sounds to me like we should call the FBI."

"No! They've thought of that. Planned for it."

"But for a job like this—"

"This isn't a job, Harley! This is my kid. Remember

how you felt when you thought I was calling because one of your kids was in a wreck? Think back two minutes."

More silence. "Goddamn it. Okay. I'll see what I can do."

"I need your word that you won't call the FBI. Your word of honor."

"I'll keep quiet until morning. But if I get a trace on that phone, we're calling in the FBI. Agreed?"

"You find that phone, I'll be begging for a SWAT team."

"Where are you now?"

"You have a pen?"

"Just a second. Okay, go ahead."

"I'm at the Beau Rivage Casino, suite 28021. Call as soon as you know anything, but not on the hour or half hour. That's when the kidnappers make their check-in calls. The next one's coming in less than two minutes."

"I can't do anything about that one, except maybe confirm that they're using the tower near Hazlehurst. I'll call as soon as I know something. Hang tough, Doctor. We'll figure something out."

"Thank you. Hey—why did you suddenly answer your phone?"

"My prostate," Ferris replied. "We don't keep a phone in the bedroom. I got up to take a leak and decided I was hungry. I heard the machine in the kitchen."

"Thank God you did. I'll talk to you soon."

Will hung up, his heart pounding. "Joe's going to call any second." He turned to Cheryl. "What are you going to tell him?"

"Wait and see, you son of a bitch. You'd better untie me."

Letting Cheryl answer Hickey's next call could be the biggest mistake he ever made. But he had no choice. He had crossed the Rubicon. There was no retreat now. He could hold the needle against Cheryl's neck as she answered, but instinct told him to show some faith. He reached out and unbuckled the belt that bound her chest.

"I don't think you want my little girl to die. You're not that far gone. You were a little girl once, too. Not so long ago, either."

She refused to look at him.

As he untied the terry-cloth belt that held her legs, the phone began to ring. The sound constricted Will's chest. "My daughter's life is in your hands. Help her, and anything I have is yours. All the money you'll ever need."

"You'd better answer that phone, Doctor."

He took a deep breath, then picked up the phone, handed it to Cheryl, and leaned down to listen.

"Yeah?" she said.

"Everything okay?" Hickey asked.

She looked at Will, her eyes inches away. As he tried to read them, an old memory flashed into his mind, the eyes of a secretary to a bank loan officer. She had kept him waiting for an hour even though she knew his loan application would be denied, reveling in the only power she would ever have over someone like him. Cheryl had a thousand times that power now. Would she exercise it to pay him back for the terror he'd forced her to endure?

"Yeah," she said finally. "Everything's cool."

He felt light-headed. He was squeezing her arm with gratitude when Hickey said, "What's the matter? You don't sound right."

The son of a bitch was clairvoyant.

Cheryl looked at Will. "I'm getting tired," she said.

"It's not too much longer now. Take one of the pills I gave you. I need you sharp."

"I know. I'll talk to you in a half hour."

Will heard the click as Hickey hung up. With shaking hands he took the phone from Cheryl and set it in its cradle. "Thank you," he said. "You just started earning your first million."

She scowled and rolled off the bed. "Fuck you very much. Now what?"

"Now we wait for the phone trace. And pray."

FOURTEEN

Huey Cotton sat on the floor in the front room of the cabin, whittling steadily. Behind him, Abby slept soundly on the sofa, the ratty horse blanket covering her body. She had been talking to Huey when exhaustion finally overcame her. She simply closed her eyes in midsentence and slipped down onto the cushions with her Belle Barbie in her left hand.

Huey had been whittling ever since.

He didn't always know what he was whittling. Sometimes he let his hands do the thinking for him. He'd found a good piece of cedar outside in the woodpile. He cut the firewood last fall, mostly oak, and while he was oiling his chain saw he'd spotted a young cedar that had been snapped off at the ground by a tornado. Cedar was good carving wood, and there wasn't a smell like it in the world. The chunk in his hands was starting to look something like a bear. Whatever it was, there was enough cedar left for something more to develop. His hands had never felt so good. His nervousness seemed to flow out through the knife blade and into the wood, and from the wood into the air, like power leaking from a car battery left on concrete.

Soon it would be morning, and he was glad. The quicker Joey got his money, the less chance there was that he would tell Huey to do something to Abby. Huey was glad she'd finally eaten some Cap'n Crunch. She was so hungry, and he had gobbled up what was left of the baloney and crackers long ago. Before the first bite, she'd asked if he knew what time her mother would be picking her up. Huey figured they would be at the McDonald's by ten in the morning, so he told her ten o'clock. A smile of relief appeared on her face, and she began chomping the cereal like birthday cake. She said her shot would hold her until ten, whatever that meant. She ate two full bowls before she was done, and even drank the leftover milk. Ten minutes later, her full stomach took its effect. Her eyes rolled up and she fell sound asleep. Huey smiled at the memory and kept peeling away slivers of cedar.

Will had set up his notebook computer on the circular dining table in the front room of the suite. He was composing an e-mail to Karen. He wanted to tell her about Ferris and the phone tracing, but he couldn't. What if Hickey came upon her while she was reading the message? For the same reason, he could not even hint at Cheryl's cooperation. If Hickey knew his wife had betrayed him, he might decide to cut his losses and run, which would almost certainly mean Abby's death.

He needed to tell her he understood her message and had taken action, but in a way that only she could understand. He needed a code. He searched his memory for some event in their past that might be applicable to the present situation, but there was nothing. It was too fantastic. But then it hit him. If their own lives did not contain a parallel he could use, other lives did. Lives on screen. He and Karen had watched thousands of movies together, some of them many times. It took him less than a minute to come up with a phrase he was sure she would understand. The message he typed was:

> **ABBY IS GOING TO MAKE IT. TRUST ME. DO YOU BELIEVE THE CONDOR IS AN ENDANGERED SPECIES?**

He could not help but smile. As cryptic as this phrase would appear to Hickey, he was sure Karen would understand it. She'd had a crush on Robert Redford for years.

"What are you typing?" Cheryl asked.

At Will's request, she lay on the sofa a few feet away, sipping from a can of Coke. She had complained when he asked her to stop drinking rum, but she seemed to realize that she needed to be clearheaded for whatever might happen in the next few hours. The question of why she seemed to be cooperating had occupied a great deal of Will's thoughts. Was it fear of more succinylcholine injections? Desire for the money he had promised, and the freedom it offered? Or had she come to believe that Hickey *did* mean to kill Abby, and wanted no part of it? The answer was probably a combination of all three, in proportions she herself did not understand.

Will plugged his Dell into the data port of the hotel

phone and logged on to AOL through their 800 number. His mailbox was empty. He sent the e-mail to Karen's screen name—*kjen39*—then logged off. Seconds after the program disconnected, the phone began to ring.

It was only four fifteen—halfway between the scheduled check-in calls. Will motioned for her to answer.

She picked up, said, "Yeah?" then handed the receiver to Will. He expected to hear the voice of Harley Ferris, but it was his answering service, making sure he'd gotten the pager message. The operator said something encouraging about "that little girl who needs the liver transplant." Assuming this was part of a cover story Karen had fabricated, Will made appropriate noises and hung up.

Almost immediately, the phone rang again.

"That has to be Ferris," he said, grabbing the receiver. "Will Jennings."

"Harley Ferris, Doctor. Our computers show a call just after four a.m., processed through the tower that serves the Hazlehurst area. It came from one of the landlines at your house."

Will's pulse kicked into hyperdrive. "Did you get any idea of the receiver's position?"

"No. Even if we'd had a tracing van there, it would have been tough. The call lasted less than fifteen seconds, and the phone was switched off afterward."

"What about the phone number? Do you have the name of the person who rented the phone?"

"Yes. But without police involvement, I can't do anything with it. I can't even tell it to you. I'm assuming it's an alias, but only the police could tell us that."

"I'm not asking you to give me the name, okay? But tell me this. Was it Joe Hickey?"

"No. Look, it's time to bring the FBI in on this. Our security people have good contacts with the local field office—"

"You gave me your word, Harley. Not until morning. What about your tracing vans? Where are they?"

"They're up in Tunica County, working with the state police on a fraud operation that involves casino employees."

Will gritted his teeth. Tunica County was practically Memphis. That meant a minimum of three hours before the vans could get to Jackson, much less Hazlehurst. "That's eight a.m. before they could even start tracing."

"Exactly. I told one crew to hit the road and come on, but you're right about the time. That's why—"

"No police. Could this equipment be flown down?"

"It's four-thirty in the morning!"

"I have pilot friends who'd get out of bed right now and go get it."

"Some of this gear is hardwired into the vans, Jennings. Listen . . . there's a guy who used to work for us, an engineer. He's retired, but he keeps his hand in. I'll give him a call. He's probably got enough equipment in his garage to do a trace from his truck."

Will's heart surged. "Do you think he would?"

"He's a good man. We're probably looking at an hour or more to get him and his equipment on site, but that beats the Tunica crew by a long shot."

"Does the FBI have the equipment you need?"

"I wish I could tell you they did, because I want you

to call them. But the fact is, when the Bureau needs cell phones traced in Mississippi, they call us."

"Damn it." Will tried to think logically, but fatigue was starting to take its toll. "You'd better call that engineer."

"Doctor," Ferris said in a compassionate voice, "You realize that we may not be able to trace this phone in time, even with a vehicle down there? If the calls don't run any longer than fifteen seconds, it's a crapshoot."

"We've got to try. It's our only option. You've got to trust me on that. My daughter's life depends on secrecy."

He gave Ferris the numbers of his answering service, the direct SkyTel line, and Cheryl's cell phone. "I should be here," he said, "but there's no telling what could happen before morning. Call me as soon as you know anything."

"I will," Ferris promised. "I hope God's paying attention tonight."

As Will hung up, he felt Cheryl's hand on his arm. Despite what he'd done to her earlier, she was watching him with empathy.

"Do you think Huey would really kill Abby?" he asked.

She bit her lip. "It's hard for me to imagine it. But if Joey pushed him hard enough . . . he might. He can't take pressure, you know? He sort of flips out, like Dustin Hoffman in the bathtub in *Rain Man*."

Will felt an enormous weight descend on his shoulders. If Ferris's people traced Huey's phone, they would have to be very careful about their next move. If they responded inappropriately, Abby could die simply because a mentally handicapped man lost control of himself for a few seconds.

"How are we supposed to get her back?" he asked. "I

mean, what did Joey tell you? After you and I pick up the ransom from the bank, what are you supposed to do?"

Cheryl hesitated, still fighting some internal battle. "I call Joey," she said finally. "Then we meet at the motel in Brookhaven."

"You're supposed to bring me along?"

"Yeah."

"Have you always brought the husband?"

She hesitated again.

"Cheryl—"

"No. This is the first time."

Will shook his head. "I told you this time is different. Joe thinks I killed his mother, and he wants to kill Karen and Abby in front of me."

"That's not it."

"Yes, it is. Only I can't believe he'd put himself, Abby, and the money in one place. If he does, he's vulnerable. He has to assume that I could torture the name of the motel out of you, which means the FBI could come down on that place like the wrath of God."

"It's the truth," she insisted. "The Truckers' Rest Motel, in Brookhaven."

"That may be what he told you. But that's not how it's supposed to go down. I've got to know where Abby is. You must know something more, Cheryl. *Think*."

She shook her head in exhaustion. "I think you should just pay Joey the money. That's the way to get your kid back. That's the way the other guys did it."

"I'm not the other guys." He picked up her Coke can and downed what was left for the caffeine. "I'm down for special treatment."

"I thought you didn't like gambling. Betting against Joey is like betting against the house."

Not with you up my sleeve, he thought. But he said, "It's that kind of thinking that keeps you where you are, Cheryl." He turned and arced the Coke can into the wastebasket from fifteen feet. "When everything's on the line, you've got to go for it."

Karen downloaded Will's e-mail at four twenty-five a.m. Getting into the study to check it wasn't difficult, because Hickey had finally passed out on the bed. The combination of Wild Turkey and the étouffée omelet had proved too much for him.

She stared at the message, trying to read between the lines. The first part was clear enough. Will had received her message and understood its meaning. He promised that Abby would make it and told Karen to trust him. But the next line stumped her. *Do you believe the condor is an endangered species?* It had to be some kind of code. Will had been worried that Hickey might see the message, so he had used something only she would understand. Or that he *thought* she would understand. Did "endangered species" refer to Abby? And what did a "condor" have to do with anything? A condor was a type of bird. A large bird. Could Will be referring to his airplane?

"Condor," she said softly. "Condor . . . condor."

And then she had it.

"Oh my God," she said, and a smile came to her face. "Condor" was Robert Redford's code name in the film *The Three Days of the Condor.* And the line "Do you believe the condor is an endangered species?" had been spoken over the phone by Redford to Max von Sydow, who played the assassin in the movie. But the significance for Karen was that the line marked the turning point in the film, when Redford turned the tables on the men trying to find and kill him. *That* was Will's message. He had somehow turned the tables on Hickey.

But how? What action could he have taken? Had he called the police? No. Not unless he had a way to keep Hickey thinking everything was still running according to plan. Tracing Huey's phone seemed the most likely option, since Will had mentioned it before. But without Abby keeping the line open, how could it be traced? Maybe he'd gotten some information from Hickey's wife. But why should she tell him anything? Had he threatened her? Bribed her? There was no way to know. She would have to do exactly what Will had told her to do. Trust him.

She hit DELETE and watched the message vanish, then looked at the clock on the study wall. She was going to have to wake Hickey to make his next check-in call. She didn't want to do it. Letting him sleep was clearly the best strategy for her own safety. But if he failed to make even one call, Abby could die. And if Will *did* have someone trying to trace Huey's cell phone, the man would have to actually switch the thing on and use it before he could be found.

Karen stood and began the long walk back to the bedroom.

Fifteen miles south of the Jennings house, Dr. James McDill and his wife sat on a leather couch in the office of the Special Agent-in-Charge of the Jackson field office of the FBI. His name was Frank Zwick, and McDill figured him for ex-Army, probably Intelligence or CID. A short, fit man in his late forties, Zwick spoke with the clipped cadence McDill remembered from certain officers in Vietnam. The SAC had been on and off the phone for the past half hour, talking to bank presidents, helicopter pilots, other SACs, and miscellaneous officials, constantly smoothing his too-black hair as he talked.

McDill's identification of Cheryl Lynn Tilly at the Jackson police station had precipitated a storm of FBI activity. After Agent Chalmers phoned Zwick, the SAC had summoned the McDills back to the Federal Building along with eight field agents. Now they all stood or sat around his spacious office, listening to Zwick arrange the logistics of his campaign over the phone. McDill could only hear one side of the conversations, but he didn't like the way the plan was shaping up. Suddenly, the phone clattered into its cradle and Zwick began addressing them.

"Here's where we stand. One: the ransom. Every bank within thirty miles of Biloxi is set to report incoming wire transfers greater than twenty-five thousand dollars to this office. Two: tactical capability. We don't have time to bring in a hostage rescue team from Quantico, so we'll use our own special weapons team. Some of you are on it, and I know you're more than capable of handling this operation. We're also coordinating a weapons team out of the New Orleans field office, for anything required on the Gulf Coast. We've got more than enough surveillance gear on site here, and we'll have twenty agents in this office by seven a.m., ready for action. We'll have twenty more out of New Orleans for surveillance duty in Biloxi. Three: air support. We'll have choppers both here and in Biloxi, ready for aerial surveillance and/or pursuit and assault." Zwick made a steeple of his fingers and looked each of his agents in the eye. "Questions?"

No one had any. Or no one wanted to voice what might be viewed as dissent by his SAC. McDill had several questions, but just as he was about to voice one, Agent Chalmers said, "Sir? I wonder if we're not jumping the gun a little on this."

"How do you mean?" Zwick asked, looking none too pleased by the question.

"Dr. McDill identified Cheryl Lynn Tilly from the JPD mug books. But that doesn't necessarily mean that the crime she took part in last year is actually being repeated this year. Does it?"

Zwick gave them a self-satisfied smile. He clearly knew something they didn't, and he could scarcely contain his excitement. "Gentlemen, ten minutes ago, our resident agent in Gulfport showed a faxed photo of Cheryl Lynn Tilly to a bellboy in the Beau Rivage Hotel. That bellboy is positive he saw Tilly in the hotel yesterday afternoon."

Every mouth in the room fell open.

"To quote Sir Arthur Conan Doyle—through the immortal voice of Sherlock Holmes—the game is afoot."

In that moment McDill had a premonition of disaster. It wasn't the quote itself. It was more the way Zwick had voiced it. And the context. At the core of all this frantic activity was a kidnapped child. A child who could die at any moment. And that took the situation about as far from a game as you could get.

"Our R.A. and that bellboy are reviewing the casino's security tapes as we speak," Zwick went on. "If they spot her, they'll do a video capture and e-mail it up here for Dr. McDill to look at. Until then, we have to assume that McDill is right. There is a kidnapping-for-ransom taking place. The same crime has been executed five times previously by the same group, and probably within this jurisdiction." Zwick laid his hands flat on the table. "Gentlemen, by tomorrow noon, those sons of bitches are going to be behind bars."

McDill held up his hand.

"Yes, Doctor?"

He tried to choose his words carefully. "Sir, after hearing all these preparations, I'm starting to wonder if the central fact of all this is being given the priority it should."

"What do you mean?"

"The kidnapped child. The hostage, as you call him. Or her. Somewhere not too far from here—if things are going as they did last year—a child is being held prisoner by a semiretarded man. That man is under instructions to kill the child if he doesn't get a check-in call from the leader of his group every half hour. Given that, it's difficult to see what you can accomplish with all this technology. Anything that alerts the leader to your presence could instantly result in the death of the child."

Zwick gave McDill a patronizing smile. "Are you suggesting we do nothing at all, Doctor?"

"No. I'm simply speaking for those who can't speak.

Right this minute, a father a lot like me is probably sitting in a room in the Beau Rivage, sweating bullets over his child. He wants to pick up the phone and call you, but he knows he can't. And he won't. For good reason. I hope you can put yourself in that man's place long enough to convince you to act with prudence."

Zwick's smile faded. "Doctor, I fully understand the complexities of this operation. But I wonder if you do. Had you and your wife reported the kidnapping of your son last year, that father you're talking about wouldn't be sweating bullets in that hotel right now. And the man behind this kidnapping would be rotting in federal prison."

Zwick looked as though he expected fireworks in response to this statement, but McDill simply sighed. "You may be right," he conceded. "But my son is alive today, and I can live with my decision. I hope that by this time tomorrow, you can say the same about yours."

The SAC's face went red, but before he could vent his anger, Agent Chalmers stood and said, "Doctor, why don't you come get some coffee with me?"

McDill took his wife's hand and rose from the sofa, but he didn't look away from Zwick as he walked to the door. He had looked away from too many officers in Vietnam, walked out of too many meetings without speaking his mind. At least tonight he would not have to feel the sickening regret he had felt then.

As he passed through the door, a chorus of voices broke into a spirited discussion of tactics and equipment. He squeezed Margaret's hand, but it was not his wife who filled his thoughts. It was that father trapped in the

Beau Rivage. McDill had never laid eyes on him, but he knew that man better than he knew his own brother.

By five fifty-six a.m., Will was close to cracking. A steady diet of hot tea and Coke had his hands shaking like a strung-out addict's, and his overtaxed mind was running in circles, like a greyhound chasing a fake rabbit. His efforts to locate Abby by tracing Huey's cell phone had come to nothing. Hickey's five o'clock check-in call had told Harley Ferris nothing new, because Ferris's retired engineer had not been close enough to Hazlehurst to do any good. But when five thirty ticked around, Will had his hopes up. Only the five thirty call never came.

He waited for ten minutes, but after that he could stand no more. For all he knew, Karen had somehow provoked Hickey into killing her. An acid lump clogged his throat as he dialed home. But when the phone was picked up, it was Karen's voice, not Hickey's, on the other end of the line.

The second she heard Will's voice, she began to sob. He was certain something must have happened to Abby, but Karen explained that her tears were simply a reaction to the stress. Hickey had missed the last check-in call because he'd passed out drunk in their bed.

"I woke him up for the five o'clock call," she said. "He told Huey he wouldn't be calling back for another hour at least. He said he had to sleep."

Hickey hadn't bothered to inform Cheryl of this change of plan. "What are you doing to help Abby?" Karen asked.

"I got Ferris. We're trying to trace Huey's phone. But if Hickey isn't calling him, we can't trace it."

"Maybe I should wake him up and tell him I have to talk to Abby."

"Do you think he'd let you?"

"Probably not. But what choice do we have?"

"Cheryl is helping us now. To a certain extent, anyway. I'll explain why later. But tell me why you think Hickey is planning to kill Abby."

"He thinks you killed his mother."

"That's what I got from Cheryl. Okay . . . I guess you'd better try to wake Hickey up."

There was a strange silence. Then Karen said, "Will, he tried to rape me."

A burning heat swept over Will's face, and the migraine that had receded after the torture session stabbed him behind the eyes.

"What happened?"

"It doesn't matter now," she said. "I cut him with a scalpel, and it stopped him. For the time being, anyway. But . . . I don't know what might happen before we leave the house. Will, if it comes to a choice between enduring that and Abby dying, I can force myself to live with it. But can you?"

He sat in the hissing silence, feeling more hatred for one human being than he had ever dreamed possible. If he came face-to-face with Hickey, he would kill the man without hesitation. But that wouldn't help Karen now.

"Karen . . . I know things haven't been what they used to be for us. I'm not sure why. I know it has to do with your leaving medical school."

"Oh *God*," she said in a hysterical voice. "At this point

that sounds so petty and ridiculous. But you're right. And all I care about in this moment is getting my baby back."

"We're going to get her back. I swear that to you. And whatever choices you have to make to stay alive, or to keep Abby alive, I can live with. Nothing you could ever do would change the fact that I love you. *Nothing.* I just hope you can forgive me for letting this happen."

Her reply was too choked for him to understand, but he thought he heard *". . . not your fault"* in there.

"Let Hickey sleep until six," he said, not wanting her anywhere close to the man now. "But if he hasn't made another call by then, you'll have to get him up and on the phone to Huey. Throw a fit. Tell him you won't wire the money unless you have proof that Abby's okay."

"I will."

They sat in silence for another few moments; then Karen whispered good-bye and clicked off.

Now it was six, and still the telephone was silent. Had Karen tried to wake Hickey? Was she trying now? Or had she succeeded, only to find herself having to submit to him to keep Abby alive?

The black sky over the gulf had changed imperceptibly to indigo. Dawn would soon break over the shrimp boats and the deep-sea fishermen heading out past the barrier islands. Will could almost see the Western hemisphere whirling eastward into the sun, like some cutting-edge CNN commercial filmed by Stanley Kubrick. Only Kubrick was dead now. And if Hickey didn't start making his check-in calls again, Abby might soon be, too.

The ringing telephone stopped his breath in his throat. He darted over to the sofa and prodded Cheryl, who was snoring softly. She rubbed her eyes, picked up the phone, then nodded to indicate that it was Hickey on the phone. She said her usual "Everything's cool," then signed off. Her eyes had the dull sheen of sleep deprivation. Will looked back at her without speaking, and in a few seconds her eyes closed.

Two minutes later, the phone rang again.

Like an automaton, Cheryl stirred and started to answer, but Will grabbed the receiver first. "Hello?"

"Harley Ferris, Will."

"What have you got?"

"The Hazlehurst target switched on his cell phone just before six. The subject in your house made a landline call that went through the Hazlehurst tower just after six. The call lasted sixteen seconds, and the trace target switched off his phone immediately after the call."

"Where do we stand?"

"My man down there has narrowed the search area to about seven square miles."

"I had that before I called you!"

"No, you didn't. You said ten or fifteen miles west of Hazelhurst, on a logging road. That could describe an area as large as twenty-five square miles."

Will groaned and rubbed his forehead. "I'm sorry. I'm going crazy here. You haven't notified anyone official, have you?"

"No. But it's long past time we did."

"Not yet. Please, not yet."

"These are very short calls, Doctor. We're looking at a minimum tracing time of an hour from now. And that's if the subject keeps making these check-in calls on the half hour. What if he skips another one? What if he skips two?"

God forbid. "Calling the FBI has to be my decision, Harley. We've still got some time. There's nothing the FBI could be doing right now that we can't. You have all my numbers."

"I hope you know what you're doing."

"I hope so, too."

He hung up and sat beside Cheryl on the sofa. She slept with her mouth open, and her snores were as regular as a metronome.

"Wake up," he said.

She opened her eyes but didn't turn her head.

"I don't think Joe would kill Abby or Karen until he knew he had his money. Do you agree?"

She swallowed like someone with a bad case of cottonmouth, then nodded and closed her eyes again. So much for reassurances. Will got up and walked back to the window.

Dawn was coming, a lighter blue hovering in the indigo, far to his left. What he had taken for pale cloud formations was actually the diffuse light of the sun making its way between much darker clouds, and the narrow strip of beach he had watched all night was resolving itself into a thin, rocky breakwater. There was no beach here. The gulf's waves actually spent themselves against the marina beneath the casino.

"Think with your head, Joe," he said softly. "Not your heart. Think about the money, not your mother. The money's what you want. The money . . ."

FIFTEEN

Karen felt hands on her body and screamed.

"Shut up!" snapped a male voice. "It's time to get up."

She blinked her eyes and saw Hickey leaning over her. He was shaking her shoulders. "What happened?" she asked, trying to collect her thoughts.

"You fell asleep."

Two facts registered with frightful impact. First, Hickey was dressed. Second, daylight was streaming through the bedroom curtains. "God, no," she breathed, unable to accept the idea that she'd fallen asleep while Abby's life was in jeopardy. But she had. "What time is it?"

"Time to shower and doll yourself up for the Man. Fix your face."

Her eyes went to the digital clock on her bedside table. Eight oh two a.m. Two hours had passed since she last woke Hickey for a check-in call. What had happened in the interim? If Will had succeeded in finding Abby,

Hickey wouldn't be standing here telling her to shower and get dressed.

"Is it time to get Abby?"

"You mean, get the money. Play your part right, *then* you get Abby back."

"Is she all right?"

"She's still asleep. I just talked to Huey." Hickey turned and walked into the bathroom.

Karen heard the shower go on. If Hickey had just talked to his cousin, that should have given Will's friend a chance to trace the call.

"Get a move on," Hickey said, emerging from the bathroom. He was wearing the same khakis and Ralph Lauren polo shirt he'd worn yesterday. He didn't look any more natural in the outfit today. "I'm going to make coffee."

"Could I talk to Abby on the phone? Would you call her for me?"

He shook his head. "You'd only upset her more. You'll see her soon enough."

Before he reached the door, Karen said, "May I speak to you for a minute?"

He stopped and turned back to her.

"I know what's supposed to happen today," she said. "I know . . . what you want to do."

He looked intrigued. "What's that?"

"You want to hurt Will. Because of your mother."

His eyes went cold.

"I understand that anger," she said quickly. "And I'm not going to try to convince you that you're wrong about Will, even though I believe you are. You think you're right, and that's all that matters."

"You got that right."

She gathered the full measure of her feelings into her voice. "All I'm asking you to do—no, *begging* you to do—is to take pity on a five-year-old girl. Use me instead."

Hickey's eyes narrowed. "Use you?"

"To punish Will. Kill me instead of Abby."

Again she saw the disturbance in the dark wells of his eyes, as though eels were roiling in the fluid there.

"You've got sand," he said. "Don't you, Mom? You really mean that."

"Yes." It was the truest thing she had ever said. If by dying she could guarantee that Abby would grow into a woman, marry, and bear her own children—or at least have that chance—then she would die. Gladly. "I think your mother would have done the same for you."

Hickey's cheek twitched, but Karen's honesty seemed to overcome whatever anger she had caused in him. They had entered the realm of truth, and offense was beside the point.

"She would have," he said. "But you don't have to. Nobody's going to die today. Let me tell you a little secret. This is the last job I'll ever pull. In a few days, I'll be in Costa Rica. A rich expatriate, like Hemingway and Ronnie Biggs."

Ronnie Biggs? "Who's Ronnie Biggs?"

"One of the great train robbers. You know, from England." Hickey looked toward the window. "Maybe that was before your time. Biggs planned a perfect crime, just like me. And he got away with it, just like me. I've got away with it five times. And today is my grand exit."

Karen felt a sudden ray of hope, like a light blinking

on in her soul. Maybe she'd read Hickey wrong. Maybe he thought twenty-four hours of hell was enough punishment. Or perhaps, deep down, he knew that his mother's death had not been Will's fault.

"Take that shower and get some nice clothes on," he said. "You've got to put on a good show for your broker this morning. Davidson gets to his office at eight-thirty. You'll call him at a quarter to nine. Then we'll drive over and you'll sign off on the wire."

"What exactly am I going to tell him?"

"I've got it all laid out for you. Just get in the shower." He chuckled. "Or do you need me to help you?"

"I can manage."

"That's what I figured."

As she walked toward the bathroom, she spied a small but fresh bloodstain on Hickey's khakis, just above the knee. "You'd better wrap that leg again," she told him. "There's more gauze in the cabinet under the kitchen sink."

He looked down at the blood and grinned. "Guess I've got a new angle on safe sex, don't I?"

His sudden levity disoriented her. There seemed no reason for it, at least none she could fathom. Maybe the impending collection of the ransom had lightened his mood. His fantasy future in Costa Rica.

She paused by the bathroom door. "Why Costa Rica?"

"No extradition to the U.S."

"Oh. Of course."

"I've got some land down there. A ranch."

Hickey looked about as much like a rancher as Redford and Newman had in *Butch Cassidy and the Sundance Kid*.

For them the pipe dream had been Bolivia. Karen looked over at the clock again, wondering what had become of Will's efforts to trace Huey's cell phone. Had it all come to nothing? Or was a host of FBI agents even now preparing to crash into the cabin where Abby was being held?

"Get your ass in gear," Hickey said. "We've got less than an hour."

She walked into the bathroom, her limbs heavy from truncated sleep. The events of the next few hours had passed beyond her control. Possibly beyond anyone's. It was like your water breaking at the end of pregnancy. That baby was going to come, and there wasn't a damn thing anyone could do to stop it, short of killing you.

Will stood at the sitting room window, wishing for a balcony. The stink of old eggs drifted from the room-service tray Cheryl had ordered. All Will had managed to get down was some tea and a biscuit, but she had eaten a massive breakfast, dubbed the "Natchez Plate" by the Beau Rivage marketing people. He wondered briefly if repeated cycles of Anectine and Restorase had a stimulating effect on the appetite.

The sun was shining full on the water now, turning the brown waves silver in its glare. Hickey's last check-in call had come three minutes ago—exactly eight o'clock—after which Cheryl had informed Will that they would be leaving for the Biloxi branch of the Magnolia Federal Bank within the hour. Harley Ferris had not yet reported in, but Will still held out hope. CellStar's first-string tracing team had reached Hazlehurst at seven fifteen a.m., but Hickey had skipped the seven-thirty check-in call making pointless the crew's hell-for-leather ride from Tunica County. But at least they'd been on station for the eight a.m. call—if Hickey had made one to Huey, and not just to Cheryl.

Any second the phone would ring, and Ferris would tell him one of two things: they had pinpointed Huey's position, or they had not. If they hadn't, Will had a decision to make. Should he call the FBI and try to convince them to start a search of the woods around Hazlehurst? Or should he pretend to play out the endgame according to Hickey's rules, withdraw all the money he could get from Magnolia Federal, give it to Cheryl to keep her cooperating, and be wearing her gun when he came face-to-face with Hickey? After the nightmares of Waco and Ruby Ridge, it was too easy to envision disaster resulting from calling in the FBI. An armed search team might panic Huey into killing Abby, perhaps even unintentionally. But the alternative was hardly more appealing. There was no guarantee that Will and Hickey would ever come face-to-face. Once Hickey knew Cheryl had the ransom, he could simply order his cousin to kill Abby and flee.

The ring of the telephone floated through the spacious sitting room. Will said a silent prayer, then walked over to the end table by the sofa and picked up the phone.

"Hello?"

"Will, it's Harley Ferris. We didn't get it."

Will stood motionless, not speaking or even thinking, the way some people reacted to the news that an emergency room X-ray had turned up lung cancer. As if by not making any move at all they could stop the terrible reality rushing toward them with the implacable indifference of a tidal wave.

"Why not?" he asked. "What happened?"

"The calls are just too short. We're very close in absolute terms, but we're talking about undeveloped land. Thick Mississippi woods. Waist-high underbrush. As far as the logging road you mentioned, there are dozens cut through there, all turning back on each other. And there are a hundred shacks in those woods."

Will could imagine it all too easily: typical Mississippi backcountry.

"Doctor, what we need now is a battalion of national guardsmen to line up shoulder to shoulder and march through those woods. And an FBI Hostage Rescue Team to bring out your little girl after the guardsmen find the place."

Will put his hand over his eyes. It would take hours to organize that kind of search. Karen would be sending the ransom wire in less than an hour. Abby's captor would almost certainly leave the cabin before then, to meet Hickey at some prearranged rendezvous. Hopefully, he would be taking Abby with him. They might have left already, Will realized, just after Hickey's last check-in call.

"Doctor?" Ferris prodded.

"I'm thinking." The only assumption Will felt comfortable making was that Hickey would keep Abby alive until he was sure he had the ransom money. He wanted revenge, but there was no reason to risk losing two hundred thousand dollars when it was an hour from being in his possession. And if he killed Abby too soon, he would lose leverage he might need if Karen or Will balked at the last minute.

Maybe that's the only card I have left, Will thought. *Hesitate at every step until I get confirmation that Abby's alive.* It would be a game of chicken. Hickey could order Huey to hurt Abby in order to force Will to proceed, but he couldn't tell Huey to kill her. Not if he wanted the money.

"Doctor?" Ferris snapped. "I've got to say this. I don't believe you're thinking rationally."

"Keep your tracing team on the job, Harley. I'm going to get them another shot at that trace."

"How?"

"Just tell them to keep their eyes and ears on their screens."

"What about the FBI?"

Will ground his teeth and looked out at the gulf. The cool air that had settled over the land during the night was taking on the yellow density of a Mississippi summer morning, as the sun baked it and sent it skyward again. *Skyward . . .*

"My God," he breathed. "Cheryl!"

"What?" Ferris asked.

Cheryl came to the wide door that divided the sitting room of the suite from its bedroom. All she wore was a towel on her head.

"What's the matter?" she asked.

"What kind of car does Huey drive?"

"An old pickup truck."

"What make? What color?"

"Last time I saw it, it was baby-shit brown. Which is

green, I guess. With lots of primer on it. It's one of those old Chevys. You know, with the the rounded cab."

"Listen to me, Harley. If you'll make me a promise, you can call the FBI."

"I'm tired of your conditions. I already regret—"

"She's my daughter!" Will shouted, blood pounding in his temples. "I'm sorry. You've already done more than I had any right to expect. But I've just learned what type of vehicle the guy in Hazlehurst is driving. And the sun is up now. If the FBI could get a chopper up over that area, they might be able to find it pretty quick."

"You're damn right they could!" Ferris cried. "And if they can't, the state police can. They can put out a statewide APB for the vehicle, too. If that guy tries to move with your little girl, they'll be on him like you know what."

"No state police. Highway patrolmen aren't anywhere close to trained for something like this. A hostage standoff with a five-year-old? It's got to be the FBI. A chopper out of Jackson could be on station fifteen minutes after takeoff." Will was excited, too, but he knew the realities. ER work in small towns had taught him that while helicopters were much faster than ground vehicles, the time required to prep them for flight often meant that conventional ambulance runs were faster, even over distances of eighty or ninety miles. But Ferris's enthusiasm knew no bounds.

"I'll handle everything," he said. "I'm so goddamn relieved. You just leave it to me."

"The FBI is going to ask you a hundred questions about me. You can't answer them. That's my condition.

You can't even give them my name. If you do, they'll have someone out at my house in ten minutes, and that could get my daughter killed."

"Damn it—"

"The kidnapper is at my house right now, Harley. He can kill Abby with one phone call. The FBI's job is to find that vehicle and that cabin. That's it. In ninety minutes you can tell them all you know, but for now, nothing. Just the vehicle."

"Jennings—"

"Don't give them my phone numbers, either. If they called at the wrong time, that could get Abby killed, too. If I think of something that can help them, I'll call you and you relay it. Understood?"

"I don't like it. But I understand."

"Use your head, Harley. Before every step you take, remind yourself that there's a five-year-old girl out there, scared out of her mind."

"I've got two of my own. College age now, but I remember what it's like."

"Good. And tell the FBI to put a paramedic in that chopper. With insulin. My daughter's a juvenile diabetic."

"Jesus. Insulin, I've got it. Well . . . I'd better make that call. Godspeed, boy."

"Harley?"

"What?"

"You don't want to know what kind of vehicle they should be looking for?"

"Shit, I forgot. What is it?"

"A green Chevy pickup with lots of primer on it. The old kind, with rounded cab."

"Got it. I'll talk to you soon."

Will heard the click as Ferris disconnected.

Cheryl was still standing in the door, but at least she had wrapped the towel around her torso. Will saw the bruises on her neck and arm, where he had injected her during the night.

"How do you feel?"

"Like I woke up with the flu," she said. "My bones ache, and all my muscles are twitching."

"That'll pass."

She cinched the towel tighter around her breasts. "Um . . . there's something I didn't tell you."

A shiver of premonition went through him. "What?"

"This is the last job. Joey's last kidnapping."

"He said that?"

"Uh-huh. He's been talking about it all year. He's had his money in the stock market a long time, and he bought some land down in Costa Rica. He's never been there, but he says it's a ranch. A Spanish ranch. Like zillions of acres with gauchos and stuff. For a while I thought it was, you know, bullshit. But I think maybe it's real."

She had held back more than he thought. But this new information only confirmed what Will had thought all along. This kidnapping was different from all the others. Hickey meant to kill Abby—and possibly Karen and himself—then vanish for good.

"You calling in the cops?" Cheryl asked.

"Not exactly."

"Are we still going to pick up the money?"

"Absolutely. And it's all yours."

She looked skeptical. "Once we get it . . . are you going to let me go?"

He ran his hands through his hair. "I need you to bluff Joe a bit longer. Over the phone, you know. Like we have been. Just long enough to get Abby."

"I'm dead," she said in a toneless voice.

"No, you're not. Hang with me, Cheryl."

She covered her eyes with a shaking hand. Fear and exhaustion had brought her to the point of despair. Will could almost read her mind. In some corner of her brain she was thinking she should pick up the phone and warn Hickey. That if she told him what Will was up to, he might forgive her and call the whole thing off before everything came apart.

"Cheryl, you've got to think straight right now. I'm going to do everything I can to help you. If you somehow wind up in police custody, I'll testify on your behalf. I swear it. But you can't save Joe. It's gone past that. I know you still feel loyalty to him. But if you try to warn him, I'll have no choice but to tell him everything you've told me. He'll know I could only have gotten it from you."

Her face closed into a bitter mask, like the face of a woman from some impoverished Appalachian hollow. "I'll tell him you tortured it out of me with those goddamn drugs."

"If anything spooks Joe now, he'll tell Huey to kill Abby, and then he'll run. But you won't get out of this room. The only place you'll go will be death row in Parchman. You'll spend ten years rotting there while you go through all your appeals. Shitty food, no drugs, no life. And then—"

"Shut up, okay? Just shut up!" Tears welled in her red-rimmed eyes. "I see I got no place to go. I never have."

"But you do. If you can keep it together for another hour, you'll get enough money to become anybody you want to be. To get free and clear for the first time in your life."

Cheryl turned and walked back into the bedroom. Before she was out of earshot, Will heard her say, "Nobody's free and clear, Doc. Nobody."

Dr. McDill accepted the magnifying glass that Special Agent-in-Charge Zwick offered him and leaned down over the photograph on the desk. It was a black-and-white high-resolution digital still, captured from videotape shot by a security camera at the Beau Rivage Casino on the previous day. A time/date stamp in the corner read: 16-22:21. Four twenty-two in the afternoon. That particular camera had been covering one of the blackjack tables at the time. The shooting angle was downward from behind the dealer, which yielded a perfect shot of the blonde in the slinky black dress standing over the king of diamonds and six of hearts.

"Is it her?" Zwick asked.

"No doubt about it."

McDill put down the magnifying glass and looked back at his wife, who was sitting on Zwick's sofa with her legs close together. The emotions running through him were intense enough to make his eyes sting. "I was right," he said. "It's happening again. Right this minute, another family is going through the same hell we did." He walked over to Margaret, sat beside her, and took her hand. "We did the right thing. Thank you for coming with me. I know how difficult it was."

She looked as shell-shocked as a war refugee. He needed to get her home.

"Has Agent Chalmers seen that picture?" he asked. McDill hadn't seen Chalmers in the past couple of hours. There were so many people moving in and out of the office now that it was hard to keep up with anybody.

"Chalmers is in the field," Zwick replied. He was already behind his desk, dialing the telephone.

"Oh my God," McDill cried, slapping his forehead like one of the Three Stooges.

"What is it?" Zwick pressed the phone to his chest.

"I'm scheduled to do a triple bypass in a half hour. My surgical team is probably calling the police right now."

"Would you like an agent to drive you to the hospital? We can have a female agent take Mrs. McDill home."

"I can't operate. I haven't slept in over twenty-four hours. May I use your phone?"

"Of course. There's another line just outside."

As McDill approached the door, a young woman burst into the room.

Zwick glared at her. "I assume you have a good reason for this interruption, Agent Perry?"

The female agent nodded, her eyes flashing with excitement. "There's a man on the main line asking for the Special Agent-in-Charge."

"Who is it?"

"Harley Ferris."

Zwick turned up his palms. "Who the hell is Harley Ferris?"

"The president of CellStar. And he says he's got to talk to the SAC about a kidnapping in progress."

The blood drained from Zwick's face.

Huey Cotton was sitting on the porch steps of the cabin, using the point of his knife to put the finishing touches on his carving. When his cell phone rang, he put down the cedar and picked up the phone.

"Joey?"

"How you feeling, boy?"

"Okay." Huey looked past the old Rambler to the line of trees. It stayed dark longer in the woods. He liked the way the light pushed down through the limbs in arrow-straight shafts, the way it did in churches. "I guess."

"What's wrong?"

"I heard something a minute ago."

"What was it?"

"A motor."

"Where? In the woods?"

"In the sky. I think it was a helicopter."

Hickey said nothing for a few moments. Then, "It's probably the Forest Service. You just heard it once?"

"No. Back and forth, like a buzzard circling."

"Is that right. Well . . . you remember the backup plan we talked about?"

Huey reached down and picked a roly-poly from the dirt below the bottom step, delighting in the way its gray segmented body curled up in the palm of his hand. "I remember."

"It's time to start thinking about that."

He felt a twinge of fear. "Right this red-hot minute?"

"Not quite. But you be ready. I'll call you."

"Okay."

"How's the kid?"

"She's nice. Real nice."

"That's not what I mean. Is she still asleep?"

"Uh-huh."

"Maybe you better wake her up."

"Okay." Huey heard the gurgling sound of the commode from inside. "She already woke up."

"Okay. I'll call you soon. Stay ready. And keep listening for that helicopter."

"I will. Are there bad people up in the sky?"

"Nobody to worry about. You just get ready."

"Okay." Huey hit END, then set the roly-poly carefully on the ground and stood to the accompaniment of creaking steps and knee cartilage. When he turned, he saw Abby standing in the cabin door. Her face was pale, her eyes crusted with sleep.

"I don't feel good," she said.

Huey's face felt hot. "What's the matter?"

"My head hurts. And my tootie feels funny."

Confusion and fear blurred his vision. "Your what?"

"Where I tee-tee. It feels funny. Something's not right."

"What should we do?"

"I need my mom. I think I need my shot."

Huey cringed at the memory of last night's terrifying injection scene. "Soon," he promised. "It won't be long now."

SIXTEEN

Karen stood in the kitchen with the cordless phone in her hand, listening to "hold" music that sounded like George Winston on sleeping pills. She was dressed in a navy Liz Claiborne skirt suit with a cream blouse, and her face was made up to cover the bruises she'd sustained during the night. At Hickey's insistence, she had even curled her hair. She had the feeling he was molding her to fit some ridiculous idea he had of the suburban yuppie wife. But no makeup was going to hide the hunted look in her eyes.

"Still on hold?" Hickey asked. He was sitting at the kitchen table, his sutured leg propped on its tile surface.

"Gray's getting something from his car."

Gray Davidson was one of the founding partners of Klein Davidson, an independent brokerage firm that handled most of the money in the wealthy suburbs north of Jackson. Karen and Will went to parties at Davidson's home two or three times a year.

"You're not going to listen in?" she asked.

Hickey shook his head. "Just stick to the script."

"Karen?" said a male voice. "It's Gray. Sorry you had to wait."

"That's all right. I know it's early. Did you get a call from Will a few minutes ago?"

"Did I ever. Two hundred grand for a sculpture. That's kind of steep, even for Will."

"It's a very important piece. But I should have gone to that convention with him. I'd have kept him at the outlet mall, instead of on his little art hunts."

When Davidson spoke again, his voice changed subtly. "Do you feel all right with this, Karen?"

"What do you mean?"

"Well, it seems odd, is all. I don't like that this guy selling the sculpture is in such a hurry for his money. Will says it's a competitive bidding situation. A New York art dealer discovered the piece three days ago in a workshop at an estate sale. He doesn't think Walter Anderson is any great shakes, so he took Will's bid, but he claims he's flying back to New York today and he wants cash."

"That sounds like an art dealer."

"But why can't we just wire the money to his account? Why does he want cash?"

"Art dealers are crazy, Gray. They carry sacks of cash all over the place. Didn't you know that?"

"All I know is that most of them are gay and all of them are crooked. There's something else. Three weeks ago, Will got nervous about the market. He sold some stock and transferred the money to various banks. He put a hundred and fifty thousand into Magnolia Federal.

He could go to any branch in the state and withdraw most of the two hundred thousand he needs. Including Biloxi."

Karen faltered for a moment, confused. Will hadn't mentioned anything about this. "Did you tell him that?"

"Yes. He said he put the money into CDs, so there would be penalties for an early cash-out. He's got two hundred thousand liquid here in his tax-free instruments trust account. No penalty for spending that."

"I'm sure that's it."

"I guess so." Davidson waited for her to say something more. When she didn't, he said, "I guess I just hate seeing that much money leave my computer in a single morning."

She forced herself to laugh. "Now, that I believe. I'll be down to sign for it in half an hour."

"Look forward to seeing you. You bringing Abby?"

She closed her eyes. Davidson was a world-class schmoozer; he knew the names of every child of every client, and it showed in his company's annual profits.

"Abby's with Will's mother today, in the Delta."

"I know she loves that. Sorry I'll miss her. Come on down."

"Bye." Karen hung up.

Hickey's chair creaked as he slid his leg off the table. "What was that part in the middle?"

"What?"

"When you said, 'What do you mean?' "

"He asked if I was all right with Will spending that much money."

"But then you said, 'Did you tell him that?' "

For some reason, Karen didn't want to mention the money in Magnolia Federal. "He said it was odd, the seller wanting cash."

"Then you said, 'I'm sure that's it.' What was that?"

When she hesitated, Hickey stepped forward and took hold of her arm. "What was it?"

"He said the guy was probably only going to report half the sale price to the IRS. That's why he wanted cash."

Hickey stared coldly at her as he analyzed her explanation. The levity he'd displayed before was gone. She suddenly wished she had Will's pistol, but Hickey was wearing it in the small of his back.

"Get your purse," he said.

She took her purse from the counter, then opened the refrigerator.

"You don't have time for breakfast."

She took two vials of insulin and some syringes from the top shelf and put them in her purse. "I want this with me in case Abby's in trouble. You have a problem with that?"

A strange light flickered in Hickey's eyes. "No problem. I told you nobody was going to die today."

"I'm glad to hear it."

"Let's go. We'll take the Expedition."

Karen picked up her keys and led the way through the pantry and laundry room to the garage. Hickey limped after her. His leg was probably burning like fire. She hoped it was infected.

She hit the UNLOCK button on her key ring, then the garage door opener on the wall. She had the Expedition cranked and in gear by the time Hickey got into the passenger seat. The pneumatic suspension hummed as it adjusted to their weight, and as soon as the garage door retracted to sufficient height, she started backing up.

"Easy," Hickey said, laying a hand on her arm. "You're going to have a wreck before we even hit the interstate."

As Karen pulled her arm away, Stephanie Morgan's white Lexus crested the top of the hill and blocked her access to the drive. She hit the brakes with a screech.

"Shit."

"Who is it?" Hickey was already reaching for the gun.

Karen grabbed his wrist. "It's Stephanie Morgan, the same woman as yesterday."

"What does she want now?"

"Something about the flower show, I'm sure. I'll get rid of her."

"You do that." He rolled down his window so that he could hear whatever transpired.

Karen got out and started toward the Lexus. Stephanie was already walking toward her, dressed more like a woman going to a cocktail party than to a weekend of volunteer work.

"I just came from the Coliseum," she said in a tart voice. "I didn't call because I knew you'd try to blow me off."

"What is it, Stephanie?"

"The same as yesterday! Only worse. The cattle show people swore they'd be out by this morning and that the whole place would be cleaned up by noon."

"And?" Karen looked past her, trying to see if either of her kids were in the car. The Lexus looked empty.

"And some *redneck* has got a pen of calves sitting in the middle of the Coliseum floor. There's hay and cow manure all over the place!"

"Calm down, Steph. It can't be that bad."

"There's cow shit all over the floor, Karen. I don't think that's going to work wonders for a flower show. You've got to come down and light a fire under those people. They just won't take me seriously."

Karen found that easy to believe. "I can't come yet, Stephanie. My cousin's in the car, and he's got a plane to catch. I'll get there as soon as I can. You'll just have to handle it until then."

"I *can't* handle it. I'm maxed out on Zoloft, and even that's not doing any good. Oh, and I left out the best part. The moving company we contracted to bring in the exhibit tables double-booked this weekend. We have no tables, Karen. *No tables.*"

Karen tried to look concerned, but she could hardly believe that yesterday she would have given a damn about exhibit tables, flowers, or even cow shit. She had to get Stephanie Morgan off her property and out of harm's way.

"Listen to me, Steph. Get on the phone and call the football coach at Jackson Academy. His name's Jim Rizzi. Tell him you've got a summer project for his football team and you'll pay real money. Tell him to get as many players he can down to the convention center with a couple of pickup trucks. Those high school boys can move those tables in half the time it would take a moving company. Okay?"

Stephanie seemed shocked by the simplicity of this solution. "Karen, that's fantastic. But I don't know Rizzi at all. And I'm no good at asking people stuff like that. And what about the cows?"

Karen wanted to scream, *Who takes you to the bathroom and wipes your behind for you, Stephanie?* But the sound of the Expedition's door stopped her cold. She turned and saw Hickey walking toward them, a concerned look on his face.

"Everything okay?" he asked.

"Oh, hello again, Mr. Hickey," Stephanie said with a Teflon smile. "I'm sorry to hold you up."

"Call me Joe, please."

Karen interposed herself between them. "I told her we have to get right to the airport."

Hickey looked puzzled; then he smiled. "We *are* late for my flight. They make you check in so early now."

Stephanie's eyes went wide. "I've got it! *I* can run you out to the airport. That way Karen can get right over to the Coliseum. Things are absolutely falling apart over there. You wouldn't believe it."

"No," Karen said quickly. "Joe and I still have some talking to do. The estate things. I told you last night. It can't wait."

Hickey looked amused by Karen's fabrication, but Stephanie's face darkened, and her voice lost its sorority-girl veneer.

"You're the *chairman* of this show, Karen. You volunteered for it. That means it's your job to—to make sure . . ."

Karen followed her gaze. Stephanie was staring at the right leg of Hickey's khakis. A bright red bloodstain ran from above the knee down to his ankle. There was blood on his Top-Siders as well. Some of the stitches must have broken loose.

"What happened to you?" Stephanie asked.

Hickey looked down at his leg.

"Joe hurt himself," Karen said quickly. "Doing some work for me."

"That looks serious."

"It's not, really," Karen said.

Hickey was watching Stephanie, his dark eyes glittering. Karen took her by the arm and started walking her back toward the Lexus.

"I'll get down there as soon as I can, Steph. You go back and slap those people into shape. And call Coach Rizzi about the tables. Okay?"

Stephanie looked back over her shoulder. "Is your cousin all right? He looks . . ." She slowed down and looked into Karen's eyes. Something was stirring in her Zoloft-padded brain. "Are *you* all right?"

"I'm fine." Karen pushed her toward the car, but she refused to be pushed.

"You don't look fine. In fact, you look like hell."

"Thanks a lot."

Stephanie looked over Karen's shoulder. Whatever she saw convinced her that something was very wrong. She took hold of Karen's wrist and, in an almost comic reversal of their previous motion, began pulling her toward the Lexus.

"Keep walking," she whispered. "When I start the car, jump in the backseat."

"I can't. Get your butt out of here, Steph. Now."

Karen risked a glance back at Hickey. His pant leg was completely soaked with blood now, and his right hand was behind his back. She turned back to Stephanie and said in a bright voice: "I'll see you in a few hours, okay?"

Stephanie's brow was knotted in puzzlement. Why didn't she just *go*? Was she trying to work out if Hickey was Karen's lover after all? Whatever was occupying her brain cells, self-preservation finally overrode it. Karen actually saw Stephanie write her off. She whirled and yanked open the door of the Lexus, all pretense of normalcy gone.

Hickey shot her through the window. A crimson flower bloomed on her upper chest, and her mouth formed an almost comical "O." Karen screamed and leaped forward, but not in time to catch Stephanie as she slid down the rear door of the car, leaving a bright trail of arterial blood on the white paint. Her eyes were closed, and blood pulsed steadily from a hole in her sternum. Karen felt her brain clicking into crisis mode, all the skills she'd learned as a nurse infusing her mind and hands. But even before she could check Stephanie's airway, Hickey's rough hands jerked her to her feet.

"Get your ass in the truck!"

"You shot her," Karen said, still not quite believing it.

Hickey aimed the .38 down at Stephanie's head. "If you don't get into that Expedition, I'll shoot her again."

His enraged eyes left no doubt that he would put a bullet in Stephanie Morgan's brain. Karen backed toward the Expedition, Hickey following with the gun.

"You said nobody was going to die!"

"She called that play. She should've handled those damn cows herself."

"She has two kids!

"You'd better start thinking about *your* kid, Mom."

Karen's mouth went dry. Abby's death had suddenly become real in a way that juvenile diabetes had not prepared her for. She climbed up into the driver's seat and sat there, trying to hold herself together. Will often joked that she could remain calm in the middle of an earthquake, but Hickey was proving him wrong. Her quest for some source of strength brought an image of her father to her mind. He had fought in Korea, then in Vietnam during the early years. God, how she wished he was here. He would know how to deal with a bum like Hickey. Hickey wouldn't know what hit him. But her father was gone, taken by cancer five years ago—

"Take hold of the gear shift and pull it over to *D*," Hickey said, as though talking to a child.

"You lied to me," Karen said. "Everything you've told me was a lie. You've been planning to kill us all along. You're going to get your money and kill us."

"Listen to me. Because your stupid gene is really showing through. Remember Costa Rica? By tomorrow night, I'll be sipping umbrella drinks in paradise. I'm not worried about who saw me shoot some airhead in a Lexus. What I *am* worried about is getting my money.

And that's what you need to focus on. Are we on the same page?"

Karen took a deep breath, then reached down and punched 911 on the Expedition's cell phone.

Hickey jammed the gun into her ribs, driving the breath from her lungs. "Your friend is dead. So hang up and start driving. Or the only mother Abby will ever know is the twenty-two-year-old Will marries after you're dead."

The 911 line rang once before Karen pressed END. She hated herself for being a coward, but she could not die here. Not in this truck, over an acquaintance who was almost certainly dead already. She had a child to raise. Nothing else mattered. She and Abby had to get through the day alive.

She put the Expedition into gear, backed onto the lawn, and drove around the Lexus and the body of Stephanie Morgan.

When the phone rang in the suite at the Beau Rivage, Will pounced on it. Now that he'd given Ferris the go-ahead to call the FBI, he wanted to hear the man report that a fleet of helicopters was combing the forest around Hazlehurst, flying at treetop level over every road and path, not a dog or a cow moving unseen. He jerked up the receiver, aware that his sleep-deprived brain was slowly but surely slipping off its tracks.

"Will Jennings."

"What are you doing answering the phone?" Hickey asked. "You expecting a call?"

"No," he stammered. "I'm just ready to move. Ready to get your money and get Abby back."

"That's good, Doc. Because it's time to leave for the bank."

"I'm ready."

"You sound sleepy. Cheryl's got some pep pills if you need them. I don't want you messing up because you can't think straight."

"I'm not going to mess up. But I need to talk to my daughter, Joe. I'm not going to the bank until I do."

"Is that right? Huh. Maybe you should talk to your wife a minute. We just had a little social call at your house."

Sweat beaded on Will's forehead. "Karen?"

"I'm here," she said.

"Are you all right?"

"Will, he just shot Stephanie Morgan."

Will blinked, certain that he'd misheard. "Did you say—"

"You heard her right," Hickey cut in. "She's busy driving now. But if I hear any more bullshit about what you will and won't do, the Lexus queen won't be the only one who dies this morning. You follow?"

"Yes."

"Now, what about this helicopter?"

Acid flooded Will's stomach. "Helicopter?"

"You been talking to the FBI?"

Harley Ferris couldn't possibly have gotten an FBI helicopter into the air and over Hazlehurst so quickly. It had to be coincidence. "Joe, I'm doing exactly what you tell me. Nothing else."

"Let me talk to Cheryl."

Cheryl was sitting on the sofa with her purse at her feet. She had gone downstairs to Impulse, a clothing store in the casino lobby that operated twenty-four hours a day, and bought a white lycra sheath to replace the torn cocktail dress. She took the phone from Will and began her litany of one-word replies.

"Yeah. . . . No. . . . Right. . . . No, he's cool. . . . We'll be there. No problem." She handed the phone back to Will. "It's showtime."

"Thank you, Cheryl." He hung up the phone. "I owe you more than I can ever repay."

She stood and slung her purse over her shoulder. "You just remember you said that."

The Klein Davidson Building was an elegant stone edifice in the affluent business section of north Jackson. It looked more like a town house than an office, but Karen knew its interior thrummed with computers churning out market quotes from around the world. There were four satellite dishes mounted on the flat roof in back, but Gray Davidson had hired an architect to construct a mansard roof to conceal them. Karen pulled the Expedition into the parking lot and parked two spaces over from Davidson's Mercedes 560.

"You only want to be thinking about one thing in there," Hickey said. "Your kid."

As Karen reached for the door handle, an older woman parked beside them, got out, gave her a little wave, and walked into the office.

"Gray's receptionist," she said.

"Go on," Hickey told her, uncovering the gun in his lap.

"I'm not taking one step until you let me call nine-one-one and report a woman shot at my address."

Hickey held the gun against her ribs again.

"If you shoot me, you won't get your money. All I'm asking is a chance to try to save a woman's life. It won't cost you anything."

"She's dead," Hickey insisted. "I shot her in the pump."

"You don't know she's dead. She has two small children, and I can't live with myself if I don't do all I can to help her."

"You won't be able to live with yourself if you kill your own kid, I'll tell you that. And that's what you're doing if you don't go wire that money."

She turned to him, unable to remain silent. "You hate Will for supposedly killing your mother, but you just shot someone else's mother. You orphaned two children. Can you explain that to me?"

Hickey expelled air from his cheeks in exasperation. "You're going to pay for this later."

She closed her eyes and leaned back against the headrest. She expected to feel the gun barrel pressed to her temple, but instead she heard four beeps, one ring, and a click.

"Nine-one-one, emergency," said a female dispatcher.

Hickey said, "A woman was just shot in the chest at number one hundred, Crooked Mile Road. She's dying."

Karen looked over at him, amazed.

"One hundred, Crooked Mile Road," said the dispatcher. "Are you at that address, sir? I'm not getting a location readout."

"I'm on a cell phone. The woman is lying in the driveway." Hickey looked at Karen as though asking if he'd done enough.

"Sir, I'm showing that we already received a call for this emergency."

Hickey's jaw clenched. "When was that?"

"About two minutes ago."

"Who called it in?"

"I don't have that information, sir. But we've already dispatched an ambulance to—"

Hickey hit END. "I think your husband has made a very big mistake. First we get a helicopter over the cabin. Now somebody's at your house reporting a shooting."

"You were outside when you shot her. A neighbor could have heard and run over."

"Your neighbors aren't that close." Hickey rubbed the dark stubble on his chin. "Get your ass in there and move the money. And remember . . . one mistake will put you in a mourning dress that you'll never really take off."

Karen got out and walked toward the entrance, his last sentence hanging over her thoughts like a pall.

The Biloxi branch of the Magnolia Federal Bank was a two-story brick building of unprepossessing architecture. There were few cars in the parking lot, but drive-through business was brisk as Will pulled his rented Tempo into the lot and parked.

"What now?"

Cheryl shifted in the seat beside him and began tapping her fingers on the dash. She had popped two amphetamines before they left the hotel, and she was wired. Will had swallowed one, fearing that exhaustion might prevent him from making the right move if an opportunity to save Abby presented itself.

"Now we wait," Cheryl replied. "Joey will call after the money's on its way."

Will took her cell phone from her lap and dialed Harley Ferris's number.

"Ferris," said a clipped voice.

"It's Will. Anything?"

"The FBI already had a chopper in the air when I called them. It's been over the woods at Hazlehurst for a while now, but the foliage is so thick, they're probably missing buildings down there, much less a pickup truck."

"What about the phone trace?"

"We're almost there, Will. We just had a quick call to the subject's number. Our crew is working its way down an overgrown logging road right now."

"What will they do if they find the truck?"

"There's an FBI SWAT team en route from Jackson. The SAC there says they can seal off the cabin without the subject's knowledge."

A chill of foreboding went through Will. "They're not going to try an assault?"

"I think they're going to play it safe," Ferris replied. "But my guess is that with your little girl's life on the line, if they get a clean shot at the guy holding her, they'll take it."

"Sweet Jesus."

"They're pros, Will. Just like you. They know their jobs."

"I've got to clear this line." Will couldn't bring himself to hang up. "Harley . . . for God's sake, tell them to be careful."

"Have faith, brother."

He hung up. *Have faith?* It took a supreme effort simply to sit in the parking lot while Abby's future unfolded a hundred and forty miles to the north. But he had to play the hand Hickey had dealt him. Hickey had to believe until the last second that his plan was ticking along like a Swiss watch.

"What happened?" Cheryl asked. "What's going on?"

"Nothing," he lied. "Nothing at all."

Sending the wire was just like everything Karen had ever done at Klein Davidson: a matter of paperwork, signing on various lines while Gray Davidson led her through the pages and made chitchat about kids and schools. With men, he probably talked kids and sports. Or women. Karen didn't know and didn't care. She was functioning on autopilot, tormented by images of Stephanie Morgan's chest blossoming red. The only thing that really registered was the receptionist handing her a receipt and saying, "The money's on its way."

"That's it? That's all we have to do?"

Gray Davidson patted her on the shoulder. "Scary how fast you can spend two hundred grand, isn't it?"

He was wearing his trademark double-breasted English suit with a spread collar shirt and rugby tie. Five years older than Karen, Davidson hailed from Hot Coffee, Mississippi, but his pretensions rivaled those of the most dedicated Anglophiles on the eastern seaboard. Some clients made fun of his eccentricities, but nobody joked about his market acumen.

"Very scary," Karen replied, wondering if Will was already in the bank in Biloxi, waiting to collect what she'd sent. "I now own a two-hundred-thousand-dollar chunk of wood."

"You look like you're going to faint," Davidson said with genuine concern. "Why don't you come into my office and sit down?"

"No. I've got to run."

"May I get you some coffee?"

"No, thanks, Gray. Really."

"Green tea? Espresso?"

Somehow Karen conjured a smile, a feat of magic under the circumstances. "It's just a summer cold. I'll be fine."

The broker didn't look convinced. She touched his arm above the elbow and squeezed with an intimate pressure. "I'm *fine,* Gray. Thanks for worrying."

Davidson's critical faculties melted. Men were so easy to manipulate. She gave the receptionist a wave and hurried toward the door.

"Go straight home and get some rest," Davidson called after her.

She held up a hand in acknowledgment but did not turn, and she barely slowed when she went through the varnished rosewood door and down the steps to the parking lot.

The parking lot of the Magnolia Federal Bank in Biloxi was filling up fast. People were cashing paychecks, hitting the ATM machines, and carrying in payroll bags. Will could see why Hickey had picked this branch. Cheryl sat beside him in tense silence, waiting for Hickey's go-ahead call. The temperature was rising fast in the parked car, so Will started the engine and switched on the air conditioner.

When the cell phone rang, he snatched it up, but Cheryl put her hand on his wrist and took the phone from his hand.

"It's me," she said. "Right. . . . Okay." She hit END and looked at Will. "The money's here. He said you should go in and get it."

Will shut off the engine and looked at the double-glass doors of the bank. "Give me the phone."

"Why?"

"I'm taking it in with me."

"You don't trust me?"

"I didn't say that. I just said I'm taking the phone."

Cheryl snapped her head away from him, but she did not resist when he took the phone from her hand. He slipped it into his pocket along with the Tempo's keys, then got out and started walking toward the bank.

SEVENTEEN

Hickey drove south along the interstate at fifty-five miles per hour, his face wet with sweat. His right thigh was thoroughly soaked in blood.

"I think some more stitches broke," he said. "You aren't much of a doctor. I think you're going to have to do some repairs here."

Karen had not given the suturing her best effort. "I don't have Will's bag. I could probably tape it up, if you stop at a drugstore."

"I don't want to stop." Hickey looked in the rearview mirror, then changed lanes. "But I may have to."

"Are we on our way to get Abby?"

"We're on our way to a drugstore."

"Are you letting us go when you get the money?"

"That's up to your husband. Let's see if he can follow simple instructions. Start looking for a drugstore."

Karen glanced to her left, searching the strip malls that

lined the interstate. She was pretty sure there was an Eckerd's along here somewhere.

"There's a cop back there," Hickey said, straightening in his seat.

She started to turn, but he grabbed her knee and said, "Don't look."

"Cops are always patrolling this interstate," she told him.

"This one's acting squirrelly. He's ten lengths back, but hanging on me like a trailer. He's running our plate."

"Were you speeding?"

"You think I'm going to speed today? This is your husband, goddamn it. The son of a bitch called somebody. That's the only way they'd know what to look for."

"What about the shooting at our house?"

"They wouldn't have issued an APB on this vehicle off that. Not yet, anyway." He checked the rearview again. "That SOB is still back there."

"You're paranoid! And you're driving suspiciously." Karen spotted the Eckerd's on her left. "Take the next exit. Northside Drive. There's our drugstore."

Hickey leaned toward her, then craned his neck backward and looked up through the moonroof.

"What are you *doing*? Watch the road!"

"Paranoid, huh? Take a look."

The moonroof was tinted against the sun, but even so, Karen could see the large dot against the sky. It was a helicopter.

"That's probably the WLBT traffic chopper," she said. But for the first time, she wondered.

"Traffic chopper, my ass." Hickey reached down and punched a number into the cell phone. After a few seconds of silence, it began to ring.

"Joey?" said Huey.

"That's right, boy. You all ready?"

"Ready."

"Were you born ready?"

"Um . . . yeah."

"It's time to go to the backup."

"Okay."

Karen's chest tightened. "You said that before. What's the backup plan?"

"Don't worry about it."

"May I please speak to Abby? *Please.*"

Hickey sighed with frustration. "Huey, is the kid right there?"

"She's in the bathroom."

Karen's maternal radar went on alert. "Has she been to the bathroom a lot this morning, Huey?"

"She sure has."

"Oh God. Her sugar's going up. She needs her shot."

"And I'm bleeding to death," Hickey said. "Stay cool. You've got stuff with you, and we'll be there in plenty of time."

"When?"

"Here she comes!" Huey sang out.

"Abby?" cried Karen.

After a brief silence, Abby said, "Mama?"

"Goddamn it," Hickey muttered.

Karen's heart leaped. "I'm here, baby. Are you all right?"

"I don't think so. I think I'm going south, like Daddy says."

Karen fought to keep control of her voice. "It's okay, baby. Mama's on her way to get you right now."

"You are?"

"I'll be there before you know it."

"Put Huey back on," Hickey said.

"I'll be there before you know it," Karen said again. "Now put Mr. Huey back on, baby."

"Okay. Hurry, Mom."

"I'm on my way!"

"Joey?" said Huey.

"I'm here. You know what to do? Everything just like I told you."

"I remember."

"We'll talk when we see each other."

"Okay. But, Joey?"

"What?"

"Is everything gonna be okay?"

"You bet. Get going, now."

"Okay. Bye-bye."

Just before Hickey pressed END, Karen heard Abby yell, "Bye, Mom!" and she filled with pride. Abby was hanging in there.

"Bastards," Hickey said, looking up through the moonroof again. "If your husband had done what he was supposed to, you'd be going straight to your little girl right now."

Karen's heart stuttered. "You said we were!"

"We're not going anywhere until I lose this tail."

"You don't know it *is* a tail."

A scornful grunt was his only comment. "Your husband had better be getting my goddamn money."

"He is! You know he is."

"He's trying to fuck me over is what I know. And I'll tell you this. If they try to stop this truck—"

"I'll say whatever you tell me to!" she promised. "All I want to do is get to Abby."

Hickey checked the rearview mirror again. "The squad car dropped back out of sight. They're playing us loose. They want to follow us to the girl."

Oh, Jesus, Karen thought. *Will, what did you do?*

Without warning, Hickey veered across two lanes of traffic and onto an exit ramp. At the bottom, he swung under the interstate and onto a wide boulevard.

"Lakeland Drive?" said Karen. "Is this the way we went last night?"

"You just sit tight, Mom."

"This is the road to the airport."

"That it is." Hickey laughed softly.

"This way, Dr. Jennings."

Will turned down a hall that led off the bank's main lobby and followed the secretary up a short flight of stairs. Upon entering the bank, he had seen that dealing with a teller was not the way to go. There were lines at the windows, and even the loan officers in the glassed-in cubicles had customers. He walked up to a secretary, identified himself, and asked to see the senior officer at the bank. When she asked what it concerned, he told her he was receiving a wire transfer of two hundred thousand dollars and wouldn't deal with anyone but the top man.

The young woman made a call, then asked him to follow her up the stairs.

The staircase ended at another hall, this one lined with doors. She led him to the one at the end, knocked, then opened it and showed him into a typical branch bank office, furnished out of mail-order catalogs. Behind a mahogany veneer desk sat a balding man in his early fifties, with shining skin and a line of sweat on his upper lip. He stood.

"Hello, Dr. Jennings. That'll be all, Cindy."

The door closed behind Will, and the man held out a plump hand. "I'm Jack Moore, vice president."

Will shook the hand and looked around the office again. There was a small door on the wall to his right, partially open.

"What's that?"

"My private restroom," Moore said.

"Oh."

"How can I help you, Doctor? Your wire came in a few minutes ago. What would you like to do with the money?"

"I want to withdraw it in cash. I also need to withdraw some personal funds. I have a hundred and fifty thousand in CDs deposited with this bank in Jackson."

Moore wiped his upper lip. "You want to walk out of here with three hundred and fifty thousand dollars in a suitcase?"

"That's right." Cheryl had retrieved a cheap briefcase from her suite as they left the Beau Rivage.

"I see. Well . . ." Moore glanced at his restroom door. "If that's what you want, I guess . . ."

The restroom door opened, and a tall man with sandy hair and blue eyes stepped out.

Will backpedaled to the door. "What the hell is this?"

"Dr. Jennings," said the stranger. "I'm Special Agent Bill Chalmers. I'm fully aware of your situation, and I'm here to help you."

Will was so stunned that he simply stood where he was. "But— How did you get here? How did you know where to go? Harley Ferris didn't know where I was going."

Chalmers nodded. "There's a sofa behind you, Doctor. Please sit down. We don't have much time, and we have a lot to do."

"I only have one thing to do. Get my money and get out of here."

"Please sit down, Doctor. I think you'll like what I have to say."

Will backed up until his calves hit something padded. He sat.

"Do you know a cardiovascular surgeon named James McDill?"

"McDill? Sure. He's a member out at Annandale. He doesn't play much golf. Collects cars, I think." Even as he spoke the word "collects," something ticked in Will's brain.

"Exactly one year ago," said Chalmers, "James McDill's son, Peter, was kidnapped in exactly the same way your daughter was yesterday."

Will blinked in disbelief.

"He didn't report the crime until last night, and nobody knows why better than you. But this week he was overcome with anxiety that it might happen again. He called our Jackson field office around eleven last night. I was on duty, and we've been working ever since to piece together what's going on."

"Have you talked to Harley Ferris? Do you know where my little girl is?"

"Mr. Ferris is working with us now. We've augmented CellStar's tracing crew with a SWAT team, and we just had a very lucky break. Get a grip on yourself, Doctor. The man holding Abby just took a call on his cell phone, and he forgot to switch it off. The SWAT team estimates they're two minutes from your daughter's position."

Waves of shock and hope buffeted Will. Even after Ferris's assurances, Chalmers's words seemed incomprehensible. "What do they plan to do when they get there?"

Chalmers walked up to the couch and squatted, so that his eyes were level with Will's. "We think we should go in and get her."

"You mean, guns blazing?"

"Not quite, no. We have special entry devices. Heat sensors and video to accurately place human bodies in the structure. They'll use special stun grenades to incapacitate the tango, then—"

"Tango?" Will interrupted.

"Sorry, that's radio slang for terrorists. These guys train to rescue hostages from terrorists."

"Can't you try to talk him out?"

Chalmers smiled patiently. "We could do that. But it's our understanding that the man holding Abby is mentally handicapped. The leader is still loose. He could call this Huey at any time and order him to kill your daughter."

Will felt as though he and Abby were standing in the

path of a truck and couldn't move. "Can't Ferris shut off Huey's phone?"

"Yes, but that might panic him. Or he might be under orders to kill your daughter if his communications are cut off. Right now—while Huey and Abby are isolated from the leader—we have a golden opportunity to go in. Before the situation deteriorates any further."

After a night spent in ignorance, Will was having difficulty processing the sudden influx of information. "I still don't understand how you got here. How you knew it would be this bank."

"We didn't. We put an agent in every bank of any size in Gulfport and Biloxi. I requested this one because it was the largest. I flew down early this morning. The minute your wire came in, I contacted my Special Agent-in-Charge in Jackson. His name's Frank Zwick. And he wants to talk to you."

"Is he in contact with the SWAT team?"

"Yes."

"Please call him. And there's a woman outside in my rental car. One of the kidnappers."

Chalmers nodded. "Cheryl Lynn Tilly. We'll leave her alone until the team hits the cabin. If she gets suspicious and comes inside, you can tell her there's some delay with paperwork. We have more agents converging on the bank right now, but they'll be discreet coming in."

"I can't believe all this."

The FBI agent smiled. "In a few minutes, your daughter will be in FBI custody, Doctor."

Will was afraid to let himself believe it.

"You did well getting Harley Ferris involved. I only wish you would have called us earlier. Trusted us."

"I couldn't."

"I understand." Chalmers got up and went to Moore's desk. The bank's vice president looked as though he didn't quite believe what was happening before his eyes. "Would you excuse us, Mr. Moore?"

"Of course." The banker made a hasty exit.

Chalmers dialed a number on Moore's phone.

"The leader's name is Hickey," Will said. "Joe Hickey. He has my wife with him, and he's one clever son of a bitch. Do you know where they are now?"

"Driving toward Jackson International Airport."

"What?"

"Don't worry. They're not going anywhere. We're watching them from a helicopter, and we've got men in the airport. Hang on." Chalmers spoke into the phone. "Chalmers here. I've got Dr. Jennings with me. . . . He's on board with us. . . . Yes, sir. Any word on the little girl?" Chalmers gave Will a thumbs-up.

"I want to talk to him," Will said, standing.

"I'll tell him," Chalmers said, and hung up. "The SAC has a lot on his plate right now, Doctor."

"What's happening?"

"SWAT found the cabin."

"The green pickup truck?"

"It's parked under the trees."

Will closed his eyes and began to pray.

Eight FBI agents in camouflage ninja fatigues and black headgear crept silently through the trees toward the cabin, their Heckler & Koch submachine guns tight against their bodies. A ninth agent was already under the structure, scanning the small floor plan with a supersensitive microphone and headphones. Their leader was Special Agent Martin Cody, and Cody was in radio contact with the agent under the house.

"Got anything?" he said into the microphone mounted inside his ballistic glass face mask.

"Not yet." Special Agent Sims Jackson was observing the cabin through a thermal imaging camera. "Nothing but a hot water heater."

Cody didn't like that. The truck was there, but the people weren't? Was there a root cellar of some kind? Could the tango have detected their approach and fled into the woods? It would be tough carrying a five-year-old girl, but Cody had been told the man was big. He could also have killed the little girl and fled alone, but even if she'd been dead a couple of hours, there should still be enough heat in the corpse to register on the thermal imaging device.

"Cody to tracing van," he said into his mike. The CellStar van was seventy yards back up the logging road. "Has the cell phone moved?"

"Negative. Still in the same position."

"We're going in," Cody said into his mike. "Prepare for explosive entry. Stun grenades through the windows, ram on the front door. It looks thin as paper, but you never know."

A staccato burst of mike clicks answered him.

"Shoot high," Cody reminded them, though they

knew the drill already. "This kid probably isn't much over three feet, which is a good break. Okay . . . deploy."

What followed was a ballet the team had rehearsed hundreds of times. Men moving forward without sound, carrying weapons they could dismantle and put back together in absolute darkness. In thirty seconds the team had deployed around the cabin, grenades and HKs at the ready.

Agent Cody had a bad feeling about the assault, but he often got those just before contact. He checked to make sure his ram team was in position to hit the door. It was.

"On my five-count," he said. "Five-four-three-two-GO!" The cabin windows shattered one second before the front door went down. Even in daylight, the blue-white flash of the stun grenades lit up the windows, followed by ear-shattering bangs. Cody saw his men vanish into the cabin. He charged forward and went through the front door five seconds behind them.

The raised cabin floor shuddered under the impact of boots. The interior was filled with smoke, but it cleared quickly through the broken windows. There were no cries of "FEDERAL AGENTS!" because no one could have heard them after the stun grenades.

"Bedroom! No joy!" cried the speaker in Cody's helmet.

"Kitchen, no joy!"

"Bedroom closet's empty!"

Cody checked the corners of the front room, in case the girl was lying dead in one of them. He found nothing.

"Cell phone!" someone shouted. "Cell phone in the kitchen!"

"Got another one!" cried someone else. "Landline in the bedroom!"

Landline? Cody had been told there was no landline in the cabin, and he had seen no wires outside. Maybe there was a buried cable running to the building. He went into the kitchen and saw one of his men holding the cell phone. He was about to take it when the phone began to ring. Cody yanked off his helmet, stared at the phone for a few seconds, then took it and hit SEND.

"Yeah?" he said, hoping the caller would mistake him for whomever he had tried to call.

"Do you have Prince Albert in the can?" asked a male voice.

Cody stood dumbfounded for a moment. "Who is this?"

He heard wild laughter; then the caller clicked off.

Cody put his helmet back on and keyed his mike. "Tracing van, did you hear that call?"

"Affirmative."

"Where did it come from?"

"Unknown. We're checking."

Cody ripped off his helmet again, pulled a digital cell phone from his pocket, and dialed the private number of SAC Zwick in Jackson.

Will paced back and forth across the banker's small office. Agent Chalmers sat behind Moore's desk, speaking quietly to Zwick. Suddenly, Chalmers groaned and covered his eyes with his free hand.

"What happened?" Will asked. *"What happened, goddamn it?"*

Chalmers looked up, his face pale. "The cabin was empty when SWAT went in. Huey and your daughter weren't there."

"What?" Will searched his mind for an explanation. "It must have been the wrong cabin."

"It wasn't. They found the cell phone inside. And someone—probably Hickey—actually called them on it while they were there. Made a joke out of it."

Will shook his head in disbelief.

"They also found a landline in the cabin, which means Hickey could have given Huey new instructions without anyone knowing. The phone company has no record of that line. It's probably an illegal tap."

A landline. He should have known Hickey wouldn't let Huey operate without some sort of backup. "But the truck was still there?"

"The truck was there, but the battery had been removed. It looks like there might have been another vehicle there. They may have gotten away in it."

"*May* have? Are you kidding me? They're gone!"

"Doctor—"

"Give me that goddamn phone!"

Will snatched the phone from Chalmers's hand and shouted into it: "Are you the guy in charge of this Chinese fire drill?"

"This is Frank Zwick, Doctor. Special Agent-in-Charge. Losing your temper isn't going to help your little girl."

"You just tell me, what do you plan to do now?"

"I'm deciding that at this moment. You can help me. Did Cheryl Lynn Tilly mention any possible destination that would require air travel?"

"Costa Rica. She said Hickey has a ranch down there. Or some land, anyway."

"Costa Rica? You can't fly direct from Jackson to Costa Rica. And there's no reservation for a Joe or Joseph Hickey on any flight out of Jackson today. So, he must be flying out under an alias, with a connecting flight to South America."

"Look, if Hickey called your men at the cabin, he knows you're involved. You may have just killed my little girl, Zwick."

"I seriously doubt that, Doctor. Hickey wants two things: his money and his freedom. Killing your daughter won't help him get either. She's half his total leverage now."

"You don't know what's going on! It's not about *money.* Hickey thinks I killed his mother on the operating table. This is about revenge. He *wants* to kill Abby. To punish me."

There was a brief silence. Then Zwick said, "That's a disturbing new perspective, Doctor."

"You're goddamn right it is."

"Do you know this Hickey? Do you remember him?"

Will heard another phone ringing. It was the cell phone in his pocket. Cheryl's phone. "Hang on, I think Hickey's calling me." He dug the phone out of his pocket and hit SEND. "Hello?"

"What's up, Doc?"

Will nodded at Chalmers. "I'm in the bank, getting your money."

"You're lying. You called the FBI."

"Joe—"

"Where's Cheryl?"

"In the parking lot. I brought the phone in with me."

"Why?"

"So I could tell you what was happening if you called."

"Well . . . the plan has changed. Your wife and me are about to take a little airplane ride. And if I see a cop or an FBI agent within a mile of me, I'm going to put one right in her ear. You follow?"

"Joe, I'm getting your money! Just tell me where you want it!"

"We'll work that out later. You just get it all ready to go. And tell your new friends to keep clear of that airport."

"I don't know what you're talking about! Joe, where's my daughter?"

"That's the sixty-four-thousand-dollar question, isn't it?" Hickey laughed. "*Hasta luego, amigo.* Just remember, whatever happens, you called the play."

The phone went dead. Will felt as though his heart had been ripped out through his chest wall. He picked up the other phone and told Zwick what had transpired.

The SAC said, "I'm going to pull back my men and let them get into the airport."

"Why? Won't Hickey be harder to stop with lots of people around?"

"Yes, but it's possible that this Huey character and your daughter are already inside the airport waiting for him. If we bust Hickey outside, they might just disappear."

"Jesus Christ. Okay. But if they are inside, what can you do? How can you stop Hickey then? What's to keep him from putting a gun to Abby's head?"

"The fact that he's dead."

"You mean you'll shoot him on sight? Can you do that?"

"Kidnapping is an extraordinary crime, Doctor. The rules of engagement allow for a great deal of discretion. And an airport is a high-security area. I can promise you this. If your little girl is in there, and Hickey makes a move toward her with a weapon, his brain will be removed from his cranium without benefit of anesthetic."

"Do you have sharpshooters there?"

"They'll be in position before Hickey gets inside the building. Now, I have a lot to arrange, Doctor. Put Agent Chalmers back on the phone."

As Will handed over the phone, several thoughts came to him at once. Any logistics that Zwick had to arrange were in Jackson, not Biloxi. Right now he was almost certainly telling Chalmers to make sure Will stayed right where he was, under FBI control. But Will's primary concern was Hickey. Even now, the man was controlling the movements of everyone involved in the situation. Five times he had pulled off these kidnappings, and the FBI had never even been told about them. At the cabin he had proved he could stay two steps ahead of the SWAT team and laugh while doing it. Opposing his proven brilliance was Frank Zwick, a man Will knew nothing about. He had to assume that Zwick knew his job, but instinct told him that the events of the next few minutes would not be as easy to control as the SAC believed. The FBI did not really know where Huey and Abby were. They *might* be in the Jackson airport; they might also be sixty miles away. As Chalmers listened to his boss on the phone, Will walked quietly out of the office.

"Where are you going?" Chalmers called. "Doctor?"

Will paused in the hall. "To get the ransom money."

"It's no good to you now."

"You don't know that. Hickey said to get it, so I'm getting it. I'll be back in a minute."

He took the stairs two at a time going down.

Five miles east of downtown Jackson, Hickey turned Karen's Expedition onto the main airport access road.

"Where are we going?" Karen asked. She was terrified that Hickey would board a flight to Costa Rica without telling her where Abby was being held.

"You just watch."

"We've got to get to Abby, Joe. Her sugar's going up."

"Just shut your goddamn mouth for five minutes. I got everything under control."

Karen leaned back and looked up through the moonroof. The helicopter was still there. It had stayed practically on top of them all the way from the interstate. Hickey was right. It had to be the police. Or the FBI. She hoped to God Will knew what he was doing.

The SHORT TERM PARKING sign flashed past. Then ARRIVALS/DEPARTURES.

"Are we flying somewhere?" she asked. "Do you have a plane here?"

"Oh, yeah. I got a whole fleet of them." Hickey glared at her. "You just can't be quiet, can you? I bet your husband thinks you are one big pain in the ass."

She sat back and tried to stay calm. Despite the helicopter overhead, Hickey had not ordered Abby harmed. Unless the "backup plan" was to kill her. Karen gripped the handle on the windshield post as Hickey swerved into the LONG TERM PARKING lane. He stopped at the barrier, took a ticket from the machine, then accelerated into the concrete-roofed garage.

He rounded the first turn at forty miles an hour. The brakes squealed as they neared the elevator on the terminal side of the building. Hickey seemed to be looking for signs of police. Seeing nothing, he accelerated around the next curve and almost ran over a young woman in a navy blue skirt suit who was pulling a suitcase from the trunk of a silver Camry. He screeched to a stop, reversed a few feet, then pulled into the parking space beside the Camry.

"What are you doing?" Karen asked.

He jumped out and closed the distance to the woman in the time it took Karen to turn and look. As the woman gaped, Hickey smashed Will's .38 into the side of her head. She dropped like a stone.

"Get out!" Hickey shouted at Karen. *"Help me!"*

A wave of nausea nearly overcame her, but she forced herself to get out and move to the back of the Expedition. Hickey was bent over the prostrate woman, rifling through her purse.

"What are you *doing*?"

He snatched his hand from the purse with a jangle of

car keys and hit the UNLOCK button on the ring. "Get in the backseat of the Camry! Move!"

Hickey grabbed the woman under the arms and heaved her upper body into the Camry's trunk. There was blood in her hair. The blow from the pistol had torn part of her ear away from her skull. She moaned in pain and confusion, but Hickey took no notice. He stuffed her legs into the trunk, then slammed it shut. When he turned to Karen, his eyes were as cold as any she had ever seen.

"Get your ass in that car, or you'll never see Abby alive again."

He didn't wait for her to obey. He jumped into the driver's seat, cranked the Camry, and backed out of the parking space.

Snapped from her trance by the realization that he might actually leave without her, Karen leaped forward and began hammering on the back door, which had automatically locked when he cranked the engine. Hickey looked back at her but did not open the door.

"Please!" she screamed, her heart in her throat. "Open the door! *Open it!*"

He waited a few seconds, then unlocked the door. Karen jumped inside and pulled the door shut after her.

"Get on the floor," Hickey ordered.

She lay stomach-down across the carpeted hump behind the front seat. Hickey drove at normal speed through the lines of parked cars.

"Are we leaving the airport?" she asked.

"Yes, we are!" he cried in his Wink Martindale voice. "That nice lady left her parking receipt right here on the drink caddy!"

Karen couldn't believe it. Hickey was going to drive right out from under the nose of the helicopter hovering overhead. The strange thing was that she wanted him to succeed. She had seen enough of his personality to know that if he were arrested, he would clam up and smile at the police while Abby died in a diabetic coma somewhere.

Hickey stopped at the exit booth.

"How would you like to pay for that, sir?" asked a woman with a Hispanic accent.

"Cash, chiquita."

"One dollar, please."

Hickey had the money ready.

"Sir, the short-term parking lot is much more convenient for brief—"

"I'd love to chat," Hickey said, "but you've got cars waiting. *Hasta la vista*."

He drove away from the booth and joined the flow of traffic leaving the airport. He drove confidently, neither too fast nor too slow. Karen raised up enough to watch him between the seats.

A sound like a muffled drum suddenly echoed through the car. She thought Hickey had switched on the radio, but he hadn't. The woman in the trunk was beating on the backseat.

"I'm glad she didn't start that shit while we were at the booth," Hickey said.

"Help!" screamed the muted voice. *"I can't breathe! Please let me out!"*

Karen shut her eyes and prayed for the woman to be quiet. If she kept screaming, Hickey was liable to pull over and shoot her. The speed and intensity of his acts in her driveway and in the garage had sickened Karen. As a nurse, she had seen the effects of violence, but never the acts that produced the damage. Real violence was so unlike what she'd seen in movies that it was hard to grasp. Slashing Hickey's thigh had been a reflex, an act of self-preservation. But he acted with a merciless dispatch that made her feel worse about the whole human race. The realization of what she had avoided by stabbing Hickey suddenly came home to her with searing clarity. Those other mothers had actually been raped by the man, had suffered the horror of becoming sexual whipping posts for all his repressed anger and resentment. And they had endured that horror for twenty-four hours. It was unimaginable.

The knocking behind Karen went on, but the cries decreased in intensity until they became a keening wail, like that of a small child.

"Traffic update!" Hickey cried.

"What?"

"I thought you might like to know, that helicopter's still hovering over the airport, three miles back. Amateurs, baby. Amateurs."

"Are we going to get Abby now?"

He laughed. "We're going somewhere, June Cleaver. That's one thing you can count on. We got an appointment with destiny!"

EIGHTEEN

Despite his belief that Agent Chalmers might try to keep him a virtual prisoner in the bank, Will had returned to the vice president's office on the second floor. He had the ransom (Moore had personally packed it into the brief-case at his feet), but he could not make a decision about what to do next until he knew the outcome of the FBI's attempt to arrest Hickey at the airport. If Hickey some-how managed to escape, Will couldn't trust him to tell the truth about Abby or anything else over a cell phone.

When the call from SAC Zwick finally came, Agent Chalmers lifted the phone, listened for a few moments, then turned paler than he had when the SWAT team had found nothing at the cabin. In his mind's eye, Will saw a nightmare scenario: FBI agents drawing down on Hickey on an airport concourse, Hickey putting a pis-tol to Abby's head, an FBI sharpshooter shooting wide, Hickey pulling the trigger. Chalmers went on listening to Zwick, but Will couldn't wait.

"Tell me!" he demanded.

Chalmers held up his hand.

"What happened?"

"I'm putting you on the speaker, Frank." Chalmers hit a button on the phone. "Go ahead."

"What happened?" Will asked. "Is my wife all right? Was my daughter there?"

Zwick's voice came from the bottom of an electronic well. "We think your wife is fine, Doctor."

"You *think*? What about my daughter?"

"We don't know."

"What do you mean? What *happened*?"

"Hickey and your wife pulled into the long-term parking garage, but they never came out. We found your Expedition with one door open. Right now, we don't know where they are. We're searching the airport, but it's just possible they got out of that garage in another car. We have a photo of Hickey from Parchman Prison, and we're faxing it down for the garage attendants to look at. We got a photo of your wife from the *Clarion Ledger*, and that's on its way down, too. We're also getting the parking lot security camera tapes."

"What about your helicopter?"

"Nothing useful. A lot of cars left that garage during that window of time."

"Jesus, you don't know anything!"

"Doctor, there's no way Hickey can—"

"Can what? It looks like he can do any damn thing he pleases!" Will stood and lifted the briefcase that held the ransom.

"What are you doing?" asked Chalmers.

"Going back to the car and waiting for Hickey's next call. And I want you to stay right here."

"That's not an option, Doctor," Zwick said from the speakerphone.

"You want to bet?"

"The only way you can participate in the resolution of this situation is our way. Otherwise, we'll have to arrest you."

"For what? I haven't done anything."

"I'll have the Gulfport police arrest you for reckless driving. You've got a hooker in your car. How about prostitution?"

"What do you want me to do?"

"By now Agent Chalmers has some special equipment at his disposal downstairs. A tracking device, which you can carry in your pocket, and which will allow us to follow you from a very discreet distance. We can wait for Hickey to arrange an exchange, then be ready to take him down at the safest possible moment. We also have an undetectable wire. With the wire, we'll know just when that moment is, and we'll also have everything Hickey says on tape."

"Undetectable, my ass. A wire helps you guys at trial, but it doesn't do squat for my wife and daughter. And they're my only priority."

"This is nonnegotiable, Doctor."

"You think so?" Will reached into his pocket and brought out Cheryl's pistol. "Ask Agent Chalmers if it's negotiable."

"Bill?" said Zwick.

"He's holding a gun on me, Frank. Looks like a Walther automatic."

"You just committed a felony, Doctor," Zwick informed him. "Don't make this worse for yourself."

Will laughed outright. "*Worse?* Are you out of your mind?" He backed toward the door. "You guys had your chance. Two chances. And you blew it both times. It's my turn now."

Agent Chalmers held up both hands to show that he had no intention of going for Will's gun or his own. "At least take the tracking device. Forget the wire. I wouldn't wear it either."

"Shut up," Zwick snapped.

"Where is it?" Will asked.

"I'll call downstairs and have it waiting for you."

Zwick said, "Agent Chalmers, as soon as he leaves that room, you will call downstairs and order the agents down there to arrest him."

Chalmers looked into Will's eyes. "They'll have to shoot him to stop him, Frank. I say we let him go."

"Goddamn it." The speakerphone crackled for a moment. "All right, just give him the tracker. Jennings, you're making the biggest mistake of your life. But if you're dead set—"

"I'm out of here," Will said. "Please don't try any cowboy stuff. I'll call you if you can help."

He aimed the gun at Chalmers all the way to the stairs. Then he gave the FBI agent a salute, turned, and bounded down the steps.

In the lobby, he made a beeline for the door. The secretary who'd led him up to Moore's office saw the gun and screamed, but a business-suited man by the front doors held up his wallet and yelled: "FBI! Everyone stay calm! It's all right!"

As Will neared the door, the FBI agent held out a small black box with a blinking red LED on it. "GPS," he said. "Military grade. We can track you down to the square foot you're standing on. Don't lose it."

Will stuck the unit in his pocket, went through the automatic doors, and raced for the Tempo. When he hit the driver's seat, Cheryl said, "Where the hell have you been? I'm peeing prune pits out here."

"You've got a real way with words, you know?" He cranked the Ford, backed up, then pulled out of the lot and onto Highway 90. Traffic was heavy, but he didn't see any obvious pursuit vehicles.

"Where are we going?" Cheryl asked, her voice jittery from the speed she'd taken earlier.

"That's up to Joe. Right now, we're headed up to I-10. Wherever the meet is, it's going to be north."

Will swung into the right lane and started around a dawdling pickup truck. As he came alongside it, he rolled down his window, tossed the GPS device into the bed of the truck, and sped past.

"What was that?" Cheryl asked.

"A pig trail for the FBI to follow."

"The FBI? Was the FBI in the bank?"

"Yes."

"Oh shit. Oh God . . ."

"The FBI raided the cabin, but Huey and Abby weren't there. All they found was the green truck and Huey's cell phone."

"Shit. I was right about the truck, though. I told you."

He turned and gave her a hard look. "They also found a regular phone. A landline. You told me there was no regular phone service at the cabin."

"I didn't know there was! I told you I never went there."

He lifted the briefcase from the floor and set it in her lap. "Open it."

"Is the money in here?"

"Yes."

She hefted the case. "It doesn't feel right. It's too heavy. Is there a dye pack in here or something?"

"No dye pack. Open it."

When the lid rose high enough to reveal the neatly stacked hundred-dollar bills, Cheryl's face lit up like Abby's did when she saw a deer walk into the backyard on a cool fall morning. "This is too much," she said in a flustered voice. "Isn't it?"

"That's three hundred and fifty thousand dollars."

She picked up a stack of hundreds and ran her fingers over it, then fanned the edges like a kid playing with a deck of cards. A high-pitched noise that was almost sexual came from her throat. Will knew the effect of cash money on poor people. He had learned it the hard way.

"Talking about money and holding it in your hand are two different things, aren't they?" he said. "I told you I'd give you enough to start over. Now you've got it. That's more lap dances than you could do in a lifetime. That's freedom, Cheryl. Mexico, Bermuda, anyplace you want to be."

She turned to him, her eyes guarded. "Can I leave now? Right this minute?"

"No. Joe is going to call any second to set up a meeting. I need you to tell him everything's still all right."

"No way." She shook her head like a two-year-old. "I've already done too much. Joey will—"

"He won't do anything! You'll never even have to see him again."

"You're lying. To bluff Joey, you're going to need me up to the very last second. Then I'll be with him. And he'll *know*."

"He won't know anything."

"You don't know him." Unalloyed fear shone from her eyes. "Joey's got this thing about betrayal. Like the mafia. He's totally paranoid about it."

"He's going to kill my little girl, Cheryl. You don't want to believe that, but deep down, you know. If he's capable of killing you, he could kill Abby without batting an eye."

"Would you let me go if you knew where she was?"

Will nearly slammed on the brakes. "Do you know where Huey's going?"

"Would you let me go if I did?"

"That depends on whether I believe you."

She pursed her lips and looked down at the money in her lap. "I was supposed to bring you to the motel, like I said. Then Joey was supposed to pick us up. I think he was going to take us back to the cabin where Huey was keeping Abby. But if the FBI raided the cabin, and Joey knows that . . ."

"He knows."

"Then he's going to his backup plan."

"What's his backup plan?"

"For Huey, I don't know. I'm still supposed to go the motel in Brookhaven. Only I don't bring you. I'm supposed to stay off the cell phone, too. Joey will call me at the motel—on a landline—and tell me what to do. I might sit tight with the money until he tells me to go somewhere, or he might pick me up."

"Where would he tell you to go?"

She looked at the money again and swallowed. "I don't know for sure. But I've been thinking about it. One time we were driving from Jackson to New Orleans, and Joey got all hot and wanted to do it. I told him I didn't want to in the car, and he said we didn't have to. About ten minutes later, he pulled off the interstate and went down this two-lane blacktop a ways and stopped at an old house. He climbed in a window and unlocked the door for me. His daddy's people owned it, I think. The house was mostly empty, but there was a bed and a stove. I think if things went to hell up Jackson way, that's where he'd go."

This was what she had held back during the torture session. "Could you find that house again?"

She shook her head. "Not by myself. It was too dark and too long ago. It's up by McComb somewhere, but that's all I know."

"You've got to try! Huey and Abby might be there right now."

"I have tried! Look, you've got the name of the motel and the general area of the house. Just give that to the FBI and let me go. They'll find your little girl."

"Not in time, they won't."

"Okay, listen. Joey calls in a minute and tells me to go to the backup plan. I'll say, 'Fine, see ya soon.' The motel's a hundred and fifty miles north of here. The house must be a hundred and twenty. That gives you guys plenty of time to set something up. I don't know what you're doing anyway. If you want to save your kid, why are you running from the FBI?"

Will sighed. "The FBI wants to bust Joe, okay? And you. And Huey. I don't care anything about that. I just want Abby back alive. And my wife. The FBI already spooked Joe twice. If he sees them anywhere close again, he might tell Huey to kill Abby. If he hasn't already."

Cheryl pulled at her hair. "But you can't do anything by yourself. Joey's closer to both places than we are. A lot closer."

"Not necessarily."

"What do you mean?"

Will pointed through the windshield. A Continental Airlines 727 was settling over Interstate 10 as it landed at the nearby airport.

Cheryl's mouth fell open. "Jesus . . . your plane. But there's nowhere to land up there. Not at the house."

"Let me worry about that." Will had once lost an engine over the Mississippi Delta and set down on a deserted stretch of Highway 61. To save Abby, he would land the Baron on a driveway if he had to. "One hour of acting, Cheryl. One hour, and you're free forever."

She covered her face with her hands. "You're making it too complicated! I told you, I don't know where the house is!"

"You know more than you think. You might—"

The ringing cell phone silenced him. There was no more time for persuasion. He pulled onto the shoulder and shoved the Nokia toward her hand.

She refused to take it.

"Answer it," he said.

She shut her eyes and shook her head.

"Answer it!"

Abby was walking through tall trees toward a gravel road when she saw Huey toss the flat tire into the trunk of the white car. He slammed the lid and looked up at her, then grinned and waved like a little boy waving at a train. Abby raised her hand to wave back. She felt like she was raising it through water.

She had seen amazing things in the last few minutes. When it was time to leave the cabin, Huey had picked up Belle and her ice chest and led her out to the green pickup truck. But instead of getting in, he opened the lid over the motor and lifted out a big black thing he said was a battery. It didn't look like any battery Abby had ever seen, but he carried it over to the white car sitting on the concrete blocks and set it on the ground. Then he opened the lid over the white car's motor and put the battery inside. While he was doing that, Abby had to run into the trees and tee-tee. Ever since she woke up, she'd had to go a lot, and that meant her sugar was going up fast.

After Huey got the battery into the white car, he went around to the driver's door and tried to start the motor. It didn't work at first, but he worked under the lid for a minute, and the car started, rattling and puffing smoke.

He looked at Abby and laughed, then went back inside the cabin. She followed. In the kitchen, he took his cell phone from his pocket, turned it on, and set it on the counter. Then he lifted Abby like she was still a baby and carried her out to the porch steps.

The white car was still running, but it couldn't go anywhere because it was sitting a foot off the ground. Huey walked to the back of the car, put his huge hands under the bumper, and started pulling on it. His face turned red, then purple. The porch steps shook under Abby's behind when the back of the car tipped off the blocks and the tires hit the ground. Huey laughed like crazy. He helped Abby into the front seat, then put his hands on the steering wheel and drove right off the blocks in front.

The car lurched forward and stopped. Huey drove backward and forward, grinding the motor and jerking the wheel left and right until the car broke loose and started across the grass. Soon they were riding under big trees whose trunks were hardly far enough apart for the car to fit between them. Huey kept saying how "NaNa's car" was going to save them, how smart Joey was, and how pretty soon they were going to hit a road.

Pretty soon they did. Two mossy ruts through the dirt. Then the ruts hit a gravel road, which got Huey laughing again until they had the flat. It didn't boom the way flat tires did on TV. Something just started flopping and grinding on the right side of the car, and Huey pulled over. He told Abby it wouldn't take long to change it, but it took long enough that she had to run into the trees to tee-tee again.

That was when she realized she was in trouble. Her

head hurt and she felt really tired. She wanted to wipe herself with a leaf, but she was afraid of poison ivy, so she pulled up her panties and started back toward the car, her eyes on Huey as he tossed the flat tire into the trunk. He was grinning and waving. She tried to wave back, but her arm didn't seem to work.

"What's the matter?" Huey called.

She fell facedown on the dirt.

The next thing she saw was Huey's face inches from hers, his eyes bugging behind his heavy black plastic glasses. He looked more scared than she was.

"My sugar's too high," she said, looking around. Huey must have carried her to the white car, because she was sitting in the front seat. "I need my shot."

"The medicine in the ice chest?"

She nodded.

Huey got the small Igloo from the backseat and set it beside her. "Do you know how to do it?"

"I've seen Mom and Dad do it lots of times. But I've never done it. You suck some medicine up into the shot and then stick the needle in my tummy and push the plunger."

Huey screwed his face up, as though the idea were unthinkable. "Does it hurt?"

"A little. But I could die without it."

He shut his eyes and shook his head violently. "We better wait till we see your mama."

"How long is that?"

"I don't know."

Abby rubbed her face where it felt itchy. "Will you give me the shot?"

Huey's lips worked all around his front teeth. "I can't. Can't do that. I hate needles."

"But I have to have it."

"I can't do it, Belle."

Abby bit her lip and tried not to be scared. "Can you open the ice chest for me?"

Huey pressed the button on the side of the Igloo and opened it. Abby reached in and took out two bottles of insulin. She picked the bottles by the "N" and the "R" after "HUMULIN."

"One of these works quick," she told Huey. "And one works later. So you mix them up."

She took a syringe from the ice chest and pulled off the cap, moving quickly so she wouldn't have to think about it long. Huey's face twisted at the sight of the needle. She drew a little clear fluid from each bottle into the syringe, making sure the medicine didn't get above the "4."

It was time to pull up her jumper, but she didn't want to do it. At least twice every day, she sat still while her mother stuck her in the stomach, but the idea of doing it with her own hands made her feel like she had to throw up.

"What's the matter?" Huey asked. "What next?"

"Can you do one thing for me?"

"What?"

Abby pulled her jumper over her right thigh and pinched up some skin and fat. "Pinch up some skin on my leg for me, like this."

After some hesitation, Huey put out his hand and pinched up the skin. "Are you scared?" he asked.

She was. But her daddy had told her that while it was okay to *be* scared, it was better not to let other people see you were. "I'm almost six years old," she said in the strongest voice she could. "I can do it."

Huey's eyes were wet. "You sure are brave."

Abby wondered how a giant who could pick up a car could think she was brave, but he did. And that gave her the courage to stick the needle in. She pressed down the plunger, and by the time she felt the pain the needle was out again.

"You did it!" Huey cried.

"I did!" She laughed and leaned back in the seat, then reached up and hugged Huey. "Let's go see my mom."

He pulled back and looked at her, the awe in his face replaced by sadness.

"What's the matter?" Abby asked.

"I'm never gonna see you again." His bottom lip was shaking. "Your mama's gonna take you away, and I'll never see you."

"Sure you will." She patted his arm.

"No." He shook his head. "It always happens. Any friend I ever make gets took away. Like my sister."

Abby felt his sadness seeping into her. She picked up Belle and pushed the doll at his hand, but he wouldn't take it.

"We'd better get going," she said. "Mom's waiting for me."

"In a minute," Huey said. "In a minute."

"Take it!" Will shouted, shoving the Nokia at Cheryl. "Answer the damn phone!"

She crossed herself, then took the phone and hit SEND.

"Hello? . . . Yeah, I've got it. . . . He's right here. . . . No, not that I saw. No cop cars. . . . We're on I-10. We turn on I-55 North, right? . . . Oh. Okay." She cut her eyes at Will. "How come? . . . Oh God. . . . Okay. Just a second." She handed the phone to Will.

"Joe?" Will said.

"You just had to play hero, didn't you?"

"Joe, I'm doing exactly what you told me to do. All I want is—"

"Don't piss down my boot and tell me it's raining. You called the FBI."

"They were waiting for me in the goddamn bank! But I didn't call them. It's your own fault!"

"What are you talking about?"

"A heart surgeon named James McDill called them. Does that name sound familiar?"

This time Hickey didn't reply.

"McDill was worried you were going to do to some other family what you'd done to his last year. He called the FBI last night. That's what started all this. The helicopters, the alerts for wire transfers, the whole thing."

"Shit. McDill? His wife was a pill, too."

"Joe, I've got the money. I'm ready to make the trade. The FBI agent in the bank tried to make me wear a wire, and I told him to stick it. I pulled Cheryl's gun on him and got the hell out of there. He gave me a GPS tracking device and I trashed it. Ask Cheryl. I *want* you to get to Costa Rica, okay? All I want is my daughter back. That's all I ever wanted."

There was a long silence as Hickey considered his

options. "All right, listen up. Tell Cheryl to take you back to the Beau Rivage. Give her the money and the cell phone, then go back up to your suite. You sit there till the phone rings. It'll be me. That phone's going to ring a lot during the next few hours, and you won't know when. You just keep your ass in that room and answer it. Watch a movie. Because if I call and you ain't there, your kid is dead. I get a busy signal? She's dead. Got it?"

Will sat speechless, watching the cars whiz past. Once again Hickey had done the unexpected. Instead of setting up a ransom exchange, or simply telling Cheryl to dump him somewhere and go to the backup plan, he had figured a way to pin Will down while he made his escape.

"I can't accept that, Joe. When would I get Abby back? How would I know you'd keep up your end?"

"You've just got to have faith, Doc. After I get the money, I'll let your wife and kid go at a public place. Same place for both of them."

"That won't work, Joe. Look . . . I know you don't just want the money, okay? You want to hurt me, and you want to do it through my family. I've got three hundred and fifty thousand dollars here. It's yours. But I've got to be there when we make the trade. When I see Karen and Abby drive away in a car, I'll give you the money. You can do what you want then. You can kill me. Just let them live. That's all I ask."

"Still trying to play hero, aren't you? The big martyr. Well, forget it. It's my way or the highway. Give Cheryl the money and tell her to drop you off at the Beau Rivage."

"I'm not giving up the money until I see Abby."

"You got no choice, son."

The phone went dead in Will's hand. He sat there in shock, all the frustration of the past twenty-four hours boiling like lye in his gut.

"What happened?" Cheryl asked. "What did he say?"

Will hammered the steering wheel with his fists. Cheryl tried to grab his arms, but he pounded the wheel until the horn cover popped off and hit the window.

"Stop!" Cheryl screamed. "What is it? What's wrong?"

He explained Hickey's last demand.

"I told you," she said, sinking back in her seat. "Joey's always three steps ahead. He doesn't make mistakes."

"He trusts you to bring him the money. That's a mistake."

"No," she said with resignation. "He knows I might think about running. But when it comes right down to it, I haven't got the nerve."

Will grabbed her arm and squeezed it hard enough to hurt. "Is that the best you can do? Are you that beaten down?"

She jerked her arm away. "What about you, hotshot? He's got you beat five ways to Sunday."

Will leaned back in the seat, his head and hands throbbing. "I could get somebody to sit in the suite and answer my phone," he said, thinking aloud. "Pretend they're me. One of my friends from the convention."

"Joey wouldn't buy that for two seconds. He knows things about you that *you* don't even know. One trick question and it would be over."

"The hotel phones, then. I could go back and smash

the junction boxes with the car. They're usually on the ground outside. A car wreck . . . that's out of my control."

"Like that's a coincidence? Get real. You're screwed."

Another plane roared overhead—an F-18 Hornet. As the thunder of its jet engine shook the car, an idea flashed into Will's mind with the brilliance of a flare at midnight. Something so simple . . .

"What is it?" Cheryl asked. *"What?"*

He took out his wallet, removed a card from the bill compartment, and dialed a number on Cheryl's cell phone.

"Beau Rivage Casino Resort," said the hotel operator.

"Give me Mr. Geautreau, please. It's an emergency."

"May I ask the nature of the emergency?"

"Life and death, damn it! Get him to the phone!"

"Who are you calling?" Cheryl asked.

"This is Mr. Geautreau. May I help you?"

"This is Dr. Will Jennings, the keynote speaker at the medical convention. We spoke yesterday when I checked in."

"Of course, Doctor. How may I help you?"

"You've had the FBI in this morning, right?"

Geautreau hesitated. "That's right."

"And they checked my room."

"Yes, sir."

"Are there still FBI agents in the hotel?"

"The last one left a few minutes ago."

"Listen, Geautreau. I don't know what the FBI told you, but they were there because my daughter was kidnapped last night. She's still missing. I'm not in the hotel now, but I need someone to think I am. One of the kidnappers. Starting in about fifteen minutes, he's going to call my suite several times over the next few hours. I need all those calls forwarded to the cell phone I'm using now. Can you do that?"

"Doctor, this sounds like a matter for the FBI."

Will had considered calling Zwick. The SAC could have an agent at the Beau Rivage in ten minutes to handle this, if Will would share his plan with the Bureau. But that would put him back under the control of the FBI, which was the last place he wanted to be.

"Can you *technically* do it?" he asked. "Just tell me that. Can you intercept the calls and patch them through?"

"Technically? Yes, we have that capability. But it's not hotel policy to—"

"Forget hotel policy. Let's talk about your personal policy. If you make sure those calls are forwarded to my cell phone for the next three hours—*personally* ensure it—I'll pay you ten thousand dollars."

"Ten thousand . . . ?"

He had the man's attention. Geautreau was caught between perceived legal risk and flat-out greed.

"Doctor—"

"Let's make it fifteen thousand. Fifteen grand for three hours' work."

There was a brief silence. Then the manager said, "Promises are easy to make."

Will breathed a sigh of relief. All he had to do was set the hook.

"I'd need some security," Geautreau said. "Earnest money."

"Would a thousand dollars cover it?"

"I think that would be sufficient."

"Connect me to Dr. Jackson Everett's room. And stay on the phone after he hangs up."

"As you say, Doctor."

The phone rang five times. Will sweated every ring. Then he heard a click, followed by a crash.

"Son of a *bitch*," said a ragged voice. "Have a little mercy on a guy."

"Jack? Wake up."

"Who is this? Crystal?"

Crystal? Everett's wife was named Mary. "It's Will Jennings, Jack. Wake up!"

"Will? What's so important it can't wait till a decent hour? I've got the hangover from hell."

"I'll tell you later. Right now I need to you go downstairs and write the hotel desk manager a check for a thousand dollars."

"A thousand dollars? What are you talking about?"

"I don't have time to explain. I just need you to do it. It's life or death, Jack."

"You're bullshitting me, right? What is this?"

"Jack, for God's sake, I need a thousand dollars at the front desk in five minutes. My life depends on it."

"Your life . . . ? You must have gone gambling last night after all. Did you get into one of those unofficial poker games with this guy?"

"Damn it, Jack!"

"Okay, okay. I'll put it on my Visa."

"That won't work. It's got be cash or a check. This is

a personal thing with the desk manager. His name's Geautreau."

"This is a casino, Will. They're dying to give people cash to lose at the tables. I'll handle it. Let me get moving, brush my teeth—"

"*Now,* Jack! The guy's waiting. His name's Geautreau. G-E-A-U-T-R-E-A-U."

"Are you down at the desk now?"

"I'm a long way from that desk, buddy. This is life or death, no shit. Will you do it?"

"I'm on my way. But you owe me big-time."

"Anything you want. Now hang up. Geautreau's waiting for me."

"Hey, don't worry. I've got you covered on the money."

The phone clicked.

"I heard," said Geautreau.

"Fourteen thousand more where that came from. Write down the number of my cell phone. It's six-oh-one, three-three-two, four-two-one-seven. Read that back to me."

Geautreau did; the number was correct.

"You can*not* screw this up."

"Don't worry, Doctor. A pleasure doing business with you."

Will hung up, threw the Tempo into DRIVE, and headed for the airport.

"Do you really think that will work?" Cheryl asked.

"I'm way past thinking."

NINETEEN

The sign beside the chain link gate read:

WELCOME TO GULFPORT-BILOXI REGIONAL AIRPORT
PRESS INTERCOM BUTTON FOR APPROVAL
AFTER GATE OPENS, PROCEED TO STOP LINE
WAIT FOR GATE TO CLOSE BEHIND YOU

The sign on the gate itself read:

FAILURE TO STOP AND WAIT FOR GATE TO CLOSE IS PUNISHABLE BY A $10,000 FINE.

Will pressed the button on the post beside his window and waited.

"Good morning," said a male voice. "Welcome to U.S. Aviation Corp. How can we help you?"

"This is Dr. Will Jennings. I flew in yesterday in Baron November-Two-Whisky-Juliet. I have a serious emergency. My daughter has been gravely injured in a traffic accident in Jackson, and I must get airborne as soon as possible."

There was a brief delay. "Understood, Doctor. We are contacting the tower. Be advised that—"

The voice was drowned by the thunder of jet engines.

"Sorry. The Air National Guard has flight operations progress, and that might cause some delay. Please wait at the gate, and we'll get back to you ASAP."

Air National Guard operations. Will didn't like the sound of that, but it explained all the activity in the sky as they had approached the airport.

"How long will they make us wait?" Cheryl asked.

"Shouldn't be long. They do all they can to help you in an emergency."

The speaker on the post squawked with a sound that made Will think someone had held a telephone up to a radio.

"Dr. Jennings, this is Gulfport Tower. We understand your situation and will do everything we can to expedite your takeoff. Please be advised that the Combat Air Readiness Training Facility is in the middle of a combined operations exercise. We have F-18 Hornets taking off from runway thirty-two, and Army C-130s landing on runway thirty-six. This is a timed exercise, and it cannot be stopped. However, we should have a brief window during which you can depart. We estimate that window to be eleven minutes from now."

Eleven minutes. They could be halfway to Hazlehurst in eleven minutes. But he had to be careful. If he sounded too upset, they wouldn't open the gate for him.

"I understand, Tower. I contacted ATIS by phone on the way in, and I have the wind conditions. I also have sufficient fuel to reach Jackson. What do you suggest?"

"When the gate opens, proceed to the white line and stop. An employee of U.S. Aviation Corp. will escort you to your plane and assist with your preflight walkaround. We're sorry about your emergency, and will do all we can to expedite. When you reach your aircraft, contact us on 123.7."

"Thank you, Tower. Much appreciated."

The gate slid open.

Will pulled up to the white line and put his foot on the brake. He could see his Baron about seventy feet away, parked between a Bonanza and a KingAir.

"We just sit here?" Cheryl asked.

Eleven minutes. Evidence of military operations was all around them. The roar of the departing F-18s shook the nearby buildings like a hurricane, and two more of the sleek fighters were taxiing past only a hundred feet away, on their way to the primary runway. The Hornets lifted into the sky one after another, every thirty seconds. It was hard to believe there were enough fighters at the Gulfport airport to eat up eleven minutes doing this, but perhaps the tower intended to bring them back in just as fast. Will also saw two C-130 transports hanging in the sky to his right, preparing to land on the shorter general aviation runway.

Ten minutes. He didn't know exactly where he planned to go, but he needed to get there fast. There was no way Hickey was hiding inside the Jackson airport, as Zwick had suggested. Hickey would want to be moving toward the money. And whether he was bound for the cabin near Hazlehurst, the motel in Brookhaven, or the house near McComb did not matter. All three towns lay on a straight line south from Jackson. Hickey was almost certainly driving south on Interstate 55. At the speed limit, he could reach Hazlehurst in thirty-five minutes, and he could have left the Jackson airport up to twenty minutes ago. By flying northwest at max cruise—and factoring in a delay for automobile traffic in Jackon—Will could probably reach Hazlehurst before him, but it would be a matter of minutes, perhaps even seconds. How he would find Hickey and Karen—or Huey and Abby—once he got there was something he'd have to figure out on the way. What mattered now was getting airborne.

He looked toward the U.S. Aviation Corp. building on his right, but saw no one coming his way. "Listen," he said to Cheryl. "When I give the word, I want you to get out of the car and follow me on foot."

"Where are we going?"

"To my plane." He pointed at the Baron. "It's right over there. If I drive past this white line without permission, all hell will break loose. But if we just walk away, they may not notice a thing."

"You go," Cheryl said in a tight voice. "I'm staying here."

"What?"

"You don't need me!"

Will started to pull the Walther, but a simpler idea struck him. Cheryl would not separate herself from the money now. He took the briefcase off her lap, got out, and walked briskly toward the plane. Before he was halfway there, he heard the door of the Tempo slam, and the sound of running feet behind him.

"Change your mind?" he said without turning.

"You bastard."

He opened the Baron's double-wide door, tossed the briefcase between the cabin seats, then turned and helped Cheryl into the plane. She slid between the aft-facing seats and settled into the righthand seat up front. Will sat down in the left seat, scanned the control panel, then switched on his avionics and started his engines. The twin Continentals rumbled to life with reassuring ardor.

"What's that?" asked Cheryl.

A high-pitched sound was cutting through the engine noise. A siren. Will looked up and saw a boxy airport security vehicle bearing down on them, its red light flashing.

"Shit." He throttled up and pulled forward before the guard in the Cushman could blockade the Baron in the line of parked aircraft. Turning right, he started down the taxiway that paralleled the general aviation runway. The Cushman was following, but it couldn't hope to keep up with the rapidly accelerating airplane.

"Beechcraft November-Two-Whiskey-Juliet," crackled the radio. "This is Gulfport Tower. You are in violation of FARs. Return to the ramp immediately."

Will increased speed. He had thought he might take off from the taxiway, but he saw now that was impossible. A giant C-130 Hercules transport sat astride the taxiway ahead of him like an alien spacecraft, its four props slowly turning. He would have to taxi beneath the wing of the Hercules and turn onto the next taxiway, which intersected the main runway at 90 degrees.

"Baron Whiskey-Juliet," said the tower, "you are endangering the lives of military aircrew and ground personnel. Cut your engines immediately."

Cheryl braced in her seat as they rolled toward the Hercules. The sight of the huge spinning props was sobering, but Will held his collision course.

"You're going to hit it!" she shouted. "Stop!"

He swerved left, buzzed under the left wingtip of the C-130, then slowed for the turn that would carry him onto the next taxiway.

"Tower, this is Delta-Seven-One," said the radio. "Who is that crazy son of a bitch?"

That had to be the C-130 pilot. Will was halfway through his turn when another C-130 dropped out of the sky to his right and touched down on the general aviation runway.

"You're going to kill us!" Cheryl shouted.

Will completed his turn, centered the Baron on the taxiway, then stood on his brakes and ran both engines up to full power. His oil pressure looked good, and under the circumstances, that was all he cared about.

Eight hundred feet ahead of him, the F-18s took off without pause, flashing left to right across his line of sight. They looked like sculpted birds of prey as they screamed into the sky. He had always thought it a sad irony that the most beautiful machines ever built by man were built to kill. But that rule held true in nature as well, so perhaps the "irony" was merely sentiment getting in the way of reality.

"You can't fly through that!" Cheryl yelled above the engines.

He was going to have to time his takeoff so that the Baron would pass between two of the departing Hornets, but he felt confident he could do it. This was the last takeoff he would ever be allowed to make from this airport, probably from any airport. It might as well be his best.

"Is this even a runway?"

"It is for us."

"Baron Whiskey-Juliet!" barked the radio. "You are not, repeat not, cleared for takeoff."

Will took his feet off the brakes, and the Baron rolled forward with nauseating slowness compared to the jets. As they approached the intersection with the main runway, an F-18 hurtled toward the same point with a roar like a perpetual explosion. Cheryl screamed and covered her eyes, but Will knew the Hornet would be airborne before they reached the runway. He gave the twin Continentals everything he could.

Seconds before they reached the intersection, the F-18 blasted into the blue. Cheryl was still screaming, but Will let himself ride the rush of adrenaline flushing through his system. All the fatigue of the past twenty-four hours had disappeared. After hours of impotence, he was finally *doing* something.

"November-Whiskey-Juliet! Cut your engines! You are not cleared for takeoff!"

They crossed the intersection at eighty-five knots.

"November-Whiskey-Juliet—God*damn!*"

The Baron rocketed into the air. In seconds it was only a thin cross section against the sky.

* * *

Will was banking north at a thousand feet when he sighted the helicopter. It was a mile behind him, but it was moving to cut the angle off his turn. He increased speed and kept climbing, his eye on a bank of cumulus clouds to the northwest.

He had turned down his radio to dampen the sound of the tower, but as they plowed toward the clouds, he detected a new voice competing with that of the furious controller.

"Baron Two-Whiskey-Juliet, this is the helicopter on your starboard side. I am FBI Special Agent John Sims. Be advised that you have committed multiple felonies. Return to the airport immediately. Please acknowledge."

"Can he catch us?" Cheryl asked.

"Not a chance. We can do two hundred twenty knots, and we've got clouds ahead. He's history."

"Baron Whiskey-Juliet," crackled the radio. "I know you can hear me. I'm patching my Special Agent-in-Charge through on this channel. Stand by."

Will kept climbing toward the cloud bank, pushing the twin engines as hard as they would go. "Can you see the chopper?"

"Getting smaller by the second," Cheryl reported.

"Dr. Jennings," crackled the radio. "This is Frank Zwick. You're putting the lives of your wife and daughter at risk by cutting us out. You're going to need backup. Without it, your family will end up dead."

Will keyed his mike. "That's a risk I'm prepared to take."

"At least tell us where you're headed."

"The best thing you can do right now is get some agents into Brookhaven, Mississippi. Put some more in McComb. I'll call you back."

Will switched off the comm radio, then the transponder, which would normally broadcast his altitude and position to air-traffic controllers.

"You've got a bigger problem than that helicopter," Cheryl said.

"What?"

"You told that guy at the hotel to forward Joey's calls through to my cell phone, right? That means that whether Joey tries to call you at the Beau Rivage, or me on my cell phone, he's going to get this phone. How do we decide who answers?"

Will's face suddenly felt cold. How could he have missed it? If Hickey called Cheryl and got "the hotel" instead, his whole plan would be blown. "We're all right for ten or fifteen minutes," he said, thinking aloud. "I'll answer. I'll say we're stuck in traffic on our way back to the Beau Rivage."

"And after that?"

"By then we'll be halfway to Hazlehurst."

"Is that where we're going?"

"North is where we're going right now. That's all we know until Joe calls and tells you something else. Where exactly is this motel you're supposed to go to in Brookhaven?"

"Right by the main exit."

Brookhaven was twenty miles nearer than Hazlehurst, and Will had once landed there to refuel, but he didn't remember what sort of rental car facilities they had. He'd have to wing it.

The Baron shot into the clouds like a stone thrown through a waterfall, and his heart lightened instantly. The FBI chopper couldn't see him now unless it had radar. And if he dropped to treetop level, it would take an air force AWACs with look-down radar to find him. He felt a brief chill as he remembered that Keesler Air Force Base was only a few miles behind them. There might be an AWACs in the air already, on maneuvers, and after his stunt at the Gulfport field, they might be glad to shadow him for the FBI. He needed to get down into the ground clutter as soon as possible.

"What about the house Joe took you to that night?" he asked. "By McComb. Anything else come to you?"

"No."

"When the FBI raided the cabin, they found Huey's truck. That means Huey and Abby probably left in another vehicle. Were there any other cars at the cabin?"

"I told you, I never *went* there."

"But you must have heard them talking."

"There's a tractor there. I know that. Huey bush-hogs fields for part-time work."

Will tried to picture Huey and Abby escaping from a SWAT team on a rusty John Deere. It didn't seem likely.

"What else?"

"What do you mean?"

"Think about Joe's family. Cars they've had. Come on. . . ."

Cheryl shook her head in exasperation.

* * *

In the switchboard center at the Beau Rivage, a young operator sat reading the unabridged version of *The Stand*. When the hotel's main line rang, he answered the way he always did: "*Beau Rivage Casino Resort.*" But when the caller asked for Suite 28021, he punched Alt-Z on his computer, executing a macro set up at the request of Remy Geautreau, the front desk manager. A digital connection was made and a forwarding number dialed. The operator verified that the macro had executed, then went back to his Stephen King novel.

Will jumped when the cell phone rang, but he dug it quickly from his pocket and checked his watch.

"I'm going to answer," he said. "If it's Joe, I'll feel out what he expects and play it by ear. Hold the phone up to my ear, and hit SEND when I tell you."

Cheryl held up the phone, but Will said nothing. He had just realized something. At maximum cruise, the Baron's engines sounded like twin tornadoes, even with the soundproofing. Telling Hickey they were stuck in traffic near the Beau Rivage wouldn't explain the roar. Hickey might even recognize the distinctive sound of airplane engines.

The cell phone kept ringing.

Will had two choices. Throttle the engines back to idle and hope they were quiet enough to be undetectable over the cell phone, or cut them altogether. Cutting the engines was far more dangerous, but only that would guarantee that Hickey wouldn't hear them.

"Are you going to answer?" Cheryl asked.

Thankful that he had not yet dived for the ground

clutter, Will pulled back to idle, feathered his props, and killed both engines. In the eerie silence, the plane began to fall.

"Shit!" Cheryl screamed. *"What happened?"*

"Hit SEND."

Her face was bone white. *"Are we going to crash?"*

"We're fine! Hit SEND!"

He heard a beep, then the hiss of the open connection. "Joe?"

"How's it hanging, Doc? You taking a nap up there?"

Up there? Will's heart thudded. Then he realized that Hickey meant the hotel suite. He'd assumed Hickey would call Cheryl before he called the Beau Rivage, to verify that she'd gotten the money. But Hickey had clearly expected Will to answer this call. That meant Geautreau had successfully patched the call. It also meant that the "stuck in traffic" excuse was useless.

"Where's Abby?" Will asked, trying to picture himself in the suite at the Beau Rivage rather than dropping toward the earth at a thousand feet per minute. "I want to talk to her."

"Everything in its season, Doc. I'll be talking to you soon."

The phone went dead. Will dropped it in Cheryl's lap and began his midair engine-start sequence.

"Start the engines!" she screamed. "We're crashing!"

He felt a rush of exhilaration as the Continentals kicked off. He adjusted the pitch of his props and felt the plane leap forward as the blades bit into the air.

"Jesus God," Cheryl whispered, when the nose of the Baron finally came level. "I almost puked."

Will began climbing to regain the lost altitude. "Cheryl, I've got to know what kind of car Huey's driving."

"If you'd keep the damn engines running, maybe I could think."

"You think like you've never thought in your life, goddamn it! We're at seven thousand feet. We can glide for seven minutes without engines before we crash. Unless Joe gets talkative, we're fine."

"Why are you so mean?" she whined, her voice like a child's. "I'm trying to help you!"

"Try harder."

The cell phone rang in her lap.

"Who answers this time?" she asked.

"You. He just called me. He's calling you to make sure I gave you the money."

"What if you're wrong?"

"If he sounds surprised, tell him you came back to the hotel."

"Why would I do that?"

"I shorted you on the money."

She nodded.

"And try like hell to find out what Huey's driving."

"Okay."

"Wait till I cut the engines."

"Sweet Mary . . ."

Once again, Will pulled the engines back to idle, feathered his props, and starved the engines into silence.

Cheryl hit SEND as the plane began to glide earthward. "Joey? . . . Yeah, I've got it." She gave Will a thumbs-up. "Three hundred and fifty thousand," she said. "He tried to bribe me with it. . . . Yeah. No problem. I think he's about wasted by the whole thing. . . . I'm on 110 now, headed up toward the interstate. Am I still going to the motel?"

Will heard a squawk from the phone, but he couldn't distinguish words.

"Yeah, I remember. . . . Uh-huh. . . . What about Huey and the little girl? . . . Joey, you're not going to hurt that kid, are you?" She jerked the phone away from her ear. "I'm sorry. . . . I know. I will. I'm on my way."

She clicked off.

Will restarted the engines, and once again the Baron began to climb.

"What did he say about Abby?"

"He told me not to talk about it on the phone."

"What else did he say?"

"Go to Paco's place."

"What's that?"

"A club. It's on the county line near Hattiesburg. I danced there for a while. They've got rooms out back for the girls."

"He said the name of the club on the phone?"

"No. The name of the club is Paradise Alley. Paco just works there. He's tight with Joey."

Will pulled out a map. He knew Mississippi like the back of his hand, but he wanted to visualize vectors as accurately as he could. I-55 was the main north/south artery, and it bisected the state. Jackson sat in the middle, with Hazlehurst, Brookhaven, and McComb straight south of it. Hattiesburg was on a diagonal, southeast of Jackson, down Highway 49. It was much closer to their present position, but there was no way he could cover both I-55 and Highway 49. And the fact that Cheryl had been told to go to Paco's place didn't mean Hickey was going straight there, or that Huey had been given the same instructions.

"Son of a bitch," Cheryl said.

"What?"

"The Rambler!"

"What?"

She was smiling at something. "Joey's mom had an AMC Rambler. An old white thing with push-button gears. It was the club that made me think of it. Paradise Alley. Joey's mom got to where she couldn't drive, and one night Joey showed up at Paradise Alley in her car. When we tried to leave, it broke down. We had to hitch. It supposedly sat up on blocks for a couple of years, but I never saw it. I was with Huey once when he went to Auto Shack to buy parts for it. Maybe the Rambler was at the cabin." She shook her head. "I haven't thought about that car in three years!"

Will couldn't suppress his excitement anymore. At last, he had something. A white Rambler. And Abby might be in it. But where was it? "The FBI found a cell phone and a landline at the cabin," he reasoned aloud. "The landline was Joe's backup for Huey. So, unless Huey had *two* cell phones, Joe can't contact him while he's on the road."

"I'm pretty sure Huey only had one," Cheryl said. "But the Rambler could have a phone, couldn't it?"

"It could. Does Huey know about Paradise Alley? Has he ever been there?"

She laughed. "Are you kidding? You can't take Huey

to a titty bar. One glimpse of a naked woman, he blows a gasket. Joey brought him to see me dance once, and he jumped up on stage trying to throw his coat over me. It took four bouncers to get him down."

"But that wasn't Paradise Alley."

"No."

"Has Huey ever met this Paco guy?"

"No way. Joey keeps him away from all that stuff."

"Has he spent any time in or around Hattiesburg?"

"Not that I know of."

"Then Huey isn't headed for Paco's place. He's probably going wherever he was supposed to go according to the original backup plan. Joe changed your instructions on the fly, but I don't think he'd do that to Huey. So, what was Huey's original backup destination? Where would Joe have told him to go if there was a problem?"

Cheryl chewed her bottom lip as she considered the question. "Joey wouldn't want him driving too far. Not with your little girl along. Too much chance of the highway patrol stopping him."

"Did Joe say *anything* about Huey during that last call?"

"Just that he would be fine."

"I think Huey's going to the motel in Brookhaven. It's only twenty minutes from Hazlehurst, which makes it less than an hour from the cabin. Joe could get there from Jackson in fifty minutes, pick up Huey and Abby, then head east to Hattiesburg to meet you."

"Makes sense to me."

"If I'm right, Joe is driving south on I-55 right now. Huey is, too. They're probably twenty minutes apart in the southbound lanes. To hell with Highway 49."

Will gripped the yoke with both hands and put the Baron into a steep dive. He would turn west after he dropped below radar level. He wanted to be over I-55 as soon as possible, but he didn't want any curious air-traffic controllers to see him getting there.

Karen looked into the trunk of the Camry and put her hand to her mouth. The woman Hickey had carjacked had beaten her hands bloody in her attempts to get out of the trunk. Several fingers were broken. The left side of her head was swollen from the pistol blow, and her eyes had the dull sheen of shock. She looked up at Karen like she expected to be raped and left for dead.

"Get out," Karen said. "Hurry! Before he changes his mind."

Hickey was sitting in the Camry, talking on the cell phone, checking on Will. At Karen's urging, he had pulled off the interstate at a deserted exit to let the woman out of the trunk. But the owner of the Camry clearly didn't understand the chance she was being given, because she wasn't moving.

"Come on!" Karen hissed. She reached in and pulled the woman up by the arms. Slowly, like a sleepwalker waking, the woman began to jerk her arms, but whether to assist Karen or fight her, Karen couldn't tell. Somehow she got the woman clear of the trunk and on her feet.

She was a pretty brunette, with a hint of Asian ancestry around her eyes, and she wore a blue skirt suit much like Karen's. But her eyes were blank.

Karen pushed her toward the trees on the side of the road. "Run! Go on! Run!"

The woman looked around. The only sign of civilization was a boarded-up gas station. "Are you going to leave me here?" she asked.

"You're safer here than you are with us. Go!"

Like a zoo-bred animal that finds its cage left open, the woman seemed reluctant to leave the familiarity of her car.

"If you don't run," Karen told her, "you're going to die."

The woman began to cry.

In the switchboard center at the Beau Rivage, the operator was heavy into *The Stand*. Trashcan Man was hauling his nuclear weapon toward the Dark Man's stronghold, and trivialities like gainful employment simply could not compete. The young man answered the primary line on autopilot, and when the caller asked for suite 28021, he said, "Just one moment," as he usually did, and made the connection.

Twenty-eight floors above him, the phones in Will's suite rang, faded, and rang again. The operator read another paragraph of Trashcan Man's journey, then blinked and raised his head from the page. He was certain that something was wrong, he just couldn't place what it was. It took a few seconds to realize his mistake, but he thought he still had time to correct it. He was reaching for the keyboard to execute the call-forwarding macro when the phones in 28021 stopped ringing.

"Shit," he whispered. *"Shit."*

Remy Geautreau had promised him a hundred bucks if he'd forward the suite's calls for the next three hours.

He punched a code that connected him to the desk manager's office.

Remy Geautreau was not in his office. He was standing at the front desk, listening to an irate guest who had left a camcorder battery in his room after checkout. Housekeeping had already checked twice for it, but the guest refused to believe they hadn't found it. At the first brief pause, a clerk stepped up and said, "Mr. Geautreau? You have a phone call."

"I want to talk to the maid myself!" bellowed the guest.

Geautreau gave him a syrupy smile. "But of course, Mr. Collins. Do you speak Spanish?"

The man went purple. "Goddamn it!" He took his wife by the arm and stomped toward the grand entrance to make his exit.

"He lost eight thousand last night," Geautreau said with a bemused smile. "You can always tell the losers."

He went into his office and picked up the phone. "Hello?"

"I screwed up," said the operator. "With the call forwarding thing."

Geautreau's face darkened.

"A call came in for the suite, and before I could think, I put it through. I tried to catch it, but I was too late. They hung up."

The manager closed his eyes and hung up. "You just cost me fifteen thousand dollars, you incompetent ass."

As he closed the door of his office, he wondered whether the doctor would let him keep the thousand dollars of earnest money. Of course he wouldn't.

* * *

The Baron roared northward above Interstate 55 at two hundred knots. Will didn't think they had covered enough distance to sight Huey's Rambler yet—if in fact he was driving the Rambler—but he was flying parallel to the southbound lanes just in case. Cheryl was glued to the passenger window. The traffic below was moderate but steady, the cars and trucks humming along at seventy-five miles per hour while Will shot past them at three times that.

He was about to cut his airspeed when the cell phone began ringing again. From habit he reached for the throttles; then he stopped himself. If he cut the engines at three hundred feet, the state police would soon be hosing them off the interstate.

"Who answers it?" Cheryl asked.

"You."

"Joey already told me where to go. He wouldn't call again."

Will considered not answering at all, but he couldn't risk it. He pulled the throttles back as far as he dared, then picked up the Nokia and hit SEND.

"Hello?"

He heard only the open connection. Then someone said, "Jennings?"

"Joe?"

More silence.

"Joe? Are you there?"

"You wanna tell me how I dialed Cheryl and got you, you clever son of a bitch?"

Will gripped the phone tighter but kept his voice calm.

"You must have dialed the wrong number. You thought you were dialing her, but you dialed the hotel instead."

Hickey didn't reply.

"Joe?"

"Put Cheryl on the phone."

Will's breath caught in his throat. "How do I do that?"

"You hand her the fucking phone, that's how."

The coldness of Hickey's voice was worse than any blast of temper. "Joe, I'm telling you—"

"No, I'm telling *you*, Doc. I'm gonna let you in on a little secret. You're never going to talk to your kid again."

Will's face went numb.

"It was always going to be that way," Hickey said. "It had to be. It's predestination. From the day you murdered my mother. You took what was precious to me, so I gotta take what's precious to you. You see that, right?"

"Where is she, Joe? Where's Abby?"

"You don't need to worry about that. In fact, if I was you, I'd go ahead and slit my wrists, to save myself the hell that's coming. Going down to a funeral home to pick out that tiny little casket? Facing your wife after going off and leaving her like that? What kind of father does that, huh?"

Hickey's words cut to the bone, but something more terrible struck Will like a hammer. There was no way Hickey could speak that way if Karen was in the car with him. She would be screaming at the least, possibly even trying to kill him.

"Where's Karen, Joe? I know she's not with you. What have you done to her?"

"You don't need to worry about that either. No point at all."

The numbness began to spread along his arms. It was like being cut adrift in space, lost in a vacuum without air or sound.

"Wherever you are," Hickey said, "you might as well just stay there. See if Cheryl will give you a little head while you shoot yourself. She's good at it. Oh, and tell her I'll be seeing her soon. *Real* soon."

"Joe, you've got the wrong idea. I don't know where Cheryl is. I kept the phone because—"

The phone went dead in his hand.

Will tasted blood. He had bitten through his bottom lip.

"What's the matter?" Cheryl asked in a fearful voice. "What just happened?"

He couldn't speak.

"He knows, doesn't he? He knows we're together."

"I think he killed Karen. And he's going to kill Abby."

"What? You're crazy."

Will's hands began to shake.

Karen closed the Camry's trunk and looked back over her shoulder. The woman was moving now, making for the abandoned gas station at an ungainly trot. Karen wished she would turn toward the trees, because Hickey could easily drive over and shoot her if he changed his mind about letting her go. Hopefully he had too much on his mind to worry about that.

Karen walked to the passenger door and climbed in

beside him. Hickey was off the phone. He was just sitting there, staring through the windshield.

"Did you talk to Will?"

He fished a Camel out of his pocket and lit it with the cigarette lighter. "I talked to him."

"What did he say?"

"It's not what he said. It's where he said it. He wasn't in his suite."

She felt a stab of alarm. "What?"

"He answered Cheryl's cell phone. I told you he was pulling something." Hickey turned and let the hatred in his eyes burn into her. "You just remember, he asked for every bit of this."

Hickey put the Camry into DRIVE, spun it in a 180-degree turn, and sped back up to the interstate. His cheeks reddened as he drove, but his lips only grew paler.

"Call the Beau Rivage again," Karen pleaded. "There must be some mistake!"

"Oh, there's a mistake, all right. But it doesn't matter. There's nothing anybody can do now."

He said this forcefully, but he didn't look like he quite believed it.

Karen reached out and touched him softly on the arm. "*Please* tell me what's happening."

Hickey backhanded her across the face.

"Don't you touch me again," he growled.

Will reduced his airspeed to a hundred knots. They were far enough north now that spotting Huey and Abby driving south was a possibility. It was more than that, in fact. It was his only hope. The greater part of him believed that Karen was dead. There was no way she could have sat silently by while Hickey explained why he had to kill Abby. It was possible she was tied and gagged, but he doubted that scenario. With Abby under his control, Hickey didn't need such measures to make Karen cooperate.

His prayer now was that Hickey had no way to contact Huey while he was on the road. That Abby would remain alive for the next fifteen or twenty minutes, while Will tried to locate her from the air.

"I'm dead," Cheryl mumbled for the twentieth time. She was hugging herself and rocking like a heroin addict going cold turkey.

"Sit up!" Will shouted. "Look for the Rambler!"

She leaned forward and looked at her knees.

He shoved the yoke forward. The busy interstate rushed up to meet them. In seconds, power pylons and oak trees rose higher than the Baron.

"Pull up!" she screamed, going rigid in her seat. *"Pull up!"*

At the last instant, Will pulled back on the yoke and began skimming along beside the southbound lanes. Cars slowed as their drivers gaped at the low-flying airplane. From eighty feet you could see individual faces, chattering mouths, pointing fingers. Most of the car passengers probably thought he was a crop duster, albeit a crazy one.

"You look for that Rambler, or I'll flip this thing on its back until you vomit."

She pressed her face to the Plexiglas. "I'm looking!"

Will switched on his radio. He had just thought of a way in which the FBI might help him after all.

"Baron November-Two-Whiskey-Juliet," crackled the speaker. "Baron Whiskey-Juliet, this is an emergency call. Please respond."

It was a little too soon to be hearing from the FAA about his treetop run over I-55. He keyed his mike.

"This is Baron Whiskey-Juliet, over."

There was a brief silence. Then a voice said, "Dr. Jennings, this is Frank Zwick."

Will shook his head. The FBI man didn't give up easily, he had to give him that. There was no telling how long they had been making that radio call. Ever since he switched off his radio, probably.

"Doctor, we intercepted part of that last cell phone transmission. We heard what Hickey said about your daughter."

Will didn't respond.

"Where are you, Jennings? Let us help you."

"Where I am doesn't matter." He kept his eyes on the interstate to his right. "Tell me one thing. Did you ever figure out how Hickey escaped from the airport?"

"We're pretty sure he carjacked a Toyota Camry from a woman who arrived in the garage at the same time he and your wife did."

"What color was it?"

"A silver ninety-two model. We got it off the garage security tapes. We just had the Highway Patrol put out a BOLO on it."

"Could you answer one question for me?"

"What is it?"

Will steeled himself. "Has my wife's body turned up anywhere?"

"No. We have no reason to believe that your wife has been injured. Doctor, we need to know where you are. We can't—"

Will switched off the radio.

"Have you seen anything?" he asked Cheryl.

"I'm looking," she assured him. "I've seen every other kind of car, but no Rambler."

"Scan. Don't focus. If you see anything that looks remotely like it, sing out. I'll come around with the flow of traffic."

"Is that Brookhaven over there?"

"Where?"

She pointed east. "Yonder way."

"Yes."

"Hey!" she cried. "There's the motel! That's the Truckers' Rest! Right by the exit."

"Can you see the parking lot?"

"We're too far away."

Will didn't think Huey could have reached the motel yet, but he couldn't afford to pass it by without a look. He pushed the engines harder and circled back to check the parking lot. Skipping the Baron over a cellular transmission tower, he floated past the exit ramp and dropped over the parking lot of the Truckers' Rest like a seagull looking for scraps.

"No Rambler," Cheryl said.

Will shot back over the interstate and resumed his course parallel to the southbound lanes coming out of Jackson. He saw Tauruses, Lexuses, SUVs by the dozen, semitrucks, Winnebagos, and motorcycles. But no Rambler.

"Be right," he said softly, holding the image of a Rambler in his mind. *"Be right."*

"Oh my God," Cheryl said, which sometimes seemed the sum total of her vocabulary.

"What is it?"

She was staring down at the interstate with her mouth hanging open.

"What?"

"I saw it."

"The Rambler?"

She turned to him and nodded, her eyes wide.

"Are you positive?"

"It was them. I saw Huey's face. I saw your little girl in the passenger window."

Will suddenly found it difficult to breathe. He craned his neck to look back, but the spot was far behind them now. Climbing skyward, he pulled the Baron around in a turn so tight the nose could have kissed the tail.

"What are you going to do?" Cheryl asked.

"Make another pass. You make damn sure it's them. And belt yourself in."

"Oh my God."

TWENTY

"Let me tell you something about revenge," Hickey said.

He and Karen were twenty-five miles south of Jackson, and his mood seemed to improve with every mile. She could see anticipation in the way he leaned into the wheel as he drove. She looked through her window. A long field of cotton was giving way to a field of house trailers. PRE-FABRICATED HOUSING! blared the banner hanging over the lot's entrance. GET A DOUBLE-WIDE DELUXE TODAY!

"You remember what you asked me this morning?" Hickey asked.

"What?"

"Would I kill you instead of your kid?"

Karen nodded cautiously. Hickey was fond of games. Like a cruel child teasing a wounded animal, he liked to probe her with a sharp stick and watch her squirm.

"You still want it that way? If somebody has to die, I mean?"

"Yes."

He nodded thoughtfully, as though considering a philosophical argument. "And you think that would do the trick? Your dying would hurt your husband enough to pay him back for killing my mother?"

"Will didn't kill your mother." *But someone should have,* she thought. *Before she birthed you, you son of a bitch.*

"See, I don't think it would," Hickey said. "Hurt him that much, I mean. And the reason is interesting. See, you're not his blood."

She refused to look at him.

"If you died, he might miss you for a while. But the fact is, you're just his wife. He can get another one. Damn easy, with all the money he's got. A lot newer model, too. Hell, he might be tired of you already."

Karen said nothing.

"But your little girl, now, that's different. That's blood of his blood. That's *him*, the same way Mama and me were joined. And nearly six, that's old enough for him to really know her. He loves that kid. Light of his life."

At last she turned to him. "What are you telling me? Are you saying you're going to kill Abby?"

He smiled. "I'm just explaining a concept to you. Hypothetically. Showing you what's wrong with your idea from this morning."

"This morning you told me I didn't need to worry about that. You said nobody was going to die." *And somebody already has,* she reminded herself, thinking of Stephanie.

Hickey tapped the wheel like a man content. "Like I said. Hypothetically."

* * *

As soon as Will completed his turn and settled the Baron back over the oncoming traffic, he saw the small white car Cheryl had seen. Box-shaped and splotched with primer, it was piddling along compared to the other traffic, constantly being passed on the left. Cheryl was right: it was a Rambler. Will reduced power, slowing the plane until it was practically drifting up the interstate toward the car.

Then he saw it.

A small head in the passenger compartment of the Rambler, sitting close to a huge figure behind the wheel. A figure so large that it seemed to dwarf the car itself. The child was moving in the front seat, and as the Baron closed on the Rambler, Will made out the form and face he would have known by the dimmest candlelight. A relief unlike anything he had ever known rolled through him. Abby was alive. She was alive, and nothing on God's earth would keep him from her now.

"Hello, Alpha-Juliet," he said softly. He waggled his wings once, then again.

"What are you *doing*?" Cheryl wailed as the plane rocked left and right like a roller coaster. "I'm going to puke!"

"Waggling my wings," he said with a smile.

Huey and Abby were singing "The Itsy-Bitsy Spider" when the airplane first appeared. It was flying straight toward them at treetop level, just to the right of the interstate.

"Look!" Huey cried. "A crop duster!"

"He's not supposed to fly that low," Abby said in a concerned voice. "I know, because my daddy flies an airplane."

The plane shot past them. Abby whipped her head around and watched it climb, then vanish beyond her line of sight.

"I rode a airplane once," Huey said. "When Joey took me to Disneyland."

"You mean Disney World."

"No, they got two. The old one's in California. That's the one we went to. Joey says they're both the same, but I think the one in Florida's bigger."

"I think so, too." Abby patted Belle in her lap. "I met the real Belle there. And the real Snow White."

"The real ones?"

"Uh-huh. And I got dresses just like they had."

Huey's smile disappeared. He reached into the side pocket of his coveralls, fished around, then brought out his empty hand.

"If I made you something," he said softly, "would you like it?"

"Sure I would."

"It probably wouldn't be near as nice as all the things you got at home."

"Sure it would. Presents you make are always better than ones you buy."

He seemed to weigh her sincerity about this. Then he reached back into the pocket and brought out what he had spent the previous night carving.

Abby opened her mouth in wonder. "Where did you get that?"

"I made it for you."

"You *made* that?"

What had been a chunk of cedar the day before had

been transformed by Huey's knife into a figure of a bear holding a little girl on its lap. The fine detail made Abby's Barbie look like a bland store mannequin. The little girl on the bear's lap had hair falling to her shoulders like Abby's, wore a jumper like hers, and held a small doll in her hands. But what riveted Abby's attention was the bear itself. It wore no clothes, but on its face sat a pair of heavy glasses, just like Huey's. The bear was clearly watching out for the little girl.

"You really made that?" she asked again.

Huey nodded shyly. "Beauty and the Beast. You said it was your favorite. I tried to make it as pretty as I could. I know you like pretty things."

She took the carving from his hand. The wood was still warm from Huey's pocket. But more than that, it felt *alive* somehow. Hard and soft at the same time. As though the bear and the little girl might move in her hands at any moment.

"I love it," she said. "I *love* it."

Huey's eyes lit up. "You do?"

Abby nodded, her eyes still on the figures.

"Maybe you'll remember me sometimes, then."

She looked up at him with curiosity in her eyes. "Of course I will."

Huey suddenly cried out and hit the brake pedal. Abby grabbed the dashboard, fearing they were about to smash into something.

"He's going to crash!" Huey yelled.

The airplane was back, only this time it was right over the road and zooming straight at them. The cars ahead were slowing down, some even pulling onto the shoulder.

The plane skated to Abby's right, toward the trees, but it was getting larger every second. As she stared, its wings rocked up and down: first the right wing, then the left, then both again.

A strange thrill went through her. "He wiggled his wings!"

The plane's engines began to overpower the sound of the car. Its pilot rocked the wings again, as though waving right at Abby, then rocketed over the car. She clapped her hands with delight.

"My daddy does that! Just the same way! My daddy . . ."

Her face suddenly felt hot, and she had to squeeze her legs together to keep from wetting herself. Her daddy was in that plane. She knew it. And nothing in her life had ever felt quite the way that knowing that did. She reached out and touched Huey's arm.

"I think everything's going to be okay now."

As the Baron blasted past the Rambler, Will saw Abby's face pressed to the glass of the passenger window. Tears temporarily blinded him.

"I told you!" Cheryl cried. "You saw them?"

"Yes," he said, wiping his eyes with his sleeve.

"What are you going to do now?"

"I'm going to land."

"On the *road*?"

"Absolutely."

Cheryl's face went so white that Will thought she might pass out.

"Tighten that seat belt."

As she scrabbled at her belt, Will climbed to five hundred feet and took the Baron to a hundred and eighty knots.

"Where are you going? You said you were going to land. You're leaving them behind."

"We've got something to do first. I want you to watch for a silver Camry."

Cheryl's hand flew to her mouth. She had heard Zwick on the radio, and she knew who was driving a silver Camry.

"Keep it together," Will said. "Everything's fine."

He hated to let the Rambler out of his sight for even one minute, but he could cover five miles of interstate in ninety seconds, and if Hickey was close enough to give him problems on the ground, he needed to know.

"When you land," Cheryl said, "what about the cars and stuff? I mean, there's eighteen-wheelers down there."

"I'll try not to hit them."

"Jesus Christ. How did I get here?"

"Joe Hickey put you here. It's that simple."

"I see a Camry! It's silver. It's the old kind, the swoopy one that looks like a Lexus."

Zwick had said the car Hickey stole was a '92 model. Will was pretty sure the '92 Camry was the "swoopy" one, not the more generic model. He climbed quickly to a thousand feet. He would have liked nothing better than to descend and see whether Karen was in that car, but if he got close enough to see her, Hickey could spot him. The silver Camry below might not be the one Hickey had stolen—there were a lot of silver Camrys in the world—but it could be. He needed to get on the ground fast.

He executed a teardrop turn, pointed the Baron south

at two hundred knots, and began to consider the task he had set himself.

There was really only one way to stop a car with an unarmed airplane. Land in front of it. That left him two choices. He could fly past the Rambler, then turn and land against oncoming traffic, which would greatly increase the odds of killing himself and a lot of other people. Or he could fly along with the flow of traffic—as he was doing now—match his speed to that of the cars below, and drop down into the first open stretch he saw ahead of the Rambler.

"There it is!" Cheryl said, pointing through the windshield.

She had good eyes. About a mile and a half ahead, a long line of cars had backed up behind a slow-moving vehicle in the right lane, while faster moving traffic shot past them on the left.

Will cut his airspeed and dropped to four hundred feet. The vehicles below were moving between seventy and eighty miles per hour. At ninety knots, he was rapidly overtaking them, but also moving into position to land in front of the Rambler. As he approached the congested line of cars, he lowered his landing gear and went to full flaps. This further reduced his speed, bringing him more in line with the speed of the vehicles below, though he was still overtaking them.

When he descended to a hundred feet, fear announced itself in the pit of his stomach. This was no deserted stretch of Delta highway. This was I-55, where cars and trucks managed to slam into each other every day without the help of rogue airplanes. He could smell the exhaust of the big diesel trucks below. From this altitude they looked like aircraft carriers on a concrete sea.

Airspeed was eighty-five knots, still too fast. He would have given a lot for a cold winter day, good dense air for the propellers to bite into and to keep his stall speed low. This was the worst weather for what he was about to do. Cheryl leaned forward, watching the concrete rise toward them and endlessly repeating Hail Marys. Apparently, if she was going to die, she wanted to see it coming. A perverse instinct, perhaps, but a human one.

"Can you do it?" she asked softly.

A brief crosswind tried to push the tail around, but Will corrected for it. "We're about to find out."

She pointed through the windshield. "There they are!"

He shut everything out of his mind but the scene ahead. In the right lane: the white Rambler, moving slowly, seeming to pull an endless chain of cars along behind it, cars which were actually trying to whip into the left lane so that they could pass the cars holding them back. In the left lane: the fast movers, cars and trucks racing up and passing the sideshow in the right lane at eighty miles per hour. In front of the Rambler, where he needed to set down, were the speeding cars in the left lane and a couple of dawdlers in the right. A Mercury Sable about sixty yards ahead of the Rambler, and a minivan some distance ahead of that. An intricate ballet of mechanical dancers that would remain in their present relationships for a very brief time.

It was now or never.

He centered the Baron on the broken white line and dropped toward the roof of the Rambler at eighty-two knots. He couldn't see what was happening behind him, but he felt sure that the sight of a twin-engine plane dropping toward the road with its gear and flaps down and a wingspan as wide as the interstate had sent a lot of feet to a lot of brake pedals.

The Baron overtook the Rambler with a speed differential of thirty miles per hour. Will flew half the distance to the Mercury Sable, then eased the yoke forward and and reduced power further. The Baron seemed to stutter in midair, as though he had applied the brakes to a car.

Then it fell like a stone.

Three miles behind the Baron, Hickey gaped and pointed through the windshield of the stolen Camry.

"Look at that crazy son of a bitch! If he's got to crash, the least he could do is get off the highway to do it."

Karen said nothing. The instant the Baron had dropped out of the sky and lined itself up over the interstate, her heart had jumped into her throat. It had to be Will. It *had* to be.

"What's he doing up there?" Hickey wondered aloud. "He's a kamikaze, this guy. He must have lost an engine."

He looked to Karen for a response, but she sat still and silent, staring at the dashboard. If Will was risking his life to land on the interstate, that could only mean one thing. Abby was somewhere up ahead. And she was alive.

"What's with you?" Hickey said. "You gotta see this. This'll make CNN tonight." He punched her on the shoulder. "You sick or something? Why are you . . ."

He faced forward again and watched the plane drop to the level of the cars ahead, then disappear.

"Son of a bitch," he said. "Son of a *bitch*!" He floored the accelerator and started to pass the Cadillac ahead of them.

Karen grabbed the wheel and wrenched it toward her, throwing the Camry into the right lane and driving the Cadillac off the road in a cloud of dust.

"Let go!" Hickey yelled, hammering her head with his fist.

Karen clung to the wheel like a sea captain in a gale. The Camry veered onto the shoulder, which dropped precipitously to the woods below. She didn't care if they flipped three times and crashed into the trees, so long as it kept Hickey from reaching Abby. She had made that decision hours ago.

"Let go, you crazy bitch!"

He slammed an elbow into her ear and yanked the car back onto the road. Karen blacked out for a moment. She knew she had, because when she came to, her hands had slipped from the wheel, and the Camry's engine was whining as Hickey streaked past the cars ahead. She saw then that he was steering with only his left hand. His right held Will's .38, and it was pointed at her stomach.

"Do it again and I'll kill you," he said in a matter-of-fact voice.

She backed against the passenger door.

As the speedometer needle went to ninety, then a hundred, Karen studied the gun in Hickey's hand. It was somehow more frightening than the idea of a wreck. A wreck at this speed would certainly kill them both, but the gun might kill only *her*. And Abby was so close—

Hickey cursed and applied the brake. A long chain of

flashing red lights had appeared ahead. Brake lights. Something was happening up there. And that something had to be Will's plane. Hickey swerved across the left lane onto the median shoulder and raced past the braking cars. The hatred in his face was like a sulfurous fire burning beneath his skin.

Fixing an image of Abby in her mind, Karen began to pray. The image she saw was not Abby as she was now, but as an infant, the miracle of flesh and bone and smiling eyes that Karen had given up her career for, that she would give up everything for. A profound sadness seeped outward from her heart, but with it came a peace that transcended her fear. In the silence of her mind, words from Ecclesiastes came to her, heard long ago but never quite forgotten. *There is a time to kill, and a time to die.* She closed her eyes.

"I love you, Abby," she said softly. "I'm sorry, Will."

"What?" Hickey said, fighting to keep the Camry moving past the bumper-to-bumper cars.

Karen curled her fingers into claws and launched herself across the console with murder in her heart.

Hickey fired.

The Baron hit the concrete hard, and Will's plan instantly began to disintegrate. The driver of the Sable must have slowed, because the Baron was racing toward it far too fast to stop. Will hit the throttles and hopped over the car like a student pilot practicing a touch-and-go landing. When the wheels hit again, he saw that the minivan which had been comfortably ahead of the Sable had also braked, probably because the vehicles ahead of it had slowed or stopped to watch the crisis unfolding behind them.

He pulled up his flaps, cut power, and applied the brakes, but he saw in an instant that he wouldn't be able to stop in time. He no longer had enough power or distance to skip over the minivan, as he had the Rambler, and his props were spinning with enough force to chop the van into scrap metal. Yet the driver wouldn't get off the damned road to avoid the crash. Like Will, he was blocked by the wooded hill of the median on the left and the steep drop into woods on the right. But either would be preferable to being hit by an airplane. Then Will saw the group of heads in the back of the van.

Kids.

He swerved left and shut off his mixture, fuel, and master electrical switch. He felt a moment of euphoria as they passed the van, but it turned to horror as his right wingtip clipped the vehicle and they began to spin.

Time decelerated with sickening slowness. Cheryl was shrieking, and at some point in the whirling chaos Will saw a log truck barreling up from behind them. Sitting in front of the log truck like a Matchbox toy was the white Rambler. The Baron's nose gear crumpled as the plane spun, and one of the props hit the cement in a storm of sparks, sending a blade hurtling off into space. As they came around to face the Rambler again, Will saw the little car suddenly scoot forward out of the log truck's path, but his relief died as it went over the narrow shoulder and plummeted down the slope toward the trees.

"We've got to get out!" he shouted, gripping Cheryl's arm.

The plane had come to rest facing north, and the thirty-ton juggernaut of steel and wood that was the log truck was speeding toward them with the sound of burning brakes. Will unbuckled both seat belts, then leaned over Cheryl and unlatched the door.

"Get out!" he shouted.

But she didn't. She was trying to look back into the cabin. Will scrambled over her and onto the wing, then pulled her from the cockpit. She was yelling something at him, but he shoved her onto the ground and jumped off after her.

"The money!" she screamed. *"We left the money!"*

"Forget it!" He grabbed her arm and tried to pull her clear, but she jerked free and jumped back onto the wing.

Will ran for the edge of the road.

As the Rambler hurtled down the grassy slope toward the trees, Huey pumped the brake, but it seemed to have no effect. Abby was screaming in his ear, and he saw the screams like red paint on the air. His mind went blank for a second, but then a thought flashed like a Roman candle. He grabbed Abby with both hands and tossed her into the backseat like a sack of flour.

The Rambler tore through an old fence and crashed into a wall of saplings, hurling Huey's three-hundred-pound body forward and smashing his head against the windshield. Abby smacked into the back of the front seat and bounced backward.

She couldn't seem to get her breath, but other than that, she felt okay. She got to her knees and looked over the front seat.

The windshield was smashed to pieces. Huey was bleeding from his forehead, and he wasn't moving.

"Huey?" she said. "Beast?"

Suddenly he moaned and held his ribs. Abby climbed over the seat and took hold of his right hand. "Wake up, Beast." She shook the hand again, then pinched it. "Can you talk? Daddy didn't mean to hurt you!"

A loud boom sounded behind her, followed by a *whoomph* that made the air around the car glow for several seconds. Terror for her father went through her like a knife.

"Beast! Wake up!"

His right eye blinked, and he groaned in pain. "Run," he whispered.

"You're hurt."

"Run, Jo Ellen," he said in a raspy voice. "I smell gas. And there's a bad man coming. Run to Daddy."

Jo Ellen . . . ? And then she remembered. Huey's little sister was named Jo Ellen. Abby looked down at the floor. Belle and the carved bear and child lay in a mosaic of shattered glass. She picked up Belle and put her in Huey's lap, then grabbed the bear and climbed out of the passenger door. She wished she could pull Huey out, but trying to pull Huey would be like trying to pull a mountain. She turned away from the car and looked up the steep hill.

A chill of fear made her shiver.

A tall man was looking down at her out of the sun. She couldn't see his face, only his silhouette. Then the shape of the man stirred something in her.

"Daddy?" she said hesitantly.

The shadow began running down the hill.

* * *

Cheryl crawled off the shoulder and onto the grass of the median. Her knees were cut to pieces. Her hair stank of gasoline, her eyelashes were gone, and her left forearm had a big red blister on it.

But she had the money.

Behind her lay what was left of the plane, a burning mass of twisted metal in the wake of a log truck that had only managed to stop a few seconds ago. A mile-long line of cars had stacked up behind the wrecked plane, and dozens of people were coming forward, gawkers and rubbernecks in the lead.

Cheryl coughed up black smoke, and the spasm hurt like a wire brush raked over the inside of her rib cage. She thought she might have breathed fire during the explosion. What the hell. It was a small price to pay.

She flattened her hands on the grass and got to her feet, then picked up the blackened briefcase and started up into the trees.

Karen lay against the passenger door of the Camry, staring at the small hole in her upper abdomen. Hickey was gone. He'd shot her and left her for dead. She couldn't tell how badly she was wounded. Abdominal wounds were tricky. They could kill you in five minutes or put you through weeks of hell. In any case, the gunshot had been enough to knock her against the door and keep her off Hickey while he raced after Will's plane.

Through the windshield she saw cars in front of her and cars behind. But no plane. She'd heard an explosion a few moments before, one she hoped was a car wreck and not Will's Baron. But it could have been Will. Landing on a busy interstate was Evel Knievel stuff. And if something had happened to Will, Abby might be alone up there with Hickey and the others.

Karen opened the Camry's glove box, found a wad of Kleenex, and stuffed it into the bullet hole. Then, steeling herself against the pain, she forced herself to turn and pop open the Camry's door.

Falling half onto the road, she decided to let her legs follow. After they did, she rolled onto her stomach and lay there, annoyed by the numbness of her midsection. Getting up seemed a theoretical impossibility, like surpassing the speed of light. Then the smell of burning aviation fuel reached her, and she changed her mind.

Will angled down the hill toward Abby, pumping his legs like an extreme skier in a barely controlled fall. Abby took several steps up the shoulder, her eyes bright.

"I knew you'd come, Daddy!"

He snatched her up and hugged her as tight as he dared.

"Where's Mom?" she asked. "Is Mom with you?"

He had no answer. "Come on, sweetie. Let's find her."

"Wait. Huey's hurt."

"What?"

"He's stuck in the car. He's bleeding!"

Will didn't especially want to help Abby's kidnapper, but he moved close enough to the Rambler to see that the man was badly hurt. The tang of gasoline was in the air. If the car caught fire, he'd be burned alive.

"Help him, Daddy!"

Will set Abby down and ran to the driver's door. It had

not been jammed shut in the crash, but Huey was most definitely jammed behind the wheel. He weighed over three hundred pounds, and Will could scarcely budge him.

"Huey!" he yelled. "Help me! *Move!*"

The man's left forearm was like a ham. Will grabbed it with both hands and pulled with all his strength. With a groan like an annoyed bull, Huey twisted in the seat and heaved himself out onto the ground. There was just enough slope for Will to roll him down and away from the car. That was all he could do.

"Let's go find Mom!" Abby called.

He had told Abby they would do that, but he really wasn't sure what to do. The smart thing would probably be to duck into the woods and wait for the police to show up. But what if Hickey *had* been in that silver Camry? And what if Karen was still with him after all? She might be bound and gagged in the backseat, or lying wounded in the trunk. He wished he had Cheryl's pistol, but there was no point in wishing. The gun had exploded with the plane.

He scooped Abby into his arms and looked up the shoulder. A dozen people stood along the crest, looking down at him. There were probably hundreds of cars backed up already. A world-class traffic snarl. If Hickey was up there with them, so be it. Somebody up there would have a gun. This was Mississippi, after all. They might *all* have guns. He hitched Abby up on his hip and started up the shoulder.

Cheryl sat down in the trees on the ridge that divided the northbound and southbound lanes and tried to catch her breath. The scene below was like something out of a

Spielberg movie. It was like watching a parade from the roof of a building. Cheryl had done that once as a child. With her real father. But this parade had gone terribly wrong.

The doctor's plane was still burning, throwing up a column of black smoke like a refinery fire. The driver of the log truck was stumbling back toward the fire, to see the damage his truck had done, she supposed. Cars were lined up behind the plane as far as she could see, and hundreds of people were beginning to get out of them. By the plane, though, there were still only a few, as if the spectators sensed that the show might not be quite over. At least the little girl was okay. Cheryl had seen the doctor carry her up onto the road.

She needed to get moving, if she wanted to stay out of jail. Her best bet was probably to go down to the northbound lanes and hitch a ride with some horny salesman. She probably looked rough after the crash, but the truth was, men didn't care. Not when you were twenty-six and had a body tailor-made for the Victoria's Secret catalog.

Cheryl was standing up when she saw Joey rise from behind a parked car and walk toward the knot of people that had gathered around Dr. Jennings and his little girl.

Will was stunned by the reaction of the people on the shoulder. They all talked at once, and he could only catch fragments of their conversations. A couple of guys slapped him on the back, but another yelled, "Where's the stupid son of a bitch who was flying that plane? Somebody needs to arrest his ass!"

Will just held Abby tight and asked someone—anyone—to call the state police and the FBI. Three men detached themselves from the crowd and trotted back toward the line of cars, presumably to use their cell phones.

"Daddy, your *plane*," said Abby, pointing at the mangled wreck.

Will heard himself laugh. "That old girl did what I needed her to do. That's all that matters."

"Look at my bear, Daddy. Huey made it."

Abby held out an intricately carved figure of a bear holding a little girl. Will was no art expert, but he was an experienced collector, and there was something in the little figure that moved him deeply.

"EVERYBODY BACK!" screamed a male voice.

Will thought it was a cop until the men around him began to scatter, half of them sliding down the shoulder behind him, the other half running back to their cars. Among the running bodies, his eyes picked out a man standing still as a pole, thirty feet away. He had dark hair and black eyes, and one of his pant legs was soaked with blood from groin to ankle. As Will watched, he raised his arm. A revolver gleamed blue-black in the sun.

Hickey.

There was nowhere to run. He and Abby were caught between the burning plane and the steep shoulder. If he made a dash down the hill with Abby in his arms, Hickey could simply take a few steps and shoot them as they tried to reach the trees.

"Who's that man, Daddy?"

"Shh, punkin." Will had thought he might remember Hickey from the time of his mother's operation, but the man's face was a cipher. It was hard to comprehend, facing a total stranger who hated you enough to kill you and your children.

"Where's my money, Doc?" Hickey asked, his eyes smoldering like coals.

Will pointed at the burning plane. "In there."

"You'd better be lying."

"I'm too tired to lie."

"Where's Cheryl?"

"I don't know." He wasn't so tired that he couldn't lie a little. He wasn't going to tell Hickey that his wife had burned up in the plane with the ransom money.

Keeping his gun trained on Will and Abby, Hickey backed to the edge of the shoulder and looked down.

"That's the way, Huey!" he shouted. "Come on, boy! You can do it!"

Will looked around for signs of help, but he saw none.

"You know what happens now?" Hickey asked, focusing on Will and Abby again.

"What?"

"This."

He fired, and Will felt his right leg buckle. He almost collapsed, but he managed to keep his feet long enough to set Abby down and move in front of her. She was screaming in terror. He considered telling her to run for it, but he doubted she would, and any such move might cause Hickey to shoot again. He felt her clutching his pants from behind.

"Shot by your own gun," Hickey said. "How does it feel?"

Will looked down. The bullet had caught him in the

meat of the thigh, but on the lateral side, away from the femoral artery.

Hickey yelled back over his shoulder: "Come on, Buckethead! Train's leaving! Show me you're not a wheelie-boy!"

"Get out of here while you can, Joe," Will said.

Hickey laughed darkly. "Oh, I'll be gettin' on soon. But you and me got an account to settle. And that little girl behind you is the legal tender."

He took a step closer, then another. Will was about to snatch Abby up and try to run for it when a female voice stopped Hickey in his tracks.

"I got the money, Joey!"

Cheryl was standing on the far side of the road, by the median. The smile on her face was as forced as an Avon lady's on a poor street, but she was making an effort. "Let's get out of here, Joey. Come on!"

"Well, well," Hickey said. "The prodigal slut." He shook his head. "Gotta finish what you start, babe."

Her smile cracked, then vanished. "There's no reason to hurt that little girl, Joey. Not anymore."

"You know there is."

"Killing her won't bring your mama back."

His eyes blazed. "He'll feel some of what I've felt!" Hickey lowered his aim to Will's legs, which hardly shielded Abby at all.

"Joey, don't!" Cheryl opened the ransom briefcase, took out her Walther, and aimed it at Hickey's chest. "It wasn't even his fault! Let's go to Costa Rica. Your ranch is waiting!"

Hickey looked at Will and laughed bitterly. "Turned

her against me, didn't you? Well . . . she always was a stupid cow."

He turned casually toward Cheryl and fired, blowing her back onto the median and spilling hundred-dollar bills across the grass. Then his gun was on Will again, his aim dancing from head to chest to legs. As he played his little game, a strange beating sound echoed over the slab of the interstate. Will recognized it first: the *whup-whup-whup* of rotor blades. Hickey soon understood its meaning, but instead of bolting, he took two steps closer to Will.

"What do I want with a ranch in Costa Rica? I can't stand spics anyhow. This is what I came for. What goes around comes around, Doc."

Will felt a hard tug on his pants. "Daddy, *look.*"

As Hickey steadied his aim, Will threw himself on top of Abby. Then, just as Cheryl had done before the crash, he turned and looked death full in the face.

He expected a muzzle flash, but what he saw was a bloody forearm the size of a ham slip around Hickey's neck and lift him bodily into the air.

"You can't hurt Abby, Joey," Huey said. "You can hurt Huey, but you can't hurt Abby. She's my Belle."

Hickey's eyes bulged with surprise. He tried to bring his pistol far enough back to shoot his cousin, but the first shot didn't come close. The bloody forearm just lifted him higher, closing off his windpipe like a clamp. Hickey's legs kicked like a badly hanged man's, and his gun barked harmlessly into the sky. He somehow managed to choke out four words, but they were poorly chosen.

"You—god—damn—retard—"

Will watched in fascination as Huey choked the life

out of his cousin, his face as placid as that of a mountain gorilla at rest. Hickey's last bullet tore off part of Huey's ear, but then the gun clicked empty. By the time the sharp snap of cervical vertebra reverberated across the road, Hickey's face was blue-black.

His limbs went limp as rags, and his gun clattered onto the concrete. After a few seconds, Huey set him gently on the side of the road, sat beside him, and began to pet his head. Then he shook him gently, as if he might suddenly wake up.

"Joey? Joey?"

The beating of the helicopter was much louder. Will rolled off Abby and unbuckled his belt, wrapped it around his wounded thigh, and tied it off.

"Look," Abby said in a small voice. "Huey's crying."

Huey had knelt over Hickey and put a hand over his mouth to feel for breath. When he felt none, he started mewling like a baby.

"Why'd you want to hurt Belle?" he sobbed. "It's not right to hurt little girls. Mamaw told us that."

"We've got to help him, Daddy." Abby started across the road, but Will limped after her and brought her back.

"I need you here, baby. We've got to find Mom."

"I'm right here," someone said from behind them.

Will turned. Karen was standing on the median side of the road, an automatic pistol in her hand. It was Cheryl's Walther. She was pointing it at its owner, while Cheryl crawled over the grass stuffing loose packets of hundred-dollar bills back into the briefcase. Both women looked like air-raid survivors, dazed beyond reason but still trying to function, their brains pushing them down logical paths without any larger perspective.

Abby started to run to Karen, but Will caught her arm and pulled her back. Karen was not herself. If she was, she would have run to Abby as soon as she sighted her.

"Bring me the gun, Karen," he said.

She seemed not to have heard. She kept pointing the Walther at Cheryl's head, which was only two feet from its barrel. For her part, Cheryl seemed not to notice. She just kept stuffing bills into the briefcase. Will saw blood on her shoulder, but apparently the bullet had not done major damage.

He limped to within three feet of his wife. "Karen? May I please have the gun? I need it."

"She's one of them!" Karen cried suddenly. "Isn't she?"

"It's over," he said, holding out his hand. "Hickey's dead. And she's not going anywhere."

Karen jerked the Walther out of his reach. As she did, Will saw a large bloodstain on her upper abdomen.

"What happened?"

"He shot me," she said, still following Cheryl with the gun.

"DROP THE WEAPON!" shouted a male voice. "STATE POLICE! DROP THE GUN AND LIE DOWN ON THE GROUND!"

Will turned and saw two uniformed state troopers pointing long-barreled revolvers at Karen.

"Hold your fire!" he yelled. "She's in shock!"

"DROP THAT WEAPON!" one trooper shouted again.

Karen turned toward them but did not drop the gun.

Will knew they might fire at any moment. He stepped forward and put his body between their guns and Karen, but even as he did, a fierce wind sprang up, driving gravel and cinders across the road in a punishing spiral.

A Bell helicopter with FBI stenciled in yellow on the fuel tank flared over the road and set down near the dwindling fire that had been Will's plane. Two men in business suits leaped out of the cockpit and ran toward the state troopers, their wallets held out in front of them. A hurried conversation resulted in one of the troopers lowering his gun, but the other did not seem impressed by FBI credentials. One of the agents interposed himself between the stubborn trooper and Karen, and addressed himself to Will.

"Are you Dr. Jennings?"

"Yes."

"I'm Frank Zwick, Doctor. I'm glad to see you alive."

"I'm *damn* glad to see you. Can you help us? My wife has been shot, and she's disoriented."

"Can you get her to put down the gun?"

Will turned to Karen and held up his hands. "Honey, you've got to give me the gun. These people are here to help us. You can't—"

Karen wobbled on her feet, then crumpled forward onto the ground.

Will ran forward and knelt beside her. Her radial pulse was weak. As carefully as he could, he rolled her over and unbuttoned the bloodsoaked blouse. The bullet had struck her in the left upper abdomen, probably in the spleen. He leaned over and put his ear to her mouth, listening and feeling for breath, watching her chest expansion. Her airway was open, and her lungs probably okay, but he could already see some distension in her belly from internal bleeding.

"What's wrong with Mom?" Abby wailed. "Daddy, what's the matter?"

"She's all right," he assured her, though the wound could be fatal if not treated quickly in an operating room.

"We've got paramedics about five miles out," Zwick said. "They're coming up the shoulder in an ambulance. I'd estimate fifteen to twenty minutes."

"I want her in your chopper," Will told him. "You can have her on the helipad at University Hospital in ten minutes."

"That's not an air ambulance, Doctor. It's just a row of seats."

"It beats waiting. Make it happen, Frank."

The SAC nodded and ran over to talk to his pilot.

"Abby?" said Karen, her eyes fluttering.

"We're all here," Will said.

"Where's Abby?" Karen struggled to rise. *"Where's my baby?"*

"Right here, Mom." Abby knelt beside her mother.

Karen seized her hand, then raised her head, looking right and left like a lioness guarding her cubs. "Where's Hickey?"

"Dead," Will told her again. "We're all safe, babe."

It took a few moments for this to register, but at last Karen sighed and closed her eyes again. Will estimated her blood pressure by checking her various pulses, carotid, femoral, and radial. Then he checked her nail perfusion. She was going into shock. They needed to get moving.

"Daddy's going to make you all better, Mom."

Karen smiled a ghostly smile. "I know, baby."

"Does it hurt a lot?"

"With you holding my hand, nothing hurts."

Abby laughed through tears.

"All set," Zwick said, coming over from the chopper. "Ready to move her?"

"I'm a little under the weather," Will told him.

"My dad got shot in the leg," Abby said proudly. "He was trying to save me."

"Whose money is this?" called a state trooper from the median. He was holding up the ransom briefcase. Beside him, his partner was cuffing Cheryl's hands behind her back.

"Mine," Will said. "That woman was shot in the shoulder, and she was in a fire. Put her aboard that ambulance as soon as it gets here."

"That's *my* money!" Cheryl yelled. She pointed at Will. "Ask him!"

"Take it with you," Will told the trooper. "We'll sort it out later."

"How much is in here?"

"Three hundred and fifty thousand."

The trooper whistled long and low.

"You lying bastard!" Cheryl yelled at Will. "I knew it!"

"I won't forget what I said," he told her. "I'll come to court and tell them what you did to help us."

"Bullshit! You'll forget about me in five minutes!"

He shrugged and turned back to Zwick. "Let's get Karen into the chopper."

Zwick motioned for the troopers and the pilot to help.

"What about Huey?" Abby asked. "Can he come, too?"

Will pointed at the spectacled giant, who was still trying to rouse Joey from his permanent slumber. "That one isn't for the county jail. He needs a psychological evaluation. If you'll take him to University, I'll get him onto the ward."

The trooper holding the briefcase nodded.

Will tried to help Zwick and the others lift Karen, but his leg buckled again. "What's the radio frequency of the ER at University?" he asked the trooper.

"One hundred fifty-five point three-forty."

"Thanks."

Someone had made a pallet of blue FBI Windbreakers on the floor of the chopper, and they laid Karen on it. Zwick rode up front. Will was thankful for the gesture. He knew the SAC would like nothing better than to grill him for the next eight hours, but the man was demonstrating some decency.

As the chopper tilted forward and beat its way into the sky, Will went forward and contacted the attending physician in the UMC emergency room. He outlined Karen's case, then requested a trauma surgeon that he knew had not gone to Biloxi for the convention, a crusty old Vietnam vet who knew how to cut and clamp and get the hell out.

When he returned to the cabin, Karen's eyes were open. She said something he couldn't hear above the noise of the rotors, so he leaned down to her mouth.

"Family," she whispered. "Again."

"We're a family again!" cried Abby, looking at Will with wide eyes. "That's what she said!"

"That's what she said, all right," he agreed. Suddenly something broke loose in him, and waves of grief and joy rolled through his heart.

"You're shaking, Daddy," Abby said.

"I'm okay. It's been a long day."

She smiled uncertainly, searching his eyes for the invincible father she had always known, for signs that everything would soon return to normal. Will took her free hand in his, just as she held Karen's. Together they formed a circle that he vowed would never again be broken. He had made such vows before, usually after seeing some tragic death in the hospital, but eventually the grind of daily existence dulled his awareness of the central truth of life. Chaos was working beneath everything, and death always waited in the wings, watchful as a crow. This time he would not forget how precious was the time he shared with the women who loved him. This time he would keep that knowledge close in his heart.

This time . . .

I stopped shooting people six months ago, just after I won the Pulitzer Prize. People were always my gift, but they were wearing me down long before I won the prize. Still, I kept shooting them, in some blind quest that I didn't even know I was on. It's hard to admit that, but the Pulitzer was a different milestone for me than it is for most photographers. You see, my father won it twice. The first time in 1966, for a series in McComb, Mississippi. The second in 1972, for a shot on the Cambodian border. He never really got that one. The prizewinning film was pulled from his camera by American marines on the wrong side of the Mekong River. The camera was all they found. The thirty-six-frame roll of Ilford HP5 made the sequence of events clear. Shooting his motor-drive Nikon F2 at five frames per second, my dad recorded the brutal execution of a female prisoner by a Khmer Rouge soldier, then captured the face of her executioner as the pistol was turned toward the brave but foolish man pointing the camera at him. I was twelve years old and ten thousand miles away, but that bullet struck me in the heart.

Jonathan Glass was a legend long before that day, but fame is no comfort to a lonely child. I didn't see my father nearly enough when I was young, so following in his footsteps has been one way for me to get to know him. I still carry his battle-scarred Nikon in my bag. It's a dinosaur by today's standards, but I won my Pulitzer with it. He'd probably joke about the sentimentality of my using his old camera, but I know what he'd say about my winning the prize: *Not bad, for a girl.*

And then he'd hug me. God, I miss that hug. Like the embrace of a great bear, it swallowed me completely, sheltered me from the world. I haven't felt those arms in twenty-eight years, but they're as familiar as the smell of the sweet olive tree he planted outside my window when I turned eight. I didn't think a tree was much of a birthday present back then, but later, after he was gone, that hypnotic fragrance drifting through my open window at night was like his spirit watching over me. It's been a long time since I slept under that window.

For most photographers, winning the Pulitzer is a climactic triumph of validation, a momentous beginning, the point at which your telephone starts ringing with the job offers of your dreams. For me it was a stopping point. I'd already won the Capa Award twice, which is the one that matters to people who know. In 1936, Robert Capa shot the immortal photo of a Spanish soldier at the instant a fatal bullet struck him, and his name is synonymous with bravery under fire. Capa befriended my father as a young man in Europe, shortly after Capa and Cartier-Bresson and two friends founded Magnum Photos. Three years later, in 1954, Capa stepped on a land mine in what was then called French Indochina, and set a tragic precedent that my father, Sean Flynn (Errol's reckless son), and about thirty other American photographers would follow in one way or another during the three decades of conflict known to the American public as the Vietnam War. But the public doesn't know or care about the Capa Award. It's the Pulitzer they know, and that's what makes the winners marketable.

After I won, new assignments poured in. I declined them all. I was thirty-nine years old, unmarried (though not without offers), and I'd passed the mental state known as "burned out" five years before I put that Pulitzer on my shelf. The reason was simple. My job, reduced to its essentials, has been to chronicle death's grisly passage through the world. Death can be natural, but I see it most often as a manifestation of evil. And like other professionals who see this face of death—cops, soldiers, doctors, some priests—war photographers age more rapidly than normal people. The extra years don't always show, but you feel them in the deep places, in the marrow and the heart. They weigh you down in ways that few outside our small fraternity can understand. I say fraternity, because few women do this job. It's not hard to guess why. As Dickey Chappelle, a woman who photographed combat from World War II to Vietnam, once said: *This is no place for the feminine.*

And yet it was none of this that finally made me stop. You can walk through a corpse-littered battlefield and come upon an orphaned infant lying atop its dead mother and not feel a fraction of what you will when you lose someone you love. Death has punctuated my life with almost unbearable loss, and I hate it. Death is my mortal enemy. Hubris, perhaps, but I come by that honestly. When my father turned his camera on that murderous Khmer Rouge soldier, he must have known his life was forfeit. He shot the picture anyway. He didn't make it out of Cambodia, but his picture did, and it went a long way toward changing the mind of America about that war. All my life I lived by that example, by my father's unwritten code. So no one was more shocked than I that, when death crashed into my family yet again, the encounter shattered me.

I limped through seven months of work, had one spasm of creativity that won me the Pulitzer, then collapsed in an airport. I was hospitalized for six days. The doctors called it posttraumatic stress disorder. I asked them if they expected to be paid for that diagnosis. My closest friends—and even my agent—told me point-blank that I had to stop working for a while. I agreed. The problem was, I didn't know how. Put me on a beach in Tahiti, and I am framing shots in my mind, probing the eyes of waiters or passersby, looking for the life behind life. Sometimes I think I've actually become a camera, an instrument for recording reality, that the exquisite machines I carry when I work are but extensions of my mind and eye. For me there is no vacation. If my eyes are open, I'm working.

Thankfully, a solution presented itself. Several New York editors had been after me for years to do a book. They all wanted the same one: my war photographs.

Backed into a corner by my breakdown, I made a devil's bargain. In exchange for letting an editor at Viking do an anthology of my war work, I accepted a double advance: one for that book, and one for the book of my dreams. The book of my dreams has no people in it. No faces anyway. Not one pair of stunned or haunted eyes. Its working title is "Weather."

"Weather" is what brought me to Hong Kong this week; Hong Kong is my gateway to China. I was there a few months ago to shoot the monsoon as it rolled over one of the most tightly packed cities in the world. I shot Victoria Harbor from the Peak and the Peak from the City, marveling at the different ways rich and poor endured rains so heavy and unrelenting that they've driven many a round-eye to drunkenness or worse. This time Hong Kong was only a way station to China proper, though I scheduled two days there to round out my portfolio on the city. But on the second day, my entire book project imploded. I had no warning, not one prescient moment. That's the way the big things happen in your life.

A friend from Reuters had convinced me that I had to visit the Hong Kong Museum of Art to see some Chinese watercolors. He said the ancient Chinese painters had achieved an almost perfect purity in their images of nature. I know nothing about art, but I figured the paintings were worth a look, if only for some perspective. Boarding the venerable Star Ferry in the late afternoon, I crossed the harbor to the Kowloon side and made my way on foot to the museum. After twenty minutes inside, perspective was the last thing on my mind.

The guard at the entrance was the first signpost, but I

misread him completely. As I walked through the door, his lips parted slightly, and the whites of his eyes grew in an expression not unlike lust. I still cause that reaction in men on occasion, but I should have paid more attention. In Hong Kong I am a gaijin, a foreign devil, and not naturally attractive to Chinese men, though MTV and pirated American films have gone a long way toward changing Eastern prejudices about beauty.

Next was the tiny Chinese matron who rented me a Walkman, headphones, and the English-language version of the museum's audio tour. She looked up smiling to hand me the equipment; then her teeth disappeared and her face lost two shades of color. I instinctively turned to see if some thug was standing behind me, but there was only me—all five foot eight of me, thin and reasonably muscular but not much of a threat. When I asked what was the matter, she shook her head and busied herself beneath her counter. I felt like someone had just walked over my grave. I shook it off, put on the Walkman, and headed for the exhibition rooms, with a voice like Jeremy Irons's speaking sonorous yet precise English in my headphones.

My Reuters friend was right. The watercolors floored me. Some were almost a thousand years old and hardly faded by the passage of time. The delicately brushed images somehow communicated the smallness of human beings without alienating them from their environment. The backgrounds weren't separated from the subjects, or perhaps there *was* no background; maybe that was the lesson. As I moved among them, the internal darkness that is my constant companion began to ease, the way it does when I listen to certain music. But the respite was brief. While studying one particular painting—a man poling along a river in a boat not unlike a Cajun pirogue—I noticed a Chinese woman standing to my left. Assuming she was trying to view the painting, I slid a step to my right.

She didn't move. In my peripheral vision, I saw that she was a not a visitor but a uniformed cleaning woman with a feather dust mop. And it wasn't the painting she was staring at as though frozen in space, but me. When I turned to face her, she blinked twice, then scurried into the dark recesses of the adjoining room.

I moved on to the next watercolor, wondering why I should transfix her that way. I hadn't spent much time on hair or makeup, but after checking my reflection in a display case, I decided that nothing about my appearance justified a stare. I walked on to the next room—this one containing works from the nineteenth century—but before I could absorb anything about them, I found myself being stared at by another blue-uniformed museum guard. I felt strangely sure that I'd been pointed out to him by the guard from the main entrance. His eyes conveyed something between fascination and fear, and when he realized that I was returning his gaze, he retreated behind the arch.

Fifteen years ago, I took this sort of attention for granted. Furtive stares and strange approaches were standard fare in Eastern Europe and the old Soviet Union. But this was post-handover Hong Kong, the twenty-first century. Thoroughly unsettled, I hurried through the next few exhibition rooms with hardly a glance at the paintings. If I got lucky with a cab, I could get back to the ferry and over to Happy Valley for some sunset shots before my plane departed for Beijing. I turned down a short corridor lined with statuary, hoping to find a shortcut back to the entrance. What I found instead was an exhibition room filled with people.

Hesitating before the arched entrance, I wondered what had brought them there. The rest of the museum was virtually deserted. Were the paintings in this room that much better than the rest? Was there a social function going on? It didn't appear so. The visitors stood silent and apart from one another, studying the paintings with almost eerie intensity. Posted above the arch was a Lucite plaque with both Chinese pictographs and English letters. It read:

Nude Women in Repose
Artist Unknown.

When I looked back into the room, I realized it wasn't filled with "people"—it was filled with men. Why men only? I'd stayed a week in Hong Kong on my last visit, and I hadn't noticed a shortage of nudity, if that was what they were looking for. Every man in the room was Chinese, and every one wore a business suit. I had the impression that each had been compelled to jump up from his desk at work, run down to his car, and race over to the museum to look at these paintings. Reaching down to the Walkman on the waistband of my jeans, I fast-forwarded until I came to a description of the room before me.

"Nude Women in Repose," announced the voice in my headset. *"This provocative exhibit contains seven canvases*

by the unknown artist responsible for the group of paintings known popularly as the 'Sleeping Women' series. The Sleeping Women are a mystery in the world of modern art. Nineteen paintings are known to exist, all oil on canvas, the first having come onto the market in 1999. Over the course of the nineteen paintings, a progression from vague Impressionism to startling Realism occurs, with the most recent works almost photographic in their accuracy. Though all the paintings were originally believed to depict sleeping women in the nude, this theory is now in question. The early paintings are so abstract that the question cannot be settled with certainty, but it is the later canvases that have created a sensation among Asian collectors, who believe the paintings depict women not in sleep but in death. For this reason, the curator has titled the exhibit 'Nude Women in Repose' rather than 'Sleeping Women.' The four paintings that have come onto the market in the past six months have commanded record prices. The last offering, titled simply 'Number 19,' sold to Japanese businessman Hodai Takagi for £1.2 million sterling. The museum is deeply indebted to Mr. Takagi for lending three canvases to the current exhibit. As for the artist, his identity remains unknown. His work is available exclusively through Christopher Wingate, LLC, of New York City, USA."

I felt a surprising amount of anxiety standing on the threshold of that roomful of men, silent Asians posed like statues before images I could not yet see. Nude women sleeping, possibly dead. I've seen more dead women than most coroners, many of them naked, their clothes blasted away by artillery shells, burned away by fire, or torn away by soldiers. I've shot hundreds of pictures of their corpses, methodically creating my own images of death. Yet the idea of the paintings in the next room disturbed me. I had created my death images to expose atrocities, to try to stop senseless slaughter. The artist behind the paintings in the next room, I sensed, had some other agenda.

I took a deep breath and went in.

My arrival caused a ripple among the men, like a new species of fish swimming into a school. A woman—especially a roundeye woman—clearly made them uncomfortable, as though they were ashamed of their presence in this room. I met their fugitive glances with a level gaze and walked up to the painting with the fewest men in front of it.

After the soothing Chinese watercolors, it was a shock. The painting was quintessentially Western, a portrait of a nude woman in a bathtub. A roundeye woman like me, but ten years younger. Maybe thirty. Her pose—one arm hanging languidly over the edge of the tub—reminded me of the *Death of Marat*, which I knew only from the "Masterpiece" board game I'd played as a child. But the view was from a higher angle, so that her breasts and pubis were visible. Her eyes were closed, and though they communicated an undeniable peace, I couldn't tell whether it was the peace of sleep or of death. The skin color was not quite natural, more like marble, giving me the chilling feeling that if I could reach into the painting and turn her over, I would find her back purple with pooled blood.

Sensing the men behind me edging closer, I moved to the next painting. In it, the female subject lay on a bed of brown straw spread on planks, as though on a threshing floor. Her eyes were open and had the dull sheen I had seen in too many makeshift morgues and hastily dug graves. There was no question about this one; she was supposed to look dead. That didn't mean she *was* dead, but whoever had painted her knew what death looked like.

Again I heard men behind me. Shuffling feet, hissing silk, irregular respiration. Were they trying to gauge my reaction to this Occidental woman in the most vulnerable state a woman can be in? Although if she was dead, she was technically *in*vulnerable. Yet this gawking at her corpse by strangers seemed somehow a final insult, an ultimate humiliation. We cover corpses for the same reason we go behind walls to carry out our bodily functions; some human states cry out for privacy, and being dead is one of them. Respect above all is called for, not for the body, but for the person who recently departed it.

Someone paid two million dollars for a painting like this one. Maybe even for this one. A man paid that, of course. A woman would only have bought this painting to destroy it. Ninety-nine out of a hundred women, anyway. I closed my eyes and said a prayer for the woman in the picture, on the chance that she was real. Then I moved on.

The next painting hung beyond a small bench against the wall. It was smaller than the others, perhaps two feet by three, with the long axis vertical. Two men stood before it, but they weren't looking at the canvas. They gaped like clubbed fish as I approached, and I imagined that if I pulled down their starched white collars, I would find gills. No taller than I, they backed quickly out of my way and cleared the space before the painting. As I turned toward it, a premonitory wave of heat flashed across my neck and shoulders, and I felt the dry itch of the past rubbing against the present.

This woman was naked as well. She sat in a window seat, her head and one shoulder leaning against the casement, her skin lighted by the violet glow of dawn or dusk. Her eyes were half open, but they looked more like the glass eyes of a doll than those of a living woman. Her body was thin and muscular, her hands lay in her lap, and her Victorian-style hair fell upon her shoulders like a dark veil. Though she had been sitting face-on to me from the moment I looked at the canvas, I suddenly had the terrifying sensation that she had turned to me and spoken aloud. The taste of old metal filled my mouth, and my heart ballooned in my chest. This was not a painting but a mirror. The face looking back at me from the wall was my own. The body too, mine: my feet, my hips, my breasts, my shoulders and neck. But the eyes were what held me, the dead eyes—held me and then dropped me through the floor into a nightmare I had traveled ten thousand miles to escape. A harsh burst of Chinese echoed through the room, but it was gibberish to me. My throat spasmed shut, and I could not scream or even breathe.

Thirteen months ago, on a hot summer morning, my twin sister, Jane, stepped out of her town house on St. Charles Avenue in New Orleans to run her daily three-mile round of the Garden District. Her two young children waited inside with the maid, first contentedly, then anxiously as their mother's usual absence stretched beyond any they remembered. Jane's husband, Marc, was working in blissful ignorance at his downtown law firm. After ninety minutes, the maid called him.

Knowing that you could walk one block out of the Garden District and be in a free-fire zone, Marc Lacour immediately left work and drove the streets of their neighborhood in search of his wife. He cut the Garden District into one-block grids from Washington Street to Maple and methodically drove them a dozen times. Then he walked them. He left the Garden District and questioned every porch sitter, shade-tree mechanic, can kicker, crack dealer, and homeless person he could find on the adjoining streets. No one had heard or seen anything of Jane. A prominent attorney, Marc called the police and used his influence to mount a massive search almost immediately. The police found nothing.

When Jane disappeared, I was in Sarajevo shooting a series on the aftermath of the war. It took me seventy-two hours to get to New Orleans. By that time, the FBI had entered the picture and subsumed my sister's disappearance into a much larger case, designated NOKIDS in FBI speak, for New Orleans Kidnappings. It turned out that Jane was the fifth in a rapidly growing group of missing women, all from the New Orleans area. Not one corpse had been found, so all the women were classified as victims of what the FBI called a "serial kidnapper." This was the worst sort of euphemism. Not one relative had received a ransom note, and in the eyes of every cop I spoke to, I saw the grim unspoken truth: every one of those women was presumed dead. With no crime scene evidence, witnesses, or corpses to work with, even the Bureau's vaunted Investigative Support Unit was stumped by the cold trail. Though women continued to disappear and still do, neither the Bureau nor the New Orleans police have come close to discovering the fate of my sister or any of the others.

I should clarify something. Not once since my father vanished in Cambodia have I sensed that he was truly dead, gone from this world. Not even with the last frame of film he shot showing an executioner's pistol pointed at his face. Miracles happen, especially in war. For this reason I've spent thousands of dollars over the past twenty years trying to find him, piggybacking my money with that of the relatives of Vietnam-era MIAs, giving what would have been our retirement money to scam artists and outright thieves, all in the slender hope that one lead among the hundreds will turn out to be legitimate. On some level, my decision to take the advance for my book was probably a way to be paid to hunt for my father in person, to tramp across Asia with an eye to my camera and an ear to the ground.

With Jane it's different. By the time my agency tracked me down on a CNN satellite phone in Sarajevo, something had already changed irrevocably within me. As I crossed a street once infested with snipers, a nimbus of dread welled up in my chest—not the familiar dread of a bullet with my name on it, but something much deeper. Whatever energy animates my soul simply stopped flowing as I ran, and the street vanished. I kept running blindly into the dark tunnel before me, as though it were nine years before, during the worst of it, when the snipers shot anything that moved. A CNN cameraman yanked me behind a wall, thinking I'd seen the impact of a silenced bullet on the concrete. I hadn't, but a moment later, when the street returned, I felt as though a bullet *had* punched through me, taking with it something no doctor could ever put back or put right.

Quantum physics describes "twinned particles," photons of energy that, even though separated by miles, behave identically when confronted with a choice of paths. It is now thought that some unseen connection binds them, defying known physical laws, acting instantaneously without reference to the speed of light or any other limit. Jane and I were joined in this way. And from the moment that dark current of dread pulsed through my heart, I felt that *my* twin was dead. Twelve hours later, I got the call.

Thirteen months after that—two hours ago—I walked into the museum in Hong Kong and saw her painted image, naked in death. I'm not sure what happened immediately after. The earth did not stop turning. The cesium atoms in the atomic clock at Boulder did not stop vibrating. But time in the subjective sense—*the time that is me*—simply ceased. I became a hole in the world.

The next thing I remember is sitting in a first-class seat on a Cathay Pacific 747 bound for New York, a Pacific Rim sunset flaring in my window as the four great engines thrum, their vibration causing a steady ripple in the scotch in the glass on the tray before me. That was two whiskeys ago, and I still have another nineteen hours in the air. My eyes are dry and grainy, stinging. I am cried out. My mind gropes backward toward the museum, but there is something in the way. A shadow. I know better than to try to force the memory. I was shot once in

Africa, and from the moment the bullet ripped through my shoulder till the moment I came to my senses in the Colonial Hotel and found myself being patched up by an Australian reporter whose father was a doctor, everything was blank. The missing events—a hectic jeep ride down an embattled road, the bribing of a checkpoint guard (in which I participated)—only returned to me later. They had not disappeared, but merely fallen out of sequence.

So it was at the museum. But here, in the familiar environment of the plane, and in the warm wake of my third scotch, things begin to return. Brief flashing images at first, then jerky sequences, like bad streaming video. I am standing before the painting of a naked woman whose face is mine to the last detail, and my feet are rooted to the floor with the permanence of nightmares. The men crowding me from behind believe I'm the woman who modeled for the painting on the wall. They chatter incessantly and race around like ants after kerosene has been poured on their hill. They are puzzled that I am alive, angry that their fantasy of "Sleeping Women" seems to be a hoax. But I know things they don't. I see my sister stepping out onto St. Charles Avenue, the humidity condensing on her skin even before she begins to run. Three miles is her goal, but somewhere in the junglelike Garden District, she puts a foot wrong and falls into the hole my father fell into in 1972.